MW01701629

TALES OF MARMIDON

THE MENTOR'S FORGE

TALES OF MARMIDON

THE MENTOR'S FORGE

Tiffany M. Rhys

Copyright

Amazon.com
Copyright © 2025 Tiffany M. Rhys
Artwork Copyright © 2025 Tiffany M. Rhys
All rights reserved.

No part of this publication may be reproduced, stored in a retrieval system, or transmitted in any form or by any means, electronic, mechanical, photocopying, recording, or otherwise.

This is a work of fiction. Names, characters, places, and incidents either are the products of the author's imagination or are used fictitiously. Any resemblance to actual persons, living or dead, businesses, companies, events, or locales is entirely coincidental, or has been obtained with their permission.

ISBN: 978-1-971392-00-4

Dedication

Written for all those that believe in a fated love.

Be the light in the dark. Hold onto hope, no matter the shadows that loom over you. Because, hope whispers in the darkest nights, and the greatest adventures begin where fear ends.

MARMIDON
2026 © Tiffany M. Rhys
Zemin Sea
North-West Zemin Sea
North Astiri Sea
DERSHJA
Meridon
Zedet
Gillas
Perradiz
Solesstriane
NORTH ALLVELORE
KERN
Mekka
Trussie
Ultaan Mountains
Ettar
Virm
Charveil
Bearing Mountains
Hemina Mountai
MARMEADA
Thyrel
Criysou
Lakes Lelielve
Etrinn
Marsh
Daurren
Valtariel
Farthvevire
Morvae
Lake Velga
Teaere Mountains
Fescha
Astiri Sea
Ferrenway
Pincer Mountains
Kerizon
Cusika
Siltis
Zeltanni
SOUTH ALLVELORE
Calanth
NARIMONI
Drauss
Laukis
Jultens
Marrore
N
NE
E
SE
S
SW
W
NW
South Astiri Sea
West Evid Se

North-East Zemin Sea
North Fleurra Sea
Tumi
Lake Melmyrstaz
VERRA
Ledra
Ischkovan
Hauph
Pikeeyis Mountains
Asagda
Corpaniese
Faine
Nattan
Tartian
Lerriteas
Feaerre
Benjin
Norran
Terrapeth
Fleurra Sea
Kallanin
Dauriel
Yaldeer Mountains
JUSHOSH
Tarbithon
Lake Benne
Farrah
Yunedale
Lake Elgavod
Liellopi
Grasslands
Serrigour
Elpha Zavar
Auksis Mountains
Barren Lands
Keppena
Tortiaine
Waste Lands
Dresdale
South Fleurra Sea
No-Man's Land
Kalnielva
Rignalda
Lielvane Mountains
Forsaken Isles
East Evid Sea

Contents

Every journey has a start and an end. If we knew what lay ahead, would we have traveled at all?

QUALIFIED

Chapter 1

Thoren Belfry
Twenty-Eighth of Touah

It should have been second nature, but it wasn't. Thoren called out the weave once more, putting everything he could into it. “Veisis Gaiza!”

The air moved like a gentle breeze, pushing the decorated pinwheels in the city garden. He did his best to hide the discomfort he felt as he drew the energy from his inner well.

“Well . . .” The city examiner made a clicking sound in his mouth and stared at the slow spinning landscape decorations in the pale light of dawn. “It’s not the best I’ve seen.”

His remark only made Thoren feel worse. He looked at the man and briefly flashed a timid smile.

“You’ve likely just exhausted yourself.” He eyed the sweat beading Thoren’s forehead and the streaks soaking into the neckline of his shirt. “We probably should have started with weaving, as I’m not sure how well you can weave based on this.” He laughed. “But if it’s anything like your physical skills, I’m sure you’ll be more than capable of competing for this position.” The examiner yawned. “Let me just finish up this form. You can wait back in the office.”

Thoren dropped his hands to his sides in tight fists.

This was my best. He left the gardens quietly, not daring to say anything that would disqualify him.

Becoming the next mentor to Marmidon’s Gift Bearer was a job he’d wanted since first hearing the announcement five months ago. He entered the City Hall building and found a seat in the commons. There he waited, hands laced tightly in his lap and nervously rubbing his thumbs over his knuckles.

A few minutes later, his name was called by one of the city workers at the long, multi-stationed desk. “Thoren Belfry!”

He shuffled up to it. The desktop rested shoulder height to Thoren, better suited for the city clerk, an atle, standing behind it.

The atle were natives of the seas, tall as a one-story cottage, and all pacifists. She smiled down at him, her dark blue lips parting a little. "You've been approved to proceed as a candidate for the Mentor Trials." She poured hot wax over a folded letter and stamped the Valdan seal into it. "Take this with you, and only open it once you've arrived in Thyrel. I suggest you leave Elpha Zavar no later than tomorrow, if you want to be there in time."

The giant atle handed him the letter. His hand looked like a child's next to hers. The blue-tinted skin of the atle always made them look cold, even though they were as warm-blooded as any other race.

"Congratulations. I hear only a handful of others made the cut."

Hearing his acceptance as a competitor didn't make it feel any more real. Thoren didn't know how he had passed. Of course, it was a dream come true for those who had applied, but to hear that he was going to participate in the Mentor Trials made it feel too easy. He left City Hall and stepped out onto the quartz landing. The golden hues of sunrise were vibrant, the speerin flora were blooming. His fingers brushed over the sealed parchment in his hand. He tucked it away into the inner pocket of his vest, over his heart.

He felt a little guilty hiding his weakness, but no other job opportunity he knew of called to him as much as this one—even if he had to fight for it. *I'll be fine. I can handle myself, so long as I have a blade.*

Thoren rushed down the stairs, and through the narrow stone pathways of Elpha Zavar. He took in the sight of his home city, wanting to remember it all. There was no telling how long it would be before he returned here—if he returned at all.

The streets of Elpha Zavar treated every person, ethrea, atle, and therrinndore with lavish spoils. He stretched out his arm and tapped his hand on the pole of a lavender lamp post, threaded with silver and gold trims. The light had blinked out as it sensed daylight, shortly before his fingers touched it. He quickened his pace, tapping at each pole he passed. In the sunlight, the city filled his eyes with color, and buildings of crystal speckled the ground in brilliant spotlights. The crystal structures were seamlessly combined with the fine workmanship of the therrinndore's more earthy sky pillars.

He worked his way toward the center of the city, where he had planned on meeting his friends. The vibrant fabrics and logo-painted stalls of the market came into view as he turned the corner, at the end of the third city block. Thoren stopped by his favorite stall for breakfast. The flaky layers of his pastry melted together in his mouth as he chewed, and he let the sweet glaze and jam roll over his tongue.

"Thoren!"

He turned to search the crowd while licking his fingers clean.

He spotted his friends on approach.

"So, how'd it go?" Janessa asked. She tucked a rogue strand of her wavy auburn hair behind her softly pointed ear.

She nudged his arm with her elbow and looked up at him expectantly. He barely moved with her effort, like the wind he'd attempted to manipulate for the exam.

Thoren put on his best frown and mustered up a tear. "I-I didn't make it."

His friends dropped their heads.

"There's always the next era. That'll give you plenty of time to train," Vance said. He was similarly sized to Thoren, but not as fit. As usual, Vance was gullible and completely fooled.

Thoren smiled and laughed.

Janessa punched his arm. "I knew it!" She held out her hand. "Give it here."

Thoren pulled out the letter and passed it to her. "I can't open it until I get to Thyrel." He noted.

She held it up to the light passing in-between the willows.

"Wow. You really did pass." She handed it over to Vance, and then faced Thoren directly. "When do you leave? I heard that the trials start soon."

Thoren nodded. "I was encouraged to leave tomorrow, so I'm guessing the trials start within this next week. I may have a day or so to pack but then I should leave on the train."

Janessa gasped and clapped her hands together. "That's not much time. I'll need to pick out my best ethrean garb." She framed her face with her hands, covering her blushing cheeks. "Oh, do you think there are many eligible men in Thyrel? It may be too late to find someone to marry this Farthven Ladayose, but surely I can find someone in time for the next celebration."

This notable ethrean celebration was well known by most across Marmidon. It was a lunar event—a solar eclipse—the ethrean took as a blessing from the heavens for newly wedded couples.

Vance cleared his throat rather loudly. "You've had eligible men hanging around you for the last decade, Janessa."

Her lips twisted askew and a brow dropped in speculation. "Hmm . . . I mean, Vance, you're not bad, and we do get along, but I'm not sure I'd want to spend eternity with you."

Thoren lifted a fist to his open mouth. "Oh . . ." He shoved Vance. "Rejected. You'll have to carry that forever." Thoren pointed between them and asked, "Are you two coming with me?"

They nodded.

"I thought it was obvious." Janessa said with a playful smile. "We can't let Thoren Belfry, master of weapons, have all the fun. It's also been a while since any of us left Elpha Zavar."

"I mean, we do have everything we could ever want here." Vance lifted his arms to the city around them. "But it won't be the same without you."

Janessa took the letter from Vance and handed it back to Thoren. "Keep this safe. I don't want to get there and find out that you left your approval letter behind."

He took his letter and tucked it back into his vest pocket. *I should have known they'd come with me.* These two had been the best of friends with him for ten years now.

He took a deep breath, smiling widely and looking about the city. "Let's enjoy today."

His opportunities felt endless.

He and his friends spent the day roaming the city, buying some of the needed supplies, and eating at the best noshes. Motor vehicles whizzed about down the paved streets and filled them with light as the sun set. Thoren walked alongside the street with Janessa. She'd grown quiet over the last hour and kept sighing while staring at others around them.

"Do you think Thyrel has food and shops as nice as these?" She finally spoke.

"I'm sure it does. They may not be as diverse as here, but I know they still accept trade from the other races and nations."

"Thoren, what exactly are the trials?"

He hummed and took in a slow breath. He wasn't exactly sure what it would entail. The application didn't say much on it, nor had the announcement for candidates revealed much more.

"I know it will test my physical skills."

She looked up at him. "Oh, you'll pass that with flying colors."

He smiled modestly and continued, "The application also listed that our mental and spiritual limits would be tested."

"Like how fast you can think? With your reactions in combat, I don't see that being an issue, and you've always been devout to Marmidon."

Thoren nodded, still unsure if it was that simple. "Well, I guess we'll find out once we get there."

Without realizing it, the three had passed from the main sky pillars to the residential area. They stopped with the crowd at the cross walk over the tracks. The lights blinked back and forth indicating the arrival of a train. The whistle of the train called out to the further darkening sky and it passed by, pulling the wind along with it.

Thoren turned his head and watched the back of the train until he could no longer see it. He would be on that train in less than a day.

"Well, we'd all best get some good rest," Vance said. "I'll see you two here tomorrow." He waved and turned left, toward the third residential district.

The blinking track lights dimmed and turned off. The lowered gate lifted and people resumed their walks across the tracks. Thoren and Janessa moved forward with the crowd. She swung her arms, clapping whenever they lifted out in front of her.

"This is going to be *so* fun!"

Thoren agreed, silently.

He was excited, but mixed in with that, was some nervousness. He didn't know what he would be tested on exactly, or who he would be competing against. There was one skill that he was woefully lacking in. One he hoped would not be vital to this position.

"See you tomorrow!" Janessa called and skipped off down the street to the right. She'd pulled her leather bag from her back and was swinging it up in the air like a little girl coming back from school.

She looks like she's the one who got accepted.

Thoren made his way home. The oaks shaded his street, and the only light came from the lamp posts peeking between the leaves. His home was quiet. He entered and shut the door behind him, hanging his key on the proper hook on the wall to the right. Taking a few steps down the short hall, he turned and checked the front room. Empty. A single lamp was left on, in the corner.

Are they still working? Thoren wanted to share the news with his parents.

He moved on down the continuing hall to the kitchen. The sterile walls of his home only held a picture or two here and there. The table was bare, the chairs neatly tucked under it, with the lights off.

Where are they? I'm sure they said they would be off in time today.

"Surprise!"

Thoren jumped at the shout from his parents behind him. He clutched at his heart and spun around to see them standing together holding a small sweet cake, with lit candles atop it.

"Ama, Ba!" His face filled with a smile.

His father passed the sweet cake to his mother and guided Thoren to the kitchen table. "So, do we get to hear good news tonight?" He pulled out a chair and directed Thoren into it.

Thoren pulled the letter from his pocket. "I've been accepted." He set it on the table.

"Congratulations! I never doubted you'd make the cut." His father picked up the letter as his mother set the cake on the table. "The letter's all official looking, too."

"Thoren, make a wish." His mother sat across from him. She patted the table, addressing her husband, "Sit down, dear." Her gaze locked with Thoren's father who took his seat between them.

"Go on." His mother watched with laced fingers and waited.

Thoren stared at the flickering flames atop the candles. He thought through everything he could wish for in this moment.

I want to be the best mentor there ever was. Thoren sucked in a deep breath and blew.

The room fell dark as the candles were blown out.

The following day, Thoren spent time packing. His parents walked him to the station and stood with him, waiting for the train.

"Don't forget to write to us every now and then," his mother said while straightening out the neckline of his side-split white tunic top.

As a candidate for the Gift Bearer's mentor, he was to wear all white—symbolic of purity and worthiness. The clothing was a bit old fashioned and styled after the Primal Horizon Era, when the first Gift Bearer, Aiden Aodh, was selected—a little over six-hundred years ago. He looked down at his mother's hand pulling at the rims of his sleeves. A brown fabric-wrap belt was set around his waist and the long white pants were tucked into light leather boots. The belt and boots were the only non-white items he had on. His longer pale golden hair was pulled back, half up, and clearly showing his ethrean pointed ears.

"You look so much more mature," Janessa stated as she arrived.

Thoren turned to face her and his mother stepped back with his father.

Janessa smiled shyly. She'd done her auburn hair up in elaborate braids with floral accents in just the right places that complimented her heart-shaped face. Setting down her travel bag, she brushed a wrinkle out of her pale-yellow dress. The hem tapped at the top of her mid-calf boots as she smoothed the skirt.

"Oh, Janessa!" His mother clapped her hands. "Both of you have matured overnight."

"You think so?" Janessa twirled, fanning out her dress some.

"It's hard to think that the both of you have passed into your second century. With nice timing, too." Thoren's father noted.

Thoren was not aloof to the fact that his parents had wanted to set him up with Janessa for some time. Now that they were both at least a century old, they could participate in Farthven Ladayose, the marriage celebration that the ethrea held for those of age. He wasn't interested in Janessa, not like that—nor was she in him.

"I think she still needs another century," Vance said, announcing his arrival at the station.

The blare of the train sounded and the station pavilion rattled with the locomotive's approach. They all faced the loading zone.

"Marmidon watch over you." Thoren's mother wrapped her arms around him for a tight squeeze and then pulled back.

His father was next. "I know you'll make us proud."

Thoren wasn't as sure of that himself, but he knew he would try his best. His stomach knotted as he thought of his one weakness. He put on a smile and stepped back from his parents.

"I'll do my best, Ama, Ba."

Steam poured out from beneath and above the engine as the train came to a full stop. Janessa picked up her baggage with one hand and pulled at Thoren with the other.

"Let's go!"

They approached the loading zone and waited in line as arrivals got off. He looked over the square windows, framed in bronze, and the little details of the tall locomotive. It looked like a two story train, but it was just one level. This train accommodated for the Atle's average height of nine feet. The seafolk came often enough to Elpha Zavar, and other near-coastal cities, that these accommodations had become commonplace here.

Thoren took a step forward as the line moved. He'd been on this train only a handful of times to a few of the nearby cities in Jushosh, and once to visit Etrinn in Marmeada. The Primal Horizon Era city was still in ruins from the first Calamity. It was a reminder of how dangerous weaving could be. Thoren often wondered what exactly happened to cause such destruction, but most records on the event were missing vital sections, or were lost altogether. Many had asked the Gift Bearer, Aiden, for such answers. He was the last living Aodh to their knowledge, except nobody had seen him in recent years. There was still a lot of mystery and rumors revolving around that whole event.

Thoren stepped forward, with the name of it at the forefront of his mind. *The Day of Peerretdyn.*

"Come on, Thoren!" Vance called from a window on the right of the onboarding door.

Bringing himself out of his deep thoughts, he stepped aboard. The tight walkways were jammed with passengers, many not ethrean, selecting their seats and securing their baggage in the overhead storage. He waited for an opening. Once he stepped up to his friend's booth, he secured his largest bag in the overhead storage and closed it. Janessa was seated next to Vance, but that was likely his doing. Thoren sat across from them and settled in.

"Did you remember your letter?" Janessa asked.

Thoren tapped at his pants pocket. "I've got it, don't worry."

"Tickets!"

They all turned to the aisle and pulled their tickets out. The ticket master stopped at their booth, taking each of their tickets one at a time, to punch a hole into the corner before returning them.

"Welcome aboard the Evercroft. You are welcome to close the door to your booth, as soon as I leave. During this full four-day trip, there will be three meals offered, at the appropriate meal times of eight in the morn, noon, and six for your convenience with reasonable prices. Water and other beverages will also be available at the far end of every cart, I suggest you wait until after we are in motion to go get any beverages." He pointed to the left side of their booth. "We hope you have a pleasant journey with us." He smiled and tipped his top hat before moving on to the next booth.

Vance stood up and shut their booth door. "That's better." He sat back down.

The train booths were separated by padded walls that softened the noise of chatter inside and out. It took another fifteen minutes before the locomotive whistled and the joined carts lurched forward, moving slowly at first, and then picking up speed.

Once the Evercroft was moving smoothly, Vance pulled out a packed snack. He popped the tree nuts into his mouth and watched the scenery through the window.

"We'll be passing over the Evid Sea twice, right?" Janessa asked.

"Have you never gone west?" Vance sounded surprised. "I thought every ethrean made a trip out to Etrinn for ancient culture and history instruction."

"I missed it," Janessa stated and shrugged her shoulders. Her eyes narrowed as Vance shoved a fistful of his snack into his mouth. Janessa stood and stepped up to the booth door. "I'm going to get a drink, does anyone else want one?"

"I'd love a lemon twist." Vance teased a cheesy grin at her.

She looked to Thoren. "What about you?"

He was a bit thirsty. “I’ll help you.” Thoren stood and ushered her out.

They turned left and walked down the narrow aisle. Janessa pressed herself to the wall as an atle passed them. Thoren joined her, standing next to the wall.

The atle’s beaded tribal shells hung in a draped loop from his waist, rattling with every step. Thoren was used to seeing the atle in the city, but had never passed by one so close. They often wore clothing styled after the Primal Horizon Era—loose draping pants, and a cross shoulder tunic with a tied cloth belt.

“Pardon me, little ethrean.” The atle spoke down to them in passing. His voice was deeper than most men Thoren had spoken to.

“Of course, sir.” Thoren did his best to give the atle room to walk by.

They arrived at the end of the cart, finding a tiered rolling shelf full of beverages. A young woman, human, was running it. She handed out some water bottles to a couple therrinndore ahead of them. Thoren stared mindlessly as the therrinndore grabbed their drinks with their meaty fingers. Their frizzy curled hair hid their faces, but Thoren had seen plenty of their kind in Elpha Zavar. Therrinndore were short, rarely reaching five feet, and always had thick locks that frizzed. Their hands were often calloused. He thought about their other traits: cheery faces, stern in tone, and stubborn. They often came bearing shipments of minerals from the Auksis Mountains east of the city.

Thoren shuffled over to let them pass and moved forward in line. They reached the front within the next minute and Janessa requested the drinks for her and Vance.

She then turned to him and asked, “Thoren, what would you like?”

“Water.”

He took his drink, and they made their way back to their booth. Light shimmered through his water from one of the windows they passed. Glancing to the window near the cart’s shut loading door, Thoren caught sight of the transition from the mainland over the Evid Sea. The waves looked like they rolled up to the train. He veered over to the window and looked out. The train rattled on the tracks that were suspended over the water and held up by supporting pillars. Thoren could almost smell the salt. Most of their trip would be along the edge of the Evid Sea as they passed around the Waste Lands and through the single archway in the large border wall between Jushosh and Marmeada. Once they passed through they would be halfway to Thyrel and the tracks would turn north to travel around the end of the Teaere Mountains. Then a quick stop at Tortiaine, before taking a south dip passing the Marmeadan city, Morvae. After that, the Evercroft would be headed straight to Thyrel.

We should be at the border by tomorrow evening.

Although Thoren was less travelled than some other residents of Elpha Zavar, the trip to Etrinn had been memorable enough for him to retain the details of this route. Due to the length of the trip, there were three rest stops along the way. The first was one in the Waste Lands, with a boulder-surrounded structure. The grounds were cemented to keep the svilis ka—overgrown sand serpents—from attacking. Red stone covered the face of the building, which rose up several stories like the sky pillars in every major city across Marmidon.

There was another rest station just past the border in the Barren Lands, and one in the grass lands south of Marmeada's capital city, Criysous.

The best part of the day . . .

The rest stops were primarily to prepare the train for the next part of the journey, and allow those travelling some room to stretch their legs. They weren't places where people ended their trip, they were simply part of the extended trip between the two countries.

Other than the closed-in rest stop in the Waste Lands, Thoren wished they had more time to explore the cities on the way to Thyrel. Either way, he enjoyed it—spending time with his friends.

The stops each evening would be a nice break from the cramped booths and halls of the train. He was grateful that they had no need to hunt down an inn. Their tickets included an assigned room in the singular sky pillars near each train stop. It made the trip more comfortable to be able to rest and bathe as needed before the next stretch of their journey.

As tall as the train was, its wash rooms were barely large enough for the atle. And the tight hallway was often filled with restless children between meal times.

Detaching himself from the spellbinding sight outside the window, he returned to their booth. Janessa and Vance were bickering over which beverages Thyrel had as they drank theirs.

It's going to be a long ride. He looked between his friends.

FATED

Chapter 2

Dessuithiel Vizule
First of Trete

It all started with a single dream. Such dreams had come before, but none as repetitive as this one—calling to her over the last twelve years. Her sight glazed over, returning her to the nightmare of the future. It filled her mind in renewed vigor. Her pulse quickened and her hands, holding tight to her silk bedsheets, grew cold.

Marmidon. What is this? What am I to do about it?

Never had a vision—of which she received regularly enough—perplexed her so.

Her senses shifted from the sweet floral scents of her room, the delicate fabric of her bed and nightclothes, and warmth of speerin, to that of a dark realm. Airborne dust mixed with the scent of iron, and a chilling mist made it hard to breathe. This place was foreign to her, yet becoming familiar from the nightmares, which grew in detail each time they occurred.

The air shook and darkened as creatures crawled out from bridges between the realm of light and dark. Chaos consumed everything. She searched the scene before her. Sky pillars of brilliant zilkan crystal crumbled to the ground. She turned her head to find the streets shifted—her location changing and echoing the cries of those in pain, afraid, and weeping in a desperate attempt to save their life.

Dessuithiel did not recognize the city that her eyes beheld. How could this be the place she called home? Her sight caught on a single ethrean. Light radiated from his face. His eyes fixed to some unseen foe. He raised a hand to the dark force drenching all that it touched—all but this man. She expected the vision to fade away as it always did in this pivotal moment, yet the scene before her continued.

She watched intently as the ethrean's mouth moved. She could not hear his words, but knew he was weaving. Debris littering the ground was tossed through the air. Energy danced, entwined with every force of nature. The ethrean shifted, bending the very air to his will. It stole her breath away as he threw it at his enemy. She lifted her arms, shielding her face as pieces of buildings were carried away in the hurricane-force winds. This was new. Such a display of power was unknown to her. Who was this man? Who did he fight? Could he have invited such horror? Then it ended.

Dessuithiel threw her covers off, back into the present. Light from her arched window burned away the dark patches of the vision. Warmth wrapped its arms around her shaking frame. She crossed her arms and rubbed at them until her skin smoothed from the chill of the vision.

If Marmidon will not tell me what I should do, I will speak with my parents.

Dropping her feet to the pale marble floor, she stood and wrapped her robe over top of her dusty-blue silk nightdress. The added details she had seen could not wait for her handmaids to dress her in an elaborate gown or brush her long, red hair. Barely finished with tying her robe around her narrow waist, Dessuithiel approached the doors of her room leading out.

“My lady, we should get you dressed for the day.” One of her handmaids left her post beside the bedroom’s double doors, taking a couple of steps in her direction.

“Later,” she answered.

Her handmaids exchanged a glance before quickly pulling the doors open, bowing their heads as she passed through.

“My lady!” Guan sputtered. “What is so urgent that you have foregone dressing, or arranging your locks?” He walked after her—like the shadow he always was. Guan was certainly dressed like a shadow, with his black garb and leather armor masking most of his body, up to the stiff, short collar around his neck. The only part of him that stuck out was his pale face between the dark clothing and his black hair pulled back in a tidy ponytail, only a small portion of shorter strands fell loosely on the left side of his face.

“I’ve seen a vision.”

“You see many visions, my lady. How is this one different?” Guan pointed out.

She paused and Guan quite nearly ran into her.

Turning around, she looked up at her personal guard. “What I saw contradicts the Seer.”

She caught the flinch that passed through his face, pulling at his chiseled features and slightly pinching his dark brows together. He blew out his cheeks, rolled his shoulders back, and gave his head a small shake.

“That, my lady, is not possible.” He brushed a stray strand of his dark hair behind his softly-pointed ear. “What the Seer prophesies is as solid as the stone beneath our feet, as strong as the zilkan from which this tower is made.”

Dessuithiel folded her arms, matching his confidence as she held her head as tall as she could muster from her short frame. “It has come more than once and now with details I cannot ignore.” She lifted one of her arms, pointing at Guan—nearly touching his black-leather, armored chest. “This *is* an urgent message from Marmidon.”

Her guard tried his best to stifle a chuckle and hide his smile. “My lady, what is this message? Surely, you can wait to discuss it with the high lord and lady until after preparing yourself for the day.”

She lowered her head, staring at the polished tiles of vein-riddled marble. “I dare not wait, or my courage may falter. I’m not entirely certain, but Marmidon has impressed upon my mind that something terrible is coming, sooner than I’d like.”

“What do you intend to do with this knowledge, my lady? The Seer’s words are practically law.”

Dessuithiel turned away from him, facing the hall that led to her parent’s bedchamber. “I intend to discuss it with my parents. There must be something I’m missing that they may be able to discern.”

It was unlike her to voice a vision without fully understanding it. Most of her past visions were of no major consequence, but had aided in the Vizules' climb to power over most of the other ethrean royal families. She had foreseen changes in the weather, saving crops. She'd seen the intent behind other monarchies when offers and deals were presented—helping them avoid the ones that would leave Thyrel at a loss. Those were better days. Days when her power did not pain her.

At times, when she visited with the ethrea's cherished children in the school yards, she would see a glimpse into their future at the brushing touch of their hands.

Touching others had become harder for her as the years went on and her mind became weighed down with the visions of her people's futures. Too many questions, not enough answers to appease them. She went looking for answers, searching fate as though it were a textbook one day. That was the day she stopped resting a comforting hand on a laden shoulder, shaking hands when greeting, or embracing the schoolchildren she taught a few times each month. It quickly became more than she could handle once word got out that she had the gift of foresight and she dared to reach further than she should.

She pulled at her robe's sleeves and shook her head to rid her mind of the past.

Hardly a sound could be heard as she made her way to High Lord Ayzgar and High Lady Miereene's rooms. As daughter to one of the most powerful royal houses among the ethrea, Dessuithiel knew anything she brought to her parents had to be of the utmost importance—to Thyrel's wellbeing. These were the only visions she had accepted and voiced over the last decade.

I can't shake this feeling. She tucked her arms against her stomach. *Marmidon, what is coming?* She almost feared that another vision would whisk her back into that darkened realm.

"Lady Dessuithiel." The guards posted outside her parents' chamber saluted, pressing their arms firmly at their sides, shutting their eyes, and leaning slightly forward in a respectful bow.

"Rise." She instructed and watched them lift their eyes before asking, "Have the high lord and lady awoken for the day?"

The guard to the right nodded. "They have gone down to breakfast, not ten minutes ago."

She thanked them, turned back the way she'd come, and hurried down the spiral stairs of Thyrel's zilkan tower. Gliding down each step, her robe and nightdress rippled as air caught beneath them.

She arrived and found her parents in pleasant conversation and enjoying freshly baked muffins, lightly topped with a sweet crumble.

"Aba, Ba," she called to them as she approached, gathering her courage.

Her mother stood and lifted her arms, inviting an embrace—one that only hovered around her, not actually touching. Dessuithiel pulled her robe's sleeves down over her hands and tried not to show her discomfort in the attempt to welcome her.

"Morning, my dear." Her mother's hand hovered near Dessuithiel's cheek, close enough to pass warmth, but not touching. Following, her mother offered her a seat beside her, opposite of her father. "We were just discussing the details of your big day. Dundaelon will be arriving during the trials."

Every muscle tensed at the mention of it. She suddenly couldn't fix her eyes upon them. What had previously been arranged between her and the son of the Valdan royal family, left her feeling uneasy. Dessuithiel had known for some time that coming of age would inevitably bring matchmaking to the top of her parent's priorities. It wasn't long after Dessuithiel hit her hundredth year that an offer was presented from all the royal ethrean houses with sons of marriageable age. The one her parents accepted was, as she had suspected, from the Valdan high lord.

Her father reached out and picked up a folded letter on the end of the glass table. Holding it at eye-level, he said, "I know this came suddenly, and we've barely had time to prepare for your wedding amid everything the trials have demanded of you and your time, but do try and get to know him when he comes. It will surely put your heart at ease before you two are wed during Farthven Ladayose."

The second mention of marriage sent her deeper into distress. She hugged herself tightly. Her brows pinched and she couldn't meet her parent's eyes.

"Dear, what has you flustered?" Her mother quickly picked up on her cues, taking note of her robe and nightdress. "Have you had another vision?" She shifted in her seat and faced Dessuithiel directly.

Of course, Aba would connect my distress to a vision and not this marriage . . .

Her mother continued, "This one seems to have upset you. What have you seen?"

Dessuithiel found it hard to bring up the very topic she had come to discuss. Her courage fled her. This was supposed to be a joyous time leading up to her union with arguably the most powerful ethrean royals upon Marmidon. How could she tell them what she'd seen—what she had kept from them, repeatedly—over the last several years.

Her voice felt smaller than ever as she spoke. "I fear I have seen Thyrel's downfall."

Her father stood so fast his elaborate iron chair crashed upon the floor. The letter from the Valdans slapped on the glass, stuck between it and her father's hand. Dessuithiel shut her eyes tight, tensing until the ringing fell still.

"Are you sure?" her father questioned.

She looked up and half nodded, half shook her head. "It is not clear to me, but—"

Her father interrupted, "You must be mistaken." His shoulders eased, and he sighed. "The Seer has said nothing of any destruction coming for our fair city. In fact, it would be wise if you were to review the Seer's most recent prophecy." He tapped the table-top with his finger. Each thud was like another lock clicking into place around her mouth.

Lowering her head she softly complied. "Yes, Ba."

Her mother tipped her head a little. "Dear, are you trying to get out of this union?"

Dessuithiel's head snapped up.

Her father laughed. "Is that what this is?"

One of their staff reset his chair, bowing as they backed away toward the cooking quarters. "Here I was starting to wonder if you'd lost your gift."

"Aba, Ba that isn't it." She huffed, turning her face from them and spotting Guan standing at the dining room's entrance. He had plastered a neutral expression to his face, but she could see the twinkle of "I told you so" in his eyes.

She held to what little courage had not fled her and turned back to face her parents. Standing, Dessuithiel stared at the letter from the Valdans as she spoke. "Aba, Ba, what I have seen, has been a repeated vision for the last twelve years."

Her father lifted his hands, lacing his fingers in front of his mouth as he waited for her to continue. Her mother settled against the back of her seat, and nodded lightly as if saying "go on."

"This dream . . ." she corrected her wording quickly. "This vision . . . varies little, and always has the same dark energy present, spreading over everything." Dessuithiel held herself with more confidence as she continued, "Buildings lay in ruins, although I admit that many of those I saw looked like what may have once been part of the Primal Horizon Era city, Etrinn." She paused as she thought of how the vision seemed to shift between locations, always ending with that ethrean man.

She'd paused for too long and her father took that as the end of her foresight.

"It is a vision of the past, my dear." Her father sighed. "There is nothing to fear for our future." He started picking at his breakfast, noticeably eased after determining her vision was not relevant. He paused, holding his fork with a cleanly cut piece of an omelet speared at its end. "But why would Marmidon show you the past? Foresight is for the future . . ." He shook his head. "Do not worry yourself over it, my dear. Let us fill that dreary mind of yours with celebration. Before we know it, Farthven Ladayose will be upon us and you will be wed." He smiled and called for more food to be brought out for Dessuithiel.

"Ba . . . That was only part of what I've seen." She tried to resume, to seek for some answer to what puzzled her.

Her mother reached out to Dessuithiel's face again, hovering and not touching, in a show of comfort. "Dessuithiel, my dear daughter, do not forget that your Ba and I remember the day of Peerretdyn. What you have described is what we experienced. Do as your Ba says." She pulled her hand back and brushed at her own face. "You should be more concerned with the wrinkles you will create with such furrows upon your brow. Smile, my dear. It is just some pre-wedding anxieties."

Dismissed. She turned to leave.

"Dessuithiel, will you not eat with us?" her father asked.

Her mouth twitched and she squared her shoulders, speaking with all the calm she could muster while facing them in a polite bow. "I should get ready for the day first. Excuse me, Aba, Ba."

"That's our girl." Her father smiled.

Dessuithiel marched back to her quarters, wishing that she could look more upset while also knowing that her petite frame, delicate build, and ethereal beauty betrayed her.

"My lady, if you attempt to punish the floor all the way back, I have a feeling your feet will be the real victim of your frustration." Guan sounded like he was holding back a laugh at her poor attempt in being upset.

She silently acknowledged his point, and walked up the last stretch of stairs, before turning off toward her living quarters, in her usual graceful stride.

Her bedroom doors swung open ahead of her, but she paused at the threshold and turned around swiftly. Guan quickly took a step back, tucking his arms behind him and looking down near her bare feet draped in her silk nightgown.

"Guan, do you think me a fool?"

He shook his head adamantly. "Marmidon take me, the day that I do, my lady."

"Part of what I have seen I do believe was Etrinn, but the rest . . ." She took a deep breath. "I fear my parents will not listen." She pointed her finger once again at the center of his chest, barely half an inch from touching. "This doesn't give you bragging rights, you know."

He bit at the inside of his mouth, clearly doing his best to hide his amusement.

"Still . . . something doesn't feel right. I can't pinpoint it, yet, but I'll figure this out." She dropped her pointed finger, folding her arms. More than in the years past, Dessuithiel would seek for the answers that eluded her. "Guan." She looked directly at him, waiting for him to meet her gaze before continuing, "Swear on your life, that you will say nothing of my actions from this moment on to anyone, not even the high lord and lady."

He stiffened, and she could see the muscles around his dark-blue eyes in a struggle to remain neutral.

"Fate is calling to me, Guan, and I am determined to listen to its demands." She released her arms, her eyes fixed upon Guan's face, and for the first time in years, she let her fingers make contact with another living being. She winced as the connection between her fingertips and the side of Guan's face opened his life to her. Fleeting moments of his life flashed across her mind, the same as every time she touched another living soul.

Dessuithiel wished she could share her vision with him—to have someone believe her. The shock of touching him intensified and she found her fingers fixed at the side of Guan's face, unable to pull away.

Marmidon!

It took no more than seconds for the repeated vision to imbed within Guan's mind as though it had been his own dream. Her hand, arm, and mind burned as her power passed through their physical connection.

He stepped back, breaking their brief touch, but not before everything she wished she could show him had been given. Dessuithiel pulled her hand back, clutching it over her heart.

What was that? Did I just show him my vision? In all the years she had been the recipient of visions and the futures of those she touched, never had she been able to show another what she'd seen.

She was certain Guan had seen the vision of Thyrel's future. The confusion and shock in his eyes—breaking his stoic neutrality—confirmed at the very least that he had seen *something*.

Guan lifted a hand to the side of his head and he shook it slowly. "My lady . . . what . . ."

Shaking herself out of the shock, she repeated her demand. "Swear on your life, Guan. Fate is calling."

His face settled as he chose and voiced his answer. "My lady . . ." He knelt at her feet, his right hand firmly over his heart, his left fist pressed against the cool marble floor. "I swear upon my life, that I will be at *your* beck and call, to serve *you* and no one else, to aid fate as it has called to you. Marmidon be witness of it."

THE COMPETITION

Chapter 3

Thoren Belfry

Fourth of Trete

The Evercroft came to a screeching halt. The whistle blew, signaling the end of their trip. Thoren yawned and wiped a hand down his face. He'd put up with Vance's endless, and mostly one-sided, discussions about the sights and cities they had passed over the last four days. Janessa was oddly quiet. She'd only said a few things here and there. Thoren stood from his seat and retrieved his baggage. His legs were sore and his body stiff from sitting so much.

"Do you need to report in first, or check in somewhere?" Janessa asked, moving up behind him as they stepped off the Evercroft.

Thoren's eyes were drawn to the distant city—barely visible from their distant and elevated position. Thyrel was situated past open grassy fields that stretched out between the tall Bearing Mountains on the north, south, and west sides of it. The towering mountains cradled the city, leaving only one way to approach it—through the rolling grassy valley. A tall tower shimmered at the back of the city, like a diamond. He couldn't make out much of the details from here.

Janessa nudged him with her elbow and cleared her throat, still waiting for him to answer her.

"Oh, I was instructed to open the letter upon arrival." His hand brushed over his pants pocket. "It probably tells me where I should go."

"Well then, let's get moving. I want to see what it says." She pulled at his arm, moving him off the station.

His sight fell back over the landscape ahead. The Bearing Mountains were far taller than any sky pillars. Snow painted the peaks in brilliant white while the ground contrasted with deep greens and pops of floral color. The Evercroft left them at the mouth of the mountain-lined valley. The stretch ahead of them had a single well-traveled dirt road with merchants and visitors driving their trucks of goods and vehicles toward the stone-walled city. It would take them all day to walk there from the station.

"Do you think we could catch a ride?" Vance asked openly, looking about after catching up to them. "I'd like to get to the city today."

Janessa shielded her eyes from the late morning light as she searched for and spotted a potential ride. She pointed and jogged, dragging her baggage behind her. "I see one available."

Janessa dropped her hand from her face and pulled Thoren with her as she passed by. He ripped his gaze from the landscape and followed them to a line of motor vehicles.

"What's the fare?" Vance asked as he leaned forward on the open passenger window of the vehicle for hire.

Thoren wasn't sure if he was more excited or nervous that they had arrived at Thyrel. Well, practically arrived. He listened to the answer and the hiss of Vance as he reconsidered.

"I'll pay it." Thoren stepped up and pulled out his coin purse.

"Thanks!" Vance patted his shoulder and moved to the back of the vehicle to load his luggage.

They piled into the vehicle and the driver pulled away from the station shortly after the door shut. They drove down the worn dirt road toward the mountain-wrapped city. Soft dips in the road rocked the vehicle, causing them to bump shoulders. It wasn't as smooth of a ride as the paved streets in Elpha Zavar.

"How many visitors do you drive to the city each day?" Vance asked.

Their driver chuckled. "More than I can count."

"Does it ever get boring?" Janessa asked.

"Who cares if it gets boring. It pays." Vance noted. "I'd do it, too."

The driver laughed once more. "Have any of you been to Thyrel before? I see you're all ethrean."

"I've been once." Vance stated. "It's been a couple decades."

"You'll find a few things have changed, but most of the city remains the same as it was when Etrinn ruled."

Since Etrinn . . . The memory of the ruins filled Thoren's mind along with a strange sense of a shadow. It was hard to describe, even to himself, but something about the ruins piqued his curiosity. *Both cities were built using the same crystalline stone, zilkan.*

The vehicle came to a stop outside the city gates a half hour later. "You'll be walking from here. The streets inside are too narrow for these bulky things." Their driver patted the dashboard of his vehicle.

They all retrieved their luggage and stepped back from their driver's vehicle, thanking him, as he pulled back and turned around, returning to the train station.

Together they passed through the open gate. The streets were crowded, far more than home. Thoren found himself bumping against someone every few steps. Only a few turned to apologize at the same time as him.

Picking up his luggage, he held it out in front of himself to better keep it from catching on those passing by. Thoren and his friends moved deeper into the city, and the feel of the pavement under each step changed. Looking down, he saw the pathways blurring from stone into a teal and blue shimmering crystal, like a fresh pearl bathed in pure aqua water. Soft hues of purple, deep blue, and gold mixed into the glossy path like the differing veins in marble. It reminded him of looking at the smooth inner side of a sea shell—only this “shell” lit up with every step placed upon it, gradually fading to a soft iridescent glow afterwards.

Looking back up, he almost ran into Janessa. She and Vance had stopped at a market stand. The smells around Thoren filled his nose. Naudder meat mixed with fresh herbs, breads, and tropical scents of fruits imported from Kern.

“I’d like a naudder skewer,” Vance stated his order and pointed at the image on the sign. He passed over his coin and turned to them with a wide grin and his fresh meal in hand. “Part one of this trip, taste the goods.” He took a bite and pulled a mixture of grilled meat, vegetables, and fruit, off the stick.

Thoren's stomach rumbled. It was noon and he had chosen to skip breakfast aboard the Evercroft in favor of more sleep. He placed his order as well. Taking their meals, they worked their way out of the crowd and into the shaded park between the buildings. Thick-trunked trees dotted the large stretch of green space.

"Where should we go first?" Vance asked.

They each used their larger luggage as a seat, sitting in a small circle while they ate.

"I want to hear what that letter says." Janessa shifted slightly, facing Thoren with eager eyes. "We're here, so now you can open it."

"All right." He passed his skewer to her and wiped off his hands with a small napkin.

Stretching his left leg out, he reached into his pocket and pulled out the wrinkled, sealed parchment. He leaned forward, resting his elbows on his knees as he picked the wax seal. It popped off and he unfolded it.

Good Sir, or Miss,

You have been selected to participate in the Mentor Trials. This is in an effort to prepare the next Gift Bearer for troubling times ahead. You will be examined in three areas: physical strength and skill, your ability to weave the elements in harmony, and lastly, your ability to connect with Marmidon.

This exam will take place on the fifth of Trete before the highly anticipated celebration of Farthven Ladayose. You are expected to appear outside of Thyrel's zilkan tower by dawn with nothing more than yourself, wearing the mentor's garb that you should have received before departing your home city or town.

Welcome to the trials.

Sincerely,
Lady Dessuithiel

Thoren stared at the words once more. *Fifth of Trete . . . that's tomorrow!*

"Wow, that's it?" Vance said with a mouthful of meat.

"I'm not sure what I expected it to say, but I thought there would be more details on what you would be doing." Janessa offered Thoren's food back to him.

Thoren folded the letter and tucked it away, taking his skewer back.

"How do you feel you'll do?" she asked.

He thought for only a moment about it. "I don't know. I want to be the best, but I'm sure that the others applying for the position feel the same way."

"You'll get the position." Janessa smiled.

"How can you say that?" Vance contested. "Don't get his hopes up. What if he gets cut early? We'll have to comfort a dejected Thoren."

"Oh, dejected?" Thoren raised an eyebrow and tipped his head looking at his friend. "You think I'll fail?"

"Nobody really knows, but Marmidon herself." Vance shrugged.

"I bet Marmidon has already chosen." Janessa said as she finished her skewer.

Has Marmidon chosen?

It was an interesting view, one that Thoren hadn't considered. He had thought it would just be about compatibility, but Marmidon could have already chosen before any of the applicants arrived.

"Either way, you're showing up in the morning. That gives us the afternoon to find housing," Janessa said.

"Housing?" Thoren questioned, "Don't you mean an inn?"

"No, I mean housing." Janessa patted her luggage. "I'm moving here."

Thoren looked between his friends, surprised. "Vance, aren't you just visiting?"

Vance shook his head. "I plan on staying, too."

Thoren laughed. "How long were you two planning this?"

"Since you applied," Janessa stated.

"About the same time," Vance answered.

Janessa stood and took hold of her bags, slinging one over her shoulder and setting the other up on its wheels. "I'm ready to go house hunting."

"How much did you save for a deposit?" Vance joined her as she started out of the park.

Thoren finished his last couple of bites and grabbed his things. He had packed for the possibility that he would be staying, but there was still a chance he would be sent back home.

I'll be fine for a couple of weeks, maybe longer if Janessa and Vance really do find a place.

"You know that you don't have to move here, just because I'm here, right?"

Janessa nodded. "I know." She sighed, pausing and facing him before she continued, "At the same time, we are old enough to be out on our own. We *should* be. A century at home is long enough." She smiled with a child-like spark and jogged over to Vance.

Vance was the first to find a place to live. To Thoren's surprise, he'd brought substantial savings for this very thing.

"You should have paid the fare for the ride." He elbowed Vance.

"Hey, you offered." Vance shrugged.

"Vance, can I dump my stuff here at your place?" Janessa asked while tapping her suitcase and travel pack. "It will be easier to hunt for a place without them."

"Sure." He waved his keys in the air. "You're all welcome to leave your things here." His grin widened. "I'm a home owner."

Janessa huffed. "You know this would have been my place if you didn't have the higher bid."

"Sure." He took a step back, avoiding her slap aimed at his shoulder. "Think what you want, but to be here you have to pay the price."

"I think you'll be working two jobs to keep this place," Janessa said as she poked Vance's gut before walking around the entry and into the larger living space with a joined kitchen.

Thoren set his bags down in the corner of the front room and looked back out the window. The curved frame made the sight of Thyrel's streets look like a painting. Vance had nabbed a nice place, but at the same time, he had drained most of the savings he'd brought with him.

His eyes caught on a group of ethrea walking west, to the back of the city. Their white garb was the same as what he wore.

The other participants?

"I'm going out for a while." He stepped up to the front door.

"I'm headed out, too," Janessa said, securing her coin inside a smaller bag hanging from her shoulder.

"I'd like to see more of the city," Vance said and pulled his keys out. "Should we all meet back here for supper?" he asked.

"That sounds good to me." Thoren nodded and left.

He scanned the busy streets and caught sight of the participants. He kept a quick pace as he wove through the crowds. His eyes drifted up to the massive tower ahead, where shimmering light moved like sunlight on rippling water. It stood at the very back of the city as though it had been carved from the Bearing Mountains. The stone shone like the pearly crystal pathways that lined the city, reminiscent of the roots of an ancient tree. This was the tower he'd barely been able to see from the train station.

How long has this tower stood? From what he understood, Etrinn's buildings were constructed of the same material—zilkan. However, Etrinn was all ruins now. Zilkan was now a rare mineral. The only standing structure left made from it, was found here in Thyrel. History on how these buildings were constructed was missing—just gone as though erased—and the ethrea that were alive during the first Calamity, oddly could not recall the details. His gut twisted as he dwelled on it. There was a reason why nobody could remember. *It must be part of what took place on the day of Peerretdyn.*

"Hey, are you here for the mentor trials?" a youthful sounding female asked.

The question had come suddenly from his right. Thoren had been walking toward the tower in a daze. He stopped and faced the person. She beamed up at him with wide eyes, wearing the same white garb.

"Y-yeah. You?"

"Yup! I arrived yesterday from Uecketev." She thumbed at the tower. "You seem fixed on the tower. Have you not been here before?"

Thoren shook his head. "No. I've spent most of my first century in Jushosh."

"Oh! Are you from Elpha Zavar?" She waved at the air. "I hear it's the only city where ethrea like living over there."

"Well, it is the only one well-wooded." Thoren laughed. "I think we tend to stick there because other coastal cities deal with a lot of seasonal storms and lack the protection our forest gives."

"Hey, Fern!"

The masculine call came from one of the other participants a few yards ahead. His sharp-featured face and speculative eyes fixed on Thoren.

"Fern?" Thoren looked at the young woman.

She smiled shyly. “My parents are botanists.” Looking at the ethrean man calling her, she shouted back, “What?”

“Are we going to train in the tower grounds, or what?”

“Do you want to join us?” she asked Thoren. “We all wanted to get a feel for where the trials will be held tomorrow and practice some weaving.”

Thoren nodded—albeit somewhat apprehensive over the idea of weaving. He was just as curious about the location, and didn’t mind getting a bit closer to the tower. It emitted a warm energy that was difficult for him to pin.

The closer they got, the more thinned out the crowds were. Thoren slowed and stopped at the pruned bushes marking the start of the tower gardens. The rest of the participants passed through the opening and turned left into one of the open green fields. Within seconds, they began shifting the elements around them, weaving water from the air, and dirt from beneath their feet.

“I’m betting these trials won’t be all that hard,” one of the men said while swirling liquid rock around himself.

“I think there’s more to it than weaving,” Fern said and noticed Thoren had stayed behind on the other side of the hedge. She stepped over to him. “Why don’t you come in? Weaving is freely permitted in the field.” She pointed to a small sign near the entrance. “It would be good to practice before being tested on it.”

Thoren shook his head. “I think I’d best save my energy.”

"Suit yourself." Her shoulders pinched and fell while her hands slapped at her thighs. She rejoined the others and began weaving the grass, twisting it and building a basket with the strands while she sat.

Thoren turned to face the tower on his right, and looked up at the point-topped arching windows. He couldn't tell if there was glass in the panes, it looked completely open from where he stood. A few ethrean guards stood at the tower's entrance, unmoving, but clearly watching the participants weaving in the field. His chest burned, drawing one of his hands to it.

What is this feeling? He broke his gaze with the tower and the feeling faded.

"Are you well?" A soft, angelic voice asked from behind.

Thoren dropped his hand and spun around.

He was met with a ring of ethrean guards around a single woman. She was hard to see as a white veil covered her face. She wore a flowing gown with a dusting of peach-pink blossoms embroidered along the skirt and bell shaped sleeves. The only main feature he could make out beneath the veil was her fiery, dark-red hair falling to the base of her back.

"I-I'm well, thank you."

"Be sure to take care of yourself. I see you are wearing the Mentor Trial's garb. Tomorrow is a big day for you . . ." She tipped her head to see better between her guards. " . . .and the others." She appeared to be studying Thoren's face, but it was hard to tell with the veil she wore.

"Do you know anything about what we'll be doing?" Thoren asked.

One of the guards coughed—half choking in response to his question.

The woman lifted one of her delicate hands and gently patted the guard's back.

"Guan, do you need some water?"

He grunted and shook his head before responding, "My lady, we should return, you have much to prepare for."

She sighed. Even that was angelic. "If I must." She turned her head to Thoren. "Good luck tomorrow. I have a feeling you'll do well." She nodded politely and walked forward, toward Thyrel's glimmering tower. Her circling guards moved with her along the crystal path.

Thoren watched until she entered the brilliant structure.

The field had become quiet as well.

"That was Lady Dessuithiel." One of the female participants noted with a slightly negative tone. "She makes a point to visit the ethrean schools every week to recite history to the children and help them improve their weaving skills. Waste of time, in my opinion. Why have teachers, if she's going to go and take over every week?"

He chanced a glance at the participant. She didn't look like she had a warm personality. Thoren's face flushed. *Was I rude? I should have used her title! I should have bowed! T-that was Thyrel's princess!* He watched the tower windows for any sign of the woman.

"Star gobbed, aren't you?" The teasing came from the same male participant that had called Fern earlier. He had dark brown hair, similarly styled to Thoren's. His square face came off just as stern as his voice. "I heard she's been betrothed this year. It's too bad only those of royal blood can marry her."

"It's been that way for centuries and I doubt it would change anytime soon." Fern noted. "I've heard that the Valdan royal family have been making preparations to unite with the Vizule family." She sighed and brushed her hand over the pruned hedge, rustling the leaves "Makes sense, the Valdan and Vizule families are the most powerful ethrea in all of Marmidon."

Thoren glanced at the competitors and then returned his gaze to the tower, catching sight of Dessuithiel passing one of the upper floor windows. His pulse quickened at the thought of her and his chest burned once more. He felt oddly drawn to her, but quickly brushed it off as pre-trial jitters.

The Valdan and Vizule bloodlines uniting? Thoren hadn't heard such rumors in Elpha Zavar. *Even if they don't, a lady of the Vizule family is beyond me.* He extinguished any wistful feelings that had faintly sparked in their brief encounter. *I'm not even looking for a soul mate.* He lightly shook his head. *Janessa and Vance must be getting to me.*

"What's your name?" The dark haired ethrean asked.

"Thoren Belfry," he answered subconsciously.

"Pleasure." The man offered his hand over the hedge, barely within Thoren's peripheral. "Balek Thrain," he announced.

Thoren tore his gaze away from the tower, and once more the burning ceased within his chest. He took Balek's hand in a firm shake.

"You've met Fern." He pointed at her. "Over there is James, Olathe, Shirra, Byran, and Finian." He pointed to each of them as he listed them off.

For the most part they all looked similar because of the garb they wore, but Thoren was able to pick out a couple defining details to help him remember. He repeated their names internally as Balek listed them off.

James is slender, Olathe has eye spectacles, Shirra is half Verran with her tawny-brown skin and not a warm personality, Byran looks strong, and Finian has cut his hair short.

The rest of the participants joined Balek at the hedge.

Olathe clapped her hands and let the water she was manipulating dissipate into the air—fading into a fine mist that fell over the grass.

"You're more than welcome to practice with us," she said—a repeated offer Thoren was starting to get uncomfortable with.

Thoren responded, "Fern offered, but I think it's best if I rest."

I'll make a fool of myself otherwise.

If there was one thing ethrea were known for, it was weaving. Paired with an ancient word, or string of them, anyone could manipulate the multitude of forms nature took, within reason. There were forbidden uses and laws on where and when weaving could be performed within city limits. However, Thoren struggled to weave even the most basic of elements—air.

"I'm sure we'll all get to know each other well over the next week," Balek said. "It may be Thoren's strategy to observe." He stepped back from the hedge. "I don't think it's a bad thing to keep strengths hidden until they're needed."

Thoren smiled lightly. *It's more like a weakness.* He didn't dare tell them, but they would find out soon enough.

"I'm going to head out." Thoren waved at the participants. "It was a pleasure to meet you all."

They exchanged a polite nod—half bow—and waved before Thoren turned and walked down the slight city hill.

What was I thinking? Follow my competitors? They've got a better shot at this position. He lifted his hand and stared at his open palm. *Even my best friends don't know.*

FIRST ENCOUNTER

Chapter 4

Dessuithiel Vizule

Fourth of Trete

The following days passed in a blur as Dessuithiel was called to her parents for floral arrangement choices, meals to be served to the royals attending her union, and the finishing touches for her dress.

She left a rather unproductive meeting with her mother and found herself in the zilkan tower's library. The smell of history eased her tension and she pulled one of the meticulously-kept books from the nearest shelf. Not caring what it was about, so much as distracting her mind from the rapidly coming visit of the Valdan royals, she looked over the pages of runic symbols that made up the language of weaves.

Steady heavy footsteps rounded the bookshelf. She noticed the familiar shade of red in the settling fabric. Lowering the book in her hands, she lifted her eyes to the cloaked figure. This man was whom she had planned all the trials with, to test the applicants for a worthy soul to carry the task of being Marmidon's chosen mentor to the next Gift Bearer.

"It's not often you leave the mountain." She addressed him.

His elderly tones passed from underneath the oversized hood that hid his face. "The labyrinth has been prepared."

She shut the book and tucked it at her side. "I do hope you didn't strain yourself."

"I will be here until I am not. Marmidon will not take me until that fateful time comes." He spoke with a surety that Dessuithiel wished she could have for her own future.

"Am I really not to know what they will be facing in there?"

The hood swayed as he shook his head. "I cannot risk anyone knowing what they may face. The test will fail to draw out Marmidon's mentor otherwise."

She nodded her understanding. "I will do my part and bring the applicants to face the first trial in the morning." Turning around she handed the book to Guan, who then returned it to the open location upon the shelf. She addressed the man once more. "About the second trial . . ."

"I heard back from Verra." He coughed, leaning forward in an attempt to ease the pain it caused him.

"Don't speak. I should have sent for paper and pen." She reached out but hesitated. Deep down she wished she could comfort the elderly man, but she stopped herself and pulled her hand back.

I already touched Guan, not even four days ago. I don't know if I could handle touching another person. She hated the side-effects of her foresight and how it separated her from everyone.

Another fit of coughs struck the man and he stumbled, losing his strength as he fell toward the wall opposite the bookshelf. Dessuithiel acted as any concerned person would, not wanting him to fall to the floor or hit his head on the wall. She reached out against her years of reservation and grabbed the man's arm—willing to take the consequence.

He recoiled at her touch, as did she—her mind filled with images: events lived, events to come, more than she could process. She gasped, snapping her hand to her head.

"My lady!" Guan rushed around to where he could see her face. "Do you need support?"

Dessuithiel let the tension leave her neck and shoulders, forcing a smile upon her face as she met her guards' concerned gaze. "My mistake, I will be fine."

"Lady Dessuithiel . . ." the man said as he stood upright. "I'm sure you saw more than you wanted. I apologize for any pain it may have caused you. I will return to my home within the mountain for the time being." He turned from her after a polite bow.

Guan still hovered at her side, partially crouched, with his arms outstretched as though she were going to collapse. Lifting a hand, she shooed him back to his usual post two strides behind her.

"I'm going to need some fresh air tonight." Her words were mostly a declaration of her desire for a change of scenery, only partially directed at Guan.

He answered anyway. "The city has been busy as of late." He straightened his back and held his hands at his sides—resuming his usual posture. "With the influx of those curious to see the trials, I am concerned that you will brush against several individuals despite my efforts. If you wish to go out, I require more guards."

She hadn't considered the increased populace. Letting out a frustrated, but dainty sigh, she nodded. "Then I shall have more guards. I need to leave the tower, if only for a short walk and fresh air."

Selecting a gown decorated in peach-pink blossoms, her handmaids helped her dress and fix her hair simply. They did so in the practiced manner of avoiding all direct physical contact with her. Tipping and turning her head, Dessuithiel smiled at the basic braids that held half her hair back and let the remainder fall freely to the base of her back.

"Is there anything else you require, my lady?" her lady's maid asked.

"No. This is perfect." Dessuithiel stood and brushed her hands over the detailed embroidery, feeling the wide bell-sleeve flowing gently with the motion. For most of her life, the brush of fabric was all she felt. This was the life she had resigned herself to. All to avoid the visions that plagued her mind when touching any other living soul.

Dundaelon will be disappointed. She stepped up to her bedroom window, staring out over Thyrel's height-varied buildings and sky pillars, which were falling into shadow. Suppertime was drawing near, but she was not hungry. Everything felt out of her control. Her heart drummed erratically over the thought of being wed in a matter of days to a man she had never met—into a union she did not want.

The setting sun would soon trade places with Ilzu and Maz and paint the city in a pale blue light, blurring the separation between those walking the streets and the shadows. The shadows that would come for her.

Will that dark realm not leave me alone for a single day?

Dessuithiel pulled away from the window and placed a hand over her heart. Deep breaths were not helping it calm.

"Guan!" she called.

Her door burst open and her guard rushed to her side. "My lady, you called? What is the matter?"

"I want to leave the tower now." She turned her back to the window and gathered up the layers of her gown.

"It is yet early for your evening walk, my lady."

"I'm going *now*." She needed to clear her mind, to separate herself from this building that caged her.

Focusing on the sensation of her cascading dress in motion, she moved hastily down the spiral stairs. It helped distract her mind from her recurrent vision.

"My lady, if you would give me just a moment to gather the rest of your guard." Guan rushed out ahead of her before she could storm out the tower doors.

She smiled curtly, but was sure it still presented upon her face as elegantly as always, and Guan was none the wiser to her true feelings.

“I will wait here.” Swallowing her pride, she acknowledged that Guan only had her best interest at heart. The city was busier than usual and taking an evening stroll would not be without risk of an unsolicited vision.

Guan returned shortly with some sort of headpiece in hand. He offered it to her, bowing his head as he did. “My lady, you are betrothed and ought to veil your face in public.”

Right . . .

She took the headpiece, securing it atop her head and setting the sheer fabric about her face and shoulders.

It wasn’t long before she was leaving the confines of the zilkan tower behind and calming her distress with the tower garden’s embrace. The fragrance of roses drew her to the maze of pruned bushes and the floral arch that led to her favorite garden bench.

She did not leave the tower grounds during her evening walks. She hardly left home at all—except to share historical insights with the school children once a week. She spread the skirt of her gown, settling on her bench where she would listen to the sounds of her people and smell the mixture of sweet and savory foods passing through the floral surround. Here, she could let her worries go. Here, she could relax.

Caught in a sudden storm, Dessuithiel's eyes shot open. Her garden was nowhere in sight. Miles of desolate city lay around her, blotted in pockets of black mist.

"Not this place." She whispered.

She stood and glanced back at what should have been her bench, to find a large collection of rubble. Monstrous cries broke the eerie silence. Spinning around, she scanned for the source. The creature let out a pained whine before ceasing altogether.

"Marmidon? What is this I am seeing?" she called out hoping for an answer. "I'm ready to know!"

She said it, but did not fully feel ready to understand the scene before her.

Motion drew her attention to a distant street. Her breath caught in her chest as she recognized the same ethrean man from every prior vision connected to this realm. He carried a unique weapon, likely formed under his own weave, and chased after the gruesome beasts of this realm.

Do I chase him? He . . . He's fighting the darkness?

It was becoming clearer to her that this man she continued to see was not the cause of the fearsome scene but was fighting it. She needed to find him, speak to him.

Dessuithiel gathered her dress and gave chase.

She'd not been running for more than a few seconds before a sudden grip pulled at her arm. The scene before her vanished as her progress was halted.

In a single blink, the gloomy realm was replaced with the tower grounds and a flood of Guan's childhood memories in Dershja.

"My lady, apologies." Guan's voice reached her ears and the grip around her upper arm released.

She stood under the canopy of the guest homes—magical residences built within the many ancient trees of the zilkan tower's grounds. She turned to face him, brows pinched in confusion. "How did I get here?" She spoke only loud enough for Guan to hear as the rest of her guard rushed to form a barrier between her and the citizens wandering the gardens. She had a hunch as to what had taken place, but wanted to be sure.

I've never traveled within a vision before. Normally that breaks me from it. Her pulse became rapid as she feared that she may soon be unable to break away from the dark realm.

"You suddenly stood from the garden bench, searching around as though something had spooked you, before running from the rose garden, my lady," Guan answered.

"I see."

Her fears were confirmed. Dessuithiel smoothed her gown and veil, squared her shoulders, and gave her guards a reassuring nod. "It appears I have startled you in my sudden rush. I wish to return to the tower."

Guan eased and took his place ahead of her, leading the way back to the zilkan tower. There was no calming the rush still forcing her heart to beat at twice its normal pace. Questions filled her mind.

Can I never rest? Must I remain awake at all times? Will the visions steal me away indefinitely?

They approached the last stretch to the tower. She lifted her aimless stare from the zilkan path as they came upon the hedged green fields at the base of her home. Oddly, someone had stopped along the path and appeared to be in awe of the zilkan tower.

Must be one of the many visitors who have come to see the trials.

She froze as she realized what he wore, and her guard stumbled to a halt.

White garb, cloth belt . . . How did I not realize this sooner? Marmidon, is that him? The man from my vision is one of the applicants!

She stared at the back of a man fitting the image of her vision with exactness. His silvery-white, golden hair rested just past his broad shoulders. Dessuithiel tipped her head shifting what she could see and noting the man's ethrean heritage by the pointed tips of his ears.

This ethrean man, staring at the zilkan tower, lifted a hand to his chest. His shoulders tensed and he turned his head from the shimmering structure. Dessuithiel watched him closely, taking in every shift of his body. His shoulders eased.

She couldn't help herself, opening her mouth and asking, "Are you well?"

What am I doing? Alarmed with herself for asking such a thing when he looked perfectly fine.

He spun around and her lungs forgot their place, seizing as his face without a doubt was what she had seen for over the last decade. She thanked Marmidon that Guan had given her the veil to wear, or she was certain her usual elegance would not be enough to mask her surprise.

"I-I'm well, thank you." His voice was deep, charming even, if not uncertain.

It ***is*** *him.*

Dessuithiel held herself with all the regal poise she could. "Be sure to take care of yourself." She thought of what this man would be facing in the coming days. Moments they had been, but she knew he had a hard battle ahead. "I see you are wearing the Mentor Trial's garb. Tomorrow is a big day for you . . ." Tilting her head she tried to get a better look at his face.

Her ears tickled at the sound of his voice. "Do you know anything about what we'll be doing?"

Guan suddenly coughed and pounded at his chest.

Reaching out to her guard, she hesitantly patted at his back—wincing under the sting each time she made contact. Her mind ached as she saw more of his past, filling in missing gaps from the first insights she'd gained about him.

His cough sounded dry, but was easing off.

Still, she asked, "Guan, do you need some water?"

Her guard grunted as he shook his head. "My lady, we should return, you have much to prepare for."

Don't remind me . . .

A sigh slipped from her lips before she caught herself breaking composure in public.

In an attempt to amend it, she responded, "If I must." Dessuithiel couldn't help getting one more look, and giving one last well-wish to the man who'd haunted her dreams for years. "Good luck tomorrow." She smiled, knowing that he had formidable weapon mastery. "I have a feeling you'll do well." Giving a soft nod, she departed.

Guan didn't miss a beat, moving forward just ahead of her as the rest of her guard maintained her protective circle.

Once the doors shut behind her, Dessuithiel dismissed the extra guard and hurried up the stairs, removing the veil from her head.

"My lady, please, slow down," Guan called after her.

She began spouting off her thoughts, excited at the revelation. "I can't believe I saw *him*! He's here, Guan. He's competing to be the mentor!"

Guan did not answer, but followed her to the royal quarters. When she approached her bedroom's door, Guan made a noise—more of a gruff guttural throat-clearing cough.

Facing him, she smiled shyly. "Do you recognize who we spoke with, down by the training field?"

"He's the one from your vision." Guan accurately stated.

Looking at her guard, she noticed his expression caught between displeasure, and confusion.

"What's wrong?" Her heart sank.

"There's something off about him." He half folded his arms and tapped a finger on his bare chin. "He didn't feel completely ethrean. I can't quite pin down why. What role does he play in your other dreams?"

"Visions, Guan."

"Right, sorry, visions. What is his role in your other visions, my lady? Has Marmidon shared it?"

She glanced around, taking note of her handmaids holding her doors open and a few distant guards down the hall leading deeper into the mountain. Waving at Guan to draw nearer, she then whispered, "He's the one fighting off the darkness."

This time she was certain of his disapproval when he groaned.

"You can't judge him, Guan. Whatever it is you sense about him, you're wrong."

He forced a smile and stood back. "I must be, my lady. I am sworn to you and your desire is mine."

Rolling her eyes, she moved back toward her doors. "Goodnight, Guan."

"Good night, my lady."

The tower had fallen still over an hour ago as she lay in bed, staring at the canopy hung over top of her bed and draping down the four posts of the frame. Wind carried through the cracked window of her bedroom, shifting the sheer fabric separating her from the rest of her room. Her fingers rubbed over her bedsheets nervously as she sought for something to still her mind.

Unable to sleep for fear of the realm that would lay claim to her, she let her eyes water, and fought the desire to shut them for any portion longer than it took to blink. What she would give to have someone sitting beside her. To comfort her.

Marmidon, this foresight is a curse!

Dessuithiel sat up in a sudden jolt as her mind attempted to slip. Her handmaids were no longer in the room, but she knew that Guan was outside her doors, on duty this night.

A distant bell tower rang, marking the hour—two hours past midnight. Dessuithiel felt restless and tossed off her bedding. Her bare arms prickled under a cold stream of air upon passing between the curtains of her bed. Pulling on her robe she went to her window and shut it. The chill remained, circling her like a crierspry.

Guan. I need Guan.

She moved toward the shut double doors, focused on the crystal knobs as her vision began to fade out.

No . . .

She reached for them, felt them under her fingers, and then . . . nothing.

A shriek broke the endless clouds of black that had swallowed her. Dessuithiel covered her ears, crouching, cowering. All hope, joy, and light within her drained as though the very mist fed upon it. The chilling air moved around her and a creature stumbled into sight.

A scream pressed up through her throat, forcing itself out at the sight of some poor soul reanimated after having half decomposed.

The creature—as she could not call it a person—turned its head, noticing her.

A sudden figure appeared ahead of her. **Him**. *He stood between her and the creature, unaware of her. His grip upon his weapon slipped, shaking as though he were experiencing some extreme sensation, be it physical or mental. Whatever had him fixed in place did not keep him long. He kicked out at the creature's chest, following up with a mastered motion as he ran the monstrosity through with his weapon.*

Did he know who he had just protected? He didn't seem in the slightest aware of her standing behind him. The hope, joy, and light that had been stolen from her, radiated from this man. It gave her the strength she needed.

She broke from her statuesque state and ran.

Not more than a few steps into her run, she hit a wall of some sort. Her shoulder ached. Feeling over the surface, she noticed it was not solid. With another shove, it fell away. Dessuithiel dared to glance behind her, searching for the one who'd saved her from the darkness of this place. He was gone. Clicks and cracks sounded from the creature as it stumbled after her.

Each breath only made it halfway in before she pushed it back out in a frenzy. She turned to the left, spotting a place to hide—a slope leading down into a vegetative ditch among the rubble of the broken city she stood within.

Dessuithiel sprinted, but as she hit the slope, she found the ground cut much like stairs. Someone called after her. Distracted by the distorted voice, she slipped.

"My lady!" Guan shouted with alarm.

His grip came from behind, once again around her upper arm and additionally around her waist. With a sudden yank, her body was pulled back and spun around into a wall. The unsettling vision collapsed, having become distorted the moment her guard had touched her. What she saw now was Guan, very close, and precariously fated to the force of whatever had just occurred. Guan's response was immediate, preventing further harm as he'd released her and caught himself, hands pressed into the wall on either side of her.

He coughed and pulled back. Avoiding eye contact as he asked, "My lady, are you hurt anywhere?"

Dessuithiel crossed her arms and held her shoulders. Her left one ached, but she was well enough. "No, Guan. I'm fine."

He grunted and took another step back. "That is good. I'm not sure what it was that you were seeing, but, my lady, I fear that your visions may be putting your life at risk."

She studied what she could see of his face, turned away from her. He was flustered, that was clear from the flushing upon his cheeks.

"What in Marmidon is going on?"

Dessuithiel tensed at her father's inquiry.

Guan saluted, slapping his hands to his sides, and bowed toward the high lord. He held it for several seconds before rising and resuming his usual straight face and stiff posture as her shadow.

"My dear, I heard you scream. What has happened?" Her father approached, reached out, but then pulled his hands back while flashing a hesitant smile.

Scared of what I'll see.

Her parent's response after discovering that every contact brought a flood of insight to her mind, had dampened their relationship over recent years. She still loved them, as they did her, but the isolation was becoming more difficult to bear. Dessuithiel didn't know how much longer she could go without a reassuring embrace from her mother, or a comforting hand upon her shoulder from her father.

Putting on a brave face, she gave an answer that would put him at ease. "I had a nightmare. It took me a bit to wake from it, it would seem. Nothing more. I'm sorry to have disturbed your rest, Ba."

Her father addressed Guan. "Is that all? A bad dream? How did she end up out here?"

"It appears that this one caused some sleep walking, High Lord Ayzgar. I caught her before she fell over the railing and she woke from the sudden motion, alarmed."

Dessuithiel's eyes grew wide and her head turned back to see if he was fabricating such a story, or telling the truth. It appeared to be the truth.

"Dear, Marmidon!" her father gasped. "I commend you for protecting my daughter from harm, dare I say an untimely demise."

"Ba." Dessuithiel folded her arms tightly and huffed. "I'm fine. Guan did his job. Now please, go rest and worry no more."

"I'll send for some calming tea that should ease your mind, my dear. It is not just I who requires rest. Your Aba and I have entrusted the trials to you, but if it is causing undue stress . . ."

"No, Ba, I am fine. I'm looking forward to overseeing the trials. Please, do not disrupt your schedule over this."

She knew very well that her parents intended to meet with several of the lesser royal families and other denominational monarchies while the trials were being held. It was important that they kept up good relations with them.

Her father hummed, nodded and turned to leave. "I'll send that tea up."

"Thank you, Ba."

Dessuithiel began up the stairs with a heavy sigh and rubbed at the side of her head. She paused at one of the windows and stared out over the twinkling city. The zilkan pathways gave off their ever-present soft-blue glow. They stretched out from the base of the tower and through the city like veins carrying vital nutrients from the heart that was her home.

Motion drew her eyes down and a calm fell over her, stilling the rapid beats within her chest that had not slowed since before supper. There he was, leaving the training field in the middle of the night right before the first trial. He stopped, as if sensing her eyes upon him. She moved out of view when he suddenly turned around and stared up at the zilkan tower.

Pressing her back to the wall beside the window, she held her hands over her heart.

Guan spoke softly. "My lady, shall I call for your handmaids to be with you for the remainder of the night?"

She nodded absently.

Guan's right. There's something about that man. It is far more than a feeling. Marmidon needs him, but for what?

A SINGLE WEAKNESS

Chapter 5

Thoren Belfry
Evening of the Fourth of Trete

He returned to Vance's house at supper time after wandering around the city. He had a good feel of the layout and found some nice looking noshes to eat at. There was one in particular that looked like a capsized ship. The smells coming out of that nosh had been most pleasant.

Thoren knocked on the front door of Vance's newly acquired home and waited for one of his friends to answer. The door opened, Vance greeted him and waved him in. Thoren stepped aside into the front room where Janessa stood.

"We were just discussing where to eat. There's a cool looking place on the north side of Thyrel that we're curious to try."

"The north side . . . I think I saw the same one. We must have been siblings displaced at birth. I was thinking about that place not a moment ago! Assuming it is the one I am picturing."

"Well, if we're ready. I think we've picked where we're going to eat." Vance pulled his front door open again and jingled his keys.

"So, where did you wander off to?" Janessa asked Thoren.

It was easy to see from the raised brows on Vance's face that he was curious as well.

He waved his hand about. "Nowhere really. I just wanted to get a feel for Thyrel's layout."

Thoren walked with his friends through the winding paths of Thyrel. His heart had been in a nervous patter since they'd asked about where he'd gone. He couldn't stop thinking of how good the other participants were at weaving. It looked so effortless for them.

Vance held up his hand and pointed out at the nosh they'd picked. "Looks like we're just in time to avoid the supper rush."

They joined the short line just outside of the entrance. Thoren stared at the structure. As he had suspected, it was the nosh he was curious about, the capsized ship—known as The Joint. The polished planks were speckled and white. It had been constructed with amur trees. Strings of lights hung from the top and draped down in a woven pattern to the front door.

Faint folk music could be heard. Thoren picked out the instruments as he listened and found his restless heart easing in the lull of the softer tunes.

They moved inside, where a welcome desk stood a few strides from the door. A tall female atle stood behind it, taking payment and directing the nosh's guests to the open dining with a wave of her blue-tinted hand. Her tightly woven hair moved like a willow's vines each time she turned her head. Her angular face shape, characteristic of her race, was striking. One of the many aspects that lent the atle the presence they commanded in any room. Beneath the gills on the side of her neck, the woman had a necklace of several shells mixed in with pearls and carved stone beads.

She's from the northern tribe . . . It had been a while since he'd seen an atle from the north. The one on the train had been from the south.

"Just the three of you?" the atle asked. Her voice was deep, yet still very feminine.

Vance nodded. "And what would you suggest for first time visitors?"

The atle smiled. "First time? Well, you can't go wrong with the cod and Thyrel's bestselling drink: the veritian." She punched in the total for their seats. "That will be four garrens and two runds per person, making a total of twelve garrens and six runds."

Vance turned to Thoren and gave his best pleading grin.

"Oh, all right." Thoren stepped up to the desk and paid.

"Thank you, you may find your seating where you please, a waiter will be with you shortly, and you will find a menu on your table."

"Nice." Janessa followed Vance to a four chaired table near the left side of the nosh.

Thoren sat down and stared over the options. He wasn't sure how much he felt like eating.

Vance leaned over and spoke. "I spotted a group of young ethrea earlier. They had the same garb on as you." He pointed with his thumb at the nosh's window.

Thoren glanced at the window, worried that he would see the other competitors. His stomach knotted over it, but they weren't there.

Vance continued. “Does that mean you’ll be competing against them for the position?”

Thoren nodded.

“Don’t worry.” Janessa patted at the table. “You’re the best at anything you do.”

Vance cut back in. “Well, at least with old time weapons, and studies. I don’t think I’ve ever seen you weave.” He scratched at the back of his head and stared off at the ceiling. “Yeah, I’ve never seen you weave.”

Janessa gasped. “Me neither.” She dropped her menu to the table. “Why is that?”

“Maybe he’s just that gifted. We all know he’d leave us flat on the ground.” Vance laughed and Janessa joined.

Thoren cringed and tried to laugh, but it came out as more of a gruntled cough.

“Good evening.” Their waiter stepped up to their table.

Thoren sighed at the timely appearance. He was not ready to reveal his weakness to his friends.

The evening was filled with music, laughter, and good food. Thoren did his best to enjoy it, but he couldn’t bring himself to completely let go. They finished and left the nosh just after sundown.

"Did you find a place?" Vance asked Janessa.

"I did, but it won't be ready for me to move in until the twenty-sixth."

"Dang." Vance jingled his keys. "I think you two are housing with me for now."

"Fine by me," Thoren said.

Thoren took a small breath in realization. "I saw a shop with bedding. We should stop by."

"Lead the way." Vance paused walking and waited for Thoren.

It didn't take much longer for them to find the shop and get what they each needed. Thoren ended up paying for them all, again, but he didn't mind. He had a hefty savings and had brought most of it with him.

They returned to Vance's house. The structure was tall, a bit narrow across, but plenty deep, and crammed between several other structures of the same brick-built style.

Thoren entered last. "Can I take the front room?"

"You know I have bedrooms, enough for each of us to have our own," Vance said. "Are you sure? I'd feel like a bad host."

Thoren shook his head. "I'll be heading out early. It won't bother me."

"Suit yourself, but I'm turning in." Vance took his bedding and marched up the stairs.

Janessa lingered.

"Thoren?" She stepped up to him with anxious curiosity, her brows pinched. "I tried to let it go, but why haven't you ever woven around us? It wasn't forbidden in Elpha Zavar."

His gut twisted and his heart stuttered, pinching within his chest.

"I-I . . ." He couldn't think of a good excuse.

"You've been very quiet since we arrived." She looked out the window at the night life of the city.

Thoren stared at the scene beyond the glass panes as well. His heart echoed in his ears. The ground held a blue-purple glow from the crystal pathway that lined the city. Street lights cast their golden beams, and buildings speckled the dark like stars.

"Janessa." He shut his eyes and took a deep breath. His entire body trembled. "I-I can't weave." He lifted his hands, opening them, palms up.

"Wait, then how did you get approved?"

Thoren clarified. "I can barely shift the air, alter the ground, or grow a single leaf. The city examiner thought I was just tired." His hand rested over his inner well, just above his stomach. "But it hurts every time I try."

He'd said it, and he felt an odd sense of relief in doing so. Opening his eyes, he found her staring up at him.

She looked confused and deep in thought with how her brows sunk to the center of her forehead. "Why didn't you ever tell us? Do your parents know?"

Thoren shook his head. "My parents don't know the full extent. I got by in the past, with the little I can do, but as the years passed, I opted not to weave."

Janessa started going through the same questions he had, now over twenty years ago. "Are you sure you're not just saying the weaves wrong, or misguiding your inner well?"

"I'm sure, Janessa. I've looked for answers. I'm ethrean. I should be a natural at it." He turned his face away from her. The shame he carried for nearly a century resurfaced.

It wasn't that he couldn't weave. He felt the draw of power from his inner well and the connection to Marmidon's life force. There was just something wrong, like a stone lodged at his inner well's opening. He'd tried more than once to unlock it—all attempts ended in failure.

"Please, don't say anything to Vance."

Janessa rested her hand on his shoulder, urging him to face her. "If that's what you want, I won't say anything. But what are you going to do? The trials start in the morning."

Thoren pulled away from her. "I don't know, I'm wondering if I should pull out. It would be far easier to get a regular job and live out my days like everyone else." He stepped up to his bedding, which he'd placed near his bags after entering Vance's house.

Janessa sighed, quite loudly. "You and I both know that the run of the mill job would be far too boring for you. You could speak of nothing *but* this position since it was announced."

Thoren wanted to hide and escape this vulnerability. He didn't know what he was going to do about his inability to weave. He felt broken, but Janessa's words pulled at him. She knew him too well, and she wasn't mad. She was still right there.

"I do still want to try . . ."

"And you should," she agreed. "As well as hold your head up high. Weaving or no weaving, you're amazing." Janessa took a step back. "Try to get some rest. Things will work out."

"Thanks." Thoren glanced at her as she walked out of sight.

He rolled out his bedding and sat, leaning on the wall, with his knees drawn up toward his chest. Resting his arms atop his knees he stared out the window, watching the streets clear of the various people roaming them. After some time, he slumped down under his blanket, resting his head on his pillow. He tossed and turned, unable to sleep.

A bell chimed, marking the middle of the night. Thoren wiped a hand down his face and rolled to his knees. He quietly moved over to his things.

I might as well practice.

He opened his larger luggage and selected a more modern outfit; one he could move around in freely without drawing attention. Thoren secured his dark brown cotton trousers, and tucked his loose beige top into the waist. Choosing to leave his pin-striped vest off, he threaded his belt, slipped on some longer socks, and laced his boots. Turning back to his luggage, he pulled out a short sword and secured it to his belt, thinking of the open field near the tower. Taking one of the spare keys from the kitchen counter, he left Vance's house.

The differences between Thyrel at day and at night were stark. The streets weren't empty, but he could see every structure unobscured. Nearing the tower grounds, he picked up on some strange housing. It looked like homes had been built into the thick ancient trunks of several trees on the pruned grounds. More likely, ethrean weavers had coaxed the trees around the structures, making them embrace the man-made homes. Weaving plants was one of the harder weaves to control. It required great understanding of the combined elements.

Thoren stepped up to the hedge, where he'd stopped earlier, now the previous day. Guards still stood at the base of the glowing zilkan tower.

It makes sense that they always have someone posted.

He stepped around to the garden entrance and turned into the field. The neatly trimmed grass stretched for over fifty feet, and was approximately forty feet wide. The waist-high hedges surrounded the entire space with only a few well-placed entry points—all with the small sign noting the permissions of the dedicated space.

Be calm. He closed his eyes and took a deep breath as he drew his sword.

Moving through each stance was natural to him. He could feel the twist of every muscle, the bend of his joints. Thoren pictured every pass and step as his arm moved his polished blade in an aerial dance befitting the front lines of an ancient battleground.

His worries melted away the more he moved. Sweat beaded his brow as the minutes passed and he continued to shift from one offensive stance into another. He reached the end of the field only to turn around and move across it once again.

His lungs begged him for relief, and only then did Thoren sheath his blade. He wiped his brow with his sleeve, and rested his hands on his hips over his belt. Thoren tipped his head up and let out a puff of air.

Lowering his head back down, he stared at the ground.

The bells rang out, signaling two hours past midnight.

Can I move it? He wondered and dropped one of his hands, palm open.

"Nevizot Netrimus," he whispered.

Thoren clenched his jaw at the pull on his inner well. That same feeling, pinched just above his gut near his stomach, like a muscle cramp.

He pushed through it, willing the dirt to shift and rise. It moved, like a mole tunneling underneath in a single location—nothing more.

His gut twisted with greater pain. Taking the hint, he returned the ground to its prior flattened state. Ending the weave with a thought. Thoren's shoulders slumped and he squeezed his eyes shut. No matter what he did, the result was always the same.

I should rest. Thoren left the large hedged field and glanced up at the zilkan tower. Something or someone moved out of sight from one of the windows near the top. *Was that . . . ?* He thought he saw Lady Dessuithiel.

Shaking his head lightly, he resigned from the gardens and returned to Vance's home, which was a solid half hour walk from the tower grounds.

Not bothering to change, Thoren locked the front door and crawled underneath his blanket. His eyes shut, heavier now, and sleep overtook him shortly after.

INTO THE TRIALS

Chapter 6

Thoren Belfry
Fifth of Trete

"Thoren, , aren't you supposed to be at Thyrel's tower?" Janessa spoke from the edge of the front room.

Thoren's eyes shot open and he sat up with a gasp. Grabbing an un-worn set of the white garb he was to wear from his luggage, he dashed to the wash room and changed.

"Thoren!" Janessa called as he ran toward the front door. "Take this." She offered some breakfast: a thick breaded meat wrap, with a sweet smelling salsa.

"Thank you." He took it and rushed out the door.

How did I oversleep? I never oversleep!

He ran, taking careful bites of the breakfast wrap.

"Excuse me! Sorry!"

Thoren slipped between two groups and his elbow caught on one of them. The sudden bump dislodged the half-eaten wrap from his hand and it fell to the ground. He stopped and quickly picked it up with a deflated sigh. Tossing it in the nearest trash bin, he resumed his rushed approach to the tower grounds.

Out of breath, he arrived at the edge of the gardens. His shoulders noticeably rose and fell. The other participants were lined up in front of the tower, their hands at their sides and facing the doors.

The crowds had gathered for the broadcasted event and cluttered the pathways and fields of the tower gardens.

"Sorry, I need to get through." Thoren did his best to be polite as he moved through the crowds.

"Out of the way!" Vance's voice shouted above the crowd's chatter.

Thoren froze and turned around to see his friends right behind him.

Vance pushed his way ahead of Thoren and forced the crowd apart. "Let him through! He's a participant," he called.

Thoren felt his face flush. He didn't like the attention it was drawing, but Vance was clearing a path for him to the front. He thanked him in passing and rushed to the line of participants—most of which had turned at the commotion.

Fern fought a smile, trying to remain serious, and ducked her head when he passed and stood next to her at the end of the line.

"Did you sleep in?" she whispered.

"That obvious?"

"Well, your hair could use some touching up." She pointed.

Thoren felt over his hair and his embarrassment reddened his face even more.

"Here, let me help." She waved, gesturing for him to bend down.

Thoren did so, taking her help gratefully.

"I was worried you weren't going to show. I mean it would get me one position closer to being the mentor, but I'd hate for you to miss out." She combed her fingers through his hair and quickly twisted the strands through his elastic hair-tie, pulling half of it back.

"Did I miss anything?"

Fern pulled her hands back. "Nope. You're just in time."

Thoren straightened up and faced the doors of the tower, mirroring his competitors.

A horn blared over every surrounding sound. It came from atop the zilkan tower and drew all eyes to it. Thoren stared at the swirling floral top to the structure. The horn was hidden, likely built into the building.

As soon as the air fell still, a shout from the guard at the base came. "Presenting, Lady Dessuithiel!"

He overheard Balek talking under his breath to James. "She's supposedly Marmidon's fairest lady."

Thoren's pulse became rapid and his eyes fixed to the opening silver doors with golden accents that bled from the edges toward the center. He hadn't gotten a good look at her the night before, but there was something about her that caused his heart to swell with excitement. The sound of her angelic voice echoed within his mind.

Not only does she sound like a songbird, she's got a kind heart. He thought of Shirra's offhanded comment about Dessuithiel's visits to the Thyrian schools. In his eyes, charity made a woman more attractive, not less. *If she's Marmidon's fairest and sweet natured, that's a hard combination for any man to ignore.*

The doors were now open, and stepping into view was the fair Lady Dessuithiel. Thoren knew, as much as everyone else, that there were two main royal ethrean families that stood above the other six. Heiress to one of them, Lady Dessuithiel Vizule carried a rare gift, one previously only seen in Marmidon's Seer—a gift of foresight. While not as strong as the Seer's, Lady Dessuithiel's foresight *could* see finite futures of those she interacted with. The lady's deeds in aiding Thyrel's prosperity were well-known, and Thoren didn't doubt it was all thanks to her rare gift. Though every ethrean revered her, she was not Marmidon's mouthpiece—the Seer was.

The other royal bloodline, the Valdans, hailed from Elpha Zavar. They had two heirs: the gentler Gailiaethere was older sister to her brother, Dundaelon, a headstrong natural-born leader. These two royal bloodlines did not rule like the magistrates of man. Rather, ethrea held high respect for the bravery of their ancestors, who brought the ethrea from the edge of extinction to the prosperity they knew now—having protected seven other royal bloodlines from ending.

Thoren didn't know much about the other royal families, but was becoming more curious.

That being said, the Valdans ruled over Elpha Zavar sticking to old traditions more than the other ethrean cities. Of these old traditions, men often held higher stations than women, and those outside of the ethrean race had to adhere to the same social structure to live there. It didn't deter anyone, from what Thoren had noticed. The last of the old traditions that Thoren knew of, was that the Valdans highly favored and pushed for arranged marriage within royal bloodlines.

He watched the fair lady reach for the edge of her veil. His rambling thoughts ceased as he looked upon her face for the first time.

It was as though the air from his lungs was stolen, set aside just like the veil Dessuithiel had pulled from her face. Soft curves melted perfectly with the angular touches of her cheekbones and delicate nose, chin, and lips. Her eyes were like Ilzu and Maz, Marmidon's brilliant double moons.

The backdrop only added to the scene before him. Lush potted plants decorated the inside of the tower behind her. They framed Lady Dessuithiel like a painting from the heavens.

He felt his jaw drop and quickly snapped it shut. Her beauty had been greatly understated in his opinion.

The hush of the crowds remained as she stepped out and up to the lined participants. She moved like a calm stream with her pale-blue chiffon dress rippling behind her. Crystal beading sparkled from her woven rich-red hair, pulling at the deep red of her tulip-shaped lips.

Her gaze passed over Thoren and the others beside him, and then her perfect mouth parted to speak. The angelic voice Thoren had heard the night before graced his ears once more.

"Welcome!" She lifted her hands and her voice carried beyond to the crowds, amplified, yet no less pleasant. "Marmidon smiles upon you, for your willingness and desire to lead our world through the ages." Her delicate hands lowered, panning at the eight ethrea garbed in white.

Thoren resumed breathing, calming himself, with forced slow breaths. His nose filled with the floral scents of the garden, helping to calm his nerves.

She's betrothed. He pushed aside any thoughts to pursue her. *I shouldn't be thinking such things. I'm a commoner, stranger, and just here to participate in the trials.*

"I'm sure you are all eager for these trials to begin—to see who will rise above the rest and secure the position of Marmidon's mentor. The details of these events have been closely guarded." She elegantly clasped her hands in front of herself and looked directly at Thoren for a few endearing seconds. "In order to preserve the trial's authentic experience, these tests have been designed to discover the next mentor who will be worthy of this divine calling."

He caught sight of the same guard, Guan, from the previous day standing at her side. He was glaring at Thoren. Thoren turned his head from the disapproving guard and glanced behind himself to see that everyone was focused on the young lady.

"Today, our contenders will be faced with the first of their trials. Within the Bearing Mountains is a labyrinth that will test their physical prowess, capacity, and weaving mastery."

Thoren became stiff at the mention of weaving. He could already feel the pain knotting just above his stomach.

Weaving, within the first trial?

"To our dear contenders: Those that solve the riddle, and reach the end of the first trial, will move onto the second."

She locked eyes with each of them for a solid second and proceeded. "Another warning I must share: your very life will be at risk. If you desire to withdraw now, or at any point during the trials, you need only say it."

L-life at risk? My life? He didn't recall anywhere along the application process that it had stated this. *But . . . if I'm going to mentor the Gift Bearer . . .* He knew that this job would come with life-threatening situations. It made sense to have risk in the trials. They needed to know who could respond well under duress. *I know how to handle a weapon. So long as I have that, I'll be fine.* He squared his shoulders.

Silence prevailed among the participants standing resolute beside Thoren.

Dessuithiel resumed, "Very well. The public will be watching an edited broadcast, monitored by me, of each trial to be held over the course of this next week." She shifted a quarter turn to her left. "If the contenders will follow me." She faced the tower and walked back inside.

Everyone's going to be watching? How much will they be seeing? What if someone gets hurt, or . . . dies? I guess that's the editing she's talking about.

There was only one way for everyone to watch, Dessuithiel would be sharing what the competitor's lapel pins captured with Marmidon's broadcast systems—an electronic signal—that allowed images and sound to be shown through thin glassy screens, by means of a complex light weave that she was particularly good at casting. The major cities all had a large screen built into one or more of the sky pillars, while smaller cities had stations where individual screens could be viewed. Other than viewing it, the signal could be relayed with just sound through projectors. Often, commentators took to this format, while well-known news anchors covered events upon the visual broadcasts.

Ama and Ba are going to be watching me. His lips pressed tight.

The scents of floral tones shifted, to a moist freshness that he could only describe as fresh rain, upon entering the crystal zilkan tower.

Dessuithiel, followed by her four guards, Guan included, led them up the curved stairs to the second floor. The lush greenery continued to fill most of the space and a rippling fountain of water fell to a rectangular pot along the left wall.

She lifted her hand to the back wall, which was bare, and the stone gave off a sudden sheen before falling away and merging with the floor of a revealed passageway.

"This way." She stepped inside and followed the narrow hall out of sight, turning a corner.

Thoren stepped up to follow first.

The smells changed once more, becoming dry and warm. He turned the corner and spotted Dessuithiel waiting patiently with one hand raised to an open archway on the right. Her guards stood split on either side of her.

Passing through the archway, it led into an open room. Lining two walls were a few shelves of supplies and armor pieces, while the back wall held a stunning display of weapons.

"Here, you will prepare. Choose wisely. You have five minutes."

Dessuithiel Vizule

Minutes later, she awaited the competitors from within a connecting hall between the zilkan tower and the Bearing Mountains that wrapped around Thyrel and connected with her home.

What if there's something I'm missing from the vision? Of course I've missed something . . . I still don't know what Marmidon wants me to do!

One of her guards noted the passing time to her softly. It was the last minute before they were to proceed. She quickly called out the limited time to those preparing to face the labyrinth within the mountain. She knew some of what had been prepared, but honestly didn't know how dangerous this first trial would be. She'd left it up to—

The sound of grinding stone pulled her back to the present. She saw everyone had returned to the hall and the supply room had been sealed.

"I am pleased to see everyone's willingness to press on." She smiled as her eyes passed over the ethrean man of her vision. "Come."

Too soft for anyone to hear, she cast a weave, bringing out light from the energy within her. It filled the carved-stone hall as they walked deeper into the heart of the mountain.

Their walk was silent, which she didn't mind.

I'm sure many of them are nervous.

After ten minutes, they arrived. The stone hall opened to the heart of the Bearing Mountains and they stood upon the highest clifftop within it. She stepped to the side, pointed out into the dark, and called out a different weave. "Lisma Tal." The light from within her faded as the vast cavern was lit by clusters of Thyrian crystal.

She watched, somewhat amused, as each of the competitors stepped near the edge and gaped at the zilkan labyrinth below. She couldn't help smiling a little. This trial had taken several days of careful preparation by the only one alive still able to manipulate the glowing mineral.

She recited the riddle and waited as her guard secured a tracing pin to each of them. A curious question was asked by a competitor similar in build to the one in her repeated visions, but with sharper—human-like—facial features and dark hair reminiscent of Guan.

"Why not just say who won't make it, Lady Dessuithiel?"

Fate is not so easily accessed. Nor do I wish to see what unfortunate futures they may have.

Her smile faded as she responded, "It is not my place. Your experiences are for you. Who am I to tamper with fate?"

She had, in fact, reached out in the past—when she was barely seventy and still of an adolescent mind—for information locked away by fate. It had been purely out of curiosity, foolish curiosity. Her pain at every touch was the consequence of that attempt. She'd been left with a scar, befitting her crime against Marmidon's will. There was only one who could, and should, access and carry out *her* will.

Dessuithiel looked up at a suspended room above where they stood. A gentle warm light emanated from behind a wall of glass. She knew *he* was there, watching.

One of the female competitors pulled her from the painful reminiscing when they asked who was pacing in the room above them.

The woman was equally as short as Dessuithiel, but younger. The participant pointed up at the suspended room.

Dessuithiel could not share the name of the one that paced within, but she gave an answer to the effect that the person they saw was very invested in the trials. A sudden thought entered her mind, a reminder from the one above them during one of their last planning meetings. "Also, I would discourage any of you from passing over the labyrinth, as I have placed a charm preventing such." *That should be everything.* "Remain here, you will know when to begin. This is where I leave. We will be observing you."

That was it. Her part to play in the first trial was over. She turned around and left the competitors there upon the cliff's edge. Her shadow, Guan, moved up into view as she revealed the hidden passageway to the room suspended over the heart of the Bearing Mountains—to *his* living space.

"My lady, I am not sure you should have drawn further attention to *him*."

“There’s nothing to worry about.” She shrugged it off and stepped up out of the stairwell in the floor of the suspended space. Still pacing in front of the glass wall, was Marmidon’s Gift Bearer.

“That one man . . . That feeling I got, but couldn’t quite pin down before, I believe I figured it out, my lady.”

Shushing, she lifted her hand to him and approached the glass wall, standing beside the Gift Bearer where he had stopped pacing.

His worn voice garbled out, strained. “That one . . .” he coughed. “Marmidon has shown him to you.”

Dessuithiel held to the skirt of her gown, rubbing the top layer between her thumbs and fingers nervously. “How do you know?”

He tapped at his chest. “Just a feeling.” Another cough forced him to lean against the glass until it subsided.

It doesn’t sound like Marmidon will sustain him for much longer.

“There, look at that.”

She turned her attention back to the two competitors atop the cliff. Everyone else had begun the trial. The two remaining were the small-framed woman and the vision man.

THE FIRST TRIAL

Chapter 7

Thoren Belfry
Fifth of Trete, preparation room of the first trial

Thoren walked straight ahead, bypassing the food and smaller gear, for the weapons on display. He reached out for a sword, not much longer than the length of his arm. The craftsmanship was exquisite. His fingers brushed over the smooth leather grip and the details etched into the handguard.

Who made these?

There was no insignia that he could find. Taking the blade off the hanging rack, he pulled it from the sheath. It glided out in a soft whisper.

"Whoa! Who brought the Primal Horizon Era to Thyrel?" Balek voiced as he entered the room.

Thoren turned around to see that everyone was inside, including Dessuithiel and her guard, Guan. The guard still held a narrowed glare when passing over Thoren.

Such a ray of sunshine. He chose to ignore Guan.

Olathe, Shirra, and Fern were clumped together at one of the tables with essential supplies and first aid.

"Each of you will have one small pack, provided by me." Dessuithiel's voice carried in the same way it had outside, silencing the chatter in the room.

Thoren watched as two of her guards stepped away and pulled backpacks from the ends of the shelves. They held them out and each of the participants took theirs. Thoren stepped up and took the last one. He moved back behind the others and waited for the rest of Lady Dessuithiel's instructions.

"I cannot tell you what you will find within the mountain." Her eyes locked with Thoren. "Be prepared for anything, and to use every skill at your disposal. For Marmidon will need one who can see her chosen bearer through the opposing forces. One skilled and able to handle anything." She then broke eye contact, looking at the other participants.

His face burned. *Does she know I can't weave? Did she really see me last night?*

She continued, "Those still wishing to participate and face their innermost fears, please meet me back out in the hall in five minutes."

The room came to life as each of the contestants started taking supplies from the shelves and selecting their weapons. Thoren joined them as soon as he secured the blade he'd chosen to his belt.

He found some of the food available looked a bit odd, like condensed bread, and there was only enough water for each person to take one water bottle. Thankfully, that was regulated by one of Dessuithiel's guards—not Guan.

"Two minutes!" Dessuithiel called.

Thoren selected some vambraces and secured them over his forearms. There weren't any shields, and it made sense. If ethrea could weave a barrier for protection, why have a physical shield. Sadly, Thoren wouldn't be able to protect himself with weaves.

He closed his bag with his food and water.

Do I have everything I need?

He scanned the room to see everyone else had stuffed their bag and had picked out at least two weapons and some lightweight armor. Balek had three weapons: a dagger, sword, and bow. He was latching them on as Dessuithiel called out their final minute.

James and Byran were leaving the room, turning right into the carved hall.

The women were fastening the ties on their bags and slinging them over their backs. They left the room next.

"Is that all you're bringing?" Balek stepped up beside Thoren. "You must be very confident." He laughed lightheartedly and slapped Thoren's shoulder before he too left the room. Finian followed him out and Thoren stood alone with one of Dessuithiel's guards.

I need to move. Thoren took a step forward, toward the hall, but his foot dragged along the floor. *Can I do this?*

With a deep breath and a silent prayer to Marmidon, Thoren peeled his feet from their place and left the room.

The moment he stepped out into the hall with the lingering guard behind him, the rock archway began moving. It rolled in its various clumps until it met the floor, sealing the entrance shut.

"Cutting it rather close, aren't you?" Balek whispered and nudged him with his elbow.

"I am pleased to see everyone's willingness to press on." Dessuithiel spoke. "Come."

A soft light filled the dark hallway. Thoren couldn't see where the light was coming from. There weren't any electrical lights installed into the stone above them. The light seemed to be emanating directly from Lady Dessuithiel in the form of a light weave. Trails of light fell from her like stardust.

They followed her and the three guards around her—her last guard walked behind Thoren still. For over ten minutes, no one dared speak.

He listened to the clop of each boot and footfall on the stone floor, and watched as the hall shimmered with ribbons of zilkan crystal. The hall began to stretch upward and out in all directions, expanding past the reach of Dessuithiel's soft glow.

They came to the edge of a chasm. Dessuithiel stepped to the side and pointed to the vast, dark, open space.

"Lisma Tal." She spoke and light sparked to life across the enormous open cavern, while her personal light faded.

The women gasped and cautiously stepped up to the edge, peering over. Thoren joined them with the rest of the men.

Below them, was the labyrinth.

It was riddled with stalagmites and made entirely of woven zilkan walls. Pale yellow and white crystals emitted light in addition to the maze, but dark moving patches could be seen throughout it.

That's odd, are those shadows alive?

Thoren turned back around and looked at Lady Dessuithiel. She was smiling and watching each of their reactions.

Her hand lifted, palm up, and she waited while Guan handed her a single scroll.

"This is the riddle you must solve if you desire to make it through this trial."

Thoren fixed his gaze upon her mouth as she read the riddle to them.

"I thrive where courage falters, born of anxieties unseen. I challenge you with darkness, a battle fought and lost, it seems. Though one strong hand can strike a blow, it's destined to defeat. Success demands a linked force, a strategy complete."

Her guards then distributed a copy to each of them.

Thoren reviewed the riddle, opening his scroll. *'Courage falters.' We'll be facing our fears. 'Anxieties unseen.' What could it be? A challenge in the dark. It is dark here, but does the dark mentioned have more to do with those shadows? 'A battle fought and lost . . . it seems.' Is it talking about the past?* Thoren clenched his fist as he repeated the next line internally. *Though one strong hand can strike a blow, it's destined to defeat.* He knew what this meant. *My strength won't get me to the end. I have my wit, but will strength and knowledge be enough?* The last line filled his mind as Balek repeated it aloud.

"'Success demands a linked force, a strategy complete.'" He slapped his hands on the shoulders of Finian and James. "This won't be too hard."

She raised a hand and her guards moved once more. They pulled something small from their pockets and began securing a small blue gem to each of the participant's collars.

"Whatever you do, do not remove these pins. If you do, you will be beyond *our* reach to help, and there will be no way to pull you out when you desire it."

"Dearest lady, how do you know any of us will falter?" Finian asked, as politely as he could.

She remained silent.

Byran knocked Finian on the back of his head. "She has the gift of foresight."

"Right." Finian clamped his mouth shut.

"Why not just say who won't make it, Lady Dessuithiel?" Balek asked.

Dessuithiel's face fell from pleasant to serious. "It is not my place. Your experiences are for you. Who am I to tamper with fate?"

She turned her gaze above and they all followed it, spotting a glass window, several feet tall and wide with a faint light within.

A figure paced from within it.

"Lady Dessuithiel, who's that?" Fern pointed.

"A *very* interested party," Dessuithiel said. "Also, I would discourage any of you from passing over the labyrinth, as I have placed a charm preventing such. Remain here, you will know when to begin. This is where I leave. We will be observing you."

She turned and walked back into the hall. The exit closed behind the fair lady and her guards like the supply room had earlier.

Thoren faced the edge once more. *Are we supposed to find a way down there? She did say to stay here . . . and that we will know when to start.* He spun around looking for any other connecting pathway. And then it struck him. *Oh no. We're supposed to weave our way down.*

Balek was the next to catch on. He lifted a hand and called out the dirt shifting weave, "Nevizot Netrimus!"

"What are you doing?" Olathe asked.

"I'm starting my trial." Balek smiled and stepped out onto a small platform he'd made. "See you at the finish line . . . well, some of you." He saluted playfully with his hand from his forehead and dropped down out of sight.

James, Byran, and Finian were the next to cast their weave and follow Balek down into the chasm.

"Are you going with the men?" Fern turned to him and asked.

Thoren took a step back. "You go ahead." He couldn't bring himself to share his weakness. His hands chilled and the pain above his stomach haunted his nerves in the face of having to weave. Clenching his hands into tight fists, he tried to hide behind the mask of confidence he had always worn.

She stepped back from the edge.

"Are you sure?" Her eyes narrowed.

Thoren nodded his head, probably a bit too soon after her statement. He needed to look proactive or tell her the truth. Thoren tried to look relaxed, releasing the tension in his hands.

Should I tell her? He thought about his friends, and about Janessa's words "What will you do?"

What will I do?

Thoren took a step toward the edge and peered over. It was easily over one hundred feet down. He knelt and brushed his hand over the wall. The texture barely varied and there weren't any grooves to hold onto. *I can't climb down this. It forces us to weave.*

"If you insist." Fern faced the edge and called out the weave, manipulating the available loose dirt to form her own platform.

She looked back at him once more while Olathe and Shirra departed. Her eyes fell to Thoren's trembling hands. Fern's face scrunched and softened while passing through internal thoughts. She dismissed them and faced the cliff edge, ready to leave him behind.

"Fern, wait!" Thoren bit his lip, fists tight once again as he stood up. "I'm not good at weaving dirt or stone. Could you help me down? I won't ask you for anything else."

Fern smirked. "Well . . . this is a competition. If I *were* Shirra, I'd leave you behind. Thankfully for you, I'm not." She moved her platform in front of him and expanded it.

He quickly took a step back. "I-I'm sorry this uses more of your inner well. I owe you one."

"It's fine. My inner well is larger than most from all the plant weaving I grew up doing."

Dropping his head in thanks, he hesitantly stepped out onto her platform. His stomach flipped, over the height, and his palms began to sweat.

She wouldn't drop me, right? Thoren watched her open hand closely.

"Hold onto me." Fern stepped onto the platform next to him, and tapped at her shoulder.

Thoren held onto her shoulder as the platform dropped. His breath caught in his throat and he thought more than once that his stomach had tucked itself behind his heart. With a glance up, he watched the top of the cliff vanish into the dark with only a few glowing crystals lighting the ceiling.

They reached the bottom and he quickly stepped off. Fern blended her platform back into the ground around their feet.

"Thoren, check out the ground." She knelt and brushed her fingers over the veins of zilkan. "I've never seen so much of this mineral."

He stared at the obstacle between him and the next step to becoming the Gift Bearer's mentor. "The entire labyrinth is made of it." Thoren's heart warmed as he stared at the glowing crystal.

Fern gasped and rushed over to the entrance. "You know what this means, right?" She waved at the labyrinth. "We can't weave our way through the maze."

Thoren added, "And Lady Dessuithiel has prevented anyone from weaving their way over it. We have to go through it."

The weave to manipulate zilkan had been lost. Nobody alive, to his knowledge, knew how to weave it. The means of constructing the zilkan cities were certainly forgotten to time, but it had been surmised that weaving the mineral must have been crucial. Due to the strange nature of events after the day of Peerretdyn, the lost memories specifically, the consensus was that the ability to weave zilkan was lost, or taken.

Just how long has this labyrinth been down here? I thought the trials were recently prepared. It was a question he would love an answer to, but would have to wait for.

As soon as Fern approached the entrance, Olathe and Shirra joined her. They'd been waiting nearby and stepped into the faint light.

"Did Balek and the others already go in?" Fern asked.

They nodded.

Thoren stepped up to their group.

Shirra eyed him. “Is *he* coming with us?”

“I thought he was a loner,” Olathe said, easily loud enough for him to hear.

“He’s welcome to join us,” Fern said.

Shirra glanced at him, judging. “Hmm, well, if he slows us down again, I’m leaving him behind. I hope you haven’t forgotten, Fern, this is a competition. We both saw how you helped him down into the chasm. Need I remind you, only one of us can secure this life-long calling.”

“You three go on ahead.” Thoren stepped back from them. “I’ll be fine.”

“He reeks of overconfidence, too.” Shirra rolled her eyes and marched into the labyrinth.

The riddle came to mind once more and he questioned stepping away from the ethrean women. His mind spun through the words and he felt he was on the cusp of understanding it.

Fern quietly followed Shirra and Olathe into the labyrinth. They turned left at the split and vanished from sight amid the zilkan walls.

Thoren walked up to the entrance and placed his hand on the wall. His chest began to burn in the same way it had when he stared at Thyrel’s tower. He quickly pulled his hand back.

What is this . . . reaction? He touched it with just a finger and the burning filled him once again. It wasn’t painful, but concentrated around his inner well like a warm blanket. He pondered what it could mean for a few seconds before pulling his finger away as he walked deeper inside.

Pausing at the split he wondered if he should follow Fern and the other two ethrean women.

They'll think I'm using them to get through the labyrinth. He sighed and turned right.

Part of him hoped to find a dead end and end up having to go back the other way.

A melodic clinking filled the silence, like many glass goblets tapping together, coming from the entrance. Thoren hadn't gone far, and rushed back to find the entrance closed off.

He looked up to the chasm's ceiling, but he couldn't see where Dessuithiel and the "very interested" person was. The clinking crystal filled the air once more and he quickly spotted what was happening.

The labyrinth is changing!

A howl split the air. He heard the girls yelp from the other direction. Thoren's hand went straight to his blade and he rushed to their aid. The zilkan ground absorbed the impact of his steps. This quality made it hard to judge how far away Fern, Shirra, and Olathe were. He stopped at another split in the path and listened.

His grip tightened around the leather handle of his sword and eased in a repeated pattern. The whimper of a wounded animal came from his right. Thoren darted toward it. When it came to combat, he had no fear. Nothing could hold him back. What he feared at this moment was the risk to the other's lives.

"Fern!" he called.

Thoren rounded another corner and spotted a dark beast leaping at the ethrean women. Olathe cast a weave, shielding herself with ice. Shirra had her spear in hand and thrust the end into the beast. It fell to the ground with a cut off whimper and Shirra ripped her spear free.

He didn't see Fern.

"Thought we needed help?" Shirra spoke when she spotted Thoren. "How *chivalrous* of you." Her words could not have been filled with any more spite.

"Where's Fern?" Thoren lowered his sword.

Shirra and Olathe shrugged.

"She may have bailed." Olathe assumed.

She can't have. Thoren turned around and walked briskly back the other way. He'd returned to the fork in the paths one turn before finding Shirra and Olathe, but everything looked the same here. The sight of zilkan in every direction was messing with his memory.

"Fern!" he called again.

"Over here!" she answered.

He followed it, turning left, and then right where the path came to an end. There was no one there.

"Wha—"

A shriek sent his mind into flight. He spun around and raised his blade to a creature of shadow. The force from the monster knocked him to the ground. Thoren rolled out of the way as a shadow-like tentacle slapped the crystal floor.

He readied his stance and let his muscle memory take over his response. The beast had no given shape that it held for more than a few seconds. The only consistent part of its body was the tentacles it attacked with. It resembled a sea creature with an indeterminate body. Thoren searched for its eyes, or a mouth, but only saw the shifting black form. He countered and threw the beast's multiple arms aside. Taking the single moment of opportunity, Thoren thrust his blade deep into the center of the morphing body. The creature shrieked once more and evaporated into the air, rising like mist in morning light.

He heaved for air. It felt thicker, making each breath more taxing.

"Thoren?" Fern's voice called to him from behind. "What are you doing?"

He spun around, raising his blade and expecting the creature, but Fern gasped and jumped back.

"Fern?" He cautiously lowered his blade and dared to reach out to touch the top of her head, which was at his shoulder height.

"Um, yes?" she stepped back, avoiding his touch, and stared quizzically at him.

"Y-you . . . didn't you see that thing?" He looked back to where he had slain the beast.

"Thoren? Are you okay?" He turned back to Fern, but she was gone again.

Creeping into panic, he backed up against the zilkan wall. Feeling the solid crystal at his back his eyes searched the pathway to the right and left of him.

Nobody was there.

He wiped his free hand down his face. *It's an illusion.* He rested his hand over his thundering heart and stared up above at the void.

It shifted.

Thoren couldn't stay. He didn't know where the real Fern was, but she wasn't here. Jogging back to where Shirra and Olathe had been, he found the body of a canine-like beast, but Shira and Olathe were gone. He checked for the stab wound, finding it by the black oozing liquid pouring out of the strange animal like tar.

I hope Fern is okay. The other two didn't seem to care that she was missing.

He wiped the gore from his fingertips on the black fur of the creature, and moved on.

Keeping his sword in hand, Thoren remained cautious at every turn. The further in he went, the colder it became and the shadows played tricks on his eyes.

Where did everyone go?

RIDDLED

Chapter 8

Thoren Belfry
Fifth of Trete

Thoren continued through the mirrored walls of the labyrinth. He made sure to move in as straight a line as possible while working through the maze, but somehow he felt like he was running in circles.

At first, his heart raced every time he heard a shriek, howl, or cry from some unknown being. Now, it only sparked his interest.

Thoren had been telling himself they were all illusions—that none of it was real.

Those canine beasts . . . they're real, as tangible as my own flesh. But, that dark monster. What was that? His eyes kept darting above to the shifting misty void that seemed to be following him. *And then there was that illusion of Fern.*

Howling mixed with feral growls.

Sheerma! he cursed internally as three canines leapt out from the next intersection. Their glowing green eyes locked on him.

Saliva dripped from the sharp-toothed open jaw of the nearest beast as it turned right toward him. Thoren dodged and caught its underside with the edge of his blade. It fell to the ground with a dying whine.

The second and third jumped at him simultaneously. Thoren altered his grip, shifting his blade to back hand. He took one breath in. Spun. His blade sliced through their skin, but they landed merely wounded. Thoren turned on his heel and drove his blade into the nearest beast. It burrowed deep and the falling creature's weight pulled him down as its life extinguished.

One left. He freed his blade from the carcass.

He no longer feared these things, but rather was curious where they'd come from. They weren't found anywhere on the surface of Marmidon. They had similarities to a few animals. Their bodies were compact like the companion animal known as a searral—a canine. Their size was closer to a vilka, with the bear-like strength and thick fur. The ends of their hairless tails varied between stone clumped clubs, to razor sharp edges.

Thoren ducked as the last canine swiped its tail at his face. It left itself open.

He stared down at the dead creature after his blade brought it a swift end. This one had a spiked tail. Slowing his breaths, he moved on.

Thoren turned left and found another dead end.

I've been at this for hours. Am I the last one here?

Tired and a bit hungry, he decided to rest. Sliding the straps of his pack off his shoulders, Thoren pulled out the condensed bread, took a bite and then a sip of water. He kept his eyes on the open end from where he sat against the zilkan wall while he ate. His gaze briefly moved up to the mist above. It was gone. He had a theory about it, and so far, he'd been right.

The canines are throughout the labyrinth, but the mist. I believe it runs off fear.

He took an additional sip of water.

Another howl cut through the momentary silence. Footfalls softly pounded upon the zilkan, down the path, somewhere to his right. Thoren rushed to his feet and drew his blade to face the black canine. Straight ahead of him was clear, behind him was a dead end. It was coming from a side path.

His heart jumped as Fern rushed out into view. She glanced his way, turning away from him before she froze. Doubling back, Fern patted her cheeks as though she were making sure she was awake.

"Thoren? Is that really you?" She held her dagger pointed at him, even though he was more than ten feet away from her. She shook the tip at him. "Tell me. Are you real?" Her voice trembled. She moved hesitantly toward him while glancing back the way she'd come.

Thoren nodded. "Fern? Are *you* real?"

She lowered her blade from him. "I haven't seen anyone else for hours. What if they're gone? What if they already finished the trial?" She hiccupped and covered her mouth.

Thoren picked up his pack, and slung one strap over his shoulder, while he approached her.

"I haven't seen anyone else either. Well, I did see you earlier, but it wasn't really you."

"So, the same thing happened to you?" Fern turned back to face the way she'd come. "It was the weirdest thing. You were talking to me, telling me to follow you, but then—"

Howling interrupted her. It was far closer than either of them liked. Fern jumped at the sound of it with another hiccup and backed up toward him.

"T-that." She pointed, with her dagger, back the way she'd come. "It's following me, and my inner well isn't ready, yet."

“You passed combat, didn’t you?” Thoren looked down at her for a second while turning his blade to the open path and crouching into position.

“I d-did, barely,” Fern admitted, interrupted by another hiccup.

“Why did you apply?” Thoren asked, genuinely curious.

“I figured it w-would be more bookwork mentoring than actual fighting. The Gift Bearer has always been an idol of mine.”

He noticed Fern’s free hand was rubbing over the pin Lady Dessuithiel had given them.

She’s going to bail.

A shadow came into view and Thoren’s instincts took over.

“Stay behind me!” Thoren rushed out ahead of her.

The black blur sped in from his right. He raised his blade, holding the flat edge to his free hand, guarding from the creature’s clawed swipe.

Thoren shifted his weight, turning his blade as the beast propelled itself forward. He thrust forward and felt the pop of the dark creature’s skin. It whined and recoiled before his blade could dig deep enough to end its life.

Fern did her best to help. She held out her hand and shouted a weave. “Ledus!”

Fizzling crackles jittered through the air and water pulled from around them freezing the moment it touched the beast. Thoren slipped out of the way as the animal snapped its daggered teeth at his arm. He countered and cut a deep wound across its neck.

Moments later, the beast lay dead and half frozen on the ground. The black oozing blood pooled beneath it.

"No wonder you've only brought one weapon." Fern stepped around the beast, keeping as much distance from it as she could. "If I moved half as well as you, I'd be confident enough to face this labyrinth alone. You don't have a drop on you."

Alone. He echoed internally.

"Have you figured out the riddle?" Thoren asked while wiping his blade clean upon the animal's fur.

Fern shook her head. "I'm not entirely sure. I haven't had much time to think about it." She eyed the dead creature.

Thoren rummaged through his pack and pulled out the riddle. "'I thrive where courage falters. Born of anxieties unseen.'" He pointed down at the lifeless beast. "These don't have anything to do with the riddle. I believe that the dark mist above the maze is what the riddle is talking about."

"Have you fought anything other than the canines?" she asked.

Thoren nodded. "When I encountered you, well the illusion of you, I faced something strange." He pointed back in the direction of the labyrinth's start. "It was the only moment I let fear get the better of me. I thought you, Olathe, and Shirra were in danger. What about you?"

Fern tipped her head with a soft smile. "Aw, I'm touched," she said. "I encountered an illusion, too. It was of you and Balek. Other than that, I haven't run into anything besides these animals. They remind me of vilka, but . . . not." After sheathing her dagger, she rested her hands on her hips, and sighed. "I may not be great with weaponry, but I'm more than capable when it comes to weaving. I would be fine if they gave me a break for five minutes to restore my well. It makes my heart jump every time I hear them."

Thoren nodded, staring at the half frozen beast. It was a bit smaller than the ones he'd fought earlier.

It could have been a young one. He pondered. *But, there are a few things different about this one.*

The animal had three horns, evenly spaced, atop its head. This was not something the others had. Its bodily fluid—black, thick, blood—was the same. His eyes moved to its tails. This creature had two tails with a single sharp pointed end on each. He tapped his boot on one. It looked like a scorpion's stinger.

He knew the feeling she spoke of. That sudden jolt that stabbed at one's heart. Fear came in a few different forms: the sudden jolt that awakened your senses and sent adrenaline through your veins, and then the fear that paralyzed the body in the face of great harm or disturbing sights. Thoren had pushed both aside to maneuver through the maze.

"We can't be afraid," he said and moved past Fern. "It will draw whatever is in the mist to us."

"You really think it's that simple?" She laughed. "Wait, there's something in the mist? More than just illusions?"

He nodded. "Hold on to your courage. If I'm right, it will reduce the chances of us fighting the monster within it."

"We? You're going to stay with me?" Fern sounded relieved.

"I think we're better off together." He scanned the open pathways around them. "The maze has been changing."

He listened as the crystals shifted, clinking like broken glass.

"Should we work on the riddle, then?"

Thoren nodded quickly. "Let's go this way."

Leaving the dead end behind them, Thoren led the way through the labyrinth while they discussed the riddle.

"A challenge of darkness." Fern tapped at her chin. "That seems obvious. You faced a monster that came out of the shadows."

"There's likely more than one based on the dark spots we saw from above." He noted.

She pointed above them. "So, the formless monster you fought first comes from those dark spots. You don't think it has anything to do with the canines?"

"I suspect they're separate entities. The canines can be heard all over the maze." Thoren turned another corner. "But the dark spots . . . the air grows cold when they pass over." Thoren recalled the shift of temperature before he'd fought the shadow being. "The challenge will come from those dark spots. But, the riddle says it's 'a battle fought and lost.'"

"We can't win." Fern concluded. "I think it's a distraction."

Thoren hummed. "That makes sense with the following line: 'Though one strong hand can strike a blow, it's destined to defeat.' Our strength isn't a factor when it comes to the mist."

"So, the question is, how do we reach the end when we're faced with a battle we cannot win?"

It was a difficult question, one that Thoren's mind was itching to answer. The following minutes, they walked through each turn deep in thought. The noises of the maze and creatures roaming it did not stir them to fright like they had before.

Thoren kept his blade ready. For nearly an hour, they walked without confrontation.

"If I hadn't run into you, I wouldn't be here anymore," Fern admitted.

Thoren glanced at her, she was rubbing a finger over the pin again.

"You thought about leaving, didn't you?"

"Yes. I was holding my own well enough, but I questioned myself."

Thoren empathized. He questioned himself even now. “I know that only one of us can secure the position, but why don’t we help each other through this trial?”

“We could, it was never stated that we couldn’t. I can lean on your strength, which from my observation . . . is weaponry.” She grinned mischievously.

Thoren gasped.

“What? Am I wrong?”

“No, that’s not it.” He waved a hand to dismiss her last comment. “The last line, ‘Success demands a linked force!’” He pointed between them. “‘A strategy complete.’ Fern, the answer is teamwork! Leaning on each other!”

She stopped walking and tilted her head in thought. “I think you’re right. But, then does that mean we need to find the others?”

Thoren tapped at his blade. “Possibly. Your strength is weaving. Mine is as you’ve said, weapon mastery.”

“I know that Balek is pretty smart. He aced all his exams in school.”

“How do you know that?” He didn’t know the extent of how the other competitors had come to be together in Thyrel.

“Thoren.” Fern stopped and looked up at him. “Balek and I are from the same city, Uecketev. Byran, James, Finian, and Olathe are from Thyrel. As for Shirra, I never heard where she came from. By the looks of her darker skin, I’d say Kern or Verra. It makes sense as those environments are harsher to live in, and Shirra is . . . well, a bit of a hard shell to crack."

"So, I'm the only one from Elpha Zavar?"

Fern nodded.

He thought of his parents and friends watching. While in thought, the maze clinked to life once more, shifting and moving its walls. The ground under them began to lift.

"Whoa!" Fern jogged forward as the zilkan behind them moved upward, blocking off the way they had just come. The wall then started moving toward them, forcing them down the path.

"Fern, get moving. It looks like things are about to get interesting." Thoren started running.

The maze pinched shut behind them as they moved forward.

"I have a feeling we're being led somewhere," Fern said as they turned the corner.

The closed walls of the labyrinth expanded ahead of them, opening into a large arena.

Is this the center or the end?

He looked up to see swirling mist over top of the entire open space.

I don't like the looks of this.

Scanning the labyrinth, he could see and hear that the walls were all moving.

"Fern, stay close."

James was the first they spotted, running out as his pathway sealed shut behind him. Byran arrived shortly after, along with Finian.

Everyone's being driven here.

Shirra, Olathe, and lastly, Balek.

"That's everyone," Fern said.

"Fern! What happened?" Shirra rushed over with Olathe. "We went in together, those creatures showed up, and next thing I knew you were gone."

Thoren was curious as to how that happened. He shifted to better watch their conversation and Fern's reactions. She didn't look upset but stared at Shirra with some annoyance.

Fern folded her arms, not meeting Shirra's gaze as she responded. "The labyrinth changed. I got cut off." She said that, but Thoren didn't believe it entirely.

"Did the maze force you here with him?" Shirra pointed to him with her eyes.

"He helped me out when my well was low."

Shirra had no immediate response to that. She shifted her weight to one leg and folded her arms. "Not the loner I thought he was." She scoffed.

"Did you two figure out the riddle?" Olathe asked. "I mean it wasn't all that hard."

“I think the only hard part was finding anyone other than ourselves.” Shirra noted.

“Well, that won’t be an issue now.” James said as he approached. “It looks like we have no choice but to beat this thing together.”

They did figure it out. Thoren was impressed. *I can’t be the only one, I guess. But if they all figured it out, why couldn’t we find each other?* He glanced at the zilkan.

Fern stepped around and tipped her face into view of his distant stare.

She spoke. “It would be best if we knew each other’s strengths and weaknesses to form a strong strategy.” She readjusted her backpack, pulling at the straps to relieve the pull on her shoulders.

At the mention of sharing each other’s strengths and weaknesses, Thoren’s stomach tensed and the pain returned within his inner well.

His weakness was not documented anywhere. He’d searched and searched for an answer, but found nothing. There wasn’t a single case where weaving had caused pain and come out weaker than the smallest of human wells. It was easier to pass it off as inexperience as a child, or that he didn’t feel like weaving, but deep down, Thoren wanted to weave the elements with the strength of a typhoon.

James spoke first. “I pride myself on intellect, I’m a fair weaver, but not very strong with weapons.”

Thoren focused on the relief he had felt at sharing his weakness with Janessa. It had felt good to say it, and she didn’t shun him.

Maybe it’s time. I’ve hidden this long enough.

Shirra shared next. “I’m not weak with a spear, fair at weaving, and smart. I think I’m pretty well rounded.”

The air became cool and Thoren looked about the group as his heart began to drum. He shut his eyes, placing a hand over his heart, and did his best to remain calm. After a few breaths he was ready to tell Fern and the others.

Fern noticed the shift in the temperature around them and pulled at his arm. “Thoren? Why is the darkness coming for us?”

When ‘courage falters.’ Thoren heard the words repeat in Dessuithiel’s voice. *Someone here is afraid.*

His eyes snapped open and he spun around to see a black cloud splitting and descending upon the labyrinth.

The shriek of the morphing monster pierced their ears. A black spear-tipped tentacle shot out from the mist, stabbing the ground and damaging the zilkan. The wide open space began to bubble and walls shot up and down at random. The only one that didn’t jump at the sight was Balek.

“Run!” Thoren grabbed hold of Fern’s arm and pulled her in the opposite direction. “Everyone, stay together!”

Fern called out to the others, "Don't be afraid!" She pulled free of his grasp. "That thing is drawn to fear!"

James stuttered, "A-are you sure? That thing is coming right for us like everything else in this cursed maze!"

Thoren glanced back at him.

James's shoulders heaved with erratic breaths while holding to his sword. "I barely escaped last time it came for me."

James drew it in. Thoren sighed.

He stopped running and faced the lagging contestant. James was frozen in place while watching the shapeless monster, about fifty feet away, crawling out of the mist. It moved over, between, and across the bubbling zilkan path like a freshly born animal still learning to take its first steps.

"I-I'm afraid," James admitted. He held his long sword out at the misted creature.

Thoren could see from here how it shook in his hands. The creature closed the space and Thoren saw the monster lash out at James. He burst into a sprint to help as one of the flailing tentacles hit James.

He flew out of sight behind the misting blob. The speed with which it hit him left droplets of blood on the ground trailing behind.

James! Thoren jerked to a stop.

Olathe shrieked and stumbled back, speaking. “Me too!” Her hand rested over the pin on her collar. “I-I can’t do this!” She crouched to the ground, holding her head. “I want to leave!”

Faster than Thoren could react, one of the creature’s tentacles shot forward at Olathe.

Sheerma! Thoren sprinted once more, holding his sword backhand and close to his side. He considered the distance he was from Olathe against the speed of the monster.

I’m not going to make it!

“Hold your ground!” Balek shouted and released an arrow at the amorphous being. It wasn’t enough to push the attack off target. The dark being’s tentacle was embedded in the zilkan wall behind Olathe.

Thoren froze and stared. *She should be dead.*

Olathe yelped and curled up smaller, unaware of the tentacle that had speared through her chest. Thoren watched the mist pull back. He followed the pointed tip as it passed back through Olathe.

She’s not real. He looked for James as the creature let out a belting roar that sounded like a building collapsing.

The creature stilled. It had no face, but gave the impression of an intelligent being in thought.

“I’m with Olathe, real or not,” Byran said. “I thought I could handle this stuff, but, if this is what training the Gift Bearer is going to be like. I’m out.”

Thoren watched him hold the pin and ask to be taken out. With a shout, he fell into a dark misting swirl beneath him. Scanning the shifting maze's open arena, James and Olathe were also gone.

"So much for their resolve." Finian readied his weapon, a blunt-ended war hammer.

Were they pulled from the labyrinth? Who's real, and who's an illusion? His eyes drifted to those that remained nearby: Shirra, Finian, Balek, and Fern.

Fern is real. I know that. He would try his best to protect them all, but Fern would hold higher priority as he knew she wasn't an illusion.

"Thoren! Cover for me!" Balek called. "Give me a barrier!" he sprinted forward at the black monster.

A barrier? But!

"I can't!" He drew his blade and ran beside Balek toward the nearing monster.

"What?" Balek hooked his bow on his back and pulled his blade from his hip. "Why?"

His throat swelled as he tried to let go of his fears. "I can't weave!" he shouted with equal resolve to the beast that barreled toward them.

"Thoren!" Fern called out the weave, "Bajerra!"

A light green shimmer spread out in front of him and Balek, but the creature broke through it as though it were a thin sheet of glass.

Pain exploded from his back as he was thrown to the zilkan wall behind them. Gasping for air, Thoren slumped to the ground, which shook as the monster smashed into the outer wall of the arena.

What happened? He'd been caught completely off guard. Calming his nerves he watched Fern and Finian running away from the monster, which was slowly peeling itself off the wall.

Picking up his sword from the ground in front of him, Thoren rushed back to help Fern, who now faced the shifting mist with Finian and Shirra. Fern dodged the tentacles, barely keeping out of harm's way. Meanwhile, Shirra's spear spun and tore through the tentacles with some difficulty, but her courage didn't falter.

Thoren was about thirty feet away.

The sound of added footfalls came from behind. Thoren glanced back to see Balek. He'd been thrown by the monster as well.

Balek is real.

"What do you mean you can't weave?" He glared, jaw and fists clenched tight.

"I can't weave!" he reiterated.

Tightening his grip upon his blade, Thoren dropped to the ground, sliding underneath an incoming tentacle. Balek attacked the morphing monster, cutting his way through it.

"Fern, steer clear of this thing!" Thoren ordered. "Can you hold a barrier for us from a safe distance?"

Without argument, she ducked her way out of reach of the creature's flailing arms.

"I'll do what I can!" she answered, and then cast the weave.

Thoren spotted the shimmer in the air around him.

"Ready when you are," Balek said.

Finian jogged over to them. "What's our plan? There's no way out of this ring. Every exit has been sealed."

Shirra joined, stomping the butt of her spear on the ground. "If I have to, I guess we can work together on this one."

Thoren's mind reeled through their options. He didn't know much about Balek and Finian, but Shirra had shared her general strengths. Fern was right. They all should have shared their strengths when they had the chance.

Thoren sifted through what he had observed in the last couple of minutes.

Balek knows his way around weapons, but he leans on long range first. He let his mind pull details for Shirra and recalled seeing her spearmanship. It wasn't anything to gloat about, but she could hold her own. He hadn't seen much of Finian's abilities. *Those two could distract it.*

Thoren pointed to Balek. "Take shots at it from a distance. When I fought it before, it left once I pierced its core."

"So, we need to get past those tentacles." Shirra took a step forward, readying her spear.

Thoren grabbed her shoulder and stopped her from approaching the monster. Holding her, he now knew that Shirra was real. Thoren glanced from her to the amorphous demon. It watched them, moving slowly closer.

It's not going to wait forever.

"I'll take it up close. I need you and Finian to distract it." He stared Shirra in the eye. "Can I count on you?"

Shirra pulled out of his grasp. "Distract it?" she scoffed. "Are you plotting to take the spotlight?"

She's not the easiest to work with. Thoren sighed.

"I'll handle killing that thing." She shook her spear and sprinted forward. "Open it up Balek!" she shouted.

"Wait!" Thoren reached out, but she was too far.

The monstrosity snapped its tentacles on the ground, cutting the air with a razor-sharp noise.

Balek jumped into action, dodging an incoming attack. Thoren couldn't wait to act, throwing his plans aside.

Letting his body take over his reactions, he moved his way closer to the amorphous monster. The tentacles passed by him in near misses.

A blur passed overhead, carrying a pained shout. It sounded like Shirra. It was confirmed when her spear fell to the ground just ahead of him. Thoren couldn't let this carry on. He twisted, ducked, and dodged. His blade scraped against the solidified mist. It sounded like ice as the metal slid, ringing out.

"Balek!" Thoren shouted as he scooped up Shirra's weapon. He dropped his sword and arced the spear, pushing aside the last tentacle in his way with it, creating an opening.

Balek sped past him and straight for the body of the thing. He pointed his blade at the mist. Thoren held his breath, waiting for impact—for the moment this monster would dissolve.

Balek's blade started into it and the monster shrieked and pulled back. Its body tightened. Condensing into an orb not much larger than Thoren's torso.

That's not what happened the first time. Is this one different? Is it smarter?

Balek pulled at his blade, but it was stuck partway within the monster's body.

"Get out of there!" Thoren warned and sprinted forward.

The orb and Balek weren't more than ten feet from him. Just as Thoren reached Balek, a flailing tentacle struck. It broke through the shield Fern was holding over him and Balek. Thoren ducked, dropping to the ground, and tried to pull Balek down but he was too slow.

Balek was thrown.

Each time Balek's body hit the ground, he cried out, and then he moaned when he slid to a stop.

Thoren turned his gaze back to the sword sticking out of the monster.

It's almost deep enough.

Thoren dropped Shirra's spear. He stood, ran, and threw his weight into the hand guard of the fixed blade. It slipped further in, but not enough.

"Finian!" Thoren called without looking.

We need his war hammer.

The orb spun, attempting to throw Thoren, but he held to the blade. It started to slip. If he held on he'd pull it out and they'd be back to square one. He let go, leaning forward and catching himself with his hands which burned from the friction of sliding across the zilkan.

"I can't get close enough!" Finian shouted and swung his hammer into a tentacle, bashing it out of his way.

Thoren shook out his hands. He wasn't far from Finian, and Balek was back on his feet with Fern actively healing his wounds.

Where's Shirra? He looked to his right, but couldn't see her.

In the next second, Shirra filled the air with a fierce battle cry. She charged toward the monster, passing Thoren on his left, with only a dagger in hand.

"Finian! Give me your hammer, quick!" Thoren rushed to him and took it without resistance as Finian retreated to a safer distance.

The weight was different than a blade or spear, but Thoren knew just how to handle it. He held near the blunt top, letting the long handle stick out. His eyes fixed on the sword still stuck in the orb.

This ends now.

He tipped his head back, watching a tentacle swipe inches above his face. Thoren fixed his gaze once more and leapt over the monster's next attempt to stop him. Shirra took another blow. She tumbled over the bubbling zilkan ground like a skipping stone.

Fern called out another weave, different from the barrier she had previously cast. "Veisis Gaiza!"

Strong wind pushed against Thoren, almost carrying him to the core. He smiled and dropped the hammer to his side, letting the handle slide into place in his grasp as he swung it.

His ears rang from the impact.

The air's momentum carried him and the hammer with more force than he ever could have mustered on his own.

Balek's blade passed through the core and shot out the other side like a cannonball.

The catastrophic chorus, that split the air, forced his hands to his ears. He covered them as best he could, refusing to drop the hammer. Thoren stumbled back from the crumbling orb. The tentacles froze and shattered into thousands of pieces. Shortly after the pieces hit the floor, they were sucked up through a swirling black hole floating in the air above the arena.

He slowly lifted his hands from his ears and stood up tall. His eyes were fixed on the vanishing mist. The labyrinth fell still and the arena cleared.

"Is that thing dead?" Fern slowly approached Thoren.

Sweat beaded his brow and a drip slipped down the side of his face. He'd never been pushed so hard before.

I struggled. He lifted his hand, staring at how it shook. *Am I fatigued or scared?* His chest pounded and his pulse echoed through every limb.

"That was impressive." Balek slapped his hand on Thoren's shoulder.

"Is everyone all right?" Thoren asked, still staring at his hand. Bright red splattering caught his attention and he shifted his gaze to the blood on the zilkan floor of the arena.

James was hurt. He scanned the open space, but there was still no sign of James, Olathe, or Byran.

"I think so," Fern said. "Those of us that are still here at least."

"Did you see that thing pass right through Olathe?" Finian said.

"Olathe wasn't here," Thoren said.

"She was here," Shirra contested. "She's been with me since the start."

"When was the last time you felt her physically here?" Thoren watched Shirra's face scrunch as she realized the truth.

"But . . . when did she?" Shirra picked up her spear from off the ground slowly and walked over to them with Finian.

Finian held out his hand to Thoren. "My hammer."

Thoren looked at him and handed it back. "Thanks."

"Seems any weapon in your hands is deadly." Finian slung his hammer back into the loop at his hip.

"Everyone, look." Fern pointed out ahead of them.

The labyrinth rang in the familiar chorus, like shattered glass being swept away, and the wall split into a single pathway.

"Do you think that's the exit?" Balek asked.

"I hope so," Fern said.

"I'm not waiting around for you lot." Shirra turned and walked toward the exit.

Everyone, except for Balek, followed. He walked over to Thoren's fallen sword and picked it up. He held it out in offering.

"Thanks." Thoren took it and slung it back into the sheath at his hip.

They headed toward the exit. The silence didn't last long. Balek stared at Thoren. He clearly had something he wanted to ask.

"What is it?" Thoren gave him the opportunity.

"What do you mean you can't weave? You're ethrean."

Thoren sighed and nodded. "True. I can technically weave, but I won't say I have any natural talent for it. I'm not much better than a human who's just learned to shift an element."

"Really? That bad?" He stifled a laugh by clearing his throat. "At least your weapon mastery makes up for it." He punched at Thoren's shoulder.

"Oh! Should we find your blade?" Thoren recalled the way it had shot out through the core. It was likely at the other end of the arena.

"Probably." He smiled and jogged over in the direction it had gone.

"Balek, where are you going? The exit is this way!" Finian called.

"He's grabbing his blade," Thoren answered, pausing to wait for Balek.

He looked up to the black sky of the cavern. The misty void was nowhere in sight and he hoped it was the last time he would see it.

Once Balek retrieved his blade and returned, they moved through the exit in the arena wall together. There were no turns for them to divert from the path. It led the group for a half hour before the zilkan blended into the gray stone of the Bearing Mountains.

"We made it!" Shirra shouted out a victory hoot and hit the ground with her spear's end.

"Congratulations." Dessuithiel's voice echoed across the chasm.

It drew their attention to the clifftop where she stood, glowing with that same stardust-like light. In addition to her four guards was another figure, standing beside Dessuithiel. From the light emanating off the ethrean princess, Thoren could see the figure was cloaked in red, their face hidden in shadow.

A portion of the ground at the base of the cliff separated and spread out until a large platform, big enough for the remaining five participants, formed.

"Come." Dessuithiel pointed to the platform being manipulated by the combined efforts of her guards.

They all stepped onto the slab. It lifted from the floor of the chasm and took them up to meet Lady Dessuithiel atop the cliff they had started this trial on. She, her guards, and the cloaked figure had stepped back from the edge by the time they arrived at the top.

From the physique of the cloaked figure's body, Thoren could tell this "interested party" was male.

Thoren and the other contestants moved toward Dessuithiel and met her halfway across the cliff top.

Dessuithiel's angelic voice soothed Thoren's ears as she announced, "The first trial is over."

Hearing that it was over, and that he was still standing, left Thoren in a state of euphoria. He hadn't needed to weave. Everyone now knew that he couldn't, but that embarrassment paled in the face of what he'd accomplished.

I'm one step closer.

"We will stop by the supply room for you to return that which you took, and then you will have one day to rest before the second trial will be given." The princess turned to the cloaked figure standing beside her. He nodded, saying nothing.

Thoren stared at the hooded man. His heart burned—the same all-encompassing warmth he felt when looking at Thyrel's tower and the zilkan labyrinth.

This feeling, again. He resisted the urge to rest his hand over his heart.

The figure hidden beneath his cloak appeared to be staring at Thoren. His head lightly tipped toward Dessuithiel as though he were having a non-verbal conversation with her. It seemed all the more likely from the way she peered up at him with intrigue and then looked over the contestants.

"Follow me. I will lead you all back out to Thyrel." She turned and moved down the open tunnel, back the way they had first been led to the chasm.

The cloaked figure walked beside her with two guards, one of which was Guan. The remaining two waited until all of them had passed into the tunnel and they sealed the chasm entrance.

After dropping off their bags and weapons, they passed through the rest of the tunnel, back into the tower. The dry air shifted to the fresh-rain scent. His eyes stung with the daylight that flooded in through the windows as they stepped into the gardens of the second floor.

Thoren watched as the cloaked figure parted ways with Dessuithiel, turning left and going up the staircase, while they were led down to the main floor. The man seemed to lean heavily on the use of the stair railing.

Could he be . . . the Gift Bearer? He shook his head.

CLARITY

Chapter 9

Dessuithiel Vizule

Midday to the Evening of the Fifth of Trete

Dessuithiel did her best to relay what each of the competitors were facing within the first trial to those watching without the mountain. It was a simple enough task for her, one that she could do and still ponder other things at the same time.

Hours passed.

One competitor bailed—Olathe.

In these hours, she had learned the names of each competitor and kept coming back to the one from her vision, Thoren. He'd proved his skill with a blade, and his wit in discerning reality. These were of no surprise to her as her visions of him had already revealed such. She found herself growing fond of him—recalling how her stolen hope, joy, and light had radiated from within her most recent vision. Still, she didn't know how he would come to play a part in the fate she saw.

Her stomach pinched, grumbling loud enough that she felt embarrassed. She couldn't bring herself to leave the suspended space to eat lunch and it would be supper in a few short hours. At this rate, she would be here pacing within the Gift Bearer's quarters through the night before the trial ends. She'd sent Guan to retrieve a snack for each of them a while ago and expected him to return any minute.

"It's time to bring them to the center," the Gift Bearer said.

Dessuithiel didn't like the idea of him weaving more than he already had through the trial, but he was ultimately in charge of it—Marmidon oversaw it.

Stepping back up to the glass, she watched the shimmer of zilkan as it moved and formed a cage for the remaining contestants. She wrung her hands just below her chest as the dark mist moved into position.

That realm . . . those things . . .

It didn't ease her nerves to know that the Gift Bearer had access to that dreaded place. He had control over these misting amorphous creatures, but it still un-nerved her—terribly.

She continued to broadcast as the monster attacked, revealing the competitor who had bailed hours earlier. Dessuithiel shifted, unable to hold still.

She gasped and flinched in response to one of the competitors being struck. "Aiden, must you let it harm them so?" she asked directly, voicing his name in the only space she could.

"It is Marmidon's will," he responded, stepping back up to her side at the glass wall.

"James wishes to be withdrawn." She faced Aiden, who promptly pulled the competitor from the labyrinth using one of the dark realm portals.

Each competitor who asked to be removed was carried from their location in the trial, by way of the misted portals Aiden controlled, to the medic room within the zilkan tower. Once they were healed from any injuries sustained, they were released, and escorted out of the tower.

Nearing steps came, followed by Guan's announcement that their food had arrived.

She didn't move, anxiously watching everything unfolding down below through the weave placed upon each person's pin, like a charm or tether that didn't require a constant stream from her inner well to work. Dessuithiel listened as they tried to work together.

"I'm with Olathe, real or not," Byran said. "I thought I could handle this stuff, but, if this is what training the Gift Bearer is going to be like. I'm out." He held the pin on his collar and Dessuithiel relayed his wishes to Aiden. In the next moment, Byran had been removed from the trial.

"So much for their resolve," Finian said as he readied for a fight.

"Thoren! Cover for me!" Balek shouted. "Give me a barrier!"

"I can't!" Thoren responded with urgency, almost fear.

Watching intently, her eyes widened with sudden clarity.

No. Could it be . . .

She pressed her hands upon the glass, eyes wide as her charm relayed the perfect recording of Thoren to her mind and then out to the world.

Marmidon, it can't be.

She refused to believe the inclination she felt at his words.

"What?" Balek switched out his bow for his blade. "Why?"

Thoren's answer put her breath on pause.

"I can't weave!"

An ethrean who cannot weave?

Dessuithiel's hands fell from the glass to her sides, brushing over the soft texture of her gown.

Her mind was split between relaying the events of the trial to the world and pondering if Marmidon's will was to help Thoren. Helping him would be challenging. She had never heard of an ethrean who could not weave, nor was she aware of how to help him. The burning confirmation within her heart only grew the more she pondered it. Thoren had clearly been weaving within her visions.

The trial was over a few minutes later and she left with Guan to congratulate those remaining. Aiden shuffled behind, following them.

"Are you planning on coming?" she asked, pausing to face him.

"I need to see something up close." Aiden continued, shuffling past her and Guan to the trial's entrance where the rest of her guard waited.

The Gift Bearer remained a mystery, to her relief, not revealing himself as she congratulated the applicants. They stopped by the supply room on their way out. Returning to the tower's main space, where the air smelled of rain, and early evening light filtered in through the east-facing windows. Aiden turned away from their group and made his way up the spiraling stairs without a word.

He doesn't leave the mountain often, but . . . The upper levels held the libraries, study spaces, the royal chambers and eating quarters, along with the access to Thyrel's Heart Stone. *Aiden is going to the Heart Stone. I wonder if Marmidon speaks to him through it . . .*

CURIOSITY AND FATE'S CALL

Chapter 10

Thoren Belfry
Evening of the Fifth of Trete

Thoren swallowed to moisten his dry throat. They stepped out, into the early evening light, to the cheers of the city. Balek soaked it in, cheesing a wide grin and lifting his hands up behind his head like what they had just done was no big deal.

Shirra was more modest, and somehow looked annoyed. Finian followed Balek, sticking close to him as they walked out through the crowd.

Fern tugged at Thoren's sleeve. "I see your friends."

Janessa waved her hand in the air with a warm smile on her face. Her auburn hair flowed free and she wore a sweetheart fitted red dress. Vance stood next to her. He even wore his fine pin-striped vest, with a loose cotton top and trousers for the occasion. Vance had a pocket watch hooked to his vest and securely tucked away in the front left pocket. The golden chain swayed as he waved to Thoren.

"Thoren!" Vance's voice carried over the crowd.

"See you the day after tomorrow." Fern patted at Thoren's forearm and parted ways with him.

"Olathe!"

He heard Shirra calling to the failed participant and turned his gaze to find them. He spotted Shirra embracing Olathe.

"What happened?" She pulled back and looked her friend over. "When did you leave?"

Thoren then spotted James. He appeared to be all right. No permanent damage had been dealt, as far as he could see.

Thank goodness.

Byran was with Balek and Finian. They exchanged laughs and left the tower gardens as a group.

“Hey, Thoren.” Janessa grabbed hold of Thoren’s hand and pulled.

Facing his friends, Thoren was met with smiles and open arms. They embraced in a group hug, tapping their foreheads together.

“How does it feel?” Vance asked. “Did I hear that right on the broadcast?” He pulled back, breaking their circle and lowered his voice to ask, “Did you say you can’t weave?”

A knot caught in Thoren’s stomach. He’d forgotten that what they were experiencing was being shared with all of Marmidon. These trials were the biggest thing since the first Calamity, and now everyone knew there was an ethrean who couldn’t weave.

“Don’t let it bother you,” Janessa said. “You were amazing.” She stood upright and pulled at his arm. “Let’s go celebrate!”

They decided to buy food and return to Vance’s house for supper. Thoren was shocked to hear that the hours he had spent in the labyrinth had taken most of the day.

“I mean, I wouldn’t be able to rest in that place, not even to eat,” Janessa said and took a large bite of the drumstick she’d taken.

“What were those things?” Vance asked.

"And the illusions. I've heard of weaves that can do that." Janessa noted. "Did they look just like us sitting here, or were they kind of see through?"

"Oh, and what about the mist?" Vance pounded his hand on the edge of the short front room table—a new addition to his home since Thoren had gone in for the trials. They all sat on the floor around it with a small cushion under them.

Thoren tried to keep up with their questions. He answered them one at a time between bites. The food tasted so much better than the condensed bread, which had been a bit on the salty side and very dry.

Vance set down his cup and let out a satisfied sigh. "Your skills are on another level. When we watched you fighting that black orb thing, the other contestants couldn't hold a candle to you."

Thoren smiled and lowered his head. Heat flushed his face as his friends gushed over how well he'd done despite not being able to weave.

"So, do you think your inner well is defective?" Vance asked, breaking the conversation from the trial and focusing more on Thoren.

Janessa tapped the tabletop, speaking before Thoren could answer. "I did some asking around while you were in the mountain, listening to the broadcast as I did so." She looked at Thoren and smiled. "I think we can fix it." Her smile widened.

"Fix it?" Thoren set down the remains of his food, intrigued. He'd searched all over in Elpha Zavar's medical libraries over the last few years for an answer and found nothing.

"You mentioned that it feels plugged, right?" She held up her cup and reached out for a small orange. Setting it into the cup—it barely fit. "Now, for a visual. I think this is what is going on." She held the fruit in place with a finger and tilted her cup of water. Drips slipped out where the fruit was not perfectly sealing around the rim. "You said that you can weave, but it's about equal to a beginning human weaver, and that it hurts when you draw from it. Like the drips slipping out from my cup, this is all you have access to." She turned it upside down. "I believe if you push hard enough . . ." She pulled her finger from the fruit and the water gushed out as the fruit fell. "Yeudins." Janessa cast a weave and the spilled water lifted from the table top and flowed back into her cup.

"You think he's going to be foolish enough to push his inner well's limit?" Vance shook his head. "We all know what happens if you exceed it."

Thoren sighed and tipped his head down as he leaned back, laying on the floor. He stretched his arms up over his head and relaxed.

"Do you think I could find someone to examine my inner well?" Thoren asked. "I'm sure that after revealing this during the trials, there's someone itching to figure out what's wrong." He was hopeful.

Janessa spoke. "I know the weave to examine it, but I wouldn't be able to do anything to fix it."

"Even if there is someone who can figure it out, and fix his inner well, I doubt they can do so within the next twenty-four hours," Vance said, deflating Thoren's hopes.

"But the next trial is bound to be on weaving. How is he going to pass?" Janessa flicked her wet fingers at him, making Vance flinch as droplets hit his face.

Thoren stared at the ceiling while his friends continued to talk about the possibility of unlocking his inner well.

I don't know if it's possible. Could it really be that I just need to push harder? He was curious about trying. Before, he had always stopped when it became too painful. *Maybe I was on the cusp of breaking through.*

He sat up and scooted away from the table.

"Hey, are you leaving again?" Janessa asked as he stood.

"Just for a bit. I'll be back before it gets too late."

She stood. "Do you want any company?"

Thinking for a moment, Thoren nodded. "Sure."

If anything goes wrong, I'll need someone who can heal me.

She slipped on her shoes and they left together. The busy daytime streets were quieting down for the evening as they walked toward the tower gardens.

"Does this venture have something to do with weaving?" Janessa asked.

It wasn't hard for her to figure out after the topic of discussion back at Vance's place.

"I wanted to test something," he answered.

"Ah, so it *is* about weaving. Are you going to try and pop the top?" She mimicked the sound of a bottle cap popping off, and waved her hand out in front of herself. "I really think it could work."

"I hope so."

Within the next half hour, they stood inside the hedged field of the tower gardens. Thoren stared at the ground with his hand extended. His chest would not calm and his throat became tight.

"Well?" Janessa folded her arms. "What are you waiting for?"

"I'm sorry. I haven't gone out of my way to push my limit." He took a deep breath.

“I’m here if you need me. There’s very little risk in trying. Start with something simple. Just manipulate a small portion of dirt. Pull it from the ground and lift it to shoulder level. You know the words, right?”

Thoren nodded. “I know them.”

“All right then. Have at it.”

He and Janessa weren’t the only ones practicing in the field that evening. Thoren counted ten others, all practicing with their own social groups.

He shut his eyes and tensed his outstretched hand, ready to cast the weave.

“Hey, Thoren!” Balek called his name and approached from behind.

Thoren lowered his hand and opened his eyes.

“You’re Balek, right?” Janessa said.

“That’s right.” He held out a hand, waiting for her.

Thoren watched as Janessa gave him her hand and Balek bent forward, leaving a kiss upon it.

“Thoren, care to introduce me to this fine young woman?”

Janessa’s face flushed bright red and she pulled her hand back.

“Balek, this is Janessa Helms.” Thoren took a step closer to Janessa, feeling defensive of her as he angled himself partially in front of her.

"Janessa." Balek spoke her name with a wide smile, pulling out all his charm. "It's a pleasure to meet you." He shifted, looking at Thoren. "Is this fine lady free later this week?"

Thoren said "no," at the same time Janessa said "yes."

Balek smirked and shifted the topic. "You wouldn't happen to be practicing, would you?"

Janessa answered for him, "We're trying to unlock his inner well."

"Unlock it, eh?" He took in a contemplative breath through his teeth while looking Thoren over. "I can sense his inner well." He reached out, placing his hand over Thoren's stomach.

Thoren stepped back. "Excuse me?"

"Oh, sorry, I thought you were open to some help." Balek held up his hands and dropped them to his sides.

Thoren looked away, uncomfortable with the idea of a fellow competitor viewing his biggest weakness. "I have enough help."

"If you insist." He eyed Janessa. "If you still need some help later, I'll be here for the next few hours." He pointed off at the far corner of the hedged field.

Thoren then spotted James, Byran, and Finian. They were actively weaving and passing large portions of morphed stone between each other, like a game of catch.

"Thank you for the offer." Janessa bowed softly with a curtsy.

"Janessa." Balek stopped as he was passing her. "Would you be open to supper after the second trial?"

Thoren rolled his eyes and pulled at Janessa's arm. "She'll consider it."

"Of course!" Janessa quickly said and gently brushed Thoren's arm off.

"Great!" Balek smiled and with a quick bow, he left to rejoin his friends.

"Are you really going to go out with him?" Thoren asked once Balek was out of earshot.

"You know I'm not just here to find work and establish myself. I am looking for suitable partners." She pushed him, forcing him back a step. "Now, let's see you weave this dirt."

Thoren conceded and stood ready once again. He let out a forced breath and called out the weave, "Nevizot Netrimus."

The ground began to lift, forming a small mound.

"That's looking good so far. Now pull it out from the field."

Thoren's stomach cramped and the pain pinched at his inner well. He tried to hide his discomfort as he pulled the ground out, but Janessa caught on. She lifted her own hand at the ready.

"I've got you covered." She reminded him. "Keep going if you can. Condense it. This ground has high levels of clay and should be able to hold its form."

He let out an extended grunt as he tried to force the dirt together into a tight ball.

It's too much! He shut his watering eyes, ready to release it.

"Thoren, don't stop!" Balek shouted encouragement.

Surprised, he opened his eyes to see Balek, James, Byran, and Finian all standing behind Janessa on the edge of their toes.

"It hurts." Thoren groaned and his extended hand shook as his gut was stabbed repeatedly by an invisible dagger. His other hand clenched at his stomach.

I can't do it!

Thoren released the weave and the dirt fell to the ground in a half clumped sphere.

Everyone groaned with disappointment and Janessa approached him.

"Let me see how your inner well is looking now." She lifted a hand, waiting for his permission.

Thoren nodded and she placed it over his inner well.

"Redztu."

The weave was cast and she shut her eyes. Thoren held still as best he could. His body was still trembling and sweat was dripping down his back and face.

"Thoren, I can't see anything blocking the way, not physically, but your aura is . . ." She pulled back, cutting off her weave.

"Thoren, you have the largest inner well I've ever seen." Her voice was calm and serious with a sense of bewilderment.

That can't be right. Thoren didn't know what to say. *I have a large inner well? How? I've hardly ever used it.*

Balek stepped up, showing the palm of his hand. "Could I take a look?"

Thoren nodded begrudgingly.

He cast the weave and viewed his inner well. "It's true." Balek pulled back. "Then, how come you can't use it?"

"That's a great question. One I'd like to find an answer to." Janessa snapped her fingers. "There's still time before it's too late. I'm going to go see what I can find in Thyrel's medical records." She patted his shoulder. "You may have searched through all of Elpha Zavar's resources, but we haven't looked here."

"I'll go with you." Balek offered. "I'm sure we can find something."

James, Finian, and Byran spoke amongst themselves in hushed tones. Thoren turned, following Janessa as she walked toward the field's exit.

"Thoren." She stopped and faced him. "You should go back to Vance's and rest. Your inner well looked strong, but for some reason it really taxed you physically."

But, I don't feel like going back. His lips pressed tight and he nodded.

"Balek, you should keep practicing or retire for the evening," James said, stepping up to them and leaving Finian and Byran to their conversation. "I know you aren't big on studying. I love that stuff and I'm no longer part of the trials. I can help her search."

Balek was reluctant, but ultimately agreed, choosing to retire for the evening instead of training with Finian and Byran.

Thoren followed Janessa out of the field. *So much for practicing.* He parted ways with her and James at the first split in the zilkan path.

Slowing his pace, he watched as Janessa sped off with James in lively conversation.

Thoren placed a hand over his inner well. He had never been able to look inside, nor had he let anyone do so until now. Unable to think about anything else, he worked his way through the zilkan tower gardens until he came to a single bench on the far west end. The seating was placed within a simple maze of various roses. They filled out the landscaped planters and iron archways with bright pops of color and rich greens that fed his eyes with a spectacular sight.

His pulse calmed and he sat relaxed while listening to the melodies of evening songbirds in the trees.

I hope Janessa can figure it out. He sighed and tipped his head up to look at the dimming sky. Wind carried the floral scent past his nose and brushed the distant willow's vines gently.

Dessuithiel Vizule

She paced in a daze in front of her bed. It was hard to comprehend an ethrean so naturally talented in battle and mind, to be utterly useless in weaving.

"My lady," her lady's maid began. "I must ask that you pause your pacing long enough for us to help you change for supper."

Dessuithiel did as requested.

Distracting her for a short while, her handmaids helped her change into a gown befitting her expected first visit with her betrothed. Passing by her full-sized mirror, she sighed as her handmaids had selected a gown that was flattering in every way upon her petite body.

She could picture it now. Dundaelon would likely compliment her on how it highlighted the rich red of her cascading hair or the touch of pink in her cheeks with its complementary pale-blue hue. She'd heard such compliments before.

Her heart dropped, weighed down by the fears of meeting Dundaelon face-to-face. He would reach for her hand, lay a kiss upon it in greeting—they would touch. Dessuithiel had no desire to fill her mind with Dundaelon's past or future. Marmidon, she loathed the headache that would follow.

"I'm not going."

"Excuse me, my lady, are you saying you do not plan to attend supper with the royals?" her lady's maid asked.

"That is exactly what I am saying. Please inform my parents. Tell them I am weary from today and plan to rest the remainder of the evening."

Her lady's maid bowed and left her bedchambers.

She moved to the window and pulled it open, letting it swing inward until it butted against the deep-set sill encasing the arched egress. Her gaze drifted to the training fields. The unease of meeting Dundaelon faded a little as she spotted three of the competitors. It was hard to tell who they were at first, but she quickly deduced it was Thoren, Balek, and Finian. There were a couple others with them, one of them looked like James and one like Byran, but James and Byran no longer wore the mentor's garb.

Her vision flashed across her mind's eye.

Marmidon must think I can help Thoren, but I can't!

She knew of no way to mend someone's ability to weave, and without a look at Thoren's inner well, she didn't know how to even start.

A knock sounded at her door.

She paused and faced it, calling, "I'm not coming!" She assumed her parents had come to insist that she join them for supper. Her words carried more frustration in them than she had intended.

"My lady, it is I." The scratchy voice barely carried past her doors. She knew exactly who it was and regretted how she had responded.

Dessuithiel gave her handmaids approval with a nod and approached the doors as they opened.

She tipped her head toward Aiden as she inquired, "I don't think you've ever paid me a visit in my quarters. To what do I owe this privilege?"

"Thoren Belfry is going to weave." He raised the crook of his arm to cover the cough that came after speaking.

"Has Marmidon shown you?" She wasn't sure exactly how much he received as the Gift Bearer.

Aiden partially shook his head. "Marmidon has only given me a distinct feeling and a memory."

"Am I right to assume that this memory will help Thoren with his weaving problem?"

Aiden nodded. "However, you are the one who will have to perform it. My body cannot withstand the after-effects of casting the weave."

"What is the weave?" She gripped tight to the skirt of her gown, letting out a nervous-filled puff of air.

Aiden held himself a little taller. "That is what I have come to teach you."

In the following half hour, she turned away two attempts to get her to join her parents and the Valdans for supper. Dessuithiel spent the time learning how to redirect the energy of one's inner well. The weave she practiced now was not the same as what Aiden had taught her to use on Thoren, but the concept was the same. Aiden provided himself as her test subject for practice—something that made her quite anxious. He'd corrected her, reassured her, and guided her through every aspect of it.

Her head hurt as she pulled her hands back, finished with Aiden's instruction on the matter and having passed a trial of her own.

"Marmidon has given you this opportunity. She needs your delicate, steady, and powerful hand. No one else can do it and it must be done *tonight*." Aiden shuffled his way over to the exit. He paused and faced her one last time before the doors opened. "A word of caution, my lady, please ensure that nobody is within the same room while you cast it. I also do not know if one time will be enough."

She opened her mouth to ask why, but he lifted a hand, shaking his head and stating, “Marmidon and I have faith in you. Only you can do this. Only you can withstand the after-effects.” His cloak billowed as he turned around, resuming his shuffle.

After-effects?

Her handmaids pulled the doors open and a very curious Guan stood in view as the Gift Bearer left.

She lifted her hands to her head, rubbing at the sides to temper the headache. Touching Aiden’s stomach—over top of his inner well—had been a part of the process, bringing far more of his life to her mind than she could process. From the contact between them, she easily gathered that Aiden had a hard life, and had lived through many threats to it. His moments of joy all revolved around his family—one that was clearly missing as he was here in the zilkan tower alone. Dessuithiel glanced at her bedroom window, knowing she would have to connect with Thoren as well. Physical contact over his inner well was required to perform the weave.

I don’t know If I can handle much more tonight. Marmidon, I’ve not connected with others in so long. I’ve only connected with Aiden and Guan recently and it’s so much to bear.

She was learning more about her personal guard than she had ever known. He’d grown up in Dershja, was a full century older than her, and became a loyal servant to the Vizule house at a century old—unmarried. He was a quiet soul and loyal without fault.

Another sigh lifted and dropped her bare shoulders as the air passed in and out, shifting the pleated, drop-shoulders of her gown against her skin and adding to the sensory overload.

However much she wanted to rest, Aiden had told her that she had to find Thoren tonight.

"You look like you could use some rest, my lady," Guan said.

Dessuithiel shook her head, knowing what she had to do. "Let's go for a walk, Guan."

He insisted that she wear the veil over her face, but Dessuithiel would have none of it tonight. Her head already ached enough. Keeping up her rebellious streak, she left the tower before Guan could call for any additional guards. He did try to take the tower doormen, but Dessuithiel refused them.

"My lady, it isn't right for you to be out here without the veil or guards." He was relentless their entire walk around the hedged training field.

Good. Thoren hasn't left yet. She spotted him quickly.

"I have *you*, Guan." She did her best to reassure her guard while choosing a spot nearby, past the training fields, to wait for a good moment to approach Thoren.

"My lady, while I appreciate your confidence in me, please do not make this more difficult than it already is. This is hardly the time for a walk." He hinted toward some other pressing matter; one she had refused three times and would prefer to forget.

They passed by the hedged training fields, nearly at her pre-selected waiting spot. She could hear the conversation of which Thoren was taking part in. Intrigued, she stopped.

"Guan, block their sight of me, would you?" she whispered.

He did as she asked, standing in the way.

She remained there, listening to a young ethrean woman as she cast a weave to investigate Thoren's inner well.

That weave will not show what is wrong. She wasn't surprised at the woman's answer.

"Thoren, I can't see anything blocking the way, not physically, but your aura is . . ."

Dessuithiel shifted, glancing over Guan's shoulder while on her tip-toes.

The woman continued, "Thoren, you have the largest inner well I've ever seen."

Marmidon, how is that possible? She ducked back behind Guan and waved him to follow as she moved further away, to her chosen spot. She kept Thoren and his companions in view as she pondered what she'd overheard. *Thoren has a large inner well? But he said he can hardly weave . . . How could it have grown?*

Anyone could increase the capacity of their inner well, but it was something that required nearly depleting the inner well—demanding that their body store more than before once it refilled to meet the demand.

She pondered this over the following minutes as the conversation between Thoren and the others came to a conclusion. Balek, Thoren's female friend, and James left. Finian and Byran resumed weaving within the field. Thoren appeared to be leaving, but slowed, holding a hand over his inner well, before he turned toward the gardens. For a moment, her heart pattered with a mix of emotions she couldn't quite pin, but attributed to her nerves over what she had to do.

Guan shifted, moving around to block her view of Thoren as he walked past. Thoren was completely unaware that she was there. Her eyes followed him until the large flowering bushes blocked him from view.

Dessuithiel followed, pondering what she had overheard. It took only a couple minutes to arrive at the garden's edge. Thoren had slipped out of her view, but she knew he was still nearby.

Her pulse slowed the moment the smell of roses hit her nose. Taking advantage of the opportunity to calm her nerves, she reached up to a fully bloomed rose, gently cupping it, and drew it to her nose. Her senses were returning to normal being out here, though her head still hurt a little.

Her guard fell silent as her shadow.

"I'll tell you the real reason we left." She faced Guan, but held to the rose with one hand, lightly rubbing her thumb over the layered petals. "I must mend Thoren Belfry's inner well, as much of it as I can."

"He's gone on without you, my lady. Will you require that I bring him to you? This sudden desire to take a walk, this was the reason for *his* visit, was it not?" His eyes widened, a bit horrified at the idea of her helping Thoren. "Can I not do it for you? Not only are you of royal blood, you are directly overseeing the trials. How is this not meddling? He'll be disqualified."

She released the flower. "I have a feeling, you'd like Thoren disqualified." Dessuithiel folded her arms, taking a step closer to her guard. "Do I detect an ounce of jealousy? Perhaps envy? I shared one of the visions with you, Guan. Trust me, trust *him,* trust in Marmidon."

Guan turned his head to the side, clasping his hands behind his back. "If I were to be jealous of anyone it would be Lord Dundaelon." He grunted, clearing his throat. "The Valdan royals were received this evening, as you are well aware."

"Are you upset that I refused to attend supper?"

"It doesn't put you in a good light when you neglect to share supper with your future husband," Guan stated. "Nor does being outside the tower looking to aid a contestant, a *male* contestant."

"I know . . ."

He was right. If anyone were to discover what she was going to do for Thoren . . . Marmidon, her parents would surely lock her in the zilkan tower and insist on conducting the remaining trials themselves.

"I understand, Guan, but *he* told me this had to be done tonight."

Guan huffed, "Do you have to do as fate says? Can you not turn a blind eye this once, my lady?"

"Guan . . ." Dessuithiel gave him a scolding look. "I'll help Thoren and then I shall apologize to the Valdans for my absence before the sun sets."

She saw his shoulders soften—slightly.

Taking his silence as permission, she resumed her walk, searching the gardens for Thoren while working her way to her secluded bench among the roses. She chose a path outside of her regular route, wondering how she was going to track down Thoren and return home before the sun set. This slight detour was to allow her more time to think, if not to extend her stay outside the tower while hoping to bump into Thoren.

She cast her eyes upon her bench and froze. Up ahead, sitting on *her* bench, was Thoren Belfry. Fate had given him to her about as directly as possible. He sat staring at the dimming sky with no one else in sight. Thoren looked as calm as the sky he gazed at. She approached silently, as did Guan behind her.

AWAKENING THE CURRENT

Chapter 11

Thoren Belfry
Fifth-Sixth of Trete

"Strange how nature calms oneself."

Thoren jumped at the sound of Dessuithiel's voice beside him. He stared at her, surprised to see her there with only one guard, Guan, who stood beside the bench on the other side of her holding a firm glare in his direction.

Oh, great he's here, too.

He noticed the change in her apparel since the end of the first trial. This dress was even more flattering to her petite frame and gentle curves. The pale-blue, off-shoulder gown complimented her lips' shade of pink. Intricate, laced gold beading wrapped her waist and trickled off down the sides into the layered light-weight fabric. As she took one step closer, the floral embroidery, starting from the hem and gradually fading out around knee-height, reflected the zilkan path's soft glow. Her arms lifted gracefully from her sides, allowing the long, wide sleeves to hang gently from her wrists. She laced her fingers in front of her waist, waiting for him to reciprocate her conversational starter. His gaze lingered on the scalloped edges of the sleeves. The entire sight of her was breathtaking, her gown a masterpiece all its own.

She is truly in another class. I can't believe she's here. It's like I'm in a dr—

Thoren realized he hadn't spoken, and quickly turned his gaze away with his answer. "Uh, yes. It does. Very calm here, my lady." Thoren stumbled over what to say.

His throat swelled and he could feel the heat rushing to his face. He rubbed at his knees to remove the building sweat.

"I must say that you showed exemplary courage during the first trial." He could feel Lady Dessuithiel staring at him with her piercing blue eyes.

Thoren glanced, unsure if he was permitted to stare at such a rare beauty. He smiled weakly and thanked her.

Is she here to disqualify me from the second trial?

She continued, "I was curious to see how you would do."

Did she know I couldn't weave? His head snapped back and he stared with wide eyes.

"Oh, don't be too surprised." She smiled with an edge of mischief.

Thoren's heart pounded and he quickly turned his gaze away once more. Why was she here talking to him? Where had she come from? There was no crowd that followed her. Nothing that announced her presence outside of the tower and he was sure he would have heard something of the kind. He hadn't been sitting here for more than a minute before she spoke to him.

"I'm naturally curious about all the competitors."

Of course, she's just curious to see who the mentor will be.

"I wasn't intending on eavesdropping, but I heard your recent conversation with your friends."

Friends? Well, I guess I could consider Balek and the others friends of a sort.

"May I?" She pointed to his stomach. "I am intrigued."

If his face could burn any hotter, he would be able to cook himself breakfast upon it. He stood and stepped back.

Dessuithiel's guard tensed and held his hand at the ready.

"Calm down, Guan." Dessuithiel sighed like an angel and waved her hand impatiently at her guard. "He's no threat. You saw him in the first trial as much as I did. He's not the type to betray." Her gaze fixed upon him. "He seems honorable."

She then stood and her pale-blue dress ruffled with each step she took, closing the space between them. Her guard Guan grew increasingly uncomfortable. Thoren's heart fluttered equally with the ruffles of her flowing dress. The bounce of her rich red hair made her porcelain skin stand out under the moons' light.

"Thoren Belfry. It's a strong name." She hesitated before resting her hand over his stomach. Her bright-blue eyes flashed wide, but for only a moment—one he would have missed if he had been looking elsewhere.

He stood frozen. He could feel, through his tunic, her delicate fingers brush over his abs and then her palm pressed inward over his well. She appeared confused, intrigued, and relieved.

"Aktuly No Patiesibu."

That wasn't the weave Janessa cast. He now questioned what Dessuithiel was up to.

Thoren stared everywhere *but* at Dessuithiel. The guard seemed amused at his reaction, struggling to keep a straight face. His glare softened. Thoren dared to look down. Dessuithiel wasn't tall, her head barely came to his shoulders. Her eyes were shut as she examined his inner well.

As he stared, his heart continued to pound. The beats felt slow, but strong. She was captivating in form, from the gentle curve of her nose to the pointed tip, and the soft edge of her jaw to the defined lips that mimicked tulips in a pleasant hue of a dusty-pink rose, as well as her intriguing character.

Despite the enchanting view, the silence was uncomfortable.

Thoren looked mostly away as he asked, “My lady, I wonder if I may inquire something of you?”

She barely moved, her eyes remaining shut as she responded, “What is on your mind?”

“I don’t know much about you or how ethrea of your status usually spend their time, outside of ruling, but why bother with someone like me? Surely, your time is precious.”

Her hand moved upward over his chest. Flustered, he took a step back as her eyes opened and she followed his retreat. For a moment, he thought he saw a glint of longing in her eyes.

“Hold still,” she said and then answered his inquiry. “I spend my time serving my people. A ruler is only as strong as those they rule over.”

“But I’m from Elpha Zavar. I’m a citizen of High Lord Nesalariel Valdan.”

She smiled. “You are still ethrean.” She paused briefly. “But, truth be told, I’d help anyone in need if I could.”

Her heart is so pure. Her touch, gentle. He took a deep breath. *I understand why everyone loves her. If I ever found a woman, I'd want her to be like this.*

Dessuithiel closed her eyes once more. "Now, don't move."

Thoren listened. He would do anything she asked of him. Obeying, like a searral to its master.

"Here." She pressed her hand over his heart. "I can see what's wrong." Dessuithiel pulled her hand back, reluctantly, but did not step away. Her eyes moved up to his once more, studying him.

"W-what's wrong, Lady Dessuithiel?" Thoren wasn't sure what she meant.

Is she able to do anything about it? As one bearing royal blood, Dessuithiel's weaving capabilities far exceed most, if not all, ethrea. He thought about what he knew of the Vizule family. *Her parents are powerful. I do remember hearing how she exceeded their strength before she was fifty. Would she be willing to help me?*

"I will describe it the best I can." She held up her hands and laced her fingers together, but crossed and wrapped them unusually. "The energy within your inner well is very strong. If you'd told me you were part of the Valdan bloodline, I'd believe you, just based on your inner well. However, this strength has knotted itself up. The flow of energy has wrapped itself into three separate knots. This is greatly disrupting your ability to draw from it." She tugged at her hands, showing how they caught between each other, and then released them. “I have an idea.” Dessuithiel glanced behind at her guard and then back up at Thoren. “I’d like you to come with me.” She took a single step to the side and continued forward, walking through the iron arch of roses.

Guan raised his hand, indicating that Thoren should follow the fair lady.

Thoren hesitated, but then followed, strangely unable to defy her and wanting to spend more time in her presence, getting to know more about her kind nature.

He paused as he passed through the iron arch.

What am I doing? I’m turning into a lovesick searral.

Lady Dessuithiel’s guard grunted. “Please, keep walking.”

Glancing back at Guan, the fixed glare had returned.

Thoren rubbed at the back of his neck and continued. The guard remained two steps behind them. Lamps filled the zilkan pathway with beams of golden light and the pathway’s blue glow barely shifted under Dessuithiel’s steps. She walked through the gardens toward the tower’s entrance.

The hedged field came into view, as well as Finian and Byran still training.

“May I ask, my lady, where we are going?” Thoren avoided turning his face to the practice field.

I don’t want them to get the wrong idea. Would walking with Lady Dessuithiel bother them? He wasn’t sure after recalling how they cheered for him as he tried to weave. *They may want to see my success just as much as I do.* He relaxed a little, but kept his gaze averted toward Thyrel's princess walking slightly ahead on his right.

Dessuithiel turned her head toward the hedged field then back at him with a raised eyebrow.

"Does it bother you, what others may think?"

She was perceptive for sure.

She's gorgeous, soft-spoken, kind, selfless, and smart. He started to wish he *did* have royal blood.

Thoren admitted, "I want to win the trials fairly, I'd hate for them to get the wrong idea about me."

"Honorable, as I would expect." She stopped walking and faced him. She clasped her hands, holding them at waist height, and posed a question to him. "How can you compete fairly, if you can't weave? This next trial will demand it. I'm sure you are fully aware of this and your limitations." She looked at the training field. "You will be disqualified."

Thoren was afraid of hearing this. "My lady, can't I push through it like I did in the first trial?"

She shook her head. "That will not be possible." She started walking again. Her dress flowed like a floral field in the breeze with every step she took.

Turning her head slightly in his direction, she asked, "What if I can help you?"

"But at the start of the first trial, you said you can't tamper with fate." He stopped walking.

Dessuithiel nodded. "That *is* true, strictly speaking. I can't meddle with larger events." She looked him over and that same mischievous smile pulled at the corner of her lips. "But, when it overlaps with *my* fate, I can take certain liberties."

Her fate? What does her fate have to do with me?

Thoren tried to understand how the line was drawn for her to take action in dealing with his inner well. *If she wants to help. I won't turn it down. I do want to be able to weave.* He walked forward after her once again, keeping his face turned from the hedged field as they rounded the corner.

They arrived at the zilkan tower and the two guards opened the doors as Dessuithiel approached. She guided him inside and they moved straight ahead into a short hallway with only three doors. One door was straight ahead, while the other two were split with one on each side.

She stopped at the door straight ahead and waited for her guard to open it.

"My lady." Guan bowed softly and held the door while she passed through it.

Thoren followed and the door was shut behind them. The room captured his attention. Floral-structured crystal decorated the ceiling, lighting the room with a soft golden glow. There was a large and long glass table in the center with twelve cushioned chairs evenly tucked in around it.

"This is a council room, I believe it will serve us well." Dessuithiel brushed a hand over the smoothed wood trim of one of the high-back chairs. "Guan, you may leave us."

"My lady?" her guard asked, clearly opposed.

"Please." She lifted her hand to the door.

Why can't he be here? Thoren wondered.

"Just wait right outside the door." Dessuithiel instructed. "I don't think this will take too long, but I also don't know what will happen as I release a portion of his inner well."

"All the more reason I should stay, my lady. Maybe we should request the help of High Lady Miereene and High Lord Ayzgar." Guan protested.

"As fate would have it, my parents need not interfere with this." Her eyes narrowed in a rare display of sternness. "Guan, you are to remain at the door and speak nothing of this to my parents. Additionally, I have been tasked with overseeing the Trials. I know I can withstand anything that may happen." She pointed at Guan. "*You* cannot." She then pointed to the door.

His expression did not ease as he spoke. “As you wish, Lady Dessuithiel.” Guan bowed deeply and left the room reluctantly.

Release part of my inner well? Thoren’s eyes widened and he feared the pinching pain within his inner well, recalling the way it hurt when he’d tried weaving the dirt. *I-I’m not ready to feel that again!*

Dessuithiel advanced toward him, and he backed into the wall, clutching at his stomach. “I-I don’t know if this is a good idea.”

“I won’t force you, but I can feel how badly you want to be able to weave.” She reached out and grabbed hold of his left hand clutching over his inner well. Her grip was firm, yet gentle. “And then, there is the matter of fate. When it comes to my future, I can’t leave you like this. I can’t say much, but fate has great things in store for you, Thoren Belfry.” Her eyes studied his face.

He felt his cheeks burning under her stare. If this were anyone else, he would be sure the way that she looked at him sought for something more.

But, she is of royal blood. I can have nothing to do with her beyond friendship. She is well aware, I’m sure.

His tension melted away, and she pushed his hand down. Thoren glanced at her hand in his. His face burned hotter.

“It will be best for you to lay down, on either the table or here.” She gestured to his options.

Thoren didn't feel comfortable with either but chose the table. He walked over to it slowly, turned and sat on the edge.

"Lady Dessuithiel, are you sure you can do it?" He stared at the floor, while a ball of nervousness wound larger within his chest.

"I am sure," she answered. "Please, lie down."

He did as she requested, keeping closer to her than the center of the table, and held to the edge with his left hand.

Dessuithiel stepped up to him, resting one hand over his and moving the other into place over his inner well. Her hand felt hot against the chills that coursed his body.

"Whatever you do, *do not* move away from me." Dessuithiel warned and cast the weave immediately after. "Aust Savingju Stauv Dauriz Lisma."

Light flashed and filled the room, blinding him. The stabbing pain hit him a second later and every part of him wanted to flee from it. Thoren's back arched and he squirmed a little as his subconscious sought a retreat. He tensed and tried to bear it. The pain was increasing beyond that which he'd felt when trying to weave in the hedged field.

It's as bad as I feared. He squeezed his eyes shut and groaned. He wanted to curl into the fetal position. In this moment, he focused on Dessuithiel's hand over his. She gave it a comforting squeeze, reminding him of what he wanted. Thoren fought against his desire to give in.

"Don't move," she warned within his mind.

His body responded as the pain increased with a shift of Dessuithiel's left hand over his well. Energy moved from within. It twisted and poked him from inside like a multi-daggered orb. Sweat dripped down the back of his neck, his body burned like hot coals, and he couldn't stop himself from grabbing hold of her wrist with his right hand. Thoren couldn't control the trembling reaction of his body and the innate desire to flee from the pain. His grip shook and pushed against her, but she dug back in harder.

"Try not to fight me." She urged and turned her hand once more.

It took everything he had to fight against the urge to roll away from her and flee. Another gentle squeeze over his left hand diverted the fear darting about within him, just enough to keep pushing through.

Dessuithiel Vizule

She turned her left hand in his grip, guiding her weave into the next phase. He was under unimaginable pain, far more than she had ever experienced—of that she was sure. Dessuithiel did the only thing she could, giving his hand at the table's edge another comforting squeeze.

The last layers of this barrier were in sight. Her heart raced, heat burning within her. His grip tightened upon her wrist.

She spoke to him once more within his mind, seeking to calm him. *I'm almost done. Hold on just a little longer.*

Aiden had shared what might happen to her as a result of this *procedure*. She wasn't sure how it would feel, or what it would be, but it was unavoidable. The waves of energy within Thoren had built to the point of bursting.

The thyrian crystals lighting the room faded.

In a single moment, the teeming energy erupted from Thoren.

It hit her as though a boulder had rammed into her gut and tried to carry her away with it. The second wave of power struck with the force of a great wind, trying once more to push her away. Thoren sensed her weakening grip and shifted his hold on the table and her wrist to her shoulders and drew her in. He held her tight in an embrace, wrapping his arms around her. She clung to his tunic near his shoulders. The position forced her head to rest below his chin, over his heart, as the energy came in a burning third wave from his inner well. She held tighter as the broken barrier of Thoren's inner well exhausted itself with a final, cooling wave of energy, reminiscent of a calm lake.

The door rattled and Guan could be heard calling to her from outside of it. The lights shattered, falling all around and over them.

Then silence.

It was over.

Thoren's grip eased and his tension dissipated. She pulled back enough to see his face, speaking mentally to him once more. *Thoren, it's over.*

Thoren Belfry

The pain was gone and the room became still as it was before. Thoren opened his eyes and quickly released Dessuithiel.

The room was aglow like the heavens above. Specs of light twinkled mid-air, filling the room and swirling with the settling wind.

His lungs sucked in a deep breath as though he had not had access to air for the last minute.

He turned his head and looked at Dessuithiel. She had that mischievous grin.

"Thoren Belfry, You are now a weaver. So, how does it feel?"

Thoren sat up slowly and rubbed a hand over his inner well. There *was* a difference, but it was hard to explain. He could feel the available energy, far more than he'd ever had access to before.

"It feels . . . good." He found himself smiling.

Thoren swung his legs off the table and at the same time found his consciousness fading. His body started falling forward.

Sheerma! he cursed inwardly as he fell toward the floor.

He felt a sudden grip on both of his arms, catching him as he fell. The scent of a fragrant rose filled his nose. His fall was slowed, but ultimately not stopped. Dessuithiel gasped, being pulled to the floor with him. His mind spun and he tried to process what he was hearing and feeling. He opened his eyes as his mind came back to him.

He stared at the floor, but his face was not directly upon it. He gasped, realizing he'd fallen on top of Lady Dessuithiel. Thoren frantically tried to push off the floor, his arms trembled. His strength was gone. Dessuithiel's face came into view as he was barely able to push himself up on his knees. He then noticed her hands pushing upward to help him. His eyes grew wide as he registered the placement of her hands firmly against his chest.

Thoren stared at her blushing face. Her eyes were as wide as Ilzu and Maz on a full moons' night. His heart thundered and he hoped she had not noticed.

"My lady, I-I did not mean to—I'm sorry!"

Contrary to her flushed pink face, she didn't seem bothered. She smiled bashfully, igniting a flurry of emotions within him.

Her words came out softly. "Do you often apologize when others help you?"

The door burst open.

UNTAPPED POTENTIAL

Chapter 12

Thoren Belfry
Fifth-Sixth of Trete

Guan stood frozen at the open doorway for several seconds, hesitant to move through the room's star-filled air. His narrowed gaze fixed on Thoren.

"Lady Dessuithiel, may I enter?" Guan asked sternly.

Thoren tipped to his side, letting Dessuithiel move freely. She slipped out from under him and stood quickly. "Y-yes. It should be safe for you now." She smoothed her dress and brushed the loose hairs from her face.

"Are you okay, my lady? What was that *commoner* doing?" Guan stepped up to her hastily, and led her by her elbow a few steps away from Thoren. It may have been his weakened state, but Thoren thought he saw Dessuithiel flinch under her guard's touch.

"I'm fine. He fell, unprepared for how weak it would leave him. I only tried to soften his fall."

Her guard took a deep breath. "My lady, you are too kind, and need I remind you of your coming engagement to Lord Dundaelon Valdan? Being discovered in such a compromised state is *not* advised."

"I understand. I'm sorry, I'll avoid it in the future." She pulled away and dropped her arm from Guan. "However, I was successful." Her eyes shifted in Thoren's direction. "Would you help Sir Belfry back to his residence?"

Guan shot him a glare and agreed begrudgingly. He bowed and walked over to Thoren's side. He lifted one of Thoren's arms over his shoulder, secured his grip, and hoisted him up.

They were moving toward the exit when Dessuithiel spoke once more. "One more thing." She approached, stepping up in front of Thoren. "As I mentioned before, I could not unlock the full strength of your well, only a portion. Be cautious. It will take more than once to unleash your full potential." She averted her eyes bashfully and left the room.

Thoren could think of nothing but her final words as Guan practically carried him back to Vance's place. He spoke when he had to give directions, but remained quiet otherwise.

"I don't understand what Lady Dessuithiel is thinking. Helping a contestant." Guan shook his head. "I expect you will show her the proper respect and gratitude the next time you two meet."

Next time? I'm going to go through that all over again! He weakly clutched at his inner well.

"This the place?" Guan asked.

Thoren looked up and nodded. "Thank you, for helping." He pulled his arm from Guan's shoulders.

"I did it for my lady." Guan gave a curt bow and left without another word.

His legs shook under his full weight and Thoren sat down on the doorstep to Vance's home.

What have I gotten myself into?

He leaned forward and buried his face in his hands. His body still shook slightly, but the stabbing pain within his inner well was gone.

Time passed and he remained there, replaying in his head the way Dessuithiel looked at him, from the gardens and within the tower.

She's had that same look every time. It was a mixture of curiosity, wonder, and . . . *No.* Thoren shook his head. *She's destined to be with Dundaelon.* His chest pounded, flushing his face as he pictured Dessuithiel in her flowery pale-blue gown. Gold beading woven through her loose waist-long hair. *She's out of my league, both in status and birth.* He pushed his thoughts of her away and sat up, dropping his hands to his sides.

The door behind him opened and Janessa's voice called to him, "Thoren, how long have you been out here?"

He tipped his head up to see her already in her nightgown and robe.

"I thought you said you wouldn't be out too late." Her hands rested on her hips. "Don't make me mother you." She reached out and pulled under his arm.

Thoren tried moving, but only managed to roll over to his hands and knees. His breaths became labored and he ducked his head as his vision faded and came back.

"H-hold on. Not so fast." His words were laced with air. His vision blurred. He was far more exhausted than when he left the zilkan tower.

"What did you do?" Janessa stopped pulling and rushed down to his side. "Don't tell me you tried weaving again without anyone to help!" She called back into the house. "Vance! Get down here!"

Thoren struggled to remain present as they helped him inside, and over to his makeshift bed in the corner of the front room.

"Do you think we should call for some help?" Janessa asked.

Vance answered, "Having a healer here would make me feel better. I'm not that great at healing, yet."

"I'll do what I can, but I'm not sure what he did."

"Fair enough to assume he tried weaving," Vance said.

Janessa answered back, "He should have waited. I didn't find anything today, but we have all tomorrow to search for a solution before the next trial."

Thoren turned his head and opened his eyes, but all he could see were blurred silhouettes of his friends.

Their conversation faded along with his consciousness.

The soft sound of birds serenading outside, woke Thoren. He squinted from the daylight pouring in through the front room window. Lifting an arm to shade his eyes, he found his strength had returned. He was sore, but now he could move. He propped himself up on one arm and looked about the room.

"Thoren!" Janessa shouted with relief and rushed to his side from the short-legged table in the front room. She wrapped her arms around him, pushing him back down.

Dull pain spread across his chest, like a bruise being pressed.

"Ow!"

Janessa pulled back, her hands over her mouth as she apologized. "What *did* you do last night?"

He sighed and sat up. *Am I allowed to say anything? Dessuithiel never said to keep it a secret.* He looked at his concerned friend.

She bit at her lip anxiously awaiting his explanation.

"Well—"

"Thoren!" Vance came barreling into the front room. He leapt over the short table and skidded to a stop at Thoren's feet. "What happened? You scared us!"

"He was just about to tell me." Janessa punched him.

Thoren smiled weakly and nodded. *I think they should know.*

"Lady Dessuithiel . . . unlocked my inner well." He held up his hand, stopping Janessa from her imminent outburst. "Only a portion of it."

"Really!" She squealed and grabbed hold of his arm, pulling at it. "So, you can weave?"

"I think that's what he said." Vance spoke with irritation.

"Show us! Let's go to the tower gardens!" Janessa stood and rushed to the front door to lace her boots.

"Hold up!" Vance stood. "Thoren needs to eat something, and I don't know if it's a good idea to have him weave so soon. Did Lady Dessuithiel say anything about how long to wait before you try?"

Thoren shook his head. "She didn't say."

Janessa paused and set her boots back down. "Sorry, I let my excitement get ahead of reason. I agree with Vance," Janessa said. "I wouldn't want you collapsing like last night." She turned, wagged her finger in the air with a silent thought, and left toward the kitchen.

"So, Thoren, how did you end up with Lady Dessuithiel?" Vance folded his arms and took a seat on the short table that wasn't much taller than a milker's stool.

He knew that his friends would press him until they got all the details. Thoren acquiesced. "Fine, fine. But let's go into the kitchen. I don't want to explain this more than once."

Thoren stood and was relieved to find he could walk again. He made his way into the kitchen, tucked in the back right corner of the home with an adjoined dining space, where Janessa was preparing some oatmeal, toast, eggs, and cutting some fresh fruit.

Thoren shared only what he needed to, keeping the more awkward moments to himself. Although, he couldn't say he didn't like those moments.

The more he thought about how she acted around him, the more he felt like she was interested in him. *That, that can't be it, can it? It's not allowed.*

Before long, they pressed him for more details about what had happened, but he refused to say more.

"Oh, come on. You can't seriously think she just did that because of fate." Janessa slapped her hand on the stone counter. "Take it from me, she likes you."

Vance laughed. "Oh, sure. I don't know about that. She may be the same age as us, but her parents already announced her betrothal to Dundaelon Valdan."

"I know that." Janessa snatched a bite out of her apple. "I don't think Lady Dessuithiel is too fond of Dundaelon." She leaned forward on the counter, standing to Thoren's left.

"What makes you say that?" Vance asked.

"Some gossip I heard yesterday."

Vance leaned in on Thoren's right. "I guess that accounts for the other big rumor I heard last night. The Valdan siblings are coming to watch the second trial."

Thoren set down his fork and pounded at his chest coughing over his half-swallowed bite. He reached for his glass of water and took a sip.

"Why?" he asked Vance.

"I heard they've struck a deal with Verra and are bringing in something big for it."

"You don't know what it is?"

Vance shook his head. "Nobody does. There's plenty of speculation."

I need to be ready. I haven't even tried weaving yet.

Thoren scooted his plate away. "I'm going to practice." He left the counter and collected his things to get ready.

A half hour later, they all left Vance's house, headed for the tower gardens. The streets were packed, more so than when they'd first arrived.

"It must be true." Janessa scoffed at the sight.

Thoren was surprised and a little intimidated at how many people had come. It was easily the most concentrated population he had ever seen. He could pick out a fair mix of humans and therrinndore. Atle loomed over everyone as they walked the paths and were forced to duck under the trees. Other than the atle, the human Verrans were easiest to notice due to their rich and varying darker skin tones and thick curly hair, traits less commonly seen in Thyrel and Elpha Zavar because Verrans didn't visit as often as those from Marmeada and Jushosh. He spotted the pale faces, willow-leaf and spear-shaped eyes, and black hair of Dershjans as well. Thyrel felt like a pot of stew, in both the heat, and diverse crowds.

Elpha Zavar had a fair mix of crowded streets but it was never this crowded. They reached the hedged field to find it full of people weaving and playing several different games.

I can't practice here. Thoren just stared.

"Oh, wow." Janessa spoke. "That's a lot of people."

"Is there anywhere else we can go?" Thoren asked.

He looked at his friends.

Vance tapped at his chin. "Not within the city."

"Then we're going out." Janessa grabbed hold of Thoren's wrist and pulled him back the other way.

It took them an hour to reach Thyrel's city wall using the underground train, saving them from a full day of walking its length. The gates were open, but unlike the first time they'd passed through, everyone going in was being checked.

"Ah, you're that ethrean that can't weave! You might be the only one." The guard recognized Thoren as they left. "Just make sure you're back before the gates shut tonight," he called.

Thoren stopped and turned back to face the guard. "The gates are closing?"

The man nodded. "We would have kept them open, but since the broadcast of the first trial, we've had hundreds showing up today. We've been ordered to close the gate at sundown."

"I'll make sure to be back before then." Thoren made the mental note and checked the current time. It was almost noon.

I'll have just a few hours to practice. It wasn't ideal, but it was better than nothing.

He caught up with Janessa and Vance after passing through the gate.

"Shall we stake out a spot over there?" Janessa pointed out in the distance. "I believe we just have to be at least a mile out from the city to weave freely."

"That's correct." Vance confirmed.

Fifteen minutes later, they spread out in the tall grasses. Janessa stood across from him with Vance completing the triangular formation.

"We should take this slow," Janessa said. "How about you try weaving a portion of dirt like last time?"

Thoren nodded and pushed away the nervous jitters with a deep breath. He cast the weave and felt the rush of energy leave his inner well without causing any pain. Gasping, he watched as a large portion of ground lifted, broke away, and condensed into a ball. He'd only just finished the thought of it, and already it was there suspended in the air between them all.

"Thoren!" Janessa's hands shot to her mouth. "That was so fast!"

A breathy laugh left his lips and he stared in wonder at what he'd done, almost instantly.

I wove.

He lifted his hand, guiding the sphere, and the dirt ball followed.

"Try stone!" Vance called excitedly. "There's a large boulder over there. Extract some of it."

"And do what with it?" Thoren asked while willing the dirt back into the ground. It left a dirt circle with a three foot diameter where grass used to be.

"Try shaping it, something more complex." Vance held his hands out shifting the stone after calling out the weave. "Form the first thing that comes to mind. Whether that's a weapon, tree, flower . . ."

Thoren called out the weave, pulling the words from memory. “Akemins Morfejemis.”

A flower. He smiled, thinking of Dessuithiel’s gown and face.

It took more energy, but there was still plenty within his well. Thoren copied Vance, taking a portion of the boulder, and willed the stone into—a small statue.

It wasn’t a large statue, but a perfect two foot replica of Lady Dessuithiel in her pink floral gown.

Thoren quickly shifted it into a rose, but not before his friends had seen it.

Vance stepped up beside him, returning his portion of the boulder with one outstretched hand.

“I’m starting to think that the feeling is mutual between you two.”

“Me too.” Janessa folded her arms and stared at him with a raised eyebrow. “You kept all the juicy details to yourself.”

“Nothing happened.”

“Sure.” She stepped up to him deliberately. “I thought you said you weren’t interested in romance.”

Thoren could feel his face flushing and quickly turned away from them. He released his weave. “I’m going to practice by myself.” He walked east, along the south Bearing Mountains.

“Oh, come on. Don’t be like that.” Vance reached out and grabbed his shoulder. “We’re just teasing.”

Thoren knew that, but it still bothered him. "I think I should see what I can do by myself."

"Thoren, I'm sorry. It's just you've never shown interest in anyone before," Janessa said.

"It's not that." Thoren spoke, but that *was* it. Even now, his heart was pounding from the sight of the stone replica.

"You shouldn't practice alone," Vance said. "We'll stop, promise." He held out a fist.

Thoren sighed and bumped his fist against Vance's. "Not another word on it."

"We promise." He traced his pointer finger over his chest, marking it with an invisible X.

Janessa nodded emphatically.

"Okay. What should I try next?"

He spent the next two hours shifting the elements under his friend's directions. They were just as amazed as Thoren with how quickly he moved through each one.

He stepped back as he completed a two story shelter made of stone with a functional front door. He'd etched intricate designs along the borders and made a copy of the floral crystal lighting he'd seen in the tower's council room.

"Wow, where'd you come up with this?" Janessa stared up at the ceiling from within the structure.

Vance tapped his knuckles on the doorway. "I haven't seen anyone weave like this before. Thoren, you're a prodigy."

And this is just one third of what's inside. Thoren rested his hand over his inner well. The energy unwound by Dessuithiel was nearly all gone.

His eyes drifted over his other creations. He'd pulled individual minerals from the ground, sorting them into piles of iron, clay, and dolomite. Thoren had also pulled water from the air and frozen it into a block of ice after manipulating it for a while. He watched as a drip slipped down the side, growing as it picked up more water on the way.

There was one element he hadn't tried. Thoren stepped back and lifted his hand. His inner well was low, but he had enough for this. It was the simplest element to manipulate. He probably should have started with it.

His friends continued chatting, within the structure, about where they planned on eating supper. He raised a hand in front of him, palm up to the sky.

Dessuithiel's warning flashed through his mind. '*Be cautious.*'

Thoren hesitated.

Closing his eyes he rested his other hand over his inner well and felt for what was left. His inner well was refilling, slowly, and there was a portion left that he was sure he could draw.

I'll be careful.

Opening his mouth, he cast the weave, the very first weave he had ever tried. "Veis."

Thoren feared his heart had stopped with the burst of air that sprung outward from him—not just his raised hand. It barreled through the sorted mineral piles, the ice block, and slapped against his stone structure.

Janessa yelped.

He caught sight of his friends ducking for cover as the wind ripped through the openings. Thoren quickly found himself on the ground, curled over, holding his stomach, but the weave continued. A loud deep crash mixed with snapping branches. Thoren looked up through watering eyes to see the upper level of his structure had been ripped off.

Horns blared in the distance along with panicked shouts.

In the next moment, his inner well relinquished to his will and the weave was cut off.

"Thoren!" Vance rushed out from the remains. "Are you okay?" He knelt and rested his hand on Thoren's shoulder.

"I think so." Thoren winced.

He dared not move with how his stomach was cramping.

Janessa arrived seconds later.

"What did you weave?" she asked.

"Air."

"Just air?" Vance sucked in audibly. "Just . . . air?"

Thoren tried sitting up.

"I don't think you should weave air," Vance concluded.

"It's like a hurricane . . ." Janessa turned in a full circle.

Looking around himself, Thoren's jaw dropped. The ground immediately around him was bare of any plant life and the top several inches of dirt. The void stretched out more than fifteen feet from where he knelt.

Beyond that, the grass lay flat, pointed away from him in every direction. Several motor vehicles lay tipped over in the grass near the road. The trees along the foothills had several broken branches hanging down and littering the ground.

I did all that?

He stood and his knees buckled. He was fatigued much in the same way he had been after Dessuithiel opened the first portion of his well.

Vance grabbed hold of his arm as he stumbled backward. Janessa jumped to his other side.

"I agree. You are *not* to weave air," Janessa said.

Vance offered to take Thoren back into Thyrel, while Janessa stayed behind to help with the cleanup. Thankfully, nobody was hurt.

"To think you've had this kind of power inside you all this time." Vance rambled as they moved through the crowded streets. "I think you'll pass the second trial," he added.

Thoren wasn't sure. *What if it's not just air, but my inner well that caused that?*

"I guess we'll be having take-out again tonight." Vance said while he unlocked his door.

Thoren sighed as he was set down near the wall.

He looked around the room—bare of anything other than the small table and his makeshift bed. "The next thing you buy for this place should be seats."

"Do you want to pay for it?"

"No." Thoren laughed.

"Then the floor it shall be until further notice." Vance yawned and stretched his arms above his head. "I'll need to go job hunting after this next trial."

"You could have done that today," Thoren said.

"Nah, I still have some savings left for a little while longer." He tilted his head and asked, "Do you need us to go get a healer?"

He shook his head. "I'll be okay. It's not as bad as last time."

"That's good to hear." Vance stood and smoothed out his vest. "If you're good. I'm going to go pick up some supper."

That evening passed in a blur. Thoren ate and laughed with his friends around the small table in the front room. Light faded from the sky and the city filled with the pockets of light from buildings, street lamps, and the zilkan path.

A low vibration shook the windows. Their lively conversation ended abruptly.

"What was that?" Janessa stood and walked to the window.

Thoren joined her as the sound projected through the air outside once more. The glass panes trembled. He moved to the front door and opened it.

"That's a nauxen's roar," Janessa said and scrambled over to the open door. "I thought the nauxen lived north in Verra."

"They live all over," Vance said. "You just don't notice them most of the time as they stick to the mountain peaks and depths of the sea."

"What is a naux doing over Thyrel?" Janessa spoke rhetorically.

Another belting roar sounded, different than the first two. It was shrill and pierced their ears uncomfortably. Thoren covered his ears along with everyone else until the air fell still.

"There's more than one." Vance dared to tip his head out to look up above. "I can't see them."

A third, fourth, and fifth sounded off.

Five nauxen. Thoren tensed. *Five competitors.*

"This definitely isn't normal." Vance stepped outside and searched the sky. "I see them! They're flying south-west over the peaks."

"Hopefully they were just passing over," Janessa said.

Thoren hoped the same, but his gut told him otherwise. He looked at his hands and clenched them tight to still the shaking.

I think I know what I'm facing next.

A SPARK

Chapter 13

Dessuithiel Vizule

Fifth-Sixth of Trete

Dessuithiel's face burned for the next hour. She could not sleep, not after what had happened. Guan was furious—rightly so. She sat on the bench at the end of her bed, staring at her hands, the hands she had pushed up against Thoren's toned chest with.

Her blush renewed.

He was so heavy, chiseled, rattled, and equally charming. She covered her face with her hands.

She cursed, wishing that Aiden had mentioned how weak it was going to leave Thoren after mending, or better described as unlocking, the first portion of his inner well. Feelings were rapidly developing—feelings she should not have.

Guan had dared to touch her following the little incident between her and Thoren. His touch stung. It had added to her growing knowledge of his past and blips of his future. From what she'd seen, Guan would remain at her side for many centuries to come. That did give her comfort despite the pain of their brief contact.

She stood and began pacing. This was bad, very bad.

Running her fingers through her hair, she didn't care that they caught on the beaded hair ornaments, causing some to fall on the floor with a soft ting.

"My lady . . . is there anything I can do?" Her single remaining handmaiden asked from her seat beside the bedroom door. The other two had retired a few hours earlier. She rubbed her eyes.

Guan had insisted that one of her handmaids remain in the room with her at night since her vision-walking episode. Dessuithiel thought it a kind gesture, but her handmaids were clearly overworked.

"I think a cup of gulsawng tea will help me sleep."

Dessuithiel didn't like using the herb to force herself into slumber, but she couldn't stay up all night either.

Her handmaiden slipped out of the room, returning a few minutes later with a steaming cup of the sleep-inducing tea.

Soft as the sheer fabric that hung from her bed's canopy, morning light warmed her shoulder as the open window of her room let it in unfiltered. A long yawn pulled her mouth agape and her hands stretched up overhead. It had been a while since she had slept that deeply. The tea had been the right choice.

It wasn't long after she'd gotten up and ready, that a knock tapped at her door. Approaching it, she gave her handmaids a nod and the doors opened.

"Aba."

Dessuithiel's restful calm slipped away some. She smiled and lowered her gaze to the floor as she welcomed her mother into her bedchambers.

"My dear, I know you are anxious about meeting your betrothed, but refusing to eat with us last night . . ."

"I know, Aba, I'm sorry." Her guilt weighed heavier upon her shoulders as she realized she had never gone to make amends for her absence the evening before.

"I do believe that you owe Lord Dundaelon a visit, where you can apologize to him yourself." Her mother stepped aside, insinuating that she was to go this very moment. "He's a good man, very knowledgeable, strategic, talented in the arts, and eager to meet you."

She had no excuse to prolong it. Dessuithiel nodded, and took hold of the skirt of her gown as she passed from her bedchambers to the floor's main landing, between the royal quarters.

"Where is Ba?"

Her mother walked alongside her, keeping several inches between them. "He is entertaining the Valdan High Lord and Lady Gailiaethere."

"And Lord Dundaelon is not with them?"

"He has gone to walk the gardens, having claimed to have seen you out among them yesterday evening after supper."

Dessuithiel stiffened.

Did he see me with Thoren?

She thought she was nervous to meet him before, but now she dreaded it.

"Aba, must I wed?"

Her mother laughed. "Must you be so against it?" She calmed and stopped walking, remaining a step above Dessuithiel as they both paused upon the spiral staircase. "My dear, you are our only child. There is no other way to carry on our bloodline, if not through you. Thyrel's future must be secure. The Valdans' military strength is no secret among the royal families. Having our families joined will keep Thyrel's borders strong from any threat."

No, it won't. She wanted to say, but knew her mother would not take her word with the weight it should have. All because the Seer had said that Thyrel would still stand centuries from now. It astounded her that the Seer felt no need to mention anything about what Dessuithiel had been seeing for years in visions. Dessuithiel gasped, startling her mother.

What if the vision is not soon, but far in the future? Does that change what I must do for Thoren now? It was hard for her to decide. The vision had come with greater frequency and deeper control over her than in the past. She was sure it was coming that year—quite possibly this very month.

"What is it, my dear?" her mother asked.

Dessuithiel lifted a hand, dismissing the brief realization. "Nothing, Aba. I will go find Dundaelon and apologize."

"I expect you back by noon. You have your final dress fitting, and we must finalize the food choices for the banquet that will follow Farthven Ladayose. Your Ba sent out invitations to every royal house, and monarchy of Marmidon. I'll not have you disappearing today."

Dessuithiel nodded. She'd asked for this when she refused to dine with the Valdan family the prior evening.

I still need to tend to my duties . . .

She picked up her skirt and gracefully retreated down the stairs. In a rare occurrence, Guan was not attached to her shadow. His four stand-ins, however, rushed to keep up with her turns through the gardens.

Holding her skirt was the only thing keeping her from wringing her hands over meeting her betrothed. She needed to calm herself first. She needed her refuge.

Her bench was in sight, and empty. Part of her had hoped to find Thoren sitting upon it. The hidden desire caught her off guard and she lightly slapped the sides of her face.

There I go again. Thinking that something could come of us. Aba and Ba would never allow it. No one would. Fate, you are cruel.

She sank into her bench, letting the ruffled layers of her gown bunch up around her like a puffed pillow—one covered in fine embroidered designs and beading. Any motivation to find Dundaelon was gone—what little she'd had.

Dessuithiel rested her hands in her lap, shut her eyes, and let the world carry on around her. The gentle morning serenades of the birds let her relax. She couldn't recall how many breaths she'd been allowed before she was carried away in another vision.

Caught off guard, she heard the ceremonial sounds of Farthven Ladayose. Dessuithiel opened her eyes, finding herself standing under a large festive, but elegant, canopy. Her breath caught in her chest as she realized what dress she wore. It was solid white—slightly ivory in hue.

Varying lengths of flowy fabric layered down to her feet like that of floral petals. The petal-like fabric brushed at the back of her arms, split sleeves falling behind her. The music faded and a figure stepped up to her, reaching out for her hands.

She recoiled, pulling her hands behind her back before the man could touch her. The air quickly shifted and the ground seemed to tremble.

"Marmidon, I'm lost to another vision!"

This was not some distant future, this vision was but a few days away. Everything blurred suddenly. When her sight cleared, she felt she couldn't breathe. Her heart had surely stopped. Her hands found refuge over it as her pulse resumed, fast and uncertain.

"This cannot be my future . . ."

Dessuithiel gathered her dress and ran.

She hadn't made it more than a few steps before her betrothed caught hold of her arm, holding just under the dropped-shoulder sleeve.

Someone called her name in the distance.

Her strength returned and she pulled free of Dundaelon, who stood faceless behind her. His form blurred—hidden from her. She ran, searching for the one calling her name.

"I know that voice!"

This voice brought calm to her inner storm, heat to her face, and desire to her heart. The one who called to her was Thoren.

Dessuithiel gasped, emerging from her vision. She had not traveled as she had in the last two visions. Standing from the bench she glanced about. Her guards stood as iron sentinels, indifferent to her behavior.

"Fair Lady Dessuithiel."

She turned around. Her dress swayed in the sudden spin to face the man that called to her. This pale-ivory ethrean was dressed to impress with all manner of gold embellishment and emerald gems upon his tunic and armored cape draping over his shoulders.

He's well off, that is plain to see.

Her eyes quickly took in his form: taller than Thoren by an inch or two, broad-shouldered, and other than his darkened brows, he had silvery-white hair—fairer than Thoren's—and equally as long as her own. She found herself comparing the two men without meaning to. The man's face was the image of ethrean male beauty and strength. Yet, she still felt more attracted to Thoren's hardened and equally refined attributes and character.

"Lord Dundaelon," one of her guards said and they all gave the Valdan heir a deep bow.

That's Dundaelon?

She felt her jaw unlatch and drop.

This is who I am betrothed to?

"My fair lady, we seem to have missed each other at supper. I do hope you are feeling refreshed today." His words were smooth, his voice the perfect pitch.

Holding her head high, tilted up in his direction, she apologized, "I am sorry for having missed supper." She clasped her hands in front of her and then diverted her eyes from his intense gaze to the garden roses. "Spending so much energy on the trial that day left me terribly weary." It was partially true, so she didn't feel bad using it as an excuse.

He lifted his arm in offering. "Would you consider taking a stroll to make up for it?"

The tone of his voice sent a shiver down her neck. She put on her best smile and nodded once. Avoiding his arm, she began walking forward. He returned his arm to his side and joined her.

"I've heard many charming things about you, yet you refuse a gentleman's arm?"

Dessuithiel only glanced at him, keeping their casual pace through the gardens. "I'm not sure if my parents have said anything, but I tend to avoid touching anyone."

Dundaelon took a step out ahead of her, forcing her to stop. "They may have mentioned that you can be overwhelmed by touch at times, that you may receive visions from time-to-time. Yet, surely you do not intend on a touchless marriage." He reached out and brushed his fingers across her cheek. "How rare a flower you are."

She flinched at his touch and a sting of energy affected her mind as his hand moved to a lock of her hair.

His motions repeated: a gentle hand reaching for the face of another woman. Dessuithiel stood as a bystander, watching uncomfortably as the ethrean prince bestowed a passionate kiss upon the woman.

"What is this?" She turned about, recognizing her home, but not the woman with her betrothed.

Pulling back, the woman asked, "What of Lady Dessuithiel?"

Dundaelon's voice chilled Dessuithiel instantly with his reply, "What of her? That woman cowers in her quarters and avoids my every attempt at love. A man cannot live that way." He reached for the woman again.

Dessuithiel gasped and stepped back, breaking Dundaelon's connection with her. "Please." She tucked her hair behind her pointed ear. "Please, don't."

He scoffed. "There is nothing wrong with reaching for my betrothed. In time we will know all about one another." He ignored her request, pulling her hand from her side and leaving a kiss upon her knuckles. "Have you had breakfast, my lady?"

She tried to remain calm, pulling at her hand, but he held firm. Her mind was flooding with more than she wanted to know about Dundaelon's character. His charming front was tainted with the future—her future, if she were to wed him.

Marmidon, I cannot marry this man.

"I've not eaten, yet, my lord." She could feel her voice on the edge of cracking, her emotions running high with distress.

"Then, let us go and eat. I'd like more time to get to know you better before Farthven Ladayose." Dundaelon's words were smooth and elegant, but Dessuithiel had seen into his heart. He would seek out others, tarnish their union with his lust from a loveless marriage—an outcome she feared would be her doing.

Noon and the call of her mother became her saving grace, allowing her to leave Dundaelon's side. She arrived within the tower, quickly making her way to the fitting room only a couple floors beneath the royal quarters.

Dessuithiel burst through the door, as much as she could with others opening it for her, and declared, "Aba, I cannot marry that man!"

Her mother froze, holding the laced hem of her dress hung on a mannequin, and looked at her. "Whatever do you mean, dear?"

Dessuithiel marched over and plopped herself on a velvet-upholstered couch. "He's a split-tongued scoundrel, holds himself well, but his heart will turn from me in time."

Her mother let the lace fall from her hand and took a seat next to her, keeping a few inches between them. "Surely, this is just—"

"Pre-wedding nerves? Aba!" Dessuithiel stood suddenly. "He touched me! He held my hand!"

What if I show Aba? The thought brought hope. She had somehow shown Guan her vision of Thoren. That couldn't have been a coincidence. *Aba will have to believe me.* She moved toward her mother, but as many times before, her mother backed away.

"Let me show you what I saw in my future."

Reaching for her mother's hand, Dessuithiel hoped that she could show the vision in the same way she had shared with Guan.

"Show me?" Her mother paused.

Taking hold of her mother's hands, Dessuithiel tried her hardest to share what she'd seen when Dundaelon had brushed her face and held her hand.

The prick of contact jabbed at her mind. Dessuithiel did her best to push aside the pieces of her mother's future streaming into her mind. Her breath caught as the horror she had endured in her recent vision of Thyrel's future played across her mind—a seamless match.

Dessuithiel's brows pinched and she tried her best to stay the tears building behind her shut eyes.

Why can't I show her?

"Now, now." Her mother pulled her hands free.

The visions and pain ebbed away, leaving a dull headache. Confused and frustrated, she opened her eyes to see her mother waving her hands in an attempt to douse the emotional state Dessuithiel was slipping into.

"I'm not sure if I was supposed to see anything, but I hate to cause you pain, dear." She rubbed at her hands. "Save any contact for your betrothed. He is only trying to get to know you, dear. Can you blame a man for wanting to court his bride-to-be?"

Dessuithiel began pacing. "I saw our future, Aba. He will reject me. I can hardly handle holding hands!" Her pulse thrummed as her anxieties rose. "It's torture . . ." she stopped and stared down at her hand where Dundaelon had left his tainted kiss.

"My dear, you will have to adjust. Marmidon may have shown you a possible future, one you can learn now to avoid. As your Ba and I have said, you must carry on our royal bloodline. This simply cannot be done living your life in solitude."

Dessuithiel fumed, expressing a hidden desire. "Then let me find someone I can bear to touch!" She thought of Thoren as she turned to leave, stopping the moment she saw Guan arriving. He looked refreshed and wore his usual garb of fitted black clothing with lightweight matching leather armor.

"My lady, the high lady is only trying to help you prepare." He bowed before entering the room. "I bring a message from High Lord Ayzgar. He requests, Your Highness and Lady Dessuithiel to come and greet the royal houses, of which have just arrived."

"I will come, but Dessuithiel will stay." Her mother moved past her, giving plenty of space as she stepped around and continued toward the open doors.

"Aba . . ." Dessuithiel began after her mother.

"Stay. Your dress needs to be properly fitted and we cannot spare any more time putting it off." Her mother pointed to one of the tailoring staff members standing silently behind the gown with a measuring tape draped from their neck. “Her dress must be ready, no later than tomorrow evening.”

The seamstress gave a respectful bow to the high lady.

Addressing Dessuithiel’s guard, her mother said, “Guan, do ensure she stays long enough for the dress to be fitted.”

He bowed. “As you wish, Your Highness.”

Her mother left and Guan uncomfortably drew near. He grunted and pointed at her dress with a flick of his eyes. “You should try it on, my lady. Get it over with.”

Dessuithiel rolled her eyes and did as he asked, but only because she wanted this to be done as soon as possible.

“This way, my lady.” The seamstress guided her back to a closed-off fitting room while two others collected her gown.

When she emerged and stood upon the raised fitting platform, the tailor and seamstresses pinned, tucked, and marked the adjustments.

She stared into the tri-fold mirror ahead of her, watching Guan’s reflection in the right panel. He sat on the couch she had been sitting on not long before. She wondered how much of the conversation with her mother he’d heard. He understood her fears and believed her words, but would he have still believed her if he had not seen her vision?

“Guan?”

He looked up from the portion of the carpeted floor he had been staring at. "Yes, my lady?"

"I tried to show my mother a vision . . . but it didn't work."

He coughed, bending forward and leaned on his knees as he pounded his chest with one of his fists. "You touched the high lady?"

Dessuithiel nodded.

His response told her roughly how much of their conversation he had overheard. *He must have come after I tried.*

"My lady, you are becoming more daring lately. I must say it is not like you to go out of your way to make contact with others."

"I know . . ." she watched the flowing ivory fabric that was being added to her gown as she continued, "I don't understand why I couldn't show her."

"Marmidon only knows why." Guan took in a deep breath and sat back, resuming his composed demeanor. "Would you like to take a walk in your garden once the tailor is finished?"

Dessuithiel shuddered. Normally she would take up such an offer in an instant, but she knew Dundaelon was seeking to spend more time with her. The only place she could go to avoid him, was here or her quarters.

She shook her head, decided. "I'll be retiring for the rest of the day."

Guan leaned forward once again, a slight smirk on his face. “Do you plan on skipping supper again? You ought not to avoid the inevitable, my lady.”

Huffing as though she were a pouting child, Dessuithiel looked directly at her guard. “Just watch me.”

THE SECOND TRIAL

Chapter 14

Thoren Belfry
Seventh-Eighth of Trete

Morning greeted him with bells ringing in the dawn. Thoren rolled over, pulling his blanket up over his shoulder. He vaguely recalled someone waking him at some point, but had fallen back asleep. Trumpets sounded—announcing a coming event. Jolting, he sat up and threw his blanket off.

The second trial!

He rushed to get ready, and combed his hair back with his fingers into a low-set bun. He secured his hair and then his belt. Running to the front door, he slid across the polished wooden floor. He stopped directly in front of his boots.

"Thank Marmidon you've finally woken up! Hold on. You can't leave without breakfast." Janessa jogged over with his breakfast, a mix of egg, bacon, and potato wrapped in thin-rolled bread. "I think I should dump ice water on you next time."

Thoren smiled and took the food. "Maybe."

He ran out the front door and ate the breakfast wrap as quickly as he could along the way. The streets were filled with people from all nations as the trial trumpets blared over the city once more.

I should be just in time.

He arrived at the same time as Balek.

"I'm not the only one cutting these things too close." Thoren glanced at him.

"Ha! I guess not."

They found their places and watched as the tower doors opened and Dessuithiel was presented in the same manner as the first trial.

Dessuithiel Vizule

Against her will to remain within her quarters, Dessuithiel stood on the base floor of the zilkan tower with Dundaelon at her side and his older sister Gailiaethere behind.

Trumpets announced the hour and start of the second trial. The tower doors opened shortly after as she and her betrothed were announced.

"Shall we?" He lifted a hand, offering her to step out into the sunlight first.

She gracefully moved out along the zilkan path, hiding how nervous she was. Dundaelon walked alongside her and when they stopped, a few strides apart from the remaining contestants, he reached for her hand.

Before he had the chance, Dessuithiel raised her arms and addressed the crowd, "We welcome all who have come to cheer on our remaining participants."

She moved her hands in a sweeping motion, prolonging the return of them to her side where she was sure Dundaelon was waiting to snatch one up. "Today's trial will take place among the harsh environment of the Bearing Mountains." Holding her hands in front of her she continued, "We usher in the second trial, hosting the nauxen of Verra and Lord and Lady Valdan!"

Taking advantage of the introduction, she motioned to the royal siblings at her sides. Dundaelon's face hid any irritations over her avoidance, but she knew the feelings that would be there eventually. She could try and overcome her aversion to touch, but the pain would always be present. There was nothing she could do about it, no control over what she would see and feel.

If only these visions could be controlled. Then I would have no strain upon my relationships with others . . . her thoughts flitted briefly to Thoren as her eyes settled upon him. He seemed to be looking at those standing beside her. *Still, the contact was nice.* Dessuithiel smiled.

Warmth and pain touched her shoulder, flooding her mind with more of Dundaelon's past and future, the lines blurring until they all felt the same. She flinched and did her best to carry on, ignoring the scenes playing through her head.

Her betrothed took over the next announcement as they had discussed that morning. "Today's trial will test these five competitors' resolve. With an emphasis upon weaving, they will not be able to complete this trial without it. If any of you wish to withdraw, do so now." Relief washed over her as he removed his hand from her shoulder and lifted it to the southern mountains. "Each of you will be given limited supplies . . ."

She zoned out, rubbing the top layer of her gown between her fingers to help distract her from the budding headache that resulted from Dundaelon's brief touch. She couldn't imagine how excruciating an embrace would be, let alone a kiss—something that would be expected of her in the near future.

Her eyes lifted from the ground to Thoren, who stared out at the mountains. His concentrated expression and passion for this coveted position was alluring.

She found herself craving companionship that would allow her the comfort of touch that she had tasted when discovering her power did not react to contact with him.

Dundaelon finished speaking and she quickly shook her head, pulling from daydreams she didn't have the pleasure of dwelling on. Taking up her duty, she continued the trial's explanation, and how she would be broadcasting it abroad. She then turned everyone's attention to Gailiaethere, who was to lead the competitors to the starting point of the trial.

Thoren Belfry

"We welcome all who have come to cheer on our remaining participants." Dessuithiel raised her arms in welcome.

Thoren smiled and sighed. *She looks amazing in anything.* He then had their awkward moment replay within his mind. The surprise on her face as he stared down at her, barely able to lift himself off her within the zilkan tower's council room. *Why can't I forget that? A woman as perfect as her isn't even available.*

He tried to pay attention to what she was saying, but his eyes drifted over the soft emerald green of her gown bleeding into the upper half of ivory as his mind kept drawing him back to that moment. Thoren couldn't get over it. He hadn't planned on falling for anyone. He'd barely spoken to her before she'd unlocked a portion of his inner well. It made no sense for him to be so drawn to her. He couldn't even claim they were friends, merely acquaintances.

Trying his best to focus, he examined the perfectly pleated green sashes adorning her gown. They fell from a decorative metal band around the narrowest part of her waist and looped around her sides to the back. The center sash was held from flowing in the breeze by strands of gold draping between the side sashes. His eyes traced the intricacy of it all to the angular neckline ending in a short collar trimmed in gold.

Thoren still found himself smiling fondly when he looked upon her face. Her words reached his ears like morning dew upon the grass, somehow vital to his existence.

Focus! He shook his head, clearing it and listening more intently to her words.

"We usher in the second trial, hosting the nauxen of Verra and Lord and Lady Valdan!" Her arms lifted again, pulling the airy, double-layered bell sleeves of her dress.

Wait, what? Thoren shook his head and then spotted both Gailiaethere and Dundaelon standing on either side of Dessuithiel. He was aware of the nauxen and that the Valdan siblings were coming. But, he hadn't registered their presence and his mind had assumed the forms beside Dessuithiel were her usual guards.

Dundaelon held every best feature of an ethrean royal. His frame was sturdy, yet refined, his face was poised and what Thoren guessed was quite attractive based on the sighs coming from the women around. Thoren was fit, but his strength was not as obvious as Dundaelon's.

The Valdan daughter was similarly beautiful, but with a womanly build and touch to her face, and her hair held more golden tones to it, much like his own.

Thoren spotted Guan standing behind Dessuithiel with his eyes locked on him in a muted glare as usual.

Dundaelon rested one of his hands upon Dessuithiel's shoulder and smiled at her tenderly. She flinched, almost as if in pain.

A fire burned to life within Thoren at the sight. *I shouldn't be upset, they're betrothed.* He acknowledged his feelings on the matter. *Still, I do find myself drawn to her.* He shut his eyes and listened as Dundaelon spoke.

"Today's trial will test these five competitors' resolve. With an emphasis upon weaving, they will not be able to complete this trial without it. If any of you wish to withdraw, do so now."

Thoren opened his eyes and watched as Dundaelon raised his hand from Dessuithiel to the southern Bearing Mountains.

Everyone turned their heads, following his gesture. Dundaelon continued, "Each of you will be given limited supplies, prepared in advance for you. You will climb to one of the tallest five peaks south of Thyrel. Upon each peak you will find a nauxen carrying a single artifact. These nauxen will attack. We will hold nothing against you if the beast dies. You must recover the artifact and return with it to pass this second trial."

A game of fetch. I wonder what the artifact is? Thoren stared at the peaks, hidden in cloud cover. Dessuithiel spoke once more and Thoren gave her his undivided attention.

"As with the first trial, I will broadcast each competitor's progress or failure." She turned to Gailiaethere and nodded, passing the spotlight to her.

The Valdan princess took a single step forward. "If the competitors will follow us, the second trial will commence."

They were directed toward the mountain's base. Guards kept the crowds from following them, and Dessuithiel's usual four guards, including Guan, stuck close to her.

Thoren walked behind Balek and Finian and watched uncomfortably as Dundaelon escorted Dessuithiel, propping up her delicate arm with his own. Again, she appeared to recoil at the Valdan prince's touch. They spoke softly to each other. He seemed pleased while Dessuithiel looked more stiff and less receptive.

That's not like her. But what do I know? I've only spent a few minutes with her. They've probably seen each other throughout their whole lives.

"Pressure's on," Fern said from Thoren's right, disrupting his internal monologue.

"Huh? Oh, right. I guess so." He barely took his eyes off Dessuithiel to see Fern.

"You *guess* so?" Fern tapped at his arm. "Last I knew, you couldn't weave."

Balek chimed in. "He *can* weave, barely."

"I'm sure he's got a plan for scaling the mountain, but this time he won't have anyone to lean on." Shirra said smugly, intruding upon their conversation.

"I'll be fine." Thoren said blankly.

"That's what you said at the start of the first trial." Fern puffed out air from her nose. "Like Shirra mentioned, I can't help you on this one, you know that, right?"

Thoren nodded.

"He's going to be cut before we leave city limits." Shirra remarked with a snide grin and picked up her pace joining Balek and Finian.

Fern pulled at his tunic's white sleeve. "I mean it, Thoren."

He tore his eyes from Dessuithiel and gave Fern the proper attention. "Something happened that night following the first trial. Don't worry."

"Well, the only way you would be so confident is if you suddenly were able to weave. I'd believe that like I'd believe Maz had gone missing." She raised her hand at the sky where the double moons hid behind the morning light.

Thoren smiled. "I mean it. I'll make it through this."

He looked back at Dessuithiel. *Fate has great things in store for me.*

Dessuithiel started walking forward, Guan and four other guards moving in unison with her. To her discomfort, Dundaelon slipped his arm under hers, escorting her and causing her further pain whether he knew it or not.

"I must say I'm looking forward to this trial. When I heard that the Verran nauxen would be a part of it, my heart thrummed with excitement." The Valdan prince beamed. "I do hope you won't wear yourself out today. Let me know if you need anything. I will be at your beck and call."

She stiffly looked up at him with a forced smile, which likely came off as natural. "I appreciate it. I will try not to wear myself out, but this trial will last longer than the first."

"Then I will have to insist that you take breaks. I'm sure the people will understand." He patted his hand upon her arm.

His words and actions did not betray the tainted character she had seen. Dundaelon in this moment was genuine and kind, but would he remain as such if he knew how much pain such simple contact caused her? She pondered the thought of telling him. Being open in a relationship was important, and maybe her mother was right. Marmidon could be warning her what might happen if she were to put distance between him and her, no matter how painful it might be to accept him.

Why can't these visions be straightforward?

Her head was a worn drum by the time they arrived at the base of the southern Bearing Mountains. She was supposed to tell the competitors how much time they had to retrieve their item and return, but instead found her mind fixed in Dundaelon's more recent past.

He gave her arm a light squeeze. "Dessuithiel?"

When she did not respond, he proceeded to give the last instruction the competitors would get and had the supplies distributed. Dessuithiel barely heard Gailiaethere calling the competitors to the switchback path, allowing them to select a scroll with their route and destination.

Thoren passed by, his face clear in her sight that blurred between reality and the visions bombarding her. She wished she could speak to him, but speaking to him out loud would create problems of favoritism, questions from her betrothed, and speaking inwardly was not possible without touching the individual.

Still, inwardly, she wished him luck.

Oddly, Thoren turned and faced her after her inward wish, as though he had heard it. It was too perfectly timed to be a coincidence. She smiled, acting as pleasant as she could and waved with her free hand subtly at him.

Marmidon, what is happening lately? She'd shared a vision for the first time with Guan, and now it appeared as though her wishes to speak to Thoren with her mental link had carried outside of sustained contact.

Thoren quickly turned away and hurried up the path, beginning his trial. A gentle breeze pushed a portion of her loose hair against her face, itching it. Pulling her arm from Dundaelon, she tucked her hair behind her ears and took a deep breath as the bombardment of visions ceased.

"My lady, what do you require to be able to broadcast this event?" The Valdan prince reached out for her hand again.

She stepped back, but recovered her avoidance with a slight bow of her head. "It requires great focus. I cannot be disturbed. I hope you will be understanding of this." She held her hands clasped at her chest.

He withdrew his hand, tucking both behind his back as he bowed slightly toward her. "Of course, my lady. These trials are your charge, not mine. I shall remain as silent as your guard."

He straightened and eyed Guan.

His words did not ease her completely, but at least he would let her be for now. Dessuithiel closed her eyes, taking several deep breaths as she activated the enchantment upon each of the competitor's pins, secured to the collar of their garb. Each sphere of sight expanded, holding a different spot within her mind. All she had to do was maintain the connection with them and the broadcast station now.

Thoren Belfry

They arrived at the base of the southern mountains. Surprisingly the area this far over was undeveloped and barren. The soft grass of the tower gardens had shifted to cold hard stone. He stared at a switchback path leading from the base, and up about a third of the mountain.

"You will each have three days to achieve your goal and return here," Dundaelon announced, still holding Dessuithiel's arm in his.

At lord Dundaelon's command, the guards presented each of them with their pack of supplies, along with a thick tieneere coat, gloves, hat, and boots.

The same blue zilkan pin was secured to their collars, and a single weapon was offered to each of them.

Thoren chose a sword again, as it was the weapon he was most proficient with. They all switched their boots, finding the tieneere ones offered were their exact size. Thoren buttoned up the coat, pulled on the gloves, and set the hat over top of his head. The fur edge covered his ears and brushed at his cheeks in the soft wind.

Gailiaethere stood at the base of the path as she called to them. "One at a time, come and receive a route."

A guard stood beside her holding a small crate with several scrolls.

Thoren took his supply pack and slung the straps over his shoulders. He lined up behind the others and waited as each of them selected a scroll blindly from the crate. He took the last one and started up the inclined path.

"Good luck."

Thoren spun around at the sound of Dessuithiel's voice within his mind. She smiled and waved her fingers subtly. Her eyes sparkled with that look she'd given him multiple times. His face burned hot and he quickly turned away.

Again, with that look. What is she getting at?

Thoren rubbed his gloved hand over his face and marched up the stone path. He was sweating before he got halfway up.

"Why must we wear such thick gear?" Finian complained loudly from up ahead.

Thoren knew why, and so did everyone else. The mountain peaks were cold and harsh year round to all daring to traverse them.

"Just stay here then and make it easier for me to claim the position." Shirra marched past Finian, huffing and grumbling to herself.

Thoren tried to ignore the others and studied his route.

I'll be going south-east.

Tucking away his scroll into his pants pocket, Thoren picked up his pace. He wasn't sure how long it would take him to reach his designated peak, and didn't dare risk being late upon return.

I've got this. I won't be beaten easily.

The hike became quiet as each of the others split off the main path, starting their routes. Thoren's began at the end of the carved path.

He sucked in several deep breaths, holding each one for a couple seconds before releasing slowly to bring down his heart rate. The air was crisp, but not terribly cold yet.

Here it is. He held his route up against the landscape ahead of him, or rather, above him. *Time to climb.*

He secured his route once again in his pocket and removed his pack. Rushed into starting, he hadn't looked at the supplies. *There wouldn't happen to be climbing gear, would there.* He looked through the items and clicked his tongue. *Thought not.*

There was more of the dry bread and water from the first trial, but generously, there was also dried meat, and some individual-sized cookware consisting of: a bowl, knife, and cup.

Not much. He sighed and packed it back up. Slinging it over his shoulders, Thoren looked to the towering mountain.

I'll have to weave.

After sleeping, the usable portion of his inner well was restored and ready for him to take on this trial. He lifted his hand to the stone and called out the weave.

"Ackmins Morefejemis."

The weave drew the energy from his well and a suspended stairstep formed, exact to the picture in his mind. Shouts and commotion sounded from the city below. Thoren glanced back down, squinting.

He couldn't see much from this height and distance, but best he could tell and hear, it was directed at him. Everyone had seen him weave. A swelling of confidence filled his chest and he stepped up onto his first stairstep while he formed another one.

I'll leave them here to use on my return.

Doing so would use more of his inner well, as he would be creating every step along his climb instead of shifting two or three revolving steps. It was an exchange he was willing to make, and so far, everything was going great.

Thoren leaned into the mountain the higher up he climbed and found his breaths harder to take, as though the air held prisoner what his lungs required. He took a moment to rest, and expanded the step he was on into a larger platform.

His entire body had a semi-cold layer of sweat beneath the tieneere coat. He stared at Thyrel below. It felt small from here. Thoren could also see how disproportionately large the tower of Thyrel was compared to the other few sky pillars within the city. It stuck out like a beacon over a stormy sea. He doubted it would ever stop amazing him.

I wonder what kind of naux is waiting for me. He turned his head east to the peak hiding within the clouds. Patches of white blotted the upper visible half of the mountains' ridges.

Plenty of snow and ice.

He rubbed his gloves together. Carefully, Thoren stood and began weaving his stairway once again, up the side of the mountain. He had a long way to go.

Dessuithiel Vizule

After the first hour, Dessuithiel made her way back within the tower. Guan and Dundaelon escorted her to her quarters where the Valdan prince reminded her that if the energy required was too great, he would address the public and allow her time to rest.

"I'm touched by your concern, my lord." She lowered in a graceful bow, holding up the skirt of her gown slightly on one side while her other hand rested over her heart. "If it comes to that, Guan here will be the one to inform you."

Dundaelon acknowledged her guard and bid her farewell for the evening.

The door of her room shut and she let out an exasperated sigh, dropping her shoulders, and tipping her head back with her eyes shut tight.

"Shall I draw a bath for you, my lady?" her lady's maid asked.

Lifting a hand to the back of her tensed neck, she nodded. "That may be just what I need."

Nightfall covered Thyrel and the city sparkled with the lanterns and sky pillar lights floating above the zilkan glow. Dessuithiel had paced the length of her room and left permanent wrinkles in her silk nightdress from holding onto it. Releasing the skirt, she pulled her hair to the front of her left shoulder and began brushing her fingers through it.

How did I speak to him?

She'd gone over that moment several times. The look in Thoren's eyes—surprise.

He heard me. I know it. How far away can I reach out? When did this become possible? She lifted her hands out in front of her, staring at her palms. *What else am I capable of? Thoren, what have you awakened in me?*

In time she drifted off, barely on the edge of her bed. She woke, gasping at the sound of a naux's cry. Jumping to her feet, she rushed to her bedroom window and peered out at the southern mountains.

Thoren!

She pushed herself back from the window, startled that his name was the first one that came to mind. Shaking her head, she checked on each of the competitors.

Fern called out as she ran for cover. "Help! I'm done! I can't do it!"

Dessuithiel snatched her robe and ran from her room. Her handmaids barely had time to open the door before she passed through it.

"My lady!" Guan jumped into action, chasing after her as she sped down the stairs and turned to the hidden passage to Aiden's quarters.

Pounding her fist on it, she shouted. "Call her back! Take Fern!"

The zilkan door dropped, falling into the floor as Aiden responded to her. Dessuithiel hurried inside and found the Gift Bearer standing in the middle of his living room, a hand outstretched, his eyes shut in concentration.

She held her breath.

His hand lowered and he looked at her. "Fern has been taken to the infirmary."

"Is she hurt?"

Aiden shook his head. "Minor scrapes. She will be fine."

The air held within her lungs released in a relieved sigh. "Thank Marmidon." She fanned her face, which burned from her sprint. "I'm sorry, Aiden. I fell asleep."

"No need to apologize, my lady. I've been keeping a close eye on them as well." He pointed at five different glass-screened boxes on the far end of his living room.

The broadcast of each competitor was clearly displayed. Fern's broadcast faded to black. The pin's enchantment disabled the moment she had passed through Aiden's portal.

"Thank you."

"You've got your hands full. Are you sure you still wish to oversee the trials?"

Dessuithiel took a moment to ponder it. *Having Dundaelon here has complicated things.* She shut her eyes and focused on her wellbeing. Her head still ached from the forced visions of the prior day and her pulse had hardly rested since the Valdan prince's arrival. Passing the management of the trials to her father, wasn't the worst thing, but then . . . *Aba and Ba will only see another area where I am incapable of serving my people.*

"I will see this through to the end," she said decidedly.

Aiden smiled. "That's good."

His shoulders shook as he suppressed a cough, lifting a handkerchief from his pocket to his mouth.

"Maybe you ought to rest a while," she suggested.

"I will when the time is right." He smiled, bringing added creases to his aged face. "I'll keep an eye on things, go and prepare yourself for the day."

Dessuithiel did as Aiden suggested and returned to her quarters. She spent the next several hours pacing and anxiously watching the remaining four competitors work their way through the mountain range. Fern's route had been the shortest of the five and her naux had unfortunately been one of the most brutal to encounter—a stone naux.

Balek was the next to reach his peak and the fire naux atop it. He was doing well, strategically setting a trap for the winged beast. She shifted her attention to Shirra. The half-ethrean woman hailed from Kern, but had the hardened personality of a Verran. She was capable, but Dessuithiel could see that her tendency to rely upon her own strength would ultimately be her undoing.

Dessuithiel watched for a while as Finian fought a wind naux. He bounded through the air, masterfully in charge of the stone he wove under his feet. His persistence was admirable, but he was no closer to gaining the item secured around the naux's neck than when he'd started his dance with the beast over an hour earlier.

"My lady, we've brought you lunch and Lord Dundaelon seeks permission to enter your quarters to join you."

She tensed and faced her handmaiden. The Valdan prince stood at her doors, his head downturned out of politeness as permission for his entrance was sought.

My last sanctuary . . .

Putting on her elegant façade, she smiled and gave a curt nod. "He may join me for lunch." The words tasted bitter as they left her lips, but she had to at least try to make this work.

A table was prepared with an array of fruits, fresh bread, select meat cuts, and crisp and vibrant vegetables. The last items to be placed were crystal goblets and a deep-red drink in a matching pitcher.

Dundaelon stood at the table, holding to the back of the seat he offered to her. She gathered her skirt and sat as he gently tucked the chair in under her.

"I must admit that I feared you would turn me away," he said as he took the seat across from her and plucked a cluster of grapes from the fruit-filled tray. "Tell me, what does it feel like to be streaming these trials? I can hardly comprehend it."

She passed her eyes over him and picked up one of the golden-crusted rolls. "It taxes my strength . . ." She tried to draw up a relatable comparison for him. "Do you wield?"

He nodded. "I'm proficient in the blade, spear, and bow."

Perfect, as Aba said. He ***is*** *talented.* "If you were to wield all day without a moment's respite, your body would be weary, no?"

He sat back and nodded.

"While what I do now does not demand of me physically, it leaves my mind weak and sleep may call to me as I walk."

“So, you remain in your quarters?” He made the connection with understanding. “Would I be intruding if I were to stay with you?”

Her heart sped up and a chill stole the warmth from her hands. She set her roll back down upon the table as her appetite fled. “I-I am not sure that would be proper.” She stammered.

Dundaelon stood, setting down his half-eaten cluster as he moved around the table and leaned over her. His hand hovered near her face. She shut her eyes tight, bracing for the sharpness of his touch upon her mind.

“There you go again.” His voice slipped into her ears. “Don’t think I haven’t noticed you recoil at my touch.”

She opened her eyes, gazing up at his inches from her own. His irises were uniquely the brightest and palest blue she’d ever seen. Her reflection stared back at her from them. She looked frightened, her true feelings on full display.

He studied her for several seconds before speaking again. “What is it that causes you to react this way? You see visions . . . perhaps you have seen one of me?”

Her hands moved up over her heart, clutching tightly. “Lord Dundaelon . . .”

“Please, address me as Dundaelon, we will have no need of titles in private.” His hand drew nearer and the heat of his palm warmed her flushing cheek. “Tell me, what do you fear? What have you seen?”

She panicked, pushing on the floor and moving her chair back. He pulled back as she stood, knocking her chair over.

I can't bear it. She knew that the future she'd seen would surely come to pass.

"Lord Dundaelon, I cannot bear your touch." She lowered her gaze, unable to meet his eyes as she confessed. "For most of my life, physical contact has brought me pain. It is hard to explain."

His breath caught and he moved closer. "Yet, we will be wed in a few days."

She quickly stumbled back. Her dress caught on the fallen chair and she was sure she would crack her head upon the tile floor.

Instead of the hardened strike, a different pain registered over her mind. A firm grip held behind her neck and the small of her back. Dundaelon stood over her, holding her suspended over the floor she had half-fallen to.

He drew her up and wrapped his arms around her. "You cannot bear this?" he asked, moving his hands to the sides of her face and turning it up to meet him.

Dessuithiel pushed him away, gasping for air that had been stolen from her. Her hand shook over her lips and she drew back to the wall, wishing it would swallow her. Worse than the kiss he had left, was the pained vision of his betrayal to come.

Pinning her in with his arms on the wall, Dundaelon whispered, "Dessuithiel, I will not stay my passion when you are my wife. Is there no way to stay your visions? Numb the pain?"

She trembled and shook her head. "I-I have no control over them." She wrapped her arms tightly around herself. "I-I'm sorry."

He pushed off the wall and stared down at her. A heavy breath left his nose as his lips pressed tight. "This union between us will happen. Tell me, my lady, is there an end to the visions once you've seen all there is to see? Must I lay myself bare at the mercy of your foresight?" He held his arms out, as though presenting himself in offering. "In time, would the pain fade?"

She ducked her head. "I don't know."

"Then I guess we will find out, dear Dessuithiel." He approached, leaned down, and bestowed what should have been a tender kiss upon her forehead, but it stung. Drawing back, he held himself rigid. "I apologize if my visit has left you unsettled. I do hope you will see me as a fit husband, one whose heart is yours." He bowed and moved to her doors, leaving.

Dessuithiel crumpled to the floor. Her hair fell around her shoulders like a curtain closing to hide her tears from her handmaidens.

Marmidon, please take this future from me.

"My lady, are you all right?" her lady's maid asked from behind.

Steadying her breath as best she could, she responded, “I am. It is just my usual ailment when touching another.”

It was far more than usual. Her head felt as though it were splitting, her heart was ready to burst, and what should have been a warm emotional attraction was nothing short of pure terror from Dundaelon’s forward action.

“I’ll be nearby if you need me, my lady.”

“Thank you. I just need a few minutes.” Dessuithiel tipped her head against the wall, taking several deep breaths.

She brushed the tears from her face until her cheeks felt raw. The only distraction she had was the competitors still working to complete the second trial. It was early afternoon, and Thoren had just arrived at the peak where a pure-white naux leapt from its perch. Dessuithiel found the strength to stand, holding onto the wall until she felt stable.

Moving across her room, she sat on the bench at the base of her bed staring at the floor absently. Thoren held his own as his battle continued, but she grew increasingly tense the more she watched.

BURNING ICE

Chapter 15

Thoren Belfry
Eighth of Trete

On the eve of his first night, Thoren wove himself a shelter and a smooth spot to rest. Exhausted from the near constant hike throughout the entire day, he fell asleep quickly.

The next day passed much like the day before for the first half, except he now dealt with the snow and ice. The clouds that blocked his view of the peaks were gone today. The pointed tip was in sight, along with a curled up nauxen atop it.

How will I get close enough? He pondered as he climbed closer to the slumbering beast.

The nearer he got, the more he could discern its features. The nauxen he would be facing was pure white like the snow it lay upon. The only way he could tell it was there was from the shadows cast under its massive wings and larger protruding scales.

Looks like an ice naux. A quadrupedal one, too.

It was rare that a white nauxen would carry a different elemental fire. There were four main classes of naux within the quadrupedal or wyvern types: fire, ice, stone, and air. Fire was by far the most difficult to deal with and often came with equally troublesome temperaments. Ice nauxen were still irritable, but their elemental fire was not as wide spread as a fire naux's burst. It would be easier for Thoren to dodge. Stone nauxen were all brute. They sometimes carried the element of fire, but in a similar manner to the white nauxen, that was rare. Air, the most basic of elements, had never been found to spew fire or ice, but their wings were twice the size and powerful enough to cause hurricane strength winds and destruction.

Thoren stood at the top of a shorter ridge leading up to the peak. There was a small valley between where he stood and the peak the naux roosted upon.

It's going to take a while to scale that, too long. He searched the peak, looking for the easiest route up. Weaving his way up would be inevitable.

He found himself holding internal conversations with himself to combat the silence. This high up, trees were sparse along with any other vegetation. He worked his way down the slope of the lower peak he'd climbed, and into the valley between. The snow had a thick layer of ice over it, of which he was grateful for. Thoren still took each step cautiously, testing stability before putting his full weight down.

Moving quickly was difficult to do with how thin the air had become.

How do nauxen breathe up here? He stared up to see the naux was gone. *Where'd it go?*

Thoren spun around, searching the afternoon sky.

There was nothing.

Striking terror into his heart, the naux cried out from the east. Thoren shaded his eyes and caught sight of the incoming, airborne beast.

Sheerma!

He sprinted north, back up the shorter ridge as the naux's claws hit the snow drifts where he had just been. The ground shook under the beast's weight and icy snow was flung in every direction.

Thoren dove to the ground and covered his head as large clumps fell around him.

Looks like I'm doing this here. He rolled over in time to see the naux pop its head out of the snow. Its head was slim and angular with small horns jutting out at the back of its jaw, under its chin, and atop its brow. Two large horns pointed out from the back of the nauxen's head and equally large frills trailed down the center of its back to the tip of a spiked tail.

The naux turned its head, taking in a whiff of the air. Thoren lay still, hoping that he would look like a clump of dirt instead of the naux's prey. The beast's head stopped and its pale-gray eye locked in on him.

In that moment of pause, Thoren caught sight of an object dangling from a chain around the creature's neck and torso.

It's chained! He was hoping to do a quick snatch and run, but dealing with a chain disrupted that plan.

Thoren couldn't waste another second. The beast mobilized, and he was its target. He scrambled to his feet and struggled to find solid footing among the tossed snow drifts.

With a shrill cry, the naux snapped out at him. Thoren clenched his jaw as he leapt and rolled out of the way, leaving the naux only the snow and ice to clamp its daggered mouth around.

He heard a metallic jingle above him. Looking up, there was the object—a shackled metal goblet.

They want me to retrieve a goblet!

His body reacted, ducking as the naux swiped one of its clawed paws at him.

Weaving, this trial is about weaving. He struggled to think of a weave to cast. The words had fled his mind in the panic of his situation.

The bulk of society would never have to handle facing a naux. The beasts kept to the mountains and deep waters for the most part. If any ventured down near civilization, the cities were well protected by casters and weaponry, and then there was Verra. The people of Verra cultivated these beasts, treating them much like one would a searral or troxen.

Makes for a pretty big house pet. Thoren slid between the beast's hind legs and under its long tail. He let the momentum carry him down the slope into the valley.

As soon as the ground leveled out, Thoren ran.

Every few steps his foot sunk into the snow, breaking through the layer of ice. His boots padded the sharp edges, and kept his legs from being torn up. Taking a moment, he drew his blade, spun around, and faced the beast.

The naux pounded the ground, flinging the snow upward with each step as it turned around to face him.

Chest pounding and hands tightly clutched to his blade, Thoren ground his back heel into the snow and pointed the tip of his blade, at an angle, toward the incoming beast.

It's fast!

He didn't have the time to strike and was forced to dodge once again. As he rolled to his knees, Thoren caught the edge of his blade upon one of the naux's hind legs. It drew blood.

This one's young. Thoren smiled.

The older a naux was, the tougher its scales became. He stood after the swinging tail whipped overhead.

Let's try changing this up! His mind calmed some, enough to focus and retrieve the weaves he knew.

Thoren held out one hand and kept his sword in the other. Selecting the weave, he shouted, "Listose Yeudins!"

He felt the draw from his well as the weave activated and water quickly gathered from the abundant snow around him. Picturing the tentacled beast from the labyrinth, Thoren clenched his outstretched hand and watched in wonder as the water met his mental form with exactness.

His liquid monster swung out at the naux with enough force to push it back and disrupt its balance.

Just what I need.

He jogged toward the naux, wary of the tail swaying overhead. The sound of slapping water formed a repetitive cadence as droplets scattered and dripped down from the naux's side. The beast's tone shifted and the next cry to leave its mouth carried a small flurry of ice shards.

Concentrating the water in front of him, the shards caught in his liquid barrier.

Thoren tensed as the naux leapt into the air and out of reach of his liquid creation.

He squinted upward to see the beast's open jaw and a pale blue light rising up its throat.

It's going to blast me! Thoren quickly shifted the water, moving it over top of him. *A dome.* He pictured it, and the water obeyed, drawing more from his inner well.

Just as his water sealed around him, the naux's inner fire hit, freezing it.

Thoren knew it wouldn't wait for him to come out. He looked to the ground and spotted specs of dirt, sullying the previously pristine blanket of snow.

We'll try something else. He took a deep breath and gauged his inner well as he cut off the weave to the water. It wasn't needed anymore as the structure would remain frozen. *How did that use up so much?* He didn't have time to analyze.

The naux crashed down upon his dome. The frozen sphere cut through the snow and hit the ground beneath, followed by a loud crackling chorus. A large crack spread across the top. Thoren caught his breath and quickly pointed the palm of his hand to the ground.

"Ackmins Morfejemis!"

With the mental image formed, he guided the separation of dense minerals out from the dirt and directly through the crack in the ice, creating a hole and additional creeping fractures. The stony pillar struck the naux's clawed paw, soliciting an angered cry from it.

Thoren didn't wait for the beast to retaliate. He leapt out from the ice enclosure through the opened crack, with the aid of another woven portion of the ground. Blade in hand, he sought an opportunity to strike.

How do I get close enough to break the chain? He glanced behind him every few seconds, tracking where the naux was as it leapt back up into the sky and pelted the ground with bursts of wind.

At this rate, I'd have to be able to fly. He jumped and rolled out of the way as a blast of elemental fire struck the ground and traced after him in an icy blue stream.

His lungs heaved and ached as he moved into action again, narrowly missing a graze from the icy attack on his face. The tip of his hat was caught by a shard and fell to the ground, heavy with the ice crusted over it.

Thoren's head felt colder than the air around him. He hurried back the other way, giving himself as much time as possible while the beast turned around for another pass.

That was a close one. His heart pounded, trying to pump his blood to his legs as he fled.

The only way I'm getting to that naux is if I weave air. His mind flashed with the afterimage of what happened outside of Thyrel. It was powerful, possibly enough to bring the beast down from the sky, but it came at a cost. Thoren wasn't confident he could push through the pain that crippled him last time.

Stone will have to do.

He turned and faced the diving beast and watched the blue light rise to its mouth.

Not yet. He tried to calm his frantic mind and the urge to flee in the face of death. *Not yet!* His knees trembled and his hands shook.

The naux drew its head back and opened its jaw wide with a shrill cry. The elemental fire burst out at Thoren.

Now!

He called the weave with a hand aimed at the ground beneath him. The stone shot upward under his feet, in an angled pillar, at a speed that forced him to his knees.

Thoren cringed as the naux's stream grazed the edge of his knee in passing. Cutting off his weave, the momentum continued to carry him. He left his stone pillar behind as he took to the air. Thoren let out a battle cry in approaching the naux's eye. Holding his sword in a back-hand position, he slashed the beast's vulnerable organ.

At the same moment the beast recoiled in pain, Thoren was hit with the edge of its wing. As quickly as he could react, he swung his blade up and over the muscular front and into the membranous skin to be his anchor. There was no pained reaction at his strike, but the wing was in motion.

He wrapped his other arm in through the torn membrane. Winded, he tried to hold on. His inner well had taken a hit with the effort of getting up here and bordered on empty.

I shouldn't risk weaving again.

The beast took a sharp turn, tipping in Thoren's direction. His grips threatened to slip and he repositioned while holding to the thick, yet flimsy, torn membrane.

I can't let go. I'll die from this height! He glanced at the distant ground.

The naux soared around the peak more than once.

It's looking for me. Thoren stared at the membrane. *It doesn't feel anything on this part of its body.* He looked up at the beast's frilled back. *I could climb.*

His motions weren't as smooth as he'd like, and more than once he slipped, sending his heart into panic. The naux suddenly changed its circular glide and flung its wings up behind itself.

Thoren, against his better judgement, yelped as he was tossed off. The beast had landed atop the peak, holding onto it with its four paws and wrapping its tail around the narrow tip as he fell past it.

I can't die!

Dessuithiel's voice entered his mind as he fell. "*Do you wish to be withdrawn?*"

Thoren stared at the ground, speedily coming to meet him. He had five seconds at most.

I-I.

Four.

I don't want to—

Three.

Thoren dropped his blade and shot both hands down at the ground as he shouted.

"Veis!"

Air burst forth from his hands. It sent the snow flying with the same force as the naux's wings. Thoren shot up through the air while his inner well cramped. He clutched at it with one hand and watched as he again fell toward the ground.

I'm not giving up!

He searched his mind for the right wind weave and called it out, "Gaiza Skret Jez!"

His descent slowed until he stood midair with gusting wind beneath his feet.

I'll run with the wind if I must. He grit his teeth, half crouching under the pain within his stomach.

"Thoren!" Dessuithiel called within. Her usually calming tone was painted with alarm.

I'll bear the consequences. He answered, unsure if she could hear him the same way he heard her.

The naux shook the air with a roar and leapt from the peak upon spotting him.

You don't have the advantage anymore. He smiled and dug into his pain as he sprinted toward the beast.

It took less effort to run through the air compared to running on the ground and each step carried him much further. His semi-frosted knee complained, but he kept going. He fixed his gaze upon the goblet chained around the naux's neck.

I can't cast two weaves at once. Thoren thought through a budding idea. *All I need is a moment.* He dropped under the snapping jaw, then bounced up with a gust over a swiping paw. His goal was within reach.

Please work. Thoren reached out and took hold of the goblet.

"Parcest Lattas!"

The air beneath him dispersed as the cast weave changed. He began to fall, but the metal holding the goblet shattered under his grasp.

He plummeted toward the ground, seconds from impact as he spun around to face it. Holding the goblet with one hand, he stretched out his other and shouted his final weave.

"Veis!"

His fall did not slow and pain tore his inner well apart from within.

"Thoren!" Dessuithiel's voice screamed. *"I'm pulling you out!"*

No!

Thoren called out another weave, one he knew wouldn't take as much from his inner well.

"Yeudins!"

He felt the painful draw and watched, with trepidation, as the snow beneath him became water and reached out to catch him. It slowed his fall, but he still crashed into the ground with enough force that he felt his left shoulder pop and a rib crack.

Dessuithiel Vizule

She froze upon hearing his response internally. Flinching, her hands shot up to her mouth as her breath was stolen in Thoren's haphazard landing. Her gasp was not the only one as a wave of concerned shouts came from the crowd outside and below.

"My lady. If this trial causes any further distress, I will have to insist that you cease the broadcast and let *him*, the trial's head designer, handle the rest." Guan said worriedly, taking a step closer to where she sat on the landing bench outside her room.

She nodded, and moved to the nearest window. The windows of the tower landings did not open like the smaller ones in her quarters. She was forced to peer out the glass with a limited view of the peaks. Turning her gaze to the people below, they appeared just as concerned for Thoren as she had been.

Dessuithiel heard voices speaking from a few floors below. One of them was Dundaelon, and the other was his sister, Gailiaethere.

"If the gasps of the citizens were any indicator, I think I shall insist she stop the broadcast."

"The contestants knew the risk." Gailiaethere responded.

He's coming back up! Her heart was immediately set into a panic, her hands chilled, and her mouth dried.

"Guan, I need to go to *him*." She hoped he understood what she needed.

He only nodded before departing down the stairs. He paused partway, turned back to her and waved her to follow. Dessuithiel rushed forward. Guan led her down two flights of the spiral stairs before steering her off. This was the tailoring level. The staff moved in and one nearly spoke, but Guan shushed them as he pointed to a fitting room, then to Dessuithiel.

"Hide Lady Dessuithiel," He commanded and left quickly.

They did as he requested, opening the door to the nearest fitting room and she rushed inside. The door shut as the Valdan siblings arrived at the floor's landing.

"Ah, you're my lady's guard. Has she left her quarters?" Dundaelon asked.

"Lady Dessuithiel was restless and insisted upon a walk."

"Without you?"

Guan didn't miss a beat. "As much as I would like to be her guard at every hour, I too am mortal and require rest and sustenance."

"It looks like we will have to search for her without the tower." Dundaelon sighed. "Is she always this hard to find?"

Guan again surprised her with the swiftness of his response, "Only when she is unsettled by a vision, or needing a change of scenery."

Dessuithiel relaxed a little as the Valdan siblings decided to return to the guest quarters for the time being. She emerged from the fitting room only after she could no longer hear their steps.

Guan returned to her, stepping into place as her shadow. "Do you still plan on going to visit *him*?"

“You’ve spared me for now.” She feared what the evening would bring. If she remained in her quarters, would Dundaelon insist upon dining with her? Would he seek further affections? The thought shook her. “Inform *him* that I wish to spend the night.”

“My lady, not only is that inappropriate, but you will have the entire tower staff searching for you if you do not show up for supper.”

“Fine.”

She checked on the competitors and picked up her skirt rushing out to the landing and down to Aiden’s level. . The Gift Bearer had seen Finian’s waning strength and pulled him as requested. The contestant had expended all his energy and still not retrieved the required item from the wind naux.

Dessuithiel paused at the zilkan door, hand raised to it when Finian’s broadcast fell dark.

He’s in the infirmary.

Her hand dropped to her side. Twice she had been too slow to inform Aiden of the contestant’s wishes to be withdrawn, and twice he had reached them. She took a step back, feeling for a brief moment that she was not enough, not needed.

Guan stepped into sight and spoke with compassion. “You should go prepare for supper, my lady. I recommend that you join them this evening if you wish to keep good graces with the other royals and your betrothed.”

With a heavy sigh, she agreed to do so. She would dine with the other royals tonight, but only to avoid Dundaelon's unchained passions.

The evening was a blur of conversation and speculation between the royals. Political remarks dominated the discussions as they ate, and as soon as she could politely leave, Dessuithiel claimed the need to retire.

Guan escorted her back to her room, pausing at the open doors. "My lady, I will be resting tonight. If you need anything, Daedrin will be on watch."

With a single nod, she acknowledged it and he turned to retire as Daedrin, his stand-in, took his place beside her doors. She never slept as well on nights when Guan retired.

He needs sleep though. She understood. *The trial will be over tomorrow . . .* Without meaning to, she shifted her attention to Thoren's stream. He looked worn, battered, and had fallen asleep atop a shallow ledge. His inner well had not recovered. Her hand moved over top of her own inner well and she anxiously bit at her lip.

She paced until her feet ached, then sat on the edge of her bed until her mind forced her into a deep sleep.

Thoren Belfry

Thoren forced the water off him, taking in a sharp breath of the cold air. It burned at his lungs. The naux sheared the sky with a belting roar and returned to the peak.

Why isn't it coming after me? He stared in wonder, grateful to be alive.

The longer he lay there the colder he became. The water he'd caught himself with had soaked through his coat and garb as he had no strength left to manipulate it further—his inner well nearly depleted.

I need to move. He groaned, rolling slowly to his right side and letting his injured left shoulder slack behind.

It hurt to move, it hurt to breathe, honestly, it hurt to live.

Sitting up, he looked at the goblet in hand, taking in the rather dull metal it was made from. *This is junk.* He sighed and looked about for his pack. Recalling the first pounce from the naux, he realized that he hadn't noticed the pack since then. It must have been bitten off.

Looks like I'm going to travel light.

Thoren stood, with some trouble, and promptly fell forward into the rising slope. He whined at the pain in his shoulder as he tried using his left hand to brace. The ice-layered snow scratched at his bare face as he slid down to the flat valley once more.

It took him more time than he wanted to reach the top of that ridge. Several times, he glanced behind to find the naux still perched contentedly atop the peak.

I wonder. He looked to the goblet again, examining it not physically, but with his inner well—something anyone could do without weaving. *There's an enchantment on this.* He tipped his head up and laughed. *I don't think the naux will be after me now.* He lowered his head and stared at the distant city. He could barely see Thyrel's tower.

Dessuithiel spoke mentally to him again. "*I should have believed in you. I'm sorry.*"

Thoren smiled. He didn't understand how she was mentally linked with him, but it was good to hear her voice.

The bitter cold wind atop the peaks made it difficult to move the longer he was out in it. At first, he thought he could make it to his shelter from the night before, marking halfway through his route, but his right knee screamed at him with any weight put upon it. His left shoulder wasn't fairing much better, and his ribs restricted his ability to take any deep breaths. It left him in a constant state of dizziness.

It took everything he had to keep moving through each passing hour. He was sure his grip around the goblet was frozen in that position, along with his bent elbow cradling it against his icy chest.

Daylight was fading and he had nothing but the goblet in hand. Thoren kept checking his inner well, hoping for something to draw out the chill in his bones, but it remained unchanged.

A fire would be nice.

He relaxed at the thought and almost felt warm just thinking about it.

He slipped on a loose rock and tumbled down the slope—which held only a couple inches of snow. Jaw clenched and holding the goblet to his chest with what strength remained, he rolled to a painful stop at the base of one of the lower peaks. He pushed at the ground with his good arm, though aching badly with bruises forming, and stared up at the sky.

The stars were peering down at him. With a delirious grin across his face, he chuckled as he thought of the stardust within the tower. What he stared at now, wasn't as beautiful as that moment when he stared down at Dessuithiel's face under the dim twinkling light.

I might as well rest here. He shut his eyes and lost himself to a most pleasant dream.

BOUND BY DUTY AND FATE

Chapter 16

Dessuithiel Vizule

Ninth-Tenth of Trete

Morning came quickly. Her lady's maid woke her and got her ready for the day before the sun had fully risen. She wove Dessuithiel's hair, beading in crystals and pearls as she twisted, braided, and secured the extravagant design. Every motion was done with the utmost care to avoid touching Dessuithiel directly.

"My lady, you are fairer than the roses of the garden today." She stepped back. "Dare I say, that any man would be hard pressed to turn their eyes from you."

Dessuithiel stared at her reflection in the mirror. She hadn't the heart to tell her handmaiden that she would rather look plain and unappealing to Dundaelon. Anything to stay his hands from her to quell the passion that only he held for her.

"Thank you," she said and stood from the stool she sat upon.

Breakfast passed with minimal conversation as her mother and father focused on preparing the details of the wedding banquette. Dessuithiel agreed to everything her mother suggested, dazed and lost in depressive thoughts over her impending union.

She left the dining hall, Daedrin following her.

Each of the competitors were out of harm's way and working their way back to Thyrel, at least Balek and Shirra were making their way back. Thoren lay asleep still as the sun rose higher in the sky, nearing noon.

If he doesn't wake soon, he won't have enough time to return before the trial ends.

Dessuithiel made her way to the gardens, and Daedrin insisted, like Guan, that she wear her veil and bring extra guards. Too tired to oppose it, she did as Daedrin requested. The comfort of the gardens was not enough to still the rising unease within her heart and mind. She was haunted by Dundaelon's visit.

Telling him changed nothing. He will still shun me in time. She felt her lips quivering and her eyes watering. *Is there no one who cares about how I feel?* Even Guan, as caring and dependent as he was, had suggested that she try to find a way to adjust to the coming union. He cared about her, that she knew, but even with his brotherly love, he still could not speak out against the marriage in her favor.

He has always been one for tradition. The acknowledgement did not soothe her mind.

She stared at the rose arch ahead of her at the other end of the clearing she sat within. The way it framed what lay beyond it was partly like looking through a portal to another realm.

Maybe I ought to vanish into a realm of my own . . .

Startling her, the tower horns blared to life. After her racing heart calmed some, she realized it was to announce the arrival of the first competitor to return. Dessuithiel stood and walked briskly to meet and congratulate Balek.

Adding to her surprise, Guan was there searching for her. He joined Daedrin and her other guards as they cheered for the first one to finish the second trial.

"My lady. Your betrothed is on his way," Guan warned, speaking softly near her ear before he took his place as her shadow.

Finishing closely behind Balek, was Shirra.

Just as Guan had forewarned, Dessuithiel's solitude was disrupted when the Valdan siblings arrived to join her in congratulating the success of the two competitors. Dundaelon carried himself regally, causing women to swoon wherever he cast his charming smile.

Dessuithiel felt sick inside watching him, and turned her attention to the mountains. She stood back within the crowd, in a small pocket of space around her and the other royals provided by her guard.

"Have the others withdrawn?" Dundaelon asked as he stepped up on her right.

"Fern and Finian withdrew," she responded without looking at him. "One remains."

Come on, Thoren . . .

Thoren Belfry

Distant horns blared, startling Thoren awake. His body jumped under the sudden consciousness and quickly reminded him of his injuries.

The trial! He turned his head toward the noise.

He was close enough to hear the cheers from the crowds.

The sun shone down directly overhead and he lay there sweating under the heat. A grateful sigh left his lips.

I'm alive. Thanks to speerin and the coming heat of tummimar.

Rolling over, he had never felt so stiff or battered. He pushed his able hand into the dirt and realized the goblet was not immediately next to him.

Thoren stood, far faster than he should have. He stumbled as his vision faded in and out under the rapid pull upon his weary heart. He grimaced from the pain all over his body and waited for his vision to clear.

He didn't see the goblet.

I can't return without it, or I'll fail the trial!

He glanced up the steep mountain slope.

Did the nauxen take it? He shook his head. *I would be dead if it had. I was lying bait all night.* He scanned the ground once more, following his slide marks. *I came tumbling down from there, if I lost hold of it at some point.* His eyes moved along different paths that the goblet could have taken.

I'll have to check everywhere.

He shuffled and limped his way around the stretch of flat ground, and searched until his eyes crossed.

The horns blared again.

Does that mean two have returned? He feared his time was running out.

He recognized the area he was in and knew with his injuries it would take him every minute of the time he had left to get back down the mountain.

"Sheerma, just my luck," he cursed and dropped his gaze to his feet.

His eyes widened and jubilee filled his chest. Crouching down he dug his fingers into the dirt and pulled at the visible rim of the goblet.

Marmidon, thank you! He tapped the goblet against his heart.

Thoren couldn't express how glad he was that he'd left his suspended stairs sticking out from the mountainside. His inner well still had not recovered what he'd used. He had the other two thirds, but of course, they weren't accessible to him, not in any useful way. Thoren began his descent down the final mountain side.

After a tense three hour hike back down the suspended stairs, he cried out as his feet touched the switchback path.

Thoren felt more relaxed and energized in the moment he came to the bottom. He took the last step off the switchback path and faced the crowd and zilkan tower.

He held the goblet tight and pumped it up into the air using his good arm. "I made it!"

Cheers erupted from the city with his cry.

The crowd could not be restrained. He watched as they ran to meet him. Ringing continued within his ears after the cheers that followed his return. The horns blared from atop the tower, announcing the end of this trial for him.

His vision clouded and his heart thundered as adrenaline kept him moving. He'd just completed a solo trial against a naux!

His dizziness escalated with his rapid heart rate, and he found his vision failing him. He stumbled backward and fell.

Gasping and worried shouts were the last things he heard.

Dessuithiel Vizule

Everyone seemed intently focused on the broadcast as Thoren made his way down the mountainside. Their eyes were glued to the glassy screen on the nearest sky pillar. The three hours were fleeting as everyone waited in near silence. Balek remained to see Thoren finish, but Shirra had withdrawn to the infirmary to tend to minor wounds. Dessuithiel found herself anxious as Thoren stumbled to the base and lifted the retrieved goblet into the air.

Thoren shouted out, but his words were numb in her ears as she could feel the light within him waning. His inner well too near depletion to maintain his life.

Thoren, no! She pulled away from the Valdan siblings and her guard. Guan rushed to catch up to her as she wove through the crowd, not caring whom she brushed against nor the crippling pain that wounded her.

Before the echoes of the horn's blare had faded, Thoren fell backward, crashing upon the ground. The goblet bounced and rolled to a stop several feet away and worried gasps filled the air.

Dessuithiel called his name as she fell on her knees beside him. Without thinking she placed her hands upon his chest and called out the only weave that could save him now.

"Parsuit!"

Thoren Belfry

Ringing.

That constant buzz irritated him. It nagged at his weary mind and pulled him back to a painful reality.

“Thoren?” a concerned Janessa called to him.

He groaned in answer.

“Oh, thank Marmidon!” Her voice cracked and he felt her head lean upon his right shoulder, trembling.

She’s crying?

Thoren opened his eyes, only to shut them immediately under the light shining down over him. It seared the image of floral crystal to the underside of his eyelids in purples and streaks of yellow.

Am I inside the tower again?

Janessa lifted her head and brushed her fingers up over his forehead and through his hair.

“You gave us a real scare, you know.” She sniffed. “I can’t lose my brother.” Her voice shook, letting out a few badly restrained sobs.

Thoren spoke, his voice dry and raw. “You know I’m not your *real* brother.”

"I wish you were." She nudged his shoulder with her hand. Her sobs subsided.

He smiled weakly and let a satisfied puff of air out through his nose.

"If Dessuithiel hadn't gotten to you in time. Oh, Thoren. It was bad." Janessa forced her next breath out with her worry.

"Dessuithiel?"

"Yes. She came rushing through the crowd the moment you fell. Her guards were flustered and struggled to keep up with her."

Really? His chest warmed over the imagery. *I bet Guan isn't too happy with me. He wasn't keen on me from the start.* The warmth fled. *Hopefully Dundaelon doesn't have the wrong idea. Dessuithiel was just concerned about my injuries. There's nothing going on between us. But . . . she seems to flinch at anyone's touch. Except when she touched me.* He wasn't sure why, but he'd noticed it several times now.

"You caused quite the stir. I mean, everyone was thrilled to watch you collect the goblet and return. That was by far the most suspenseful two and a half days of my life!" She gripped his shoulder. "I wanted to sprint up the mountain and bring you back myself."

"I matter that much to you?" He watched her turn her face from him with a hidden smile.

"I only would have come after the naux, mind you."

"Right." He turned his head back to the ceiling and shut his eyes.

It felt good to rest. The bed was a welcome reprieve from the sleep he had on the ground the night before and he lay in a fresh set of the white garb. He took in a deep breath and noticed the pain in his ribs was gone, as was the pain in his left shoulder and right knee. He felt achy, but nothing like he did when he'd reached the base of the mountain.

"Who healed me?" he asked.

"Well, that's another odd thing. Dessuithiel did not call the healers, but took you on herself."

She refused them?

Thoren opened his eyes and sat up, propping himself on his elbows.

"Hey, just because you're healed, doesn't mean you get to go anywhere." Janessa pushed him back down.

His head rested back against the pillow on the medical bed he'd been placed upon.

"Who else finished the trial?" he asked.

Janessa stood and leaned on the edge of the bed. "Balek finished first." She spoke his name fondly.

Thoren looked at her with a raised brow. "Janessa, do I detect a crush?"

She averted her gaze and smiled. "Shirra was the other one to complete it."

What? He propped himself back up, and more, sitting upright. "What happened to Fern?"

"She withdrew. Thank goodness for that, too. She got landed with a stone naux." Janessa pursed her lips and blew a whistle out through them. "Finian was holding his own against the wind naux, but ultimately he wore out and couldn't retrieve his goblet."

"They're alive, right?"

She nodded.

Relief washed over him and his pulse calmed.

So far, the trials had not claimed anyone's life. He hoped it would remain that way.

Dessuithiel Vizule

"How could you do such a thing!" Dundaelon shouted at her within the walls of a tower council room. "You spared him! Gave part of your inner well to a competitor!" He fumed.

She had managed to avoid him for the rest of the day following the end of the second trial, but now that she'd left the only real sanctuary she had left—Aiden's quarters—Dundaelon had dragged her away to discuss her actions of the previous day. Even Guan was upset with her for having stayed the night within Aiden's space.

Her guards remained outside of the room, but she was certain they could hear Dundaelon's angered expression of his opinion.

Dessuithiel avoided eye contact, holding tightly to the skirt of her laced, ivory gown—a simple dress her mother had selected for that day, and one that only mirrored the coming union. "You would have let him die?" Her voice cracked as she spoke.

Dundaelon sighed, lifting a hand to partially cover his face as he shook it. "I would have sent for a healer." His tone softened and he pointed between them. "We are *royals*." He reached out and took her hand. "You are my bride-to-be." He brought his other hand to her chin, tipping her face up to meet his gaze. "Please think of how it makes me feel when you so readily run to the aid of a competitor in these trials, yet flinch at my touch, as though I carried poison."

She searched his face. The words leaving his lips were genuine, but she couldn't forget what she'd seen and what she continued to see at every touch from him.

"I understand." She did her best to hide her discomfort and remedy what little hope she might have at a happy marriage. "I may have acted rashly out of my devotion to these trials."

"You are *very* invested." He chuckled. "I admire that about you."

He pulled his hand from hers, bringing it up to cup her face. "I took some time to speak with your parents . . . I am sorry for any pain I have caused you." He pulled back realizing that his touch was only adding to it. "Maybe, if it would help, you could share what you have seen with me?" He looked between his hands and her face. "I find myself drawn to you more each time I see you. Tell me you can at least learn to love me?"

Dessuithiel cursed her body's poor timing as a shiver pulled her back and away from him. She wasn't sure if she could tell him what she'd seen. The Dundaelon of the future was not the man that stood before her now. She didn't want what she saw to come to pass before they'd even wed.

Giving her best answer to his last question, she said, "I-I will try."

It was all she could muster, and looked to be enough, at least for now. Dundaelon smiled and rested his hands behind his back. He bowed. "My lady, that is all I ask."

She wrung her fingers and bit at her lip. "Would you mind if I were to check on Thoren Belfry?"

There was a slight flinch in the corner of his eyes, but he stood tall, offered an arm and smiled. "If it would help you relax."

Dessuithiel did not mean to nod as eagerly as she did. "It would, thank you, my lord."

Bearing the pain, she took his offered arm and he led them from the council room, where Guan, Daedrin, and the remaining three guards took up their posts around them as they moved to the infirmary.

It took most of her concentrated energy to push down the repeated visions filling her mind of her future with Dundaelon as they made their way to check on Thoren. Doing so, left her conversational responses short. The Valdan prince was trying to have a discussion with her. She felt terrible for her seemingly uninterested responses.

Guan stopped at the infirmary's door briefly to knock before opening it. Dessuithiel pulled away from Dundaelon and entered. Thoren's friend, whose name she'd come to learn was Janessa, bowed deeply thanking her.

"Please, rise."

Her eyes fell upon Thoren. "How are you feeling?"

"Good as new, my lady."

The sound of his voice made her heart swell. She shut her eyes, doing her best to swallow emotions that were not appropriate for her to have. Relaxing, she lowered her gaze to the floor. Images of Thoren's future fight flashed across her mind. His courage radiating in the dark. She wished she could face her future with the same courage. As the images faded, she realized that Dundaelon had not come into the infirmary with her and Guan.

Does he not approve of this?

Her voice shook as she did her best to express her feelings. "I'm so glad you're all right. I-I only intervened due to the severity of your condition and too little time in which to reverse it. Otherwise, I would have sent for a healer." Looking to the ceiling, she struggled to remain composed and did not understand why. "Don't push your well like that, ever again." She took a deep breath. "One more weave, just one second longer, and my power wouldn't have been enough."

Stinging zapped at her mind under a gentle touch to her elbow, causing her to flinch.

Guan spoke. "You've seen him, and he is well." His eyes flitted to the hall where her betrothed waited.

"There's always something to prepare for, Guan." Her words spoke not only of her fast-approaching wedding but the future she knew was coming as well.

Her guard led her out, speaking back to Thoren and his friend Janessa. "You two can see yourselves out."

The door shut behind them and Guan released her into Dundaelon's care. From one pain to another, she passed. Like the years long ago, her mind was adjusting to the increased contact, growing numb and leaving her in a daze.

She looked back at the shut door, mentally reaching for Thoren beneath the visions clouding her sight. The door shifted, becoming the rose-covered archway of her gardens.

She was swallowed within a new vision. A realm of giant crystals grew around her until they stretched out of sight in the dark ceiling above. Soft golden light fell off the towering minerals to a cavern's rough floor. She turned about and spotted Thoren. He walked between the natural sky pillars. Her heart calmed and she felt the overwhelming urge to confide in him.

The knotted mass of energy within his inner well brightened. The call of Marmidon settled upon her mind with clarity. It was time to release the next seal of Thoren's inner well. She saw the moment it was opened, and felt what it would demand of her. Her heart shook.

The scene faded and she saw the infirmary door once again and the mental connection between Thoren and her stabilized. As Dundaelon led her away, up the spiral stairs, she relayed a single message—a call from Marmidon and her heart.

Thoren Belfry

The room fell still after Lady Dessuithiel left. He'd noticed how she shut her eyes for a moment following his response and released the tension in her lace-covered shoulders, dropping them a full inch.

She would be worried about any of the competitors.

He also noticed that her change in attire was a little different from what she normally wore—elaborate gowns dipped in pastels and glittering with beads and gems. The dress he'd just seen her wearing wasn't simple by any means, but it was all ivory, from the lace and beading to the sheer layers over the silk.

It looked like a wedding gown. She looked . . . sad. It was subtle, but hidden under her thick lashes and behind the pale blue wall of her irises. It was in the tears she blinked away before her glaring guard pulled her back out of the infirmary. She'd flinched yet again at the touch of another when her guard had taken her out.

I wonder why she does that . . .

Thoren scooted to the edge of the bed, facing the door, and dropped his feet. Standing, he started after Dessuithiel and caught himself against the wall as his balance was not yet back.

Why am I chasing her? His heart knew, but his mind fought it. *She was upset about something.* He had, for a split moment, had the strong desire to comfort the ethrean princess. *Who am I to comfort her?*

"Thoren, let's go. Vance has been waiting to hear how you're doing." Janessa walked around the bed and pulled gently at his arm.

"Right," he whispered and followed dolefully.

Before reaching the door, Dessuithiel's voice permeated his mind like it had during the second trial.

"Meet me in the gardens tonight."

He stopped walking, looking at the shut door.

"Oh, come on." Janessa stepped behind him and pushed at his back, forcing him forward once again.

They exited the tower and walked down the zilkan path, passing the hedges and pruned trees. Something didn't feel right about leaving. Thoren stopped and looked back at the tower, hoping to catch a glimpse of Dessuithiel through one of the windows.

"My lady, you should retire. I can see how weary you are." Dundaelon surprised her as he pulled her to the spiral stairs and led her up to her quarters. He brushed his hand over the side of her face as he stood over her, ready to deliver her to her quarters. He studied her pained face, smiling. "Thank you for making an effort. I know it is not easy for you."

Without warning, he moved in, stealing a kiss before turning to leave.

Her handmaidens couldn't help giggling after they shut the doors behind her.

"My lady, you two were made for each other," one of them said.

She turned her head, and her confusion must have been all over her face for how quickly her handmaiden fell quiet.

"Please, leave me tonight. I wish to be left alone."

They left and she heard Guan questioning them as the doors shut. Dessuithiel moved to her window and stared down at the tower gardens—her gardens—where Thoren would be coming to meet with her.

Marmidon, what you ask of me may be more than I can bear.

She should have been developing feelings for her betrothed, but instead found an increase in attraction each time she thought of Thoren. Fate had brought them together to save the future of Thyrel, but she now wanted her own future saved. Feelings of rebellion rose up within her and she grasped hold of them, clinging to them as she visualized the rose archway.

I need some way to reach the gardens.

Dessuithiel knew what she would do once she got there, but there was the matter of getting there without Dundaelon knowing.

Opening her door, Guan turned and bowed. "Is there something I can do for you, my lady?"

"Guan . . ." She stepped out into the hall, fidgeting with her fingers. "Do you think you could help me meet with Thoren?"

He tried to hide his feelings, but she could see it as his smile faded. "What for, my lady? You know how it unsettled your betrothed after today's incident."

"Marmidon needs his inner well fully unlocked. She's telling me it's time to break the next seal." She dropped her hands to her sides. "Could you keep Dundaelon from following me?"

"Following you where?"

Dessuithiel gasped and turned around to see Dundaelon standing at the top of the stairs with a tray of steaming tea.

"My lady, are you trying to avoid me?" He approached.

Her chest constricted and heat fled her fingers and face.

"I-I . . . there's someone I have to see." She looked to Guan for help.

He sighed and relented. "Lady Dessuithiel will be meeting with the trial's head designer to finish the preparations for the third trial."

"And this is something I cannot attend? My lady, you really should be resting."

"I'm afraid that only I may visit the trials' head designer. I will rest after, I assure you." Dessuithiel reclaimed her composure and stepped around the Valdan prince. "Please understand."

Guan followed her after bowing to Dundaelon.

She gathered her skirt and hurried down the stairs to Aiden's floor. Once there, she waited anxiously at his zilkan door, the only place within the tower she could not freely enter, as zilkan could only be manipulated by Aiden.

The door opened and she made her way inside. Aiden greeted her and offered some fruit from a bowl upon his table.

"Thank you, but I need a way to get down to the gardens without being seen." She rubbed her arms thinking of how hard it would be to explain what she was about to do to Dundaelon.

"I can get you there by way of a portal." He nodded and raised his hand. "I had a feeling Thoren's inner well would be further released today."

Guan stepped up between them. “Is it absolutely necessary for her to do this?” He looked to Dessuithiel, concern written over his face. “Teach me, and I will go do it.”

“I’m sorry, this is something only Lady Dessuithiel can do with her innate strength in light weaving.”

Guan fell quiet.

“Here, my lady. Go and fulfill Marmidon’s will.” Aiden raised a shaking hand and called forth a swirling portal of black mist. “Be careful. There is no room for error or it will claim your life, my lady.”

Guan raised his voice in protest, rushing to stop her. “My lady, wait! Don’t do it!”

Before her guard could reach her, Aiden had moved the portal over her. She’d passed through into a realm so cold it was as though tieneere had fallen, and the gate shut behind her as an exit formed in front of her. Emerging within the tower gardens, she lifted her hand, picturing the cavern Marmidon had shown her. To perform this next task, she needed a place apart from reality, a place where only she and Thoren would be allowed.

“Illithan Tal Lisma nin Amina.”

Light shot out from her fingers, each stream fading as they struck a wavering barrier under the garden arch. The sight of what lay beyond the arch, swayed as though a layer of water had filled the space between the roses and the ground. Dessuithiel stepped forward and passed into her illusory realm.

She stood in the cavern, in awe of how exact it was to the scene from her vision. Here she would wait for Thoren, here she would open the next seal of his inner well.

DESTINED FOR GREAT THINGS

Chapter 17

Thoren Belfry

Tenth of Trete

Waiting for the sun to set felt as hard as it would be to have every nail pulled from his fingers. He kept to the front room of Vance's house and stared out the window as he paced.

"Did he break or something?" Vance asked from the edge of the room.

“No.” Janessa sighed and pulled him away.

Was that it? Thoren had fought the idea of falling for anyone since before he left home. He slapped the side of his face.

“See! He’s inflicting harm on himself!” Vance resisted Janessa.

Thoren listened to the scuffle and their banter until Janessa successfully pulled Vance away, by the sounds of it, she’d gotten hold of his ear.

Their supper would soon be delivered, coming from a nosh with emphasis on atle delicacies. As rare as an opportunity to eat the upper-classed seafood was, Thoren almost felt like skipping it and heading straight for the gardens.

His heart wouldn’t stop its rapid beating, no matter what he tried to distract himself with. He kept seeing Dessuithiel in that ivory gown. *I bet this has something to do with Dundaelon’s visit.* He stopped pacing suddenly with a gasp.

Without telling Janessa or Vance, he left the house and jogged through the streets toward the tower gardens. He hated how thick he’d been, not noticing why sooner.

Dundaelon’s come to claim her! ***This*** *Farthven Ladayose is going to be their wedding celebration! Dessuithiel . . . does she not want this union?*

He arrived at the gardens, jogging through them to the rose-wrapped iron arch and bench where Dessuithiel had found him that first night.

I'm here.

He spun around, searching the flowers for her. Others walked around him, most in pairs as they took in the garden's beauty.

"Hey, you're that Thoren guy!" Someone recognized him. "What you did was mind blowing! None of us saw that coming after you said you couldn't weave." The man laughed and slapped his arm. "Of course you could weave!"

"R-right . . ." Thoren chuckled uncomfortably. "If you'd excuse me."

"Yeah, I'm sure you have things to do. The next trial is being held tomorrow."

Tomorrow!

Thoren thought back over the last few hours and faintly recalled Janessa mentioning that he'd been out for a full day. The next trial was taking place in the morning.

I'm too distracted.

He patted his hand over his heart and questioned why he came. At this point it was foolish to ignore how he felt about Dessuithiel. She stirred his heart like no other and drove him to exceed his limits at the risk of his own life. He ran his hands up through his shoulder-length, pale-gold hair in a frenzy.

What am I doing? I came to become the Gift Bearer's mentor, not fall in love!

Thoren backed away from the rose-encircled bench. He turned and passed back through the iron arch, feeling a cool rush pass over his body.

His surroundings changed.

He no longer stood in the gardens south of Thyrel's tower, but in the soft glow of massive mineral structures. The sky was masked in the large crystal columns, each equally as large as a sky pillar. He heard water rippling to his right.

How did I get here?

He shifted his gaze from the crystal structures to the pool of water. Energy pulsed from somewhere nearby.

Thoren turned back the other way, spotting a softly traveled path leading deeper within the tipping crystals. He had nowhere else to go, the iron arch was gone.

Each step echoed off the various smooth surfaces. The ground was a mix of orange dirt and clay with a red tint and stuck to the underside of his boots a little. Taking in a deep breath, algae filled his nose.

The deeper in he went, the stronger the energy was that filled the air. Each breath became strangely sweet as it passed down his throat into his lungs.

"Hello?" he shouted.

"Thoren," Dessuithiel called back and stepped out from behind one of the columns. "You came." She sounded relieved.

"What is this place? I-I mean, my lady, how did I get here?" He raised his hand to their surroundings.

She approached him, stopping only a step away and tipped her head up to meet his curious gaze.

"I've cast this illusory realm; we are still standing within the tower gardens. And while an illusion it may be, what you see and feel is in fact real, and a sacred place within Marmidon. While this realm surrounds us, nobody can see or hear us. We may speak plainly." Her voice shook slightly, just enough for him to catch.

He had the distinct feeling that there was something happening behind her smiles and calm public approach. Something she was trying to express to him.

"Is something the matter?"

Her gaze moved to one of the crystals, her eyes glinting under the warm glow. "There's always something, Thoren. This world is vast and evil abounds when left unchecked . . ."

"I don't know if I can help, but is there anything I can do? At the very least, I can offer a listening ear."

She smiled and glanced at him, fidgeting with her fingers in front of her. Dessuithiel took a deep breath and faced him. She held her hands tightly against her chest, looking up at him with a rosy glow across her cheeks.

"If I could, I would remain here indefinitely. Where time cannot bend or flow to that which is to come . . . perhaps I ought to bring all those I hold dear." Dessuithiel's hands dropped to her skirt and she brushed her fingers over the flowing fabric. "Although that would be an impossible task."

What does she fear from the future? The trials must be for something that is coming. He studied her face, wondering what else must occupy her mind for someone of her status and unique power. *Knowing the future must be hard on her.*

She shifted her weight and moved her eyes from him to a new part of the cave every few seconds. He worried he'd made her uncomfortable by staring and diverted his gaze to a distant part of the cavern.

She broke the silence after a few seconds, facing him again. "I can't explain why, but . . . fate has brought us together to face the future."

His thoughts reeled. *What do I have to do with the future? I just came to compete in the trials. Do I win? Do I lose?* His nerves were becoming increasingly unstable. *I shouldn't be here!* He scanned their surroundings, wondering if anyone else was hidden away behind the mineral structures. Her grumpy guard was nowhere in sight. Thoren was alone with the princess. His eyes settled back down on her.

"I don't know if you've ever felt the same way, but for some reason, I feel a kindred soul in you."

Thoren thought of all the times her eyes had lingered on him like this, almost smiling like a distant friend he'd been apart from for years.

"I'm flattered, my lady." Thoren tried to understand what she was getting at while also keeping himself from getting too attached to the idea of being Dessuithiel's friend. "How are we alike? I am a common citizen of Elpha Zavar, and you are royalty."

Her eyes moved back to him. "We share what every mortal does, but more than what the public sees, more than my bloodline, we both have a greater purpose in life." The intensity of her stare sparked to life that very connection she'd spoken of. "I called you here because I want to make sure you're prepared."

"You mean, for the third trial? Lady Dessuithiel, you're doing the very thing you said you could not! I cannot be told the future." Thoren stepped back. "Aren't there consequences for meddling with fate?"

As much as he enjoyed her company, talking with her, and getting to know her, he feared further interaction would disqualify him. He still wanted to win the trials.

"Thoren Belfry," she spoke sincerely—intensely. "You *are* my fate."

BEYOND THE THRESHOLD

Chapter 18

Thoren Belfry

Tenth of Trete

Panic. Anticipation. Confusion. Desire.

"My lady, what do you mean, I'm your fate?"

Dessuithiel remained where she was. "You know what I mean."

Did he? Was what she was inferring really what he was thinking?

"But, you're betrothed to Lord Dundaelon!"

This was more than Thoren wanted to get involved with. He'd rather be shunned as a non-weaver than get between two royal families. He had feelings for Dessuithiel, *that* he could not deny, but he had sense enough to avoid them. Nothing could come of a love between a royal and common citizen.

This was a mistake.

He took another step back.

She moved forward, closing the distance he'd made, and clasped her hands over her heart. "I've seen your face in my dreams for over a decade, Thoren Belfry." Her eyes remained locked on his. "As I have watched you in these trials, your determination, courage, and care for others—including your competitors—I have been drawn to you. I know what our customs state, and I *should* be keeping my distance." She tapped her hands against her chest. "Marmidon knows the guilt I feel over these emotions, but if I am to have a future I can stand to live in, then I must chase after it."

Thoren froze in his retreat.

She turned her head, downcast and unsettled as she shook it. Her hands clenched tight. "I do not understand this twist of fate. Yet, I have seen what is coming and can do nothing, save help you prepare."

Her eyes contained fear, heartache, and sorrow as they lifted back up to him. These emotions tainted her elegance and the desire to banish them filled Thoren. That blasted desire to comfort her filled his chest.

I should never have gotten involved.

He shut his eyes and lowered his head, pushing back the prohibited emotions.

"Lady Dessuithiel. I-I cannot accept your affections." He turned his face from her, staring at the crystal structures.

The illusionary cavern fell silent.

He could barely see her hand tap over her heart in his peripheral vision.

She softly added, "I know we have barely spoken to each other, barely had any chance at building a relationship, but I can't help but feel that in some way, you and I were meant for each other. Tell me I am not alone in this."

Her fingers brushed his own. He wanted to pull away, but a force unfamiliar within him compelled him to remain—to let her hold his hand. Thoren could not deny that he had pondered such a relationship, but this was not one he could chase. He convinced himself that this was all the comfort he could give her.

Her words held more passion than Thoren had ever expressed in his life. It was admirable—and terribly attractive.

"Thoren . . . few know that I experience physical pain any time I touch another person. I've grown distant to even my own parents. I have lived *years* in physical isolation. No one to comfort me when saddened, no one to love beyond words. But when I touch you . . . it is not pain I feel, nor visions that bombard my mind. I feel alive. I feel hope."

Every time she flinched . . . Her stiffness under everyone's touch . . . It all made sense now. He felt for her, knowing pain in his own way each time he had tried to weave and failed in the past. He had been liberated from that through her power, and it seemed that fate had liberated her through him.

Her eyes shone, and a tear slipped from one. "Thoren, your heart is pure. Your goals are honorable. You are the very kind of man I would have at my side, if given the choice. Even if fate hadn't sealed us together, I would seek you out to the ends of Marmidon, after seeing who you truly are. If I could, I would renounce my bloodline to have your companionship."

Her words struck the strings of his heart, ringing out purely and drawing him in even more. His heart was tied around her fingers in his hand.

Thoren kept his gaze from her, afraid that upon seeing her face, his heart would give in.

Dessuithiel stepped even closer—only inches left between them. Thoren intended to step out of reach, break the hold she had upon his hands, until he made the mistake of glancing at her face.

He knew now, from the moment their eyes had met on his first day in Thyrel, she was his soul mate. Thoren was powerless under her influence. He'd felt the connection she spoke of, but feared the consequences of acting on it. Her fingers held tighter, brushing his skin with hers—smooth as silk, and gently warm.

The thought of her betrothed stopped him from giving in completely to her words, her touch.

Let me leave, before I make a mistake. He closed his eyes, reviewing the illusionary realm he had traversed. *Every illusion has a weakness.*

Dessuithiel released his hand. He thought she was pulling back, reconsidering what she had suggested between them, but then she cupped the sides of his face.

She whispered, "I will fight my fate, for you."

She guided his face down to hers. Her lips brushing over his—hesitant but hopeful.

He no longer fought it.

"Dessuithiel," he whispered and lost himself.

Marmidon, forgive me for this.

He was utterly enamored with her. Drawn in by her gentle nature, selfless service, and indeed her beauty. Thoren thought his heart had taken flight in the few seconds their lips had met. He wrapped his arms around her, pulling her closer.

He did not care how long they remained. He was lost in the moment. Dessuithiel pulled away sooner than he wanted—drawing her hands back from his face. The loss of warmth upon his cheeks woke him from the daze of love and awakened him to the crime he had just committed against his own ruling house.

What have I done? His hands brushed over her back stiffly; fingers laced between her beaded hair. *How could I?* He withdrew quickly, and stepped back. Deep regret doused him.

"My lady, I-I'm sorry."

She smiled shyly, only adding to his infatuation. He lifted a hand to his chest feeling each rapid beat of his heart. *I really shouldn't have.*

He searched her eyes and listened as she spoke, igniting his heart on fire. "Thoren Belfry, you *must* win."

Win? I should withdraw.

He knew there was a delicate balance of power between the ethrean royals. If he sought after Dessuithiel, it would break the union set to take place. Thoren had no royal lineage, no right to lay claim to her. Dundaelon Valdan would be humiliated—furious. Would they bear it?

I do not think they would.

Brushing stray hairs from her face she cleared her throat, stood tall, and cleared the air with a question. "How aware are you, of the balance in power between the monarchies?" She redirected their conversation, and he didn't doubt that she knew the thoughts passing through his mind. Her blushing face turned away slightly.

She looks so confident in public, but here she's so bashful.

Thoren cleared his own throat, pushing away the rush of emotions that had overtaken him. He tried to swallow his guilt and rationalize it as effects of the atmosphere and her forward remarks. He was grateful that his lapse in judgement had taken place in this illusory realm. Nobody else would know what had happened here, not even her grumpy guard.

He told her what he knew of the ruling monarchies, realizing she had asked not about his knowledge of *ethrean* power balance, but the monarchies in general. "Marmeada and Jushosh sit at the top, in both influence over trade, land, and military strength. Although, I believe Dershja's military has been on the rise along with Elpha Zavar—even though my home city is not a country of its own. Verra prides themselves on their nauxen breeding and uses the beasts as their leverage politically. Kern cultivates most of the rare foods and linens, and while not militarily powerful, they do hold a monopoly on fine goods. Narimond's desert terrain limits their agriculture, but they more than make up for it with brute force in manual labor both of their people and the animals native to their lands. Lastly, the atle of Allvelore rule the seas and bring fine sea treasures to the surface to trade, they don't involve themselves in politics, and it's easy for them to avoid conflict."

"You've been well educated." She smirked. "It's important to be aware of the balance between the ruling nations. If one is not aware of history, one cannot avoid repeating past mistakes in the future."

He caught onto where she was leading the conversation.

"These trials. It's not just to find a mentor, is it?"

"The trials are necessary and would have taken place regardless of society's growing tensions, but you are correct. There is more to these trials than meets the eye. The only reason society continues, is because of the ruling hand of Marmeada and Jushosh. However, something *is* brewing, be it in Dershja or Elpha Zavar. I'm not entirely sure where or what it is, as those visions have not been shared with me directly."

Thoren thought about the small northern country—Dershja. Their population was largely human. They all had pale porcelain skin, black hair, and a rich history of technique, strength, strategy, and discipline. Plainly, they were very skilled in a variety of martial arts—something that the rest of the world would be hard pressed to match. If something was going on in Dershja and Dessuithiel was concerned about it, Thoren could only assume that the monarchy of that nation was plotting something.

"This peaceful era is coming to an end, Thoren. I'm scared of what the future holds." She returned her hand to his. "I don't have all the answers, but please, do not give up. Marmidon needs you, or things will get shaken, and not in a good way. Farthven Ladayose will be upon us in two days, directly following the third trial." Dessuithiel gazed up at him, her eyes filled with pain. "If I'm being honest, Thoren, I don't want to wed Lord Dundaelon. Maybe I never should have acted upon these feelings that draw me to you . . . but I know that I will never have the kind of love with him that I could have." She wrung her hands, turned away and sighed. "Maybe it was all wishful thinking."

He felt hurt at her words, even though he knew that it would never work for them to be together, not in the way her and Dundaelon could. Even with the pain she would feel at his touch, the Valdan prince could openly love her. He thought of the coming union. It was soon—very soon. *Farthven Ladayose*. He'd seen the festival decorations being prepared on his way to the gardens this very evening. *Does she not have a say in who she marries? Even if it can't be me, surely there is someone else besides Lord Dundaelon, someone she can bear to touch.*

"Have you shared this with your parents, my lady, that you're in pain when you touch others? Have you told them you don't wish to get married? As for the future, why not announce what you've seen to the world if it worries you so?"

Dessuithiel huffed, shutting her eyes for a moment.

"My parents will not listen to me on this matter. I'm not the Seer and they say it is just my nerves. Even if I have proven my foresight in the past, I don't hold the same influence as the Seer. My foresight will not change the monarchies' minds. They still believe a union between the royal families is in Thyrel's best interest, and that there is no threat to the future."

Thoren asked, “Lady Dessuithiel, what is coming?”

Is it another Calamity? If there will be another Gift Bearer this would make the most sense. I wonder how much time we have.

Her lips pressed tight before she changed the topic, leaving his question unanswered.

She calmly said, “Thoren, I’m ready to unlock the next portion of your inner well.”

He blinked several times, confused. She presented herself formally, as in the past.

“We’re going to open it, now?” It caught him off guard.

Dessuithiel laughed sweetly, like the songbirds at dawn. “Remember, I said it would take more than once for you to reach your full potential?”

Right . . . But, do I want it unlocked? He thought about how strong the wind was every time he wove it. Every ethrean had a knack for one element over the others. It looked like wind was his, but using it caused pain. Would unlocking the next portion cause even more havoc?

Thoren stood tall and bowed deeply. Upon rising he spoke. “Lady Dessuithiel, I fear that I will have to decline, again.”

Her smile slipped from her face. “Do you fear the power you wield?”

He took a moment to ponder her question. He was deeply grateful for Dessuithiel’s help in opening a portion of his inner well, granting him the ability to weave like every other ethrean—which he never thought he would be able to do. As he was now, Thoren was just as powerful as Janessa, Vance, and the other competitors from what he'd seen. He didn't have full control over air, but if that was the only thing he couldn't weave, he could bear that. *I don't need more. I don't want to feel that pain again . . .*

He gave her his answer. "I do fear it."

She closed her eyes and sighed heavily while holding tightly to the ivory skirt of her dress.

With sincere affection she spoke again. "I cannot reveal at this time why, but you *must* open your inner well," she begged, dropping to her knees and bowing forward over them.

Thoren's chest grew tight and he rushed to her side, pulling at her shoulders to lift her from the ground.

"You shouldn't do such things, my lady."

Dessuithiel lifted her hands, taking hold of his sleeves, keeping him there beside her. Her gaze was intense and held the same fear from earlier.

There's a reason she needs my well unlocked. What is it? She could not say why. Do I dare risk going against fate?

He wasn't fond of feeling that unbearable pain again, but Dessuithiel knew more about what was to come than anyone else, save for the Seer herself. Thoren studied her face, felt the slight tremble in her frame as he held her shoulders in his hands.

I'll do it. He dropped his head and pulled his arms back. Her grip loosened, and her spirits lifted with hope.

Thoren diverted his gaze from her as he said, "All right. Unlock it."

Dessuithiel had him lay upon the ground. She knelt beside him, on his right, and placed her right hand over his inner well. "This time will be worse, I'm afraid." She briefly rested her left hand over his heart.

His skin prickled at her touch and he tried to ignore the rush of heat building in his face.

Thoren noticed her hand shook as she pressed down over his stomach.

Why is she worried? Worse than last time, by how much? Thoren lifted his head to ask in the moment she cast the weave.

His scream caught in his throat as his inner well swelled and shot sharp daggers of energy throughout his body.

"You can do this!" she shouted, holding to his tunic with her left hand at his chest to stabilize herself.

He ground the back of his head into the dirt and his spine jolted in sporadic movements. Thoren rarely cried out in pain, but he could not restrain himself. He scooted his feet, drawing his knees up and back down, fighting against himself. This pain tested him far more than the last time. Thoren could feel his consciousness fading in and out.

"Stay awake!" Dessuithiel entered his mind. "*Do not give in. If you lose consciousness, your well will be permanently locked!"*

Thoren bit at his cheek, drawing blood, to stay awake. *My well will lock? Permanently?* He fixed his gaze upon her.

Dessuithiel began twisting her hand and the energy within him. Thoren cried out. His fingers clawed at the ground, but found it to be stone and not the clay from the illusion that surrounded them. The cavern blinked in and out revealing the tower garden's overhead trees and the night sky.

The illusion is breaking!

Raising a shaking hand he held to her upper arm. His eyes watered and every cell sought an end to the torment.

"Stop!" he screamed and tightened his hold around her arm.

His eyes watered and he thought he saw her crying and biting at her lip, trying to remain focused on her task. Her fingers brushed over his abs and up toward his heart. If it was like last time, then his torment was almost over.

He held to this task clutching his free hand into a tight trembling fist.

Dessuithiel bowed forward, resting her forehead upon his chest. Her left hand moved from it and slipped underneath his neck, pulling at his hair.

Her voice echoed within his mind. *"Prepare yourself."*

The grip under his neck tightened and she held onto him with all her strength as the second portion of his inner well released. She gasped in fear as the energy passed through her, pushing her away.

Thoren could feel her grips slipping.

I've got you. He reached up and around her, holding her close as a second, third, and fourth wave of energy shattered the unstable illusionary realm.

His head spun and his heart pattered furiously, or was it hers? Dessuithiel lay upon his chest within his embrace, closer than the time in the tower.

Just like the first time, the air immediately around them was filled with twinkling stardust. He listened, hearing only faint conversations in the distance. The illusion had withheld his cries from reality—nobody was rushing their way.

They were alone, for the moment.

Thank Marmidon it's over.

He relaxed, taking each breath slower. His hands still shook from the experience, and he wondered if he would be as weak as he was after the first time this had happened. Thoren didn't feel as weak as last time. That was promising.

"Lady Dessuithiel, are you all right?"

She did not respond.

His heart ignited with worry. He shook her gently and called to her again.

Nothing.

Against the dizzying effects blanketing his mind, he sat up, holding her in his lap. She was limp.

Was this the fear I saw in her eyes? He quickly placed his fingers at her neck. *Why then, why would she do it?*

Once, twice, and then steadily, her pulse strengthened. Thoren pulled her into an upright position, wrapping his arms around her tightly as tears of gratitude fell from his eyes.

Dessuithiel. How can it be that my heart belongs to you?

Racing footfalls drew near as someone approached the rose gardens. Thoren flinched, ripping his gaze from Dessuithiel's peaceful face. He looked around for a bench to move Dessuithiel to. Thoren scooped her up and positioned himself—ready to stand. The air still carried the little lights, mimicking luminescent insects. He took a deep breath and stood, grateful that his strength did not waiver. Just as he turned around and took a step toward the nearby bench.

"You!" Guan's voice came from the shadows just beyond the rose archway behind him.

Why is it always him? Thoren squeezed his eyes shut and carefully turned to meet Guan with a forced smile.

"Lovely evening, isn't it?"

"My lady!" Guan rushed to steal her away from him. "What did you do?" he accused, and took her from Thoren's arms.

He wanted to keep her, but knew that Guan would not allow it.

"She's okay, calm down. I-I didn't do anything." Thoren questioned that internally.

She was the one to unlock the next portion of my well, but was it my power that caused her to pass out?

"I see the specs. I'm no fool as to what she promised you." Guan stepped away. "She unlocked the next portion of your well, didn't she?"

Thoren moved to his knees and bowed his head. "She did."

"I knew it!" Guan took several breaths to calm himself. "She'll not do it a third time."

Thoren looked up to see Guan's intensity firing down at him from his eyes.

He said the only thing that he could, "I'm sorry."

Guan left with Dessuithiel in his arms.

Thoren knelt there bent forward staring at the zilkan that made up the rose garden's many pathways.

She'll be okay. He tried to remain calm. *Guan must have been searching for a while. How long were we hidden in her illusion?*

He struck the ground with his fist and then brushed his trembling fingers through his hair, pulling it out of his face. *I can feel how strong I am.* He dropped his hands in front of himself.

Thoren stood and walked slowly back to Vance's house. After a few minutes, he spotted his friend's home in the distance, he tried to free his mind of how it had felt to hold Lady Dessuithiel. The sensation of her lips against his own. He groaned and wiped a hand down his face.

I'm a dead man if anyone ever finds out about that.

He hoped his face would not betray him. His cheeks still felt warm, too warm for the comfortable night air to have caused. Coming up with a cover story, he rehearsed before reaching out for the door handle. *I just took an evening stroll. Preparing myself for the last trial, I did some weaving in the tower gardens.* He paused. *The third trial. I wonder what it will be . . .*

He stepped through the door, shutting it behind him quietly. It was late, he wasn't sure how late, but most of the streets of Thyrel had been empty.

Light shone from the kitchen out to where he stood. Thoren walked over to turn it off.

"Where have you been?" Janessa spoke, startling him.

She sat at the counter with a cup held between her hands and a kettle within reach.

"I went out for a walk." Thoren hoped that would be a good enough answer.

Janessa released her cup and turned to him. She looked tired. "You left without eating. Tell me you at least got something to eat while you were out?"

Thoren scratched at the back of his head and then shook it.

"I thought that might be the case." She sighed and stood, walking over to the cold box. Opening the door, she pulled out some packaged food. "Eat."

He stepped up to the counter and nodded. "I'll do that. Thanks."

Janessa looked him over. "Do you know how late it is?"

Thoren shook his head.

Her brows lifted expressing some surprise. "It's two hours past midnight. How could you lose track of time?" she snapped her fingers with a sudden thought. "You met up with Dessuithiel. That's it, isn't it?" She folded her arms and her eyes were fixed upon him. "I'm no fool. I saw the way she looked at you. You're going to get caught, you know."

His face burned hot and he tried to defend himself. "I wasn't seeking her affections." He thought of the way Dessuithiel had reached for his face and the moment that followed. Thoren smiled.

"Thoren!" She shoved him and he stumbled over a step. "You know that the Valdan are here! How could you be so careless? Even if you aren't seeking after her, to be seen *with* her could be counted as a crime against her betrothed."

Thoren fended off her punches, catching them and holding tight as she pulled against him.

"I don't think anyone saw us together, other than her personal guard," he said.

Janessa gasped. "Her guard! Thoren, what if he tells High Lady Miereene or High Lord Ayzgar?"

He released her hands and she backed up a step patting at her cheeks. He then realized his folly.

She's right! Guan is Dessuithiel's personal guard. His job is to protect her.

"Where did you meet with her? Did she come find you? How can you be sure that Dundaelon won't hear about you two meeting?" She rattled off faster than he could answer. "Thoren you're meddling in royal affairs. You know how the Valdans are. If they find out you two have been meeting with each other . . ." She jabbed her finger into his chest and he recoiled.

"I know . . ." His voice trailed off.

It wouldn't be good.

Janessa calmed, folding her arms. "I know she's pretty, and you've been lovestruck over her for the last few days, but you need to let her go. This is serious."

He nodded. "I understand."

"Good." Janessa's lips pressed tight and she looked at the food she'd set out for him. "I'm heading to bed. You should, too, after you eat."

"Yes ma'am." Thoren sat on one of the four bar stools and began eating the cold sandwich.

"I'll see you in the morning." She walked back toward the front of the house, where the base of the staircase was. "I've got an alarm set. You won't be late this time. I'll use ice water if I must." She turned up the stairs, grinning.

Thoren set down the sandwich. *I really can't pursue Dessuithiel. What if doing so triggers what she has seen?* His mind hurt trying to sort through fate and his feelings.

Moving a hand over his inner well, he shut his eyes and focused on the power swirling within him. This *was* more than he could ever have dreamed to have access to, and all thanks to Lady Dessuithiel's power.

Fate may have great things in store for me, but what about the world? What will suffer for my gain?

LOST LOVE

Chapter 19

Dessuithiel Vizule

Tenth of Trete

Whispers at her feet pulled her to consciousness. A shiver shook her and soft crystal light touched her eyelids tempting her to open them. Her memory failed her and she wondered when and how she had come to her room or if she had ever left it.

“I think she’s waking up.” Her Ba spoke and moved closer.

“Dessuithiel, dear. How are you feeling?” her Aba asked.

She peeled her eyes open and looked at her parents. They held to each other lovingly, looking down at her.

"Guan was right. It may be too much for her to handle," her Aba said.

Too much? What's too much? Not the trials!

Dessuithiel sat up, faster than she should have and her vision glazed over with specs of light. "I'm fine," she declared.

"Guan was very concerned when he came to us last night," Her Ba said and looked at her Aba. "He said you had exhausted yourself and required immediate attention. When we came to you, the light of your life was barely lit."

"It was the greatest scare of our lives," her Aba added. "I think it would be best if your Ba handled overseeing the last of the trials."

"No!" she protested and leapt from her bed.

Her nightdress swayed as much as her body. She leaned into the post at her bed's end for support.

"This was my charge, and I will see it through!"

"You've expended too much energy."

She scrambled for some way to hold her position in the trials. "I won't broadcast it! The third trial . . . won't be broadcast."

Her parents looked between each other, and slowly nodded before her Ba said, "If you promise not to overexert yourself, not broadcasting the trial as you said, then I will permit it."

She sighed thanking them profusely all the way to the doors of her room and out upon the landing as they left.

Her strength had returned a little, enough for her to hold herself up and balanced. Dessuithiel turned and faced Guan. If there was anyone that might have known what had happened, it was him.

"Tell me what happened." She waved him to follow her back into her quarters and sent her handmaidens out.

Guan folded his arms, his muscular build popping out with the positioning. "You nearly lost your life is what happened, my lady."

She did not meet his eyes, but stared at the floor near the small dining table of her room.

"As soon as Aiden mentioned your life would be at risk, I tried to stop you." Anger radiated in his tone. "The Gift Bearer was faster, and sent you to the gardens." He shifted, turning partially away from her and looking hurt emotionally, which was rare to see. "I searched for over an hour before running into *that* competitor." His hands tightened upon his arms, the indentations at the tips of his fingers clearly visible. "You were limp in his arms, my lady. I do not know how you came to be unconscious. I can only assume it was due to the after effects of releasing the inner well. Tell me that was the last time it will happen."

Guilt rose up her throat, constricting it as she listened to how worried her guard had been for her life. Guan truly cared.

He glanced up at her before continuing, “He claimed innocence, but I know if he had not come to Thyrel, you would not have acted so rashly, putting your life on the line!”

“Guan . . .” she reached out to him, willing to bear the pain, but he pulled away. His hands dropped to his sides in tight fists.

“I am sorry, my lady.” He calmed, but she could see there was still a fire within him. “I pledged my fealty to you. Forgive my outburst.”

Compassion swelled within her. “I forgive you, Guan. I know that you care, more than you show, about me.”

His head snapped in her direction, eyes wide.

“I also know that you will be there when I need you, always. Thoren may not be important to you, but he is to me. He is who Marmidon needs at this time. Aiden is too weak, and his heir is not yet ready to face the darkness. Like it or not, Thoren is who she has chosen, and I am the only one who can prepare him.”

“You’ll not do it again!” He resumed his grumpy mood.

“And if Marmidon requires it?”

“Then I’d rather see the destruction come to pass than lose you.”

“Oh, Guan.” She stepped around to face him directly. “What if he’s the only person I can bear to touch?”

His shoulders dropped along with his anger. She watched his face as it softened and he met her eyes. “Truly? You can touch him without pain?”

Dessuithiel nodded.

She could see him working through how complicated things were about to get. He sighed. "My lady, what would you have me do?"

Dessuithiel shut her eyes and thought through the vision of Thyrel's impending dark day. Thoren fought the darkness. She watched as he moved to cast, and a shadowed form moved not against him but to aid. She gasped.

"Guan!" She held her hands out in a physical expression of her realization. "Let me try again to share a vision with you. Watch closely."

Before he could pull away, she lifted her hand to the side of his head, doing exactly as she had the first time she'd shared her vision with him. The sting of contact registered and she secured her connection. Warmth spread down her arm to the tip of her fingers at the side of Guan's head. This time she shared every vision she'd had of Thoren and that dark day.

Her guard stepped back when she severed the connection and withdrew her hand. She stared at her fingers. *It is possible to share my visions! Aba and Ba will have to believe me now!* Her chest swelled in her success.

"You're there, helping him, Guan." She smiled, and asked, "Did you see?"

He nodded.

"I think I understand how this part of my power works. This could solve so many things!"

She moved toward her doors when Guan caught hold of her wrist. She stared up into his dark-blue eyes. He shook his head.

"You can't show them, my lady."

"What? Why not?"

"Just as fate has called to you, you cannot bend it to your will. There are consequences for that, ones worse than pain at every touch."

"But if they see what is at stake. They'll . . . They'll . . ." She realized what Guan was saying. *They'll stop the trials. Marmidon will not have her champion.* What she'd seen could become something far worse. Her brows pinched and she shut her eyes. *Is there nothing I can do?* She lost her mind to a vision alongside Guan.

Her mind reeled through her guard's future. He fought beside Thoren, casting his own strength against a foul evil. She couldn't tell if the one behind such cold, dreary, and depressive energy was a specter or a physical being. Dark energy shifted through the black mist pouring out of the ground throughout Thyrel. Creatures cried in bloodthirsty harmonies as people fled.

Her lungs forgot how to breathe as Thoren was thrown harshly into a nearby structure. She heard the bricks crack, his own cry of pain cut in and out. Her royal guards were falling under the hand of a shadowed figure from which all the evil present was flowing.

Guan rushed to Thoren's aid. The dark energy was repelled before putting an end to Thoren's life.

Dessuithiel took a step forward, desiring to heal Thoren's wounds, but she was fixed in place. Her betrothed fought at her side, protecting her from the feral beasts. Moving apart from herself, she felt a rise of light emanating from her. It filled the air, forcing back the encroaching darkness until Thoren charged to the heart of it.

The scene shifted, replaying but the events this time grew darker. Thyrel was not just in battle, but overrun. There was an army among the dark creatures, and Thoren, as skilled as he was, fell.

Dessuithiel gasped. "How could this be?"

Guan responded, experiencing this new vision alongside her. "Marmidon has given you a choice."

The vision faded. Tears streamed down her face as she knew what Marmidon was asking of her. No matter what she chose, losses would be had, and she was being asked to accept the lesser grief or there would be worse consequences. *I must let everything come to pass in the way that it should, no matter how terrible it is.* She sniffed and blinked back the remaining tears.

Guan released her. "I will be where I need to be when the time comes." He stared at her bedroom wall in a daze over what he had seen with her.

"I don't know if I can do it." She spoke truthfully. Even now, her hands shook and heat drained from them.

Standing tall, hands at his sides as he bowed, Guan did his best to reassure her from his own shocked state. "I'm sorry, my lady." His tone became grim. "Try to accept Marmidon's will."

Dessuithiel sat at the base of her bed. *He made it look easy.* She thought of how Guan had left her room after their shared vision of the coming terror. He was calm, albeit dazed, but he had accepted it without question.

Her handmaidens returned and rushed her through getting dressed and ready for the third and final trial. Morning light bled through her doors, more ominous than any day prior. She stepped out to find Aiden, her parents, and the Valdan siblings waiting for her.

“We have decided to address the crowds at the start of the trial today, and High Lord Nesalariel wishes to speak on behalf of your coming union.” Her Aba and Ba stepped aside, revealing the high lord of Elpha Zavar himself.

Dessuithiel stared at a man who resembled his son, but with whiter hair, a leaner build, and irises so light-blue they nearly looked completely white.

He had not come to the last couple of meals that Dessuithiel had attended with the other royals. This was her first time meeting Dundaelon’s father, and he froze her heart with a single glance.

“Shall we go and call the contestants for the final trial?” Dundaelon offered his arm to her as he approached, breaking her line of sight to the high lord.

Without speaking, Aiden turned and stepped down the stairs, leading the way. Her parents and Dundaelon’s father followed the Gift Bearer. She watched her parents, tenderly holding each other’s hand with loving gazes and smiles. She couldn’t hold back the tears, knowing what her future would not have.

“My lady, have I upset you?” Dundaelon asked, pulling his arm back.

She shook her head. “No. I fear that all the stress has made me a bit emotional today. Let us go and greet the competitors for the final trial.” Doing her best to compose herself, she held her hand out, waiting for him to take it.

I will accept your will, Marmidon. Let fate lead me into your guiding hands for the better good of all.

He hesitated, but ultimately took her hand and rested his arm under it, leading her down the spiral stairs. The visions she'd grown accustomed to, filled her mind once more, but changed. With every step they took, what she had seen, the betrayal of their union, shifted to one that remained true and loyal, but ever painful for her. *Her* heart swayed in time's unforgiving pull, becoming cold.

Dessuithiel looked up at him. He had a warm face and was willing to try and make their union work. She didn't understand why his future had changed. The events unfolding in each of Thoren's futures had not changed, yet the Valdan heir's course had taken a turn.

Is this really what my efforts will bring to this marriage?

Thoren Belfry

True to her word, Janessa woke him early—thankfully without the ice water. Thoren groaned and rolled over.

"What time is it?"

"Six." Janessa prodded him with her foot. "The trial starts at eight."

"Why so early then?" He pulled his blanket up over his head.

Janessa ripped it off. "Because, we have to have you looking your best."

Thoren rolled back over to see a wry smile on her face.

Janessa forced him out of bed and he relented, getting ready. After washing off and dressing in his white garb, he left the wash room to find Janessa leaning against the wall with a brush and small ties in hand.

"Come on. I'm going to have you looking like a true competitor." She smiled.

Thoren was seated on the floor of the front room while Janessa sat on the short table and braided the top half of his hair into a style befitting an ethrean warrior. She finished and stepped back.

"I think that will do." Her next breath caught in her throat and she reached out, pulling a few strands out and letting them fall to the sides of his face. "There." Her smile widened.

"You two got up early." Vance yawned as he stepped down off the stairs.

"Well, it is the *last* trial," Janessa said.

Vance nodded and added to the morning conversation. "I wonder what it's going to be."

Thoren wondered this as well. The first two trials had been physically demanding, and pushed him to limits he didn't know he had.

She looked worried about me facing this trial with only one third of my inner well.

Thoren stood.

"Have you two eaten any breakfast yet?" Vance asked.

Thoren shook his head. "Not yet."

"Then, let's go out and get something for this big day."

"I know where a great nosh is." Janessa noted. "Hold up for me, I just need to change really quick." She rushed back up the stairs.

"I think we both need a quick minute." Vance chuckled. "Thoren's the only one ready."

They were all out the door by seven and Janessa led the way to the nearby nosh.

Thoren found his nerves unsteady and a near constant jittering feeling coursing his body. He couldn't tell if he was nervous or excited for the trial to start.

"Good luck out there today!"

A call caught his attention and he found the stranger waving to him with a smile.

Thoren bowed slightly in thanks.

"Up on time today." Balek's voice sounded from up ahead. "And you are looking radiant as ever, Janessa."

Thoren watched his competitor approach, and tensed as Balek lifted Janessa's hand to his lips, bestowing a kiss. Thoren moved up past Vance. He took Janessa's hand from him.

"She always looks . . . radiant." He fumbled over his words.

Balek cleared his throat. "Seems we all had the same morning plans." He nudged his head at the nosh they stood outside of.

Thoren glanced at the brick building.

It had a large front-window display with several purposefully placed pastries, breads, and meats.

"You should join us!" Janessa offered.

Thoren opened his mouth to protest, but Janessa squeezed his hand tightly and bumped him.

"Right, Thoren?"

He faked a smile and agreed.

Once they were all seated inside and awaiting their food, Balek laced his fingers atop the decorated table and leaned forward.

"Are you ready for the final trial?" He stared at Thoren.

"I think so."

"Better hope so. After you barely made it out of the second, I'd hate for something to happen to you."

"I don't think Lady Dessuithiel will let anyone die." Janessa joined in.

"Then why mention their lives would be at risk?" Vance noted. "We've clearly seen how dangerous these trials have been."

"The mentor has to be strong enough to face these kinds of things." Thoren shared his thoughts.

"You're right." Balek leaned back with a heavy sigh. "I know you want this position as much as I do. But, there can only be one."

Janessa looked between Balek and Thoren, clearly torn on who to root for.

'There can only be one.' He echoed Balek's words internally.

The bells rang, signaling the eighth hour of the day. Thoren stood in a line with Balek and Shirra awaiting the moment the tower doors would open.

"Good luck," Balek said.

"You too," Thoren responded.

Shirra shook her head, standing between them. "You two *need* the luck."

"Confident, are we?" Balek shot back, holding his head up a little higher.

The tower horn blared and the doors swung open with the announcement of the Valdan siblings and Lady Dessuithiel. Dundaelon stepped into view with Dessuithiel at his arm. He led her forward toward the awaiting contenders. Gailiaethere followed her brother and stepped up beside Dessuithiel—who shone like a vibrant flower, wearing a soft-green gown edged in gold.

The crowds behind hushed and the horns blared once more. Thoren caught sight of two others stepping out from the tower.

"Presenting, High Lady Miereene and High Lord Ayzgar!" The guards announced and their voices carried over the crowds—amplified through a weave like the last two trials.

Another horn blared and a third announcement was given. "Presenting, High Lord Nesalariel!"

Thoren quickly bowed along with everyone else, using the sincere salute of Elpha Zavar. He held his right fist over his heart, crossing his left behind his back as they bent forward and awaited the call to rise.

Dessuithiel Vizule

Time ticked by in the back of her mind as they exited the tower with the trumpet's sound and call of their titles. Her parents emerged after her and the Valdan siblings. They introduced Elpha Zavar's high lord. The man walked out into the morning light like glistening snow.

Her father addressed the crowd. She watched as he looked at her, love and kindness in his eyes—full of life. He brought up the impending marriage and the crowds fizzled with excitement.

Dessuithiel filtered out the gasps and mixed squeals of excitement. They didn't know what would come of such a union—they would never know her pain. She caved inward to the constant visions of her and Dundaelon's future. She was left, bitter, angry, and hurt while putting on a façade of love in marriage. Thyrel's bleak future became overshadowed by her own pains. She was held hostage under the same dark influence she had felt in each of Thoren's visions. At the thought of the dark visions, it clouded her sight, showing her people left fractured, yet she did not understand how or why it had happened.

Her father continued, "Betrothed for the last two months, our daughter will join not only her hand with the son of High Lord Nesalariel, but all of ethrea kind into a new nation."

Her entire body grew tense, enough that Dundaelon had taken notice. He rested his free hand over hers and gave it a soft squeeze.

Whispering, he asked, "How are you holding up?"

She shook her head, masking her emotions. "I'm fine," she whispered back.

"High Lord Nesalariel, please." Her father turned the time over to him, and a chill shook Dessuithiel.

There's something very off about him.

The ethrean high lord scanned the crowd after thanking Marmidon for such an honor. He spoke of those he had already sent to begin restoring the Primal Horizon city of Etrinn that had laid in ruins for over two centuries. His smile chilled her spine.

Nesalariel's voice was deep like his son's, but devoid of emotion and as pale as his icy skin. She was sure that if the high lord were to stand atop a snow-covered valley, he would have blended in.

He mentioned when the union would be taking place, and reminded her how soon Farthven Ladayose would be upon them.

Dessuithiel felt physically ill at the mention of her union with Dundaelon. A recent memory flashed to the forefront of her mind, blurring out the visions of her betrothed. She recalled confessing something to Thoren—but she couldn't remember what. *Did I tell him about the future I saw or my desires to avoid this wedding? Darn these after effects!* She gave her head another light shake, grasping for her lost memory. Part of her wondered if fate had intended this all along. She couldn't recall much, if any, of her conversation with the competitor. Dessuithiel only recalled leaving the tower and casting an illusory realm within the gardens. She had intended on opening the next portion of Thoren's inner well, and based on how Guan had found her, she assumed it had been successful.

High Lord Nesalariel then concluded with an invitation to all the monarchies of Marmidon.

Her father joined, welcoming all to celebrate. None of the magistrates of men, atle, or therrinndore would arrive in time for Farthven Ladayose, but the celebrations would take place for a full week—leaving enough time for them to join at various points.

The spotlight was then given to her. Pulling out of her dazed stare with the ground, she spoke the rehearsed introduction.

Her eyes fixed upon Balek, who was the first to finish the second trial. As such, it would be his honor to be the first entering the third trial. "The first to be tested will be Balek Thrain." She caught a look from her father and quickly added, "The third trial will *not* be broadcast."

Complaints erupted, as she could have predicted. It was a big shift from how the first two had been handled—an unexpected shift in her own plans.

Nesalariel scolded the public and silence drowned the crowd under his unfeeling gaze.

Eager to step away from the situation, she called Balek. "Come."

Thoren Belfry

High Lord Ayzgar's voice carried over the city. "Arise."

Everyone did so and waited anxiously to hear the reason for the high lord and lady's presence.

Ayzgar continued. "Today, we usher in the final trial for an event we have shared with the world. Marmidon has given the call to a new Bearer as her last passes on the Gift. As such, the trials were prepared for one worthy to mentor Marmidon's chosen."

Thoren felt his heart swell with a mixture of excitement and anticipation. He recalled the day this announcement was given across Marmidon, calling to the ethrea for a worthy mentor to rise to the occasion.

This is what I want. His previous resolve renewed.

"Our daughter, Lady Dessuithiel, has made us proud by taking on this task, to spare nothing from these trials. With Marmidon's guidance, and our daughter's meticulous mind, these trials have narrowed down these privileged few. Today, Marmidon will choose her mentor, forged through a fire that only *one* can truly withstand."

Ayzgar turned his gaze from the three of them, to his daughter. "In light of this historical event, we will add upon history, joining the two royal houses of Vizule and Valdan!"

Thoren heard gasps among the crowd mixed with rumored confirmations of Dundaelon's presence having been with the intent on forming his union with Dessuithiel this Farthven Ladayose.

"Betrothed for the last two months, our daughter will join not only her hand with the son of High Lord Nesalariel, but all of ethrea kind into a new nation."

A new nation? Do they intend to create their own country? How? Both Thyrel and Elpha Zavar are within the domains of Marmeada and Jushosh. The rest of ethrean cities are held among the other nations. Thoren was sure that everyone had the same questions running through their minds. *If this is being broadcast, the monarchs of Marmeada and Jushosh are both watching this!*

Will they stand by and let it happen? Who will lead the ethrea nation? Surely, High Lord Valdan won't concede his power to the Vizule.

Thoren looked at Dessuithiel. She had that uncomfortable tension again. She said nothing, standing like a statue with her arm stiffly upon Dundaelon's.

What has the Seer told them? He wondered how they could make such a declaration. His eyes then went to High Lord Nesalariel. He had a soft smirk on his face and stood with his hands clasped behind him.

Thoren's gut knotted when he looked at the ethrean that led his home city, Elpha Zavar. He had never seen High Lord Nesalariel in person before this moment. His eyes were cold, his stance dominant.

He won't share a throne. Thoren realized. *Dessuithiel knows this.*

"High Lord Nesalariel, please." High Lord Ayzgar turned the spotlight to Nesalariel.

Thoren's shoulders were increasingly becoming more tense and his hands clenched tight. *Nesalariel can't be trusted.* He couldn't shake the feeling.

"I thank Marmidon for this honor." Nesalariel's iron gaze moved from Ayzgar and Miereene to the audience standing before him. "I have taken the liberty of sending my finest weavers and architects to the ruins of Etrinn to clear the way for this new nation. That land has laid in waste for the past two-hundred and eighty-eight years. No nation has dared set foot in it since the first great Calamity claimed those who used to rule it. This land rightfully belongs to the ethrean race, and so it shall once more." He smiled, but even his smile felt cold.

"Following the third and final trial, my son, the great Lord Dundaelon, will be wed and our people will lay claim to the land that has, and always shall be, for the masters of weaving—the ethrea."

Etrinn! Thoren's breath caught in his throat. The ruins of Etrinn were on the other side of the Bearing Mountains that surrounded Thyrel. *That's not far from here.* He gazed up at the mountains behind Thyrel's tower.

The stretch of land that belonged to Etrinn's once great nation, stretched from the north tip of Marmeada to Narimond at the south, with Kern lining the entire west end.

I can see why High Lord Nesalariel wants it. That land is in a prime spot to oversee the affairs of three large nations. With Elpha Zavar as the fourth, he would have eyes on the most powerful of Marmidon's monarchs. *He's always been big on buffing his military strength.* Thoren had served his required time already, and most ethrea of Elpha Zavar remained enlisted. *He's planning something.* The knot in his stomach shifted, causing his heart to stir with unease. *Dessuithiel mentioned Dershja as well. Is there a war coming?*

It was the most logical answer to everything he knew and understood. Thoren stared at Dessuithiel, waiting to catch her eye, but her gaze remained lowered at the ground.

High Lord Nesalariel then extended an invitation. “I now offer this invitation to the rulers of every nation. Come, and celebrate with us, for history will speak of this day for eons to come.” He waved his hand to High Lord Ayzgar, turning it back to him.

“I second High Lord Nesalariel’s offer. Come, dine and meet with us as we reestablish the eighth nation of Marmidon.” Ayzgar waved his hand to his daughter. “Lady Dessuithiel, I turn the time to you to announce the third trial.”

She looked up from the ground, but avoided Thoren’s gaze as she spoke. “The first trial tested our contenders’ resolve to move forward. The second trial challenged their weaving ability to find creative solutions when left on their own. This last trial will test more than just their physical resistance and weaving. Combined with their mental prowess, our contestants will be faced with the power of Marmidon.”

The power of Marmidon? Thoren wasn’t sure what that meant. *The Gift Bearer carries Marmidon’s power.* The image of the red-cloaked figure from the first trial flashed to the forefront of his mind. *That was him.* His eyes widened. *Are we going to face off with the Gift Bearer?*

"The first to be tested will be Balek Thrain." Dessuithiel lifted her free hand and moved it to the open doors of the tower. "The third trial will *not* be broadcast."

The crowds shouted their displeasure.

Thoren stood firmly in place, clenched fists still at his sides.

High Lord Nesalariel called out above the noise of the complaining crowd. "Have you forgotten your place?"

Silence fell.

Dessuithiel called to Balek.

Dessuithiel Vizule

Her betrothed led her back within the tower after both their parents had returned inside. Dessuithiel nearly forgot about Gailiaethere. She hadn't said a single word since her father had joined them that morning.

They all climbed the spiral stairs to where the third trial was to be held. A floor containing a powerful object that Aiden had often paid visits to—the Heart Stone of Thyrel.

A zilkan door barred the entrance, but Aiden stood nearby ready to open it.

Dessuithiel presented the trial to the first competitor. “Beyond this door, you will face the last trial Marmidon has for you, Balek Thrain. She will examine your mind, heart, and soul. This is your last chance to withdraw, as once you begin, you *must* see it through to the end, be it in victory or loss of life.”

Balek stood resolute, not even a hint of fear. She thought she saw the corner of his lips turn up in a slight smile, showing some excitement.

“I will proceed,” Balek declared.

Dessuithiel paced outside of the Heart Stone’s chamber. The high lords and lady departed within the first few minutes following Balek’s departure into the chamber. Her mother had suggested that she join them to socialize with the other ethrean royals that had come from across Marmidon, but she couldn't bring herself to leave.

"I'll go and cover for you, my lady." Dundaelon offered with a smile and a kiss upon her hand.

I know he's trying . . . She felt terrible about everything that was about to take place.

Folding her arms tightly she swallowed against nausea and fought the urge to crumple her dress in her sweaty hands. Minute after minute she eyed the shut zilkan door. Balek did not wear a pin this time. She could not *see* what was happening.

Sensing her distress, Aiden offered, "My lady, would it help you to know how each contestant is progressing?"

She paused in her pacing and nodded.

Aiden monitored Balek, giving her updates on his progress. His descriptions were far from what she wanted, but it was better than being left completely in the dark.

As the first hour mark drew near, Aiden announced Balek's success in completing the trial and had moved him to the infirmary.

"He may not wake for some time. I suggest that you go and bring in the next contestant," Aiden said.

Returning to the base of the tower, Guan asked, "Should we call for Dundaelon to join you, my lady?"

She shook her head. "This is my charge. We need not pull him away for something as simple as guiding in the next competitor."

He stepped back behind her. "Would you consider your veil?"

"Guan . . ." She rolled her eyes and shook her head.

He sighed and signaled to the guards to announce her as the doors opened and the trumpets signaled. She stepped outside and called Shirra Namarie to step forward and follow her.

Just like Balek, she presented the trial, explaining the risk—there was no pulling out of this one. Shirra accepted it, entered, and the door was shut behind her.

She paced once again, more nervous this time as even Aiden appeared on edge. Over an hour passed and she started to wonder if Shirra was going to be okay. Aiden had become very quiet. His brows drew together and he moved to the door, placing his hand upon it. The seal broke and he moved inside.

"Aiden?" She followed him.

Her mouth fell open and she stopped, frozen at the end of the hall before the Heart Stone's chamber. Shirra lay upon the floor, scraped a bit, but no mortal wound was visible. Aiden knelt beside her, resting a hand over her face as he shut her eyelids.

His tone was somber as he said, "Prepare a casket."

Dessuithiel had sensed it before Aiden had said anything. The light of life had fled Shirra's body.

Dessuithiel's hands had moved to her lips, covering her open mouth. Shutting her eyes tight she nodded. She'd had her doubts when it came to Shirra, but Dessuithiel had not foreseen this outcome.

Another hour came to an end, since she'd followed Aiden into the Heart Stone chamber. The news of Shirra's passing had traveled through the tower staff and reached her parents. As the fallen competitor was prepared and placed within an open casket, Dessuithiel's Aba did her best to give her words of comfort.

"This was a possible outcome to these trials, as dangerous as they have been. Don't blame yourself, dear."

She nodded, unable to speak as she began fearing for Thoren. If only Balek was awake and she could ask him about what he faced. She had known that the third trial would be something she would know nothing about. This trial was Marmidon's and hers alone. Aiden had told her as much.

"Do you want us to join you as you address the public to return Shirra Namarie to her people?" her Ba asked.

Dessuithiel shook her head. "I will handle it."

"You don't have to shoulder it alone." Dundaelon stepped up to her. He reached out and touched her hand, wrapping his fingers around it.

Dessuithiel pulled back when a sharp sting penetrated her mind. Before he could say anything, she sought his forgiveness. "I need some time to recover."

He nodded, trying to hide the hurt in his eyes at her withdrawal. "Okay. I shall give you some space."

Her words barely sounded in her response, "Thank you." Leading the pallbearers to the base of the tower, she waited as the trumpets sounded. Dessuithiel moved through the following minutes, half present.

Thoren Belfry

Another two hours passed before the horn signaled Lady Dessuithiel's return. Upon the opening of the doors, several guards carried an open casket out. Dessuithiel stood at the door solemnly.

A hush fell across the crowds as the open casket passed by Thoren. His heart rate became rapid at the sight of Shirra lying within.

She's dead?

"Thoren Belfry," Dessuithiel called his name.

Murmurs broke out across the crowd as Shirra's lifeless body was carried between them.

"What happened?" a Verran man shouted above the worried conversations. "What is this third trial?"

"How did she die?" An atle's booming voice passed over the crowd.

Thoren turned back around to face the tower and Dessuithiel.

She lowered her head as she spoke. "Marmidon was too much for her."

"What does that mean?" a therrinndore shouted and pushed his way to the front of the crowd. "Are we just to sit here and believe that?" He shook his fist and pointed at Lady Dessuithiel. "Only a coward hides the truth!"

The crowds were quickly getting out of hand. Dessuithiel could sense it as well, and several tower guards marched out to meet those on approach with demands.

"Thoren Belfry. The time has come for your third trial." Dessuithiel's voice sent chills down his spine.

What is this trial? He glanced back at the pallbearers moving through the crowd toward the city gate.

Dessuithiel spoke to the crowd next. "She will be returned to her loved ones with our condolences. Every participant was given multiple opportunities to withdraw, and I warned from the beginning that their lives were at risk if they proceeded." Her reminder silenced the people.

Her gaze locked on Thoren.

"It's time," she called to him once more.

Thoren moved down the zilkan path to the open tower doors. Once inside he spotted Guan at the base of the stairs. His usual glare was cast not at Thoren, but the floor. He looked just as shaken as the crowd over what had happened to Shirra. The usual calming smells of rain did nothing to still his restless heart this time as he followed her up the stairs.

They passed by the second floor, where the first trial had been taken, and moved up for more than twenty stories of the tower.

Guan walked behind him silently.

How far up are we going?

His legs began to burn from the constant climb and he wondered how many floors were within Thyrel's tower. Each time they passed by the east-facing windows, he looked out to see the silent city waiting to hear the results.

Janessa must be worried. He thought about his friends. *Would Vance have pulled out if it were him in my place?* His mind passed from his friends to his parents. *Ama and Ba! I never wrote to them.* He regretted how he'd spent some of his free time.

Dessuithiel diverted from the spiraling stairs to the next floor. This floor was bare of anything. There were no shelves, fountains, plants, nor rugs, nothing—other than the Valdan prince who welcomed them.

Thoren bowed to Dessuithiel's betrothed as he took the ethrean princess's hand. She hid her pain well, but now that he knew, Thoren couldn't ignore it. *Does he know it pains her to touch him?* He felt protective and guilty at the same time thinking of the moment he and Dessuithiel shared within her illusory realm. *She acts like it never happened . . . Was it real?* The thought didn't linger long as he looked to the only change in the entire room's surround. It was better to occupy his thoughts with the trial, locking away any emotions that he clearly had misread. Straight ahead was a single door. It was made of zilkan and intricately designed. Symbols marked the border of the doorway. They felt familiar and he studied them a moment longer.

That's the tongue of weaves! He realized and tried reading it. *It's not the same dialect. Far older than any script I've ever read.*

"Thoren Belfry, beyond this door awaits the final trial. Part of what you experience within this room will be unique to you as Marmidon examines your soul, and your worthiness to serve her." She spoke formally and raised a hand to the door. "As before every trial, if you wish to withdraw, you may do so now, for when you pass through this door, there is *no* turning back."

"Are you ready?" Her voice spoke within his mind.

Thoren tried to gauge her, but she kept her emotions in check.

"My dearest, Dessuithiel," Dundaelon said from the right side of the open space. "Would you prefer I present this trial to Thoren here?" He stepped up to her side and reached out for her hand.

She turned her face from him with a sigh and flinch, as he took hold of her hand. Returning with a forced smile, she nodded her head toward him. "I have strength enough for this, thank you. Your presence is enough."

Guan stepped up to the zilkan door, knocking upon the stone.

"Have you made your decision?" Dundaelon asked Thoren.

What is beyond that door? He looked at the writings. There was something ominous about it. Powerful, for sure. *Do I really want this?* He thought of the cold face of Shirra in the casket. *She gave her life in pursuit of this job. Where's Balek?* He wondered.

Thoren dropped his gaze and fought internally.

From the moment I heard the announcement, my heart has sought this. But was this just wishful thinking? Do I have what it takes to be Marmidon's mentor?

He faced the door and felt a burning within his chest. It was familiar by now. He'd felt this throughout the trials, and from the first time he stepped foot within the tower gardens. Something was calling to him, and that something was beyond this door.

Should I?

His brow pinched and he clenched his jaw as he swallowed the fear within.

"I'll go in." He locked eyes with Dessuithiel.

She looked relieved and yet troubled at the same time.

"Then, you will be presented before Marmidon."

Her words repeated within his mind—that Marmidon had great things in store for him—as he was led up to the door and it opened by some unseen force.

"May you be worthy of this post," Dessuithiel said as he stepped through the door into a long hallway that turned out of sight.

The door shut behind him and Thoren stood there alone, under the soft crystalline glow within the Bearing Mountains. His stomach twisted and he felt nauseous.

No turning back now.

THE THIRD TRIAL

Chapter 20

Thoren Belfry

Tenth of Trete

Moving forward was the only thing he could do. Energy passed over the shut door, and upon looking back, he could see a strong barrier had been placed over the carved walls, floor, and ceiling—he would *not* be leaving.

The stone hall echoed his steps as he moved down it. Thoren followed the curve to the right and slowed to a stop as it opened into a large cavern. The ceiling held the streams of zilkan lighting the space in a soft blue glow. Jutting up in the center, on the ground, was a golden crystal, about waist high.

This one feels different from zilkan, yet . . . He walked up to it. *No. Not different, but familiar. This is the energy I've been feeling through the zilkan.*

History books spoke of a crystal that held the very life of their world. Coincidentally, Thoren spotted a single book on the floor in front of the crystal.

Reaching out, he cautiously picked it up.

History of Etrinn: A combined record of the day of Peerretdyn.

He didn't understand how it would be used for a trial. *Why is it here?*

Thoren opened the book, turning to the first page, and began reading.

For a city as great as Etrinn was, the fall was even greater.

This is a record of all that is known of the events on the day of Peerretdyn—the day of destruction.

Our gracious and kind rulers, Arda Barratos Aodh and Zoran Aodh, had organized and declared a world-wide festival and celebration. It was to be held in the central plaza of the city.

The day couldn't have been fairer as we ushered in the celebration of peace between the eight nations. Queen Arda and King Zoran arrived in the plaza amid the great sky towers of Etrinn. Here was the single largest crystal structure known to all of Marmidon—the Heart Stone.

Within every linked atom of this crystal flowed the power that binds, shifts, grows, and sustains life. For, Light and Dark were a song of harmony within it.

Every nationality and race could be found roaming the streets on this day, and many came to witness the gift declared by her majesty, the Queen.

To usher in the Era of Peace, Queen Arda and King Zoran crafted a weave of their own. One that was said to share Marmidon's Heart Stone with the world, letting the power flow freely. To give a power that few, at the time, could use. This power I speak of, is what we know as weaving. A fascinating connection with our world.

Thoren dropped the book and stared at the crystal. *This is a Heart Stone.* It dawned on him. *But . . . weaving? Their gift to the people was weaving?* It didn't make sense. Anyone could weave. His stomach knotted, drawing his hand to it, as it reminded him of the very thing that not long ago was out of reach.

Something felt off about what he'd read. It was taught in all schooling institutions that weaving was a natural ability given at birth. The words they used to control the elements were passed down since the dawn of time, or so it seemed.

Is this really how weaving came about? Almost in sync with his thought, a strong wave of energy poured out from the Heart Stone. Thoren found his breaths labored. *Calm down.* He moved a hand over his heart, and continued reading.

The festival started as most of that time, with music, song, food, and drink a plenty. Many danced with their loved ones, while others conversed around the edge of the plaza. Only one stood near their majesties, as their advisor and friend, known as Sirds Mednekai.

Time passed, and the appointed moment arrived. Their Majesties took their place beside the Heart Stone, placing a hand upon it while casting their new weave together.

This was where everything fell apart. The next thing we knew, the ground was cracking and splitting beneath our feet. It was all we could do to flee the plaza with our loved ones. Marmidon withdrew her Heart from us and Queen Arda and King Zoran—

vanished. The first great Calamity ensued, swallowing large portions of our beloved city, Etrinn, and the nations were left in ruin. Countless were lost that day, and little remained unscathed by the quaking, storms, and great upheaval.

Many have theories of what caused this day, you will find them in this compilation.

Thoren re-read the page again. *That's it? Something just went wrong? Was it their weave? Did they intend such destruction? Why did they vanish? Maybe they fell into Marmidon with the Heart Stone.* Thoren flipped through the other pages, skimming the accounts. There was little variation to them, and all of them were missing the finer details.

There's something more to it. I'm sure of this.

The Heart Stone swelled with light, and he backed away. With the increased radiance, he felt a rise in the energy within the cavern.

What is this?

Everything around him suddenly shifted. Thoren fell, or so he thought. Gone in a blur of shapes and color, Thoren no longer stood in the cavern. The book was no longer in his hand, either.

His breath caught in his lungs as he stared at his surroundings. He was in a city far beyond anything present among the nations of Marmidon. Flying shuttles zoomed overhead between sky pillars that made the ones in Elpha Zavar look like miniatures. For these truly reached into the sky.

The streets were filled with sleek-looking motor vehicles, more advanced than those which roamed the roads of the current era. The structures were true to the ruins that lay scattered across Etrinn. Zilkan filled his eyes in every direction in exquisite designs with refined metals and smooth glass.

A horn blared and Thoren spun around in a panic as a vehicle was about to hit him. He braced, opening his mouth to weave.

“Veis!” Wind burst out from his hands, lifting him into the air as the vehicle passed underneath him.

He landed with decent control of the current that carried him. Releasing the weave, he moved to the crowded walkways alongside the road.

This is Etrinn!

He stuck out like a sore thumb among the people, but nobody seemed to care. Thoren stopped and gasped as the form of a passing ethrean went right through him.

It's not real. He looked about at the city. *Then, what is the purpose of showing me this?*

Thoren stumbled back at the sudden change of scenes. The flourishing city now lay in waste. Fires consumed everything that would burn, screams ripped through the air mixing with the shrieks of creatures that covered the city. The smell around him became putrid, turning his stomach as death filled his nose.

He observed the creatures laying waste to the city, recognizing them.

The black misting monsters that darted about the ruined city were the canine beasts from within the maze. Large swirling portals could be found in every direction, along with a range of fearsome beasts pouring out from them—ones the like he'd never seen.

Thoren spotted several of the tentacled monsters murdering civilians as they crawled across the debris-strewn city.

This is terrible! Thoren gasped as one of the beasts leapt at him. *It's not real.* He reminded himself, relaxing to his detriment.

The canine sunk its teeth into his shoulder and knocked him to the ground. He cried out and threw his fist into the beasts' face.

It dug in deeper. Thoren struck again and again.

Why? I thought this was an illusion!

Thoren had no weapon to lift against the canine. It clawed at him, cutting across his chest. Thoren shouted out in pain. He reached for anything. His hands hit a loose chunk of debris.

I can touch the city, too?

He shouted out the morphing weave, shaping the stone debris into a weapon he could defend himself with. He drove the long dagger up through the beast's chest. It let out a whine and released his shoulder as it became limp.

Thoren tossed it off and sat up, scooting away from the creature.

This. This is how Shirra died! He looked once more at the scene around him.

Firelight painted the shadows in red, and the cries of the people lessened as the seconds passed.

This event. It wiped out most of the ethrean race. This was well known across Marmidon. *What am I supposed to do?*

There was a reason he was here and he just needed to find it. *Am I looking for the answer to why the city fell? Should I help those still alive? Or am I supposed to escape?* He touched his wounded shoulder and brushed his fingers down over his torn flesh. *I need to heal before any more of those things attack me.*

He held his right hand to his wounds and called out the weave, "Salabotte."

The draw upon his inner well moved to his wounds, knitting them shut. Within seconds he was healed.

That was fast.

He cut the weave off and rubbed his thumb over his shoulder. Normally, healing a wound like that would take several minutes, not seconds.

A chill passed over him and he turned his head up to see the black mist. It rose from a distant part of the city, like a sky pillar of its own, and stretched its dark hand over all of Etrinn.

An overwhelming sense of dread struck him to his core. *What is that?*

The screams were gone now, leaving only the snarls and shrieks of the shadow beasts behind.

Everyone within the city is dead.

Thoren stood as a strong wave of cold passed through him. Something was different about the city. The shadows had found him. This was more than a vision of the past.

This is the trial!

Holding his newly formed weapon in hand, he slew the beasts leaping at him. Thoren moved in practiced form, letting his senses run his motions between each attack.

Whether it had been a matter of minutes or a half hour, Thoren couldn't tell. The sky remained the same as he slaughtered the foul beasts. In time, the beasts thinned down to the last few around him.

His shoulders rose and fell heavily as he killed the last canine. The mist that came with the creatures dissipated, revealing their corpses at his feet. At a glance, he estimated he'd slain well over a hundred of the animals.

Otherworldly shrieks sounded from the mist beyond the circle of carcasses at his feet.

Those belong to something new. Thoren lifted the dagger in his hand. *I don't think this will be enough.* He scanned his surroundings and his eyes caught on some refined metal debris. *That will do nicely.*

He stretched out his hand and called the words from memory, "Lattas Morfejemis!"

The metal headed his call and reshaped into a weapon worthy of his hand. Thoren reached out and took hold of the newly formed blade. The darker metal almost blended in with the mist. His hand tightened into the perfectly shaped grip. Of the many different weapons he could have crafted, this mid-length sword suited his skills best. *I can't imagine that will ever change.*

The mist was closing in on him, but he still had a little time left.

Dropping the stone dagger in his other hand, he called out a second time, forming another sword, and took hold of it. Swinging the blade in his left hand into a comfortable backhand position, Thoren braced for the monsters emerging.

I'm ready for you.

He caught sight of one of the shrieking monsters. His body froze as he processed what he'd seen.

That, that looked like a—

Clicking came from behind him. He spun around and swung his blade at the source. The edge cut across bare bone and a few remaining strands of ligament and muscle. A creature fouler than any he had faced thus far, stared back at him with an eerie green glow in its eyes. Black mist poured out of the ground endlessly, like the tears of the dead laying in the rubble throughout Etrinn.

Pain seared throughout Thoren's body, deeper than any flesh wound, touching his very soul.

The humanoid creature's jaw unhinged and a paralyzing shriek pierced Thoren's ears. His pulse clanged rapidly while his heart burned.

What is this thing? Thoren broke the momentary stare with death and kicked out at the exposed ribs of the creature. The soul-biting pain faded.

He didn't wait for the staggering being to regain control of itself and drove his sword through its chest where he figured its heart was.

Like the cold air that settled all around him, his body lost heat when the creature grabbed hold of his blade. It was unfazed by the mortal wound.

Thoren ripped it out and stepped back. The creaking clicks and shrill shrieks of these creatures sounded out all around him.

Do these things not die? He tensed. *No, the canines weren't what killed Shirra. It was these things.*

Thoren did the only thing he could. He spotted a pocket between the nearing shadows of death and bolted for it.

Long after that disturbing encounter, Thoren wiped the sweat from his brow as he watched a third tentacled monster fade away into the mist. He dropped his arms to his sides, letting his blades rest on the ground. His lungs ached from the prolonged strain upon his body.

There's no end to it.

He scanned his surroundings. He'd traveled around the ruins of Etrinn for longer than he cared to keep track of. Everywhere he went, he passed through an open graveyard.

There was still no weakness to the human-like beings. They embodied everything his imagination could think of when picturing death personified.

They're already dead. I can't kill them. He sighed, feeling the sweat beading down his back and soaking in where his tunic pressed against his skin. *What is the point of all this?* He revisited his earlier thoughts.

When I entered through the door, it brought me to a Heart Stone. That book was there intentionally. Was the answer within those pages?

He shut his eyes for a moment as he tried to recall every detail.

The Calamity. This wasn't what they intended. What is the link between what I've seen and experienced?

Upon opening them, his eyes were drawn to the pillar of mist. At first he thought that he needed to avoid it, but now he wondered if it was his goal to reach it.

There's only one way to find out.

Thoren tightened his hold upon his blades and started forward.

Dessuithiel Vizule

Just as she thought, Thoren accepted the trial. He entered and the door shut like it had for Balek and Shirra, despite Aiden's absence. She knew that the Gift Bearer could control the mineral's manipulation without having to be right next to it, but she did wonder where he had gone off to.

"My lady, do you intend to remain here, or would you be willing to join me for lunch?" Dundaelon gave his most charming smile with his offer.

He's trying so hard to love me.

With Aiden gone, she had no way to know what Thoren's progress was. She sighed softly and nodded. Sooner or later, she would have to get used to spending more time with Dundaelon.

She tried to hide her pain at his touch and respond in kind with the only thing she could offer him—words. "I should have some time to spare," she replied, surprised at how the Valdan prince's face beamed.

Every minute that followed their meal was uncomfortable. She kept looking to the exit of the tower's dining hall, where Guan stood with his back to them, giving them some privacy. It was getting harder to sit still.

Where did Aiden go? What if Thoren has finished? She thought about the two competitors before him. Balek had completed it quickly, but Shirra failed after just over an hour. Her eyes darted to the clock. *It's almost been an hour.*

"Does it really bother you that much that you don't know what is going on?" Dundaelon chuckled. He moved from the seat across from her to the one beside her, blocking her view of the exit.

"I prefer to know what's going on, yes." She averted her gaze down to her plate, taking hold of her fork and picking at a remnant of meat she had not been able to stomach.

"I'm sure I could help distract you." He leaned on the table and edged forward, demanding her full attention as his face stopped inches from hers. "I admit that I don't know what your favorite things are. Would you care to enlighten me?"

Dessuithiel leaned back in her chair, resting fully on the mid-back riser. "Flowers. I love roses."

"Ah . . ." he wagged his finger and clicked his tongue. "I should have guessed that, by how often you go out to the rose garden."

"Maybe you should take a guess as to what else I like?" She was partially curious, but also too distracted to really hold up the conversation. Without thinking, she reached out to Thoren. She linked with him quickly, surprising her. She tensed, sitting upright.

"Oh, I got that one, didn't I?" Dundaelon clapped his hands together once. "I didn't think that there were many others out there that enjoyed watching the sun rise. My sister prefers to sleep in."

Dessuithiel shut her eyes, shocked to find that her mental sight filled with what Thoren was experiencing. Dundaelon mentioned something about landscaping, but she couldn't focus on his words.

Her hands held tight to the fabric of her skirt. She fixated on what she was seeing. Watching from Thoren's eyes, she could clearly make out a misting pillar in the distance that he looked at. He was surrounded by a fallen city, the one from her vision.

What if I had it wrong all this time? What if there is no disaster coming for Thyrel? Marmidon! Dessuithiel stood suddenly, pushing back on her chair so fast it cried out against the marble flooring. *But Guan was there, too. He cannot enter the trials. Are they two separate incidences?* Her shoulders drooped.

Dundaelon stood quickly as well. "What is it? Is something wrong?"

She looked at her betrothed. "I-I just had a realization . . ."

But then how is this coming for Thyrel? She tipped her head up, eyes shut, and took in a deep breath.

"My lady, would it help if you were able to take a stroll?" Guan approached from the dining hall's door.

"I don't think the garden would soothe me right now, Guan." She leaned forward on the table, watching as Thoren moved through a mist-ridden, broken-down city. He slashed through countless beasts of shadow that resembled the canines Aiden had brought from the shadow realm to the labyrinth during the first trial.

"I think your guard—Guan, was it?" Dundaelon eyed Guan, who nodded to confirm, "I believe a walk would do us both some good. I don't like being cooped up, and the day is breathtaking." He stepped away from the table and his chair, offering his arm to her. "If you would do me the honor of escorting you, I would be most pleased."

She looked down at his arm and slowly pushed off the table. *If I want his loyalty, I must make an effort.* Swallowing hard, she lifted her hand to him. At their touch, her connection with Thoren was severed, replaced by the all too familiar visions of her future with Dundaelon.

Guan led the way this time, only stopping briefly to gather more guards to join them. Sun bathed her skin with speerin's gentle warmth. It helped, but she still found her pattering heart unable to calm from her recent revelation. What could her visions mean? The dreaded future she had seen for years was just a moment among the trials for Thoren. Maybe a defining moment, but she would not know as long as Dundaelon held her hand around his arm. And then, there was the more recent vision with Guan fighting alongside Thoren, in the same dark energy, in what she had assumed was Thyrel. The Valdan prince led her to the rose garden, pulling every charming string he could to gain her favor.

"You know, I didn't realize there were so many varieties of roses before I came and first strolled through here."

He stopped and released her as he reached out for a half-bloomed bud. The soft pink hues bled in from the edges and the center popped with deep red. He carefully plucked it from the bush and peeled off the thorns. Satisfied with it, he offered it to her.

"I know that this marriage isn't what you would have chosen." He wrapped his hands around hers as she held the rose. "But life is full of thorns. We just need to know how to remove them."

She stared at the rose. "But not all thorns can be removed."

He pulled his hands back, resting them behind his back, clasping one of his wrists as he continued walking at a leisurely pace. "When my Ba told me who I would be marrying, I wasn't sure what to think. Even as far as Elpha Zavar, word of you had reached me. You were mysterious. Many spoke about your visions and how you brought Thyrel from the bottom to the top of the royal ladder, second to the Valdan, of course." He turned partially to face her. "I eagerly arrived, curious to see the one I will be spending my life with, blessed under Ilzu and Maz."

Dessuithiel's steps felt heavier as they moved through the gardens.

"I must admit that I had not heard that your visions came at a cost until you told me." He sighed, stopped, and faced her.

"I'm sorry to disappoint." She lowered her hand and the rose dropped against the skirt of her gown—a soft green and earthy design selected by her lady's maid.

He reached out and lifted her downcast face, lightly holding his finger under her chin. "What can be done? If we do not have the answers now, we'll have to make things work. Who knows, maybe there is a way to stay the pain you feel at my touch." He lifted his hand from her chin and brushed his thumb over her cheek, admiring her. "These gardens suit you."

His tender actions and sweet words would have made any woman happy, Dessuithiel was sure of it, but still she found it hard to find the same attraction to him that he so easily found toward her.

"You're a sweet talker," she responded and moved forward, twirling the rose in her hand slowly.

"I aim to please," he smiled and walked alongside her, keeping pace.

They rounded a turn in the zilkan path and came to her favorite rose arch and bench. Dessuithiel slowed as she passed under the arch, and thought of the recent visit she had made here to open the next portion of Thoren's inner well. Her mind grasped for the lost memory. Her grip tightened around the rose stem, frustrated with all that she couldn't recall.

Something else happened. The way Thoren looked at me . . .

As her thoughts shifted to him, her neural link clicked back into place. Her sight was taken, replaced with Thoren's. Horrific beings attacked. She gasped and reached out for the bench she knew was just ahead—dropping the rose. Finding it with her shins, she cringed and sat. Her breaths were fast and shallow as the creatures fought with him. Black mist poured from their empty sockets; a shriek pierced the air.

"My lady, you appear to have lost your sight." Dundaelon sat beside her, but did not touch her. "Is she having a vision?" He asked openly.

Guan responded, "It appears so."

"I can hear you," she said.

"Is that not normal?" Dundaelon again sought further understanding.

She took deep slow breaths, flinching with every creature, beast, and rotting monster that filled her vision. Thoren fled the grotesque humanoid beings, running between varying sized falling pillars of mist from the sky and the ground portals where the creatures emerged from. He moved toward the largest misting pillar at the center of the storm overshadowing the fallen city.

The Valdan prince rested his hand upon her shoulder, pulling her back out. Again, she gasped, sucking in sharply as her sight returned, but her mind filled with the painful visions.

"Is there a pattern to when these visions come? I thought it was only through touch."

Dessuithiel shook her head, she wasn't keen on telling him about her link with Thoren. Playing it off as though it had been a sudden vision, she said, "Some come without warning, and most happen upon contact."

She relaxed and lifted a hand to the side of her head. The near constant visions and neural link were building quite the headache.

"Maybe we ought to return to the tower." Dundaelon stood from the bench. "I've had enough fresh air, how about you?"

Dessuithiel nodded.

Thoren was progressing through the trial, the very thing she had seen for years. There was no telling when he would finish, but she was eager to be there when he did.

Thoren Belfry

It became harder to avoid the attentions of the humanoid beings the closer he got to the misting sky pillar. Pushing his body to its limits, Thoren cut his way through dozens of the misting canines, and more than ten of the tentacled monsters. There were other beasts taking similar forms to that of a rajum—a large feline with a crown of horns amid a thick collar of fur—and some that were as small as a beynin, bouncing about and difficult to dodge.

He broke into a small clearing and panted heavily. Each breath added to the cold that was slowly freezing him from the inside out. His joints felt stiff, and his grips were weak.

I'm almost there. His eyes locked on the pillar stretching to the sky just ahead of him. It was no more than a hundred feet from where he stood. A low rumbling whoosh surrounded the mist that billowed up to the sky. The noise was constant. Static electricity flashed in vibrant green lightning here and there within the black cloud.

Thoren kept his ears tuned on the many monsters' various cries and sounds around him, but any of the remaining foul beasts were distant now. He turned back the way he'd come to see he'd cleared a wide swath through the mist and the broken city was laid bare before him.

I feel like the last person alive. Thoren clenched his jaw as a wave of fatigue pulled at him. *I can't stop here.*

Facing the misting pillar, he steeled himself.

As if sensing his resolve, a deep cry tore through the air, followed by a dramatic shift in the black pillar. Thoren tensed and tightened his hold upon his blades.

A face formed within the mist, turning around until it fixed its green gaze upon him.

Overcome by instinct, his body moved at the same time the face above him spoke a single word—a weave.

Thoren looked back with wide eyes where he had stood only a second before. The ground was struck by an invisible force. It collapsed violently.

The shockwave pushed Thoren back, forcing him to cast a weave of his own.

"Gaiza Skret Jez!"

The wind came to his aid, catching him mid-air and supporting him beneath his feet.

This being . . . Thoren stared up as the face turned, tracking him. *This is what I must defeat!* He wondered if he could accomplish such a task.

The being called out another weave and the mist shot out in all directions forming tendrils aimed at him.

Sheerma!

Thoren's body reacted with trained speed, despite his fatigue. Still, one of the tendrils caught the side of his right shoulder, cutting through his sleeve and into his flesh about half an inch. It stung like it was freezing over.

Eyes wide and tracking the multiple tendrils in motion, he dodged and ran on the streams of air at his feet. Rising higher into the air, Thoren made his way behind the misted face, hoping to find a blind spot to attack.

But how do I kill it? It's tracking me somehow, but doesn't seem to attack until it locks onto me. He caught his breath watching the pillar shift. *It's large, making it slow. I have the advantage there, but those weaves. They're so strong and fast.*

He scanned the sky for the tendrils, but they were gone.

Were those limited to time? He couldn't be sure.

His heart thundered as the green gaze pushed out from the pillar locking onto him.

He tensed and darted to the left.

The misted mouth opened, calling another foreign weave. The words were as convoluted as the inscriptions around the zilkan door he'd passed through at the start of this trial.

Every step he took pulled from his inner well. Thoren knew he couldn't maintain this forever.

I have to kill this thing before my well is depleted.

Thoren came to a sudden stop as a swirling pillar shot down in front of him. It sucked the air from his lungs and around him.

What! He turned back the other way, struggling against the pull of wind behind him.

The face was on the move again, calling out another weave. Thoren released the wind that held him up, hoping to drop out of range of the incoming weave. Instead, he found himself pulled into the vortex. He'd dodged the second weave, but at the cost of being dragged inside the first.

He screamed as the vortex threw him.

Thoren landed hard on the ground, gasping for air, with more than one injury.

My arm. He shakily turned his head to see his arm twisted in a way it wasn't meant to bend. He squeezed his eyes shut and let out a whimper.

"S-salabotte!" he wove, and directed the power from his inner well to his arm.

He bit his lip as his bones straightened out and the break was healed—again, within seconds. His legs weren't much better than his arm and he healed them next.

Rolling over, his entire chest felt bruised and battered. There was no telling how much time he had before the face would catch up and call out another deadly weave.

Calling for the third time, Thoren healed the rest of his internal wounds.

Catching sight of the deadly glare above him, Thoren called the wind to his aid once more. "Veis!" Leaping up into the air faster than the weave cast against him, Thoren shifted to his next weave. "Gaiza Skret Jez!"

He felt the upward pressure of air under his feet and ran. Clenching his hands, he realized he no longer carried his blades. Unarmed, he glanced below. The mist covered the ground, concealing his blades.

This thing has to have a weak spot. He moved around it, not daring to stop. *It moves like the tentacled monsters, slow overall, but when it attacks, it's faster than the canines. And then, there's those eyes.* The green glow was the same as what the walking undead had.

I doubt physical attacks will do any good. He sighed, letting go of any lingering thoughts to retrieve his blades.

Thunder sent a shockwave of sound through the air, drawing his eyes to the clouds above. Rain fell. The cold drops hit his skin, stinging like the tendril that had cut his shoulder. Acid or ice, neither possibility was good.

I can't stay in this. He stopped and watched as the shifting pillar turned to meet him. His exposed skin continued to sting in the burning rain. *I'm out of time and options.*

Lightning reached down to the ground, striking at the pieces of metal strewn about it. The city was aglow, his view expanding as the bolts renewed and sent piercing fear through Thoren.

It's so powerful. What can I do against something like that?

He lifted his hand, staring at his shaking palm. His inner well was all he had left available to him.

I won't stop. Not here, not ever.

He clenched his hand tight and stared back at the massive green gaze.

Pulling at the limit of his inner well, Thoren bounced between weaves. Casting an offensive weave and falling toward the ground a few seconds at a time, and then reinstating the air beneath him, rising back up.

The near constant shift between weaves kept the face in the pillar distracted, but didn't seem to be doing anything to it. Worse still, Thoren's inner well was nearly exhausted.

If weaving isn't the answer . . .

Sound blurred with every other of his senses as he crouched.

I'll just have to take a look inside.

He twisted his foot against the air that held him level with the titan before him.

Ready or not, here I come!

Thoren screamed, bursting forward with the wind behind him. With every step, he urged the wind to push him further—faster.

The mist-wrapped titan's mouth opened.

Thoren braced, breaking every barrier of fear within himself as he pushed straight for it.

Before the enemy's weave was cast, Thoren passed in through its mouth. He slid to a stop, hovering within the pillar. Just as it looked, the mist wasn't solid. He searched the darkness enveloping him. Flashes of green passed by, filling in the details of his bleak surroundings.

He took a step forward, and to his surprise, found solid ground underfoot. Risking a fall, he cut off his weave. He remained in place. Chilled completely, the air took all the heat he'd worked up from fighting. Thoren rubbed his hands. His environment shifted, similar to when he was dropped into the ancient city.

Now where am I?

A distant golden glow pierced the darkness. It made his heart pound and burn.

The Heart Stone!

Thoren burst forward. He ran toward the light with everything he had. The desolate city was nowhere in sight, nor was the face within the pillar he'd passed inside of.

Was it like crossing dimensions? he wondered as he ran. It didn't make any sense to him, but at the same time, he only cared that he was still alive.

Steadily, the air became warm and the mist fell behind him. The soft glow from the Heart Stone washed away the terror of Etrinn.

Thoren slowed as he stepped up to the crystal. He reached out gently, and wearily placed his hand upon it.

Light blinded him for several seconds.

The sensation of the mineral beneath his hand vanished.

Not again!

Thoren rubbed at his eyes, blinking away the afterimage of light. His ears picked up a most confusing sound—a child's laughter.

His surroundings came into focus.

He stood in a small village. It was not elaborate. In fact, it was the opposite. Children ran through a clearing playing a game of chase. Thoren turned around and spotted a single young boy sitting on the edge of a rustic wooden porch. In human years, he looked to be about twelve. His ears had a soft point to them.

He's half-ethrean. He realized this child could easily be over twenty with ethrean blood.

The boy stared back at him, aware of his presence.

The child had auburn hair, and striking green eyes. However, looking in the child's eyes was nothing like the feeling from the green eyes of the titan he'd faced.

His chest burned warmly.

His eyes widened as he listened to the boy speak.

This child . . . Thoren took a weary step toward him.

His action sent the scene before him fleeing. He stood within the cavern of the Bearing Mountain as his foot hit the ground.

Thoren turned about.

I'm back? He spotted the Heart Stone glowing softly beside him and the book on the floor in front of him. *It's like I never left. Is it over? Did I pass?* Thoren checked over his body, finding the blood-stained tears in his tunic still there.

A soft melody could be heard within the cavern. It came from the waist-high Heart Stone. The burning warmth called to him, swirling within the mineral. Thoren dared to reach for it once more.

Dessuithiel Vizule

Upon their return, she asked Guan to find Aiden, calling him by the same title Dundaelon had heard before, the trial's head designer—maintaining his hidden identity.

The Valdan prince escorted her to the Heart Stone's floor and within the next ten minutes, Aiden arrived with Guan.

"Can you tell how close he is to finishing?" Dessuithiel pulled her hand from Dundaelon and held the skirt of her gown. She stared at the zilkan door separating them from the Heart Stone chamber. The Gift Bearer's enchantment was still enacted on the passageway and chamber, preventing anyone from weaving their way in or out.

"It is hard to say, my lady." He spoke from under his drawn hood, masking his face as he always did when outside of his quarters in the mountain. "Marmidon only knows."

"It's been an hour . . . Balek was finished at this mark, and Shirra . . . shortly after."

"It is up to each competitor as to how quickly they solve the trial and face Marmidon's judgement."

Dundaelon interjected, "And once he finishes, how will we know who Marmidon's chosen mentor is? That is, if Thoren survives."

Dessuithiel tensed. She trusted that Thoren would survive, her visions had shown her as much, but it still pressed worries upon her.

"I will know." Aiden tapped at his chest. "With a single question, I will know."

Dessuithiel became restless. She began pacing back and forth across the length of the floor, watching the door and listening as Aiden updated them on where Thoren was. She was tempted to reach out to the competitor, connect her mind with his again, but worried that doing so would cause concerns for her to rest and resign from the remainder of the trial.

Another hour passed.

Dundaelon had a set of chairs brought for them, and sat, conversing with Guan about Thyrel's coming festival. He hadn't experienced one here before and noted the differences between Farthven Ladayose in Elpha Zavar and Thyrel.

She ignored their discussion as she sat down in the chair beside her betrothed. Even then, she couldn't bring herself to sit all the way back, she barely sat upon the edge, ready to jump up at a moment's notice. Her hands rubbed over her knees, then along the golden edge of her loose-draped sleeve.

"You look like you have a headache, and I heard that water helps." Dundaelon stood when Guan returned with a tray holding glasses of water. He took one and approached her, insisting.

Dessuithiel only drank the water when Dundaelon forced the cup into her hands. Her lips pressed tight in a forced smile as she passed it back. The water cooled her throat and pulled the heat from her face. Her worry had caused her to sweat more than a midday walk in the gardens during the middle of tummimar.

Standing, she again began to pace.

Thoren Belfry

His hand slid over the crystal's pointed tip.

Its light mixed with the air, swirling above him like fire. It fell from above, crashing upon him and the Heart Stone. His hand became fixed in place atop the crystal by an unseen force.

What's happening now?

All at once, Thoren cried out and fell to his knees. He leaned forward on the crystal. Trembling, he clutched at his inner well. His forehead pressed against the Heart Stone as the energy within him moved, controlled by the force within the Heart Stone. It twisted and turned through his inner well. The last portion—released.

He didn't know if his screams were heard outside of the cavern, but his throat was raw by the time the pain subsided. Sweat dripped off his nose, falling to the floor. He could swear he saw blood.

The power holding his hand to the Heart Stone withdrew and his arm fell to his side. Then he fell to the floor, staring up at the ceiling.

The stardust energy in the air moved, traveling out through the cavern and back to the door that sealed him inside.

Thoren's sight blurred as his consciousness gave out.

Dessuithiel Vizule

She hadn't crossed the floor once before a muffled scream sounded from within the chamber. Dundaelon stood, as did Aiden. They all moved to the zilkan door.

"That doesn't sound good."

Dessuithiel glanced at the Valdan prince. "No, it doesn't." Her gaze moved to Aiden. "Can you open it?"

"I will try." He lifted his hand, mumbling the ancient weave that controlled the mineral.

Nothing happened and Thoren's scream intensified.

"What's wrong?" Her hands hugged her chest, feeling every thundering beat of her fears.

Aiden dropped his hand and shook his head. "Marmidon will not allow us to enter."

"But you cast the enchantment!" she cried.

"Is this what happened when Shirra died?" Dundaelon asked.

She shook her head, stepped up to the door, and placed her hand upon it. Shutting her eyes she reached out for Thoren's mind. She felt nothing and his screams ceased.

This isn't right.

Familiar energy passed through the door.

The mineral cracked. She pulled her hand back. A second wave struck seconds after along with a third. The cracks grew and the door buckled out toward them. Guan moved in and pulled her back from it as the fourth wave of energy passed through, shattering the door.

The energy tickled her mind. Dessuithiel's hands shot to her mouth as she gasped. Her face grew hot as her lost memories returned all at once. She brushed her fingertips over her lips, the lips she'd pressed against Thoren's within her illusory realm.

Dundaelon moved in, taking her from Guan and wrapping his arms around her protectively. His warm breath brushed across the top of her head as he asked, "Are you unharmed?"

Hands trembling, she looked up at her betrothed, feeling a wave of guilt. Her eyes lingered upon the Valdan prince's lips.

I kissed Thoren!

She pushed back, breaking out of Dundaelon's hold. Golden specs of light danced gracefully in the air, pouring out from the Heart Stone's chamber. Picking up her skirt, Dessuithiel ran inside.

Guan chased after her, along with her betrothed who called to her. She turned the corner. Her heart stopped, seeing Thoren upon the floor. His clothes were bloodstained and torn in several places. There was no pool of blood beneath him, but the sight was familiar.

Rushing to his side, she knelt and pressed her fingers into his neck. The tremor in her hand made it too hard to tell if Thoren had a pulse. Dropping her head, she pressed her ear to his chest.

Don't take him. Marmidon, don't take him!

"My lady!" Guan dropped to Thoren's other side. "Let me handle this."

Every beat of Thoren's heart echoed within her ear. Tears flooded her eyes.

Dundaelon crouched beside her. "Guan is right. This is not your place." He reached around her, holding to her shoulders as he guided her back up to her feet.

Aiden stepped up to Thoren. "I will take him to the infirmary, my lady. Fear not. He is alive."

She walked in a daze back to her quarters, led by Dundaelon and shadowed by Guan. Her handmaidens opened the doors and she was led inside. Dundaelon guided her to the bench at the foot of her bed and sat beside her.

"My lady. I wish you wouldn't act so rashly."

She pulled from her daze and glanced up at him before returning her gaze to the floor. "I'm sorry. I know how it reflects on my status, but the public is not here to witness my behavior this time."

Dundaelon sat up stiffly. "And that makes it okay?" He grabbed hold of her chin, turning her to look at him directly. "Dessuithiel, we have barely a day and a half before we are sealed together beneath Ilzu and Maz. I would have you restrain yourself from rushing to the aid of any other male, competitor or not." His touch burned against her paled skin. His eyes traversed her face, studying the pinch of her brow, the fall of her lashes with every blink, and then her lips. "Do you know the effect your natural charm has on a man, my lady?"

Her eyes moved frantically between his and his nearing lips. His hand brushed from her chin, along her jaw, and to the back of her head. Pushing against him, she only delayed it. Dundaelon kissed her for the third time.

She held no fire for him.

The Valdan prince pulled back, resting his cheek against hers as he whispered, “Do you know? If not, you soon will.”

Her heart stopped. Her mind fell into the visions of her future. The gloom and veil over her home city crawled into her. Whatever love she thought she could garner for him, fled—lost from this moment and every second to come with Dundaelon.

BREAKING FATE

Chapter 21

Dessuithiel Vizule

Eleventh of Trete

Gasping for air, Dessuithiel woke from a nightmare. She touched the side of her head, rubbing at the headache still present from the previous day. A chill wrapped its arms around her and she pulled her blanket up to her shoulders, drawing in her knees as she leaned upon them.

She buried her face in the fine linen, wishing she could as easily expunge the memory of her future as she did the tears falling from her eyes. Her eyes ached when she lifted her head minutes later and stared at the blurry image of her window. Light gently brushed it, beckoning the day's start and the end of her freedom.

Today was Farthven Ladayose.

A knock sounded at her door. She did not turn her head, but held tighter to her knees beneath her blanket.

"My lady, shall I answer your caller?" her lady's maid asked.

Dessuithiel sighed and nodded. She wiped the remnants of her tears from her face as the door cracked open. Lifting her head from her arms, she listened.

It was her mother.

"She has only just woken up, High Lady Miereene."

"Well enough, I did hope to be able to help her prepare for today."

The door opened wider and her mother entered. Her soft taps upon the tile floor grew louder as she neared and stopped at the base of the bed.

"My dear, let's get you ready." Her mother turned and called to her own staff of handmaidens. "Bring in the dress, let's hurry." She clapped her hands twice.

Dessuithiel stared at her reflection. The trifold mirror of her washroom showed an ethrean princess adorned from head to toe in glittering ivory, lace, and layers reminiscent of her favorite flower. Her mother carefully tugged at her hair, working the last of the crystals and pearls into it.

"Aba . . . did you and Ba love each other when you were wed?"

Her mother paused and tipped her head around, looking at her through their reflection with tender eyes. "My dear, I don't know if I'm the best one to ask. Your Ba was the one that took time to warm up to me when our union was sealed under Ilzu and Maz." She stepped out and set aside the few hair gems she had left. "What would you have me say?"

Dessuithiel's shoulders dropped as she let out a pent up breath. "Aba, what if I don't love him? What if this marriage takes away any love I might have for someone else?"

"And which royal would you be harboring love for? The only other eligible choices are not of age for another five years. Not only that, what better opportunity to secure Thyrel's future would you have than to be paired with Marmidon's most powerful ethrean house? Dessuithiel, I know it seems impossible right now, but give it a chance."

She turned from the mirror and faced her mother, tears already welling. "Aba, I've seen my future with him. Please, don't make me. I'll be miserable."

Her mother reached out for her, desiring to give her comfort, but held off just before holding Dessuithiel's face. "And you've seen this? You know how fickle the future can be. One choice can alter the balance of civilization. What if you don't marry Lord Dundaelon? Will Elpha Zavar leave Thyrel alone when they come to rule New Etrinn? I'm sure you can tell as well as your Ba and I that High Lord Nesalariel has high ambitions. This was the only way your Ba and I, as well as the lessor houses, could see balance for all ethrea. We, the Vizule house, have always been reserved and calculated in our decisions. We do what is best for the greater good. Being part of the Valdan house gives us more pull in what they do." She pulled her hand back. "This is how we prevent future conflict. If you find it hard to love Lord Dundaelon at this time, think of your love for your people. Let that be your reason, until there comes to be a place for him in your heart."

She picked back up the gems and moved behind Dessuithiel to place them.

"But what if Thyrel will be worse off this way?"

Her mother chuckled lightly. “Hardly, dear. The Seer has foreseen Thyrel, still standing, hundreds of years from now. You know this, yet you continued to say otherwise. You may have visions that have proven helpful in the past, but they are limited, even you know this.”

Dessuithiel sighed. “Yes, Aba.”

They won’t listen, and I cannot tell them what is coming. Though she was terribly tempted. *Marmidon, I have no one else to turn to . . .* She shut her eyes, tears falling down her cheeks as she sent a silent plea to Marmidon.

“Dessuithiel, dear!” Her mother fumbled for a tissue, bringing one to her face and dabbing at the tears. “Oh, sweet Dessuithiel, if it weren’t for the balance of Marmidon, I wouldn’t force this upon you.”

For the first time in years, her mother wrapped her arms around her, holding her tight. Dessuithiel’s eyes opened in surprise, and before her mother could pull away, she closed the embrace, holding her as she sobbed upon her mother’s shoulder.

“I don’t know what I’m going to do without you, Aba.” Again, she was tempted to tell her mother of what she had seen, but the alternative future held her back. Her heart filled with warning, but she had no right to give it. Against the premonition, she voiced her concerns, “Aba, what if continuing down this path leads to your passing, both you and Ba? I could lose you this very day.”

Her mother patted her back gently. “I don’t know what you’ve seen, but I don’t plan on going anywhere. Your Ba and I are well guarded. If it would ease your anxious heart, I will ensure we have extra guards with us through the festival.”

“And if that isn’t enough?”

“Then I will accept what Marmidon has chosen for your Ba and I, all for the greater good. I’ll never be far away whether physically or from the hereafter. But don’t dwell on such needless worries. Everything will go smoothly, you’ll be wed, and travel with Lord Dundaelon to New Etrinn, which is just a jump, skip, and hop over the mountains.” She teased, but her voice cracked with emotion.

Dessuithiel’s tears fell faster as she saw the impending moment among the visions of her mother’s future. She held tighter, not wanting to let go, not wanting time to continue in its endless revolution.

“If only I could stop time, turn it back,” Dessuithiel choked out.

A knock sounded at the door to Dessuithiel’s quarters. Her mother pulled back. Dessuithiel reluctantly released her. Her Aba smiled and brushed her thumbs over Dessuithiel’s cheeks.

“Find your strength, dear. It’s time to put on a smile.” She stepped away and spoke to one of the handmaidens on her way out. “See that you touch up her make up. She’s a bit emotional right now.”

“Yes, High Lady Miereene.”

Dessuithiel tried to steady her breaths, but the tears kept coming. Her face scrunched the more she sobbed, uncontrollably.

"Oh, dear me, my lady, we can't have this." Her lady's maid entered the wash room and quickly pulled several tissues from a box on the counter. She rushed over and dabbed at the streaks. "You should sit down. It will be easier for me to keep any stains from your dress as well."

Dessuithiel nodded, taking a seat on a padded stool near the counter and a smaller oval mirror.

"Let it all out, my lady." Her lady's maid urged. "Most women would run to be in your position, you know . . . but may I say, I admire your courage and sacrifice."

Dessuithiel took in a sharp breath, feeling it stutter. She didn't hold back, letting it all out until she couldn't cry any more. Her handmaidens helped her clear the redness from her face and made her fit to be the splendor of the festival.

Walking out into her bed chamber, her fate rested upon her, heavy and cold. She neared her door and waited the moment it took for it to be opened. As she lifted her eyes from the floor she was met by Guan's smile.

"My lady . . ." He could say nothing more, lifting his arms toward her before tucking one behind his back and directing her to the stairs.

Dessuithiel knew what came next. Her betrothed would parade through the city with her, enjoying the celebrations, and then bring her to the center plaza as Farthven Ladayose darkened the sky with its solar eclipse.

Each step was like a nail being driven into her heart, breaking her hopes of love into shallow pieces. Her betrothed met her near the stairs, on the guest quarter's landing.

"My lady, you are as radiant as Ilzu and I, like Maz, shall orbit you always." He offered his arm.

They descended the tower floor by floor. She slowed as they neared the infirmary. Her eyes drifting to the closed door where the surviving contestants lay tended.

Pulling upon Dundaelon's arm, she sought one last opportunity. "Would you allow me to check on the contestants? It would help me be more at ease today, if I were to see their condition first hand."

The Valdan prince looked between her and the shut door. "I suppose I can allow it. I wouldn't want you distracted through the celebrations."

She pulled her arm from him, bowing in thanks before approaching the door. Guan opened it, eyeing her.

He whispered as she passed, "Caution, my lady. Marmidon's power may still be lingering upon them. I advise that you withhold any contact."

She nodded, but wanted more than anything to hold Thoren's hand. To feel alive in the passion he had given her all too briefly that single night. Thoren no longer wore torn and bloodied clothes, but a fresh set of the mentor's garb. The royal healer bowed with a firm salute, hands at his sides, and reassured her of both Balek and Thoren's health. He stood between the beds, blocking most of her view of Balek and another person sitting at the competitor's bedside. She took a single step to the side to see them.

Janessa? Thoren's friend sat hunched over, asleep on the edge of Balek's bed. Looking down at the one Dessuithiel wished could be at her side, she asked, "Is there any indication as to when either of them will wake?" She hoped that Thoren would open his eyes for her.

"We'll have to wait and see."

"Thank you, for checking them over."

He bowed once more before leaving the room.

I can't wait. Thoren . . . please, break my fate. She reached out to him mentally, but his mind was still out of reach for her. *I'll fight it. I meant what I said. Marmidon, please let him wake.*

A faint male voice reached through the abyss of Thoren's sleeping mind.

"We'll have to wait and see."

Lady Dessuithiel spoke next. "Thank you, for checking them over."

The soft click of a shutting door sounded, followed by silence. Thoren tried to pull himself from the depths of his weary mind, but found it hard to do.

The door sounded once more, followed by heavy footsteps and Dundaelon's voice. "I hear he is stable."

Dessuithiel hummed in response, sounding melancholy.

"You should let the healers tend to him. I know you feel like it's your responsibility to oversee the contestants, but we have a ceremony to prepare for."

She didn't say anything, only softly humming again.

"Come on. Ilzu and Maz will be in position in just over an hour."

Farthven Ladayose. Thoren had been unconscious for nearly a full day.

Thoren fought to open his eyes, but they were sealed shut like the door that closed after Dundaelon and Dessuithiel's departure from the room.

Barely over an hour? She'll be wed to Dundaelon! Thoren couldn't still his heart beating rapidly over the thought. He tried once more to open his eyes, but to no avail. *Maybe it is for the best that I remain here. I won't have to see her wed.*

Dessuithiel Vizule

Dundaelon retrieved her, and she left, more reluctantly than she had ever left anyone before. Her heart wished to remain at his side. Her mind yearned for him. Dawning the mask she had so often worn the last few days, Dessuithiel faced the public as Dundaelon presented her before them. They followed the high lords and ladies of all the ethrean royals who'd come for this very day.

The sun betrayed her, beaming down warmth and joy upon the city while the moons crept ever over it—embracing the coming moment. The cheers felt numb against her ears. Her mind was lost in a dreary future. The aisle of citizens and visitors closed behind the guards trailing them. She kept her eyes fixed upon Guan, who walked ahead of her. Her parents were too far ahead to see and her heart ached for them.

Music filled the air as they arrived at the center plaza forty minutes later. Dundaelon bowed, took her hand and waist, leading her through the first dance of Farthven Ladayose. Her steps followed those she had practiced through her younger years. She moved gracefully, but her mind was nothing but pain. The dimming light eased the ache of her eyes, but only increased the panic within her. Her hands chilled, unable to warm in Dundaelon's grasp.

"My Dessuithiel," he leaned in close, "I wanted to keep it a surprise, but I've requested a rose garden to be made in New Etrinn for you. My gift to you, the most beautiful rose of all." He pulled back, guiding her through a gentle spin.

The thought of his kind gesture should have stirred loving feelings within her, but it only pressed the return of tears to her eyes. He tugged her gently, pulling her back through the spin and into his arms. His hand slipped back into place and lifted to the middle of her back. He was one of the finest, and first, dancers she had ever been with.

The music swelled and fell, moving each of the celebratory couples through a dance reminiscent of a flame's delicate roll. She was the only woman in straight ivory and glistening white crystal and pearl. The citizens being wed this day wore various hues of red, orange, and yellow, while the men wore white.

The sight of the men drew her thoughts back to Thoren, back to the moment they had shared. How her heart ached. A tear slipped from her eye as she blinked.

"My lady." Dundaelon slowed and lifted his hand from her back to her face, brushing the tear off. "Why do I feel as though our union does not bring you the same joy as it does me?"

"I'm sorry." She blinked away the rest of her resurfacing sorrow, putting on the best smile she was capable of. "There's been a lot on my mind."

He nodded. "I can relate, at least in part."

The clock tower chimed, marking the hour. Noon. Farthven Ladayose had arrived. Her fate about to be sealed. Her life locked in a one-sided love. She searched Dundaelon's face, looking for features that resembled the one that held her heart.

Thoren . . . I wish . . . I wish it were you!

THE TRUE FACE OF EVIL

Chapter 22

Thoren Belfry

Eleventh of Trete

Warmth spread within his heart, a sense of urgency contrary to his thoughts. It spread to his limbs giving him strength. His eyes drew open as though Marmidon herself was telling him to chase after her.

He stared up at a zilkan ceiling decorated with floral vines and a softly lit crystal chandelier. The room he was in was otherwise plain, and he lay upon a bed, one of three, wearing a new set of the mentor's garb. *Ah, here again.*

He spotted Balek, hooked up to a monitoring system and asleep upon the infirmary bed next to him. Surprisingly, Janessa was sitting in a chair beside him, bent forward—also asleep.

Wait, she's tending him and not me, her adoptive brother? Thoren felt a little hurt, but was relieved to see Balek had survived the third trial.

He knew that Janessa held feelings for Balek and was relieved that she had found someone to care for. With a rush, the feeling of urgency that had spread through him only a minute earlier returned along with thoughts of Dessuithiel hand in hand with Dundaelon. It did not feel right. He looked about the room. *I need to get out of here.*

He sat up quickly, immediately feeling dizzying vertigo that forced him back down. He huffed like he'd just sprinted, and a cool rush passed over his head.

I can't stay here . . . Something is telling me that Dessuithiel needs me! Thoren rolled off the bed, falling to the floor. He barely caught himself. Short of breath, he crawled across the floor to the door he'd heard Dessuithiel leave through. His arms trembled and the fatigue hanging over him almost numbed his sense of touch.

His hand wrapped around the door's lever-like handle, and he pulled it down, unlatching it. His face beaded in sweat from the effort of making it this far.

I'll never make it in time like this!

"Sir!" A tower guard rushed to his side. "You shouldn't be out of bed!"

The man lifted Thoren to his feet and steered him back to the medic's room, where groggy hums sounded from Janessa.

"No, I need to leave." Thoren protested and pulled against the guard who held him.

"You don't need to leave in this state. I assure you that we will see to your full recovery. The trials are over, and a healer is on his way."

Thoren knew the trials were over, but something else was about to be over if he didn't get out of this tower. He staggered back and slipped out of the guard's hold. Barely able to balance himself, Thoren went straight for the swirling stairs of the tower before the guard could cut him off.

"Mr. Belfry, please wait!" The guard followed him. "It'll only be a few minutes."

"I'm sorry, I'll be foregoing that healing session." He dismissed the guards' attempt at convincing him to stay a while longer." Thoren wheezed and clenched his teeth as he pushed himself forward. "I can't miss today's event."

"If it's the celebrations you're trying to get to, you can watch a broadcast of it here within the tower." The guard persisted. "At this point, you won't be able to get near the center plaza due to the crowds."

Thoren paused on the stairs. *The crowds, I hadn't considered how that might impact my ability to reach her. Not only that, how do I stop a royal wedding without putting my head on a chopping block?* He didn't know if death would be his punishment for interfering with such a royal affair, but there would be dire consequences. He might lose a century of his life to prison, or be disqualified from the mentor trials.

"Lady Dessuithiel is being wed, as I'm sure you heard. There won't be a better place to watch it than here."

Thoren faced the guard, gave a nod of thanks for his persistence and offers.

"I'm afraid that I must decline."

With that, Thoren turned back around, held to the railing, and rushed down the stairs as quickly as he dared.

Music rang through the air, penetrating the tower windows from outside. The daylight shining in through the windows was fading. Thoren's strength was slowly returning, but not fast enough. He stopped at one of the windows and peered down at the ground. He was at least five stories up. He would lose several minutes to these stairs. *Falling would be faster . . .*

He pressed his hand against the glass as the thought stuck. Gauging his inner well, his eyes widened. It swelled with energy, more than he'd thought he could possibly hold within himself. Thoren didn't need to wait for a healer. He had enough to heal himself and cast weaves all day. Risking it, he wove within the tower. A nearby guard called out a warning that he shouldn't weave without permission and someone else was rushing down the stairs. Healing took mere seconds with what he had access to. It was just as fast as in the third trial.

I'm coming, Dessuithiel!

Glass shattered and fell to the tower grounds below as Thoren burst through the window and began to fall. He heard Janessa's yelp of concern and shout to him from the broken window. He called out an increasingly familiar weave, feeling the rush of air slowing his fall. He landed, but not as smoothly as he'd hoped. Rolling to a stop with a grunt, he stood and kept going.

People gasped as he pushed his way between them.

"Isn't that Thoren Belfry?"

Another shared their surprise. "Did he just leap out through the tower's window?"

Thoren picked up speed. The fatigue he'd felt when waking up was gone, his strength returned.

"Thoren?"

He thought he heard Vance's voice, but he did not stop.

Thoren rushed through the streets, counting the seconds and minutes that passed. He grew increasingly worried the longer it took to get to the center plaza. The trains sat empty and the stations deserted. Even the conductors had left for the celebrations. His chest heaved as he slipped between alleys to cut time. Echoes of fast-falling steps sounded behind him. With how close the peak of the eclipse was, others were rushing to the plaza just like him.

Emerging from an alley, the streets ahead brought him to a screeching halt. They were packed to the brim with celebrating ethrea, man, therrinndore, and atle alike. Sweat beaded his brow from having run all the way here. The plaza had taken him a half hour to reach.

He spotted a large elegant canopy in the center of the masses. The celebratory song for those being wed had already started. Thoren glanced at the sky to see the two moons nearly in position over the sun's beaming light.

They'll be taking their vows any minute!

There had to be something he could do to delay it, giving him more time to figure out how to stop it altogether. *I can't reach her without drawing attention to myself. If I create a distraction elsewhere that could help draw the guards, then maybe I could reach her and stop the vows. I need some way to hide beyond the dimming light . . .* A thought came to mind and he eyed a short building's roofline near the central plaza.

Thoren skirted around the crowd and broke the city law, weaving the air at his feet outside of all permitted zones. He bounded up to the roof as graceful as a deer. Landing atop ceramic roof tiles. Taking several of the tiles from the roof, he wove them into a fine powder, hoping it would be enough to draw some of the guards away to investigate. Calling the wind to his aid, he sent the dust up into the sky several roofs over before guiding it up where people could see it.

He grew more concerned with each second that passed and nobody moved or mentioned his makeshift smoke signal. He made sure to keep out of sight, peering down over the edge at the canopy straight ahead. Before the clock tower finished its chimes, the sky darkened as completely as the eclipse would blanket it. The music came to an end. The dancing among the crowds became still. Time was up. If he was going to do anything to stall the wedding, now was the time.

His mind filled with the sudden plea of Dessuithiel. "*Thoren . . . I wish . . . I wish it were you!*"

His entire body tensed. She had shown no hint of her feelings since she'd opened the second portion of his inner well—until now.

My lady, did you have to push it so close to the last second?

He looked about, prepared to crash the royal wedding. Lanterns, made specifically for Farthven Ladayose, lit up around the plaza, dusting it with sparkling light like falling fireflies. The scene was magical, and he was about to ruin it.

The vows . . .

Heart ablaze, Thoren broke Thyrel's law once more as he cast his weave. The air burst from his open palm down at the plaza, forcing the crowds to duck and huddle together. The canopy ripped from its supports and flew off over the city, falling to the ground beyond the nearby structures. Some spotted his falling smoke signal, pointing to it. A pair of guards left to investigate, but not as many as he would have liked. Moving into the next part of his impromptu plan, he released the wind and called refined droplets from the air with another weave. A thick fog settled down across the central plaza. Thoren stared at Dessuithiel standing with Dundaelon at the heart of the celebration. The Valdan prince held her close, scanning the area with scrutiny.

She was angelically dressed and her fiery hair was loose across her back with intricate beading. Thoren's eyes took in the elaborate ivory gown within seconds. The folds and layers fell to her hidden feet like rose petals swaying in the settling wind. Her bare shoulders, as delicate as the sheer ruffles draped behind her arms. Her shoulders pinched up near her ears. Her eyes were likely shut but he couldn't be sure as her back was to him. He could tell that she was uncomfortable under Dundaelon's touch.

"Who cast this weave?" The call of a familiar guard carried over the crowd. It was Guan. "High lords and ladies, allow me to investigate."

Thoren thickened the fog further, maintaining his weave and hoping Guan could not see above the veil of mist. He realized that not only the house of Valdan and Vizule were sitting around the perimeter of the central plaza. It looked like every royal ethrean house was present. He recognized the high lords and ladies from the royal houses of Stabranga, Malduin, and Gudrovs. Each of them had several children, most of which were wed. There were three other royal high lords and ladies with their mix of younger and older children that he did not recognize, but knew had to be the lesser royal houses: Dailuma, Drosmane, and Varonar.

"Clear the air! A gust and fog will not delay this sacred ceremony!" High Lord Nesalariel stood from his seat across from his son, Dundaelon, and nearest to Thoren.

Several guards did as the high lord demanded, clearing the air, and forcing Thoren to increase his output to maintain some level of fog. This wasn't working. As the air cleared, the high lord of Elpha Zavar scanned the crowd. His gaze was hardened and impatient.

"I can feel an active weave," Nesalariel growled.

High Lord Ayzgar stood from where he sat across from Dessuithiel, and said, "This is not a permitted zone, guards, find the weaver!"

Thoren cut off his weave and ducked lower, hoping the high lords had not figured out where he was.

"Thoren, what are you doing?" Vance made himself known whispering from behind. His friend had followed him.

"Vance . . . dear Marmidon, you scared me!" Thoren ducked down, turned, and faced his friend.

"Are you deliberately trying to crash a wedding?" Vance's eyes flicked at the central plaza just on the other side of the roof ridge. He balanced on the balls of his feet, crouched on the roof tiles. "Why on the good face of Marmidon would you do such a thing? This is a wedding between two powerful ethrean royals!"

Thoren sighed. It was going to take too much time to explain it to him, nor did he know if his friend would accept that Thoren had fallen in love with Dessuithiel and she had fallen in love with him. Only Janessa had a hint of what was going on between them and warned that he should steer clear of it.

"Thoren, she opened your inner well. Of all the things to do, why?"

Thoren couldn't skirt around it. Vance needed an answer, one that made sense. Lady Dessuithiel's plea echoed from memory. He shut his eyes, defensively tensed, and told him. "Dessuithiel asked me to stop her wedding."

"What!" Vance hushed himself quickly and crouched closer as he continued with a hushed tone. "Is this something she had foresight about? Her wedding has to be stopped?"

Thoren shook his head. "It's hard to explain . . ." He thought of her words that still echoed within his mind. She hadn't outright said that she wanted him to stop her wedding, but he could feel it. "I just know that this isn't what she wants."

"Did she tell the high lord and lady?"

Thoren half nodded, expressing what he understood. "They have excused her warning as pre-wedding nerves."

Vance fell quiet.

Thoren took the time to return his attentions to those below. He spotted Dessuithiel, out of Dundaelon's grasp now, holding to the skirt of her gown tightly and glancing about. The ceremony was resuming and they were about to exchange vows.

She's waiting for me . . . but If I show myself, it will be plain how I feel about her. All of Thyrel, the world, will know.

His gut twisted, not with the pain of his inner well, but with emotions he knew he couldn't publicly have. He wanted to jump down there and stand tall as he opposed the wedding, hoping that

Dessuithiel's parents would permit it, but Thoren knew how it would turn out—nothing like that.

I never thought I would risk my reputation, freedom, and my life for love. How do I stop this wedding?

"Thoren. Get down there. I'll disperse the crowd," Vance said suddenly.

"Really?" Thoren slid back beside his friend. "You realize that you could very well be caught and charged? The royal guard are actively looking for a weaver."

Vance nodded. "Go, I think I know what's going on here." His gaze held a seriousness Thoren had never seen in his friend before. "Janessa may have slipped a few things to me . . . I don't entirely approve, but I'm your friend. I know you wouldn't do this if you didn't feel it was right."

Janessa . . .

A half chuckle and disapproving puff of air slipped out his nose and his lips pressed tight trying to hide a smile. "Thank you."

Thoren slipped down and dropped into the alley. He could hear the crowd quieting as Dundaelon began his vows.

His chest swelled and pained listening to the words that left the ethrean's lips to a woman he barely knew. The air shifted. Energy pulled around him. Vance had begun. The dim light provided by the eclipse dimmed further as storm clouds gathered, thick and dark. It cast the city into the dead of night. Gasps sounded from those below and many pointed to the formed clouds.

Vance, be careful.

His friend was best at weaving water in various forms and one of his specialties was storms. Static built in the air and bumps spread over Thoren's arms. Thunder rumbled as the energy built above and flashes lit up the clouds.

"Where did that come from?" someone nearby asked, pointing at the storm that spread out over the plaza.

Thoren glanced up to where he knew Vance was, wondering how much of his inner well he was using up. Pushing a weave like this was bound to leave his inner well exhausted.

I'll only have one chance at this.

Crouching, he readied to sprint to *his* maiden. For at this point he had claimed her in his heart.

The high lords and ladies stood as rain threatened to put an end to their celebrations. Vance guided a strike of lightning to the nearby clock tower and broadcast station, sending sparks falling to the ground. Heavy rain fell moments after, drenching the plaza and everyone there. Hollars mixed with the sounds of those leaving the plaza in a hurry. Thoren made his move, weaving through the crowd as fast as he could, but still barely at a brisk pace, having to move against their retreat from the plaza Guards did their best to mitigate injury as everyone rushed for cover in the nearby noshes, inns, and shops.

Thoren heard in passing. "You don't suppose there's someone against this? One of the other ethrean royals perhaps?" The question came from a stocky therrinndore.

A response came from an elderly human beside the therrinndore. "Feels like Marmidon herself is against this union."

I know I needed cover, but Vance, this is a little much.

"Make way! Make way!" guards called in unison as they led the royal families from the plaza.

Thoren hoped to avoid being seen as he stepped out past the crowd, sticking to the darkest patches, and lifted his hands to the nearby lamps. With a simple weave, he darkened the plaza, breaking the tether within each crystal holding light. Vance's storm now provided the only light in split moments, strobing everyone's movements.

"High Lord Ayzgar, this does not feel natural," one of the guards said.

Thoren moved into the open space filled with the most powerful ethrea alive. Only the royal families and their guard stood in the plaza with him. Dessuithiel held his full attention. In each flash of light, he drew closer. His hand reached out for hers. Their fingers brushed.

“You!” A familiar voice called and he grabbed hold of Thoren’s shoulder from behind. Before he realized who it was, Thoren moved swiftly in self-defense, landing a punch squarely on Guan’s nose.

Guan shook it off and grabbed hold of him again, pulling him away from the royals. “What are you doing here? You should be in the tower resting. Don’t tell me this is your doing?” He waved a hand at the storm, flicking rainwater from his fingertips.

The High Lord and Lady Vizule were quickly walled off by the Thyrian guards. They were moving back toward the tower in the distance with the other royal houses. Some of the guards held their hands out, clearly holding an active weave to keep the rain from soaking the royals.

“I’m doing what my heart tells me I should do,” Thoren answered Guan, unsure if he would allow him to proceed and fulfill his lady’s wishes. “She doesn’t want this.”

“Dundaelon, take your bride!” High Lord Nesalariel commanded. “Clearly, there is someone here intent on disrupting your union. This storm reeks of weaving.” he spoke above the rain, and in an extended flash locked his gaze with Thoren. Nesalariel stiffened, the look of recognition in his eyes.

Darkness cut their locked gaze off and Thoren had the distinct feeling that he should run. He pulled, but Guan tightened his hold.

"Why would my lady ask you to ruin her wedding?" he hissed. "I see no reason for it. You have only blinded my lady, clouding not only her mind but her heart."

"I won't deny that I have been enchanted by her as many others have, but I don't know the reasons behind her request."

Thoren was only told that the future would be shaken in a bad way. She had not mentioned anything about her wedding. Beyond that, he only knew the desperation he'd heard within his mind, but was stopping the ceremony enough? Was that all she needed of him? They still could not be together. Ethrean customs and laws, the monarchies, would not allow it.

Another weave was cast, fizzling through the air. Crackling pops sounded, followed by a stillness blocking out the sounds of rain, thunder, and distant onlookers. A glimmer of green passed over the center plaza, passing overhead before falling toward the ground just behind Thoren and Guan. The scene around them changed and the storm no longer drenched him.

Wait, is this an illusory realm? He recalled the one Dessuithiel had cast in the gardens to meet with him privately. *Who cast it?* He hoped it was Dessuithiel, but the pit in his gut and the scene unfolding around him told him otherwise.

Thoren broke free of Guan's hold. "Guan, we need to break out of this realm."

"You didn't cast this?" Guan tensed and lifted his hands, ready to cast at a moment's notice.

All Thoren could see were shadows. He turned around, scanning for anything that didn't belong, a portion of the illusion that would give away its weak point. *This is an illusory realm, outside forces can't see or reach this space. We're locked in until the caster ends it, or we find the weakness within. I don't know if there is anyone powerful enough to break it from the outside.* The center plaza was gone, replaced with black sand, and shifting pillars of mist. *Is it just Guan and I in here?*

He called to Dessuithiel and listened for her to respond—unsure if it was better that she was locked in here with him or outside of it. She didn't answer. For all he knew they were taking the royals somewhere else to finish the union. He wouldn't be able to stop it from in here.

"Thoren, be careful!" Her voice entered his mind, startling him. *"He's in there with you!"*

Who? What's going on? Dessuithiel, what do I do?

Nesalariel's voice broke the silence as he angrily asked, "You would dare to oppose this marriage, one blessed by Ilzu and Maz?"

Thoren tensed, momentarily freezing in place. The shadowed forms shifted in an oddly familiar way. One drew near. The black mist fell from Nesalariel, peeling away—revealing him.

The high lord approached with a cold glare.

“Aren’t you one of the competitors from the trials?” he asked, stopping a couple feet from him, he ignored Guan standing beside Thoren. “What force has possessed you to interfere? You are one of my citizens, are you not?” He folded his arms, setting his head high.

“I-I . . . You are correct, High Lord Nesalariel. I am from Elpha Zavar, and one of the competitors from the trials.” Thoren’s hands clenched at his sides as he tipped forward in a slight bow. “My actions . . .” he struggled to give the reason as his thoughts flitted about in a panic.

I never had a chance at reaching her. How much of this did Dessuithiel know? What will be the consequence? Would Nesalariel grant me a pardon if I tell him why? He met the high lord’s cold gaze, rising upright.

Before Thoren could continue, Guan grabbed hold of his arm and cast, “Saisette.” Thoren was bound in invisible chains on the spot by the weave. Guan bowed to the high lord of Elpha Zavar.

“High Lord Nesalariel . . .” He rose. “I apologize for the disruption.” He then looked at Thoren sternly. “I will see to it that he doesn’t interrupt and the ceremony proceeds.”

The high lord still watched Thoren closely. Nesalariel let out a fiery breath. “Answer me. Why interfere with my son’s union?”

Thoren glanced at the realm still active around them. He dared to say it. “This marriage cannot happen.” Thoren spoke, perhaps too plainly, taking advantage of their closed off space from the public's eyes and ears. "Lord Dundaelon is not meant for Lady Dessuithiel. Their union will bring disaster to Marmidon." He felt his words resonating with the feelings he'd seen in Dessuithiel's eyes.

Guan took hold of Thoren's arms and pulled them behind his back, where he quickly physically bound them with a weave that shifted the fibers of a handkerchief into a firm rope. In doing so, the weave holding Thoren in place was released, and the princess's personal guard pulled him close.

"What in Marmidon do you think you're doing?" he whispered into Thoren's ear.

Nesalariel closed the two steps to reach Thoren, grabbed hold of his tunic, by the collar, and took him from Guan.

"How *dare* you assume ruin from this union." He fumed. "I ought to have your life for this offense!"

The same coldness Thoren had felt before, seeped from High Lord Nesalariel. Daring to meet the gaze of his high lord, Thoren opposed him again.

"Lady Dessuithiel wants nothing to do with your son! She begged me to interfere."

The realm masking them from the public shook, sending tendrils of green light across the barrier as it broke down. The walls of illusion fell the moment Nesalariel drew his fist back.

"You insolent—" He struck Thoren to the ground.

"High Lord Nesalariel!" Guan shouted, nervous energy in every word as he held a hand out between the high lord and Thoren, stopping further punishment. "Thoren is a contestant to be Marmidon's chosen mentor. His actions here are inexcusable, but his life is not yours to take."

Thoren's head spun and pulsed from the side of his head where Nesalariel had landed his punch. He sat up, hands still bound at his back, and stared up at the guard. The man who'd hated him from the start just defended his life.

Rain drizzled down upon them.

Nesalariel growled and pulled back, noticing the failing of his illusory realm. The rain fell harder and lightning flashed with echoes of thunder, guided by the one Thoren knew was behind it. *Vance.* Guan pulled Thoren to his feet, but before they could go anywhere, Thyrel's high lord approached.

"Nesalariel!" Ayzgar stepped between Elpha Zavar's high lord and Thoren. "Such violent outbursts are beneath our station! You would hide your actions from us? Where is your dignity?"

Ayzgar must have been the one to break Nesalariel's weave. He was in awe at the high lord's ability. Breaking an illusory realm from the outside required expertise only few had ever attained.

Thoren pulled at the binds around his wrists and looked up at the arguing high lords.

The only royals that had remained in the plaza were the Valdan and Vizule's. Nesalariel turned his anger to Ayzgar.

"This union is but a step to the expansion of my domain. The moment Ilzu and Maz pass, Thyrel will no longer belong to you!" He shoved Ayzgar back.

The royal guard rushed to put themselves between the two high lords and High Lady Miereene rushed to her husband's side, wrapping her arms around her beloved. "What are you talking about?"

"You fools thought there could be a true union between us?" Nesalariel laughed. "I might as well celebrate a little early." He raised his hand at both the High Lord and Lady Vizule.

Dessuithiel screamed. "Aba, Ba, get out of there!"

Thoren jerked free of Guan's hold, hoping to intercept in time, but he watched in horror as a green glow flashed from High Lord Nesalariel's eyes as he spoke foreign words. The high lord cast a fatal weave at High Lady Miereene and High Lord Ayzgar.

It happened too fast for either of them to react—for anyone to stop. The royal guard turned around, gasping in horror.

Dessuithiel's sorrowing cry broke Thoren's heart.

What kind of weave was that? He'd heard it, as did everyone around who remained and now turned to flee. Several guards carried away the bodies of their high lord and lady, rushing to safety, while the rest faced High Lord Nesalariel ready to defend.

The air broke out with monstrous cries of terror—the cries of creatures from a dark realm. *That voice, that dialect! Those things!*

Thoren stared with wide eyes and clarity.

The face. The weaves from the trial! He looked upon the threatening high lord's face. *It was High Lord Nesalariel I fought! That trial was preparing me for this moment!*

The remaining ethrean guards sprang into action, casting offensive weaves at Nesalariel. The high lord deflected and canceled out the weaves cast at him with ease. Nesalariel countered, weaving foreign words at the ethrean guards. They fell to the ground, lifeless, like High Lady Miereene and High Lord Ayzgar.

Nesalariel cast his weaves in near identical form to the speed and ferocity of the misting pillar. However, unlike the misting face, the high lord was quick on his feet. This fight would be a challenge with as great a risk as the trial.

I cannot hesitate, not even for a moment. I cannot let fear get the better of me.

The ensuing chaos spread as sounds of the beasts Thoren had slain among the trials emerged from various points in the city. Vance's storm ceased, and gradually daylight returned with the waning eclipse.

Thoren looked at Guan. "I can fight him! Just take this off!" He nudged his head back at the binding on his wrists.

Guan rushed to Thoren's side, removing the bind. His voice was barely audible and trembling. "I've seen your strength. I'm taking a risk, but please, save Lady Dessuithiel."

"Ba!" Dundaelon shouted. "What have you done?"

The ethrean prince stood with an arm out protectively in front of Dessuithiel, and his older sister Gailiaethere, just outside the plaza. Several guards were urging them to leave.

Guan released the binds and Thoren rubbed at his wrists. He sensed the danger that was turning back toward Dundaelon and Dessuithiel. He leapt into action, wrapping his arms around High Lord Nesalariel and tackling him to the ground before harm came to the prince or princess.

"Run!" Thoren shouted. His tone carried a warning not just for the betrothed couple, but the guards as well. Dundaelon wore confusion and cutting pain upon his face over what his father had done.

The ground rumbled and crackled. Thoren was shoved off with strength beyond that of a normal ethrean. He scrambled to his feet, holding himself at the ready. Glancing back, he still saw both Dundaelon and Dessuithiel.

"What are you waiting for? Run!" Thoren screamed.

Dundaelon snapped out of his daze and grabbed hold of Dessuithiel's hand, pulling her away from his father.

Gailiaethere stumbled after them.

Misting geysers shot out from the ground all over Thyrel. Screams echoed as people were met with the dark beasts held within.

Nesalariel's gaze moved from his fleeing children to Thoren. "You seem strangely familiar." The green gaze of the titan stared into Thoren's soul. "I see." His mood soured. "Marmidon thinks you can stop me."

His words confirmed Thoren's feelings. "I will not let you take hold of this city." He readied to strike, tensing every muscle and reviewing every weave he knew.

High Lord Nesalariel staggered with laughter. "What can you do?"

"More than you know."

Thoren raised his hand calling out multiple weaves. He shifted his inner well between each one, casting and cutting them off within seconds. The high lord kept up with Thoren's throws. Deflecting and canceling each weave that came at him.

I can't defeat him the same way I did the misting face. His body is real, mortal as my own. I'll have to kill him. If I wasn't already in trouble, I will be after this . . .

Shifting his tactics, Thoren called the wind to his aid. The air whistled as it whipped around Thoren. It threatened Nesalariel's footing, pushing him back as he raised his arms to shield his eyes from everything being tossed about in it.

Thoren morphed pieces of metal from nearby, pulling them from buildings, turned over stands, and benches. He gripped tight to his newly formed sword-like weapons and dashed ahead with intent to slay the corrupted high lord.

Nesalariel shouted a weave of his own with the ancient dialect and voice that was not his.

Thoren dodged at the last second, dropping to the ground and rebounding with a gust of air. He moved with the wind's aid, slashing upward at Nesalariel's face. His steel connected, ripping through the high lord's jaw and cheek.

Confidence swelled within him. *I can do this.*

Another weave left Nesalariel's lips and it sent Thoren flying backward. His woven wind couldn't keep up with the force that threw him back, and he crashed into the brick-faced side of a building. Windows shattered from above and beside him.

Thoren fell to the ground coughing up blood and wheezing.

I took a direct hit. Another one like that and I'll die!

Battle cries sounded from ethrean guards, reinforcements likely sent by those who'd fled. They charged past Thoren toward the threat. He tried to stand, but fell back against the brick wall of the building. He sat struggling through each breath and watched as Nesalariel dispatched the ethrean guards in a similar fashion to the first group before them, cutting through them with a weave like a blade through tall grass. The hardest thing to process was how he had done so. Thoren saw nothing but a green flash of light following Nesalariel's sweeping hand.

"Get up, Thoren!" Dessuithiel called within his mind.

HER LOVE

Chapter 23

Dessuithiel Vizule

Eleventh of Trete

Her nightmare was made real. Everything had happened faster than she had time to process it. Tears still streamed down her face as Dundaelon actively protected her from creatures of the mist overtaking Thyrel. Her parents were gone. She never had a chance to stop it. Nobody did. In her pain, she found herself searching for Thoren among the sparks and weaves being cast in the plaza. She recalled the faint brush of his hand over her own before everything turned upside down.

He came for me? She wondered if perhaps her heart's desire and plea had somehow found Thoren before she was forced to recite her vows. *When did he leave the tower?* She realized that he must have followed them shortly after. *How? When did he wake?* The answers to her questions would only be found if they survived this.

She called light to her aid as the cold mist stretched out to her and Dundaelon. The creatures within shrank back with whines of pain. She shifted the light, spearheading it into one of the braving canines. It steered away.

"Keep it up, my lady!" Dundaelon shouted and then called a weave of his own. The ground groaned and he moved his hands and body in sync with the stones he pulled from beneath the dirt. He flung large rocks at the creatures, striking several down on the first shot.

He glanced back at her. "Aren't these the beasts from the first trial?" he asked while shifting the ground again, keeping the black canines at bay with the aid of her light.

Dessuithiel confirmed and continued to aid him while looking for Thoren among the increasing darkness. A pained scream passed through the mist, followed by cracking stone and shattering glass.

She reached out for Thoren, feeling the mental link between them flickering. Before it faded, she sought it, focusing everything into it. Shutting her eyes, she secured the neural link, grateful that it had returned. Pain registered. Thoren was hurting, his inner light shaken.

She called to him, *Get up, Thoren!*

Guan stood behind her, dutifully protecting her. She turned to face her shadow. "Guan! Thoren needs you!"

He left without a word.

Dessuithiel did what she could to aid Dundaelon, turning her light into a deadly weapon against the darkness. Everything playing out around them matched the vision she'd seen with Guan. The environment of Thoren's trial was surrounding them. The ground groaned. She watched every step Guan took. He sprinted across the battlefield of the central plaza, finding Thoren in time to cast a barrier.

Guan, thank you! Dessuithiel returned her focus to the beasts around her and Dundaelon. Her light weaving struck the dark creatures, shattering their dark forms and scattering her light. Her eyes drifted to Thoren again and her breath caught in her chest. Her scattered light was the light from her visions. It was not just Thoren that was to fight this battle. *Marmidon! I'm supposed to help him!*

She did not know the outcome of this battle, but she pleaded with all her heart. *Marmidon, let the light prevail! Protect the one I love!*

A SEALED FATE

Chapter 24

Thoren Belfry

Eleventh of Trete

He looked for her, spotting her fighting with Dundaelon several yards to his right. The Valdan prince fought skillfully against a pack of misting canines with weaves shifting the ground into a deadly weapon. Dessuithiel shielded them with light, striking with the same force when openings presented. She was a beacon in the darkness, cutting through the mist with her golden glow.

The air crackled, sending tendrils of green lightning ripping across the ground like an underground beast burrowing near the surface. One of the tendrils was headed straight for Thoren. He groaned as he tried to move out of the way, but he was not fast enough to evade it.

"Bajerra!" Guan cast, leaping in front of Thoren and taking the hit. He stumbled back from the impact, shoulders heaving as he repelled the dark energy.

Guan shouted to Thoren, "Don't make me regret saving you!"

Thoren cast his next weave, healing his wounds. He thanked Guan in passing as he rushed back to fight the high lord. He called forth another weapon with a weave, after he was unable to spot his prior ones.

The high lord shoved the last of the fallen guards with the heel of his boot. A smile stretched across his face at the sight of Thoren.

"Back for more?" Nesalariel chuckled, amused. "Shame this world has lost sight of what true vision is."

Thoren listened to the cries throughout the city and the sounds of the beasts being slain as those able to defended the weak.

Vision? He's insane!

"Listose Yeudins!" Thoren drew the water from the nearby fountains and air. With a flick of his hand, it shot forward and struck Nesalariel.

I got him! His success was short-lived as the water split just ahead of the high lord who held out a hand, parting it like it was child's play.

Thoren quickly changed it, he shouted the weave, "Piersings Ledus!"

The parted water froze over and broke into sharpened shards. Willing it, Thoren sent every shard at Nesalariel.

The shattering sound blinded his ears to the weave the high lord cast. It sent his shards flying away in every direction.

Thoren shielded his face and chest with a barrier, holding his arms like an X in front of himself, as several shards embedded themselves in his legs. He winced and quickly plucked the ice from his body before ending the weave and healing his wounds.

"Now, that is interesting. You're adept and fast." Nesalariel's grin widened. "That well of yours. It's rather large."

Thoren crouched, ready to sprint at a moment's notice. He let his instinct take control. "Akemins Morfejemis!"

The ground burst with sharp stone beneath the high lord. The tips crossed over each other as Thoren trapped Nesalariel within and closed the space.

The draw upon his inner well increased as a force within his trap pushed against him. Nesalariel was still alive and fighting back.

"Thoren," Dessuithiel called to him mentally. *"I'll give you one shot at Nesalariel. You must stop his heart. Don't miss!"*

Thoren looked back where he'd last seen her. She stood in the open road with a hand raised at the ready. Guan was back at her side, vigilant and adeptly protective.

Dundaelon ran to Thoren. "What are you doing?"

Thoren looked wide-eyed at the ethrean prince. "Your Ba murdered Thyrel's high lord and lady! He'll kill everyone here! I'm doing what must be done!"

Dundaelon grimaced, hurt by his words, but acknowledging his father's error. "How can I help?"

"Have Dundaelon call to his Ba, distract him. There must still be a part of his Ba in there. We need only a moment."

Okay. Thoren nodded and turned back to his struggling enclosure. "Call to your Ba, what little is left of him," he ordered.

The stone cracked and burst with a green light from within. Nesalariel stepped over the crumbling stone, dusting his shoulder off.

"Nice try."

Thoren ground the tip of his boot on the debris-dusted path under him. His grip tightened around his make-shift blade. He was ready.

Dundaelon took a cautious step toward his father with a raised hand, calling his attention and asking, "Why would you do this, Ba? This was to be a joyous day!"

"Now!" She shouted internally.

Thoren sprinted forward as Nesalariel's eyes shifted from him to Dundaelon. Each step pounding into the zilkan beneath him. He thought he saw blue sparks bursting with the contact. The air lifted behind him, and a bright light blinded Nesalariel.

Thoren lifted the tip of his blade, his aim true with his next step and drove the sharpened tip into the high lord's chest. Thoren's momentum came to a stop as he crashed into Nesalariel.

Nesalariel cried out with more than one voice. It shook not only his heart, but stole the Valdan prince's courage. At a glance, he saw Dundaelon faltering while shaking his head in disbelief. Nesalariel fell backward to the rubble-covered ground where Farthven Ladayose had been held. Thoren drove the dagger-shaped weapon deeper as he knelt over the high lord. Nesalariel's jaw clenched tight and he sucked in through his teeth.

"It would seem . . ." Nesalariel coughed up blood as he spoke. "My era . . . has yet . . . to come. A parting gift . . ." His mouth moved, but Thoren could not make out what he was saying.

The light from his eyes faded and he fell limp. Thoren peeled his blood-covered hands from the dagger in Nesalariel's chest, leaving the weapon behind. He stood and stumbled back.

Thoren cried out in the next second as his inner well knotted up. He fell to his knees and bent over from the pain, placing his face an inch from the ground. Seconds later, the pain vanished. Bits of stone and dirt bounced out of the way as each forced breath left his nose. He dared not stand.

The sounds of distress throughout the city fell into a cold silence. He lifted his head. Thoren remained frozen in place, staring at the dead high lord. Black mist bubbled up around his body, pulling him into its cold abyss.

Fast-paced footfalls echoed down the zilkan path to him. Each step brought the ruffling sounds of flowing fabric.

“Thoren!” Dessuithiel slid to his side. She wrapped her arm over his back, and held to his shoulders. “Are you all right?”

Tears streamed down her cheeks. Her eyes wide with worry, but still she held his wellbeing above her own.

“I don’t know.” He risked sitting up, relieved to find no pain with the movement. “Did we do it, Dessuithiel? The future you saw . . . Did we avoid it?”

“Yes . . . Thoren.” Her eyes glistened, and a small smile graced her face, solemn but hopeful. “We avoided the worst of what I saw. This outcome, while still burdened with sorrows, was the best future available to us, the one with the least measure of pain, and by Marmidon’s will we found it . . . but . . . what did High Lord Nesalariel do?” She turned his face to meet hers. “You were in pain.”

“As far as I can tell I am uninjured, but you have lost both your parents. How are you?”

Her lips trembled and she looked to the sky, blinking away what tears she could, but more streamed down her face. Her voice quivered as she spoke. "I will be okay in time . . ."

Thoren's heart broke seeing her grief. He couldn't imagine having to watch his own parents murdered before his eyes. He clenched his hands, still held over his inner well applying pressure. Her eyes drifted down to them and she quickly removed her arm from his back. She pulled his hands away from his stomach. With a shaken sigh, she eased as she confirmed that it was not his blood covering his hands. Calling out the weave, she collected a small orb of water from the air and washed the blood from his fingers and palms.

Suddenly, she gasped, and cut the weave. The water fell to the ground and she pressed a hand to his stomach.

"Aktuly No Patiesibu." Her voice shook as she cast the weave and examined his inner well. She slumped back, dropping her hands in her lap. "Everything we did."

"What did he do?" Thoren feared the answer.

"He sealed half of your inner well."

Sealed? Not locked? He found the change in descriptive words unnerving.

He shut his eyes and gauged his well's strength. It was true. The power he'd had—half of it was gone. He couldn't even sense it.

"My Lady!" Dundaelon joined her, kneeling at her side.

They both turned to face him.

“Are you unharmed?” He reached out for her.

Dessuithiel flinched at his touch, despite how tender it was.

His eyes narrowed on Thoren. “Tell me, how this happened.” He wasn’t asking Thoren directly, but it was clear that he felt Thoren was in part to blame. “I do not understand how my Ba could turn to such dishonorable violence so quickly. He called monsters, ones like those fought in the trial.”

Dessuithiel held Dundaelon’s hand, gently guiding it off her. She answered with all the kindness she had, “Lord Dundaelon, I saw this day in a vision. I did not know where the destruction would come from, and it grieves me to have seen life taken from both the house of Vizule and Valdan.” Thoren could tell she was barely holding together, on the edge of sobbing. Her gaze turned to Thoren briefly. “I asked him for aid. Forgive him. He did not seek to end your Ba, only to protect the lives of those here. Your Ba’s life was sadly an unavoidable price, paid to avoid the loss of those I have vowed to protect.”

With his mouth hanging open, he scoffed, “You saw this coming and did not think to tell me?” He stood, indifferent to her grieving tears, and stepped back with emotional hurt pinching at his brow. “Does our betrothal mean so little to you?”

Dessuithiel stood, hands clenched at her sides. "Lord Dundaelon, you are a good man, but even my parents would not listen. Would you have?"

"Would you have given me a chance?" He took another step back with increased hurt.

"Our parents are dead. I think it best that we call this wedding off." Dessuithiel's voice cracked as she stepped up to the Valdan heir. "Thyrel . . . is under my rule." She pulled the marital band from her left pointer finger and shoved it into his hand.

"You never intended on honoring the betrothal." He looked away, tensed, and growled with the ring tightly clenched in his fist. "You've lost any support of the Valdans from this moment on! Looking at you only brings me pain."

"Dundaelon!" The distant call came from Gailiaethere. "Brother, where are you?"

"Think what you will. It's time for you to go home," Dessuithiel spoke softly.

Thoren stood up beside Dessuithiel, wishing he could give her comfort openly, and watched as Dundaelon's face scrunched into a restrained scowl. He turned, voicing another displeased huff, and marched away toward the sound of his sister's call. The few guards of the Valdan house that remained rushed to the orphaned siblings, and their new ruler, High Lord Dundaelon.

Dessuithiel eased and let out another shaken breath as though she'd held it for the last minute. They stood in silence, watching and listening to the efforts of those working to remedy the mess around them.

No support from the Valdans? Thyrel will be left vulnerable if ever attacked in the future! Dundaelon's words echoed within his mind.

"Dessuithiel." Thoren watched her turn to face him. He avoided her glistening eyes. "I don't know if it was wishful thinking that kept drawing me back to you. All of Marmidon is aware of what the Valdans seek now. Thyrel will be at risk if you don't take his hand in marriage. I have no army to protect you with."

She eased his heart in a single moment with the touch of her hands cupping the sides of his face. "Thoren Belfry, have you forgotten? You are my fate, and *nothing* will stand between us."

Thoren pulled back and quickly glanced to the right and left, ensuring that nobody had seen her forward action, even if just her touch.

He continued, "But, what about the Valdans?"

She smiled. "They were destined to this fate from the beginning. Come, let us leave the plaza's restoration to Guan." She wiped her face dry and eyed someone standing behind Thoren.

He turned around to see Guan was inches from him.

"My lady, I would prefer to remain at your side." His brow was lowered, his glare afresh upon Thoren.

"Stay, organize my parents' burial, the cleanup, and make sure the wounded are tended to." Dessuithiel lifted her hand, cutting off his protest. "That's an order from your new high lady."

Guan grumbled and gave a stiff bow. "At your command, my lady."

Vance shouted Thoren's name, rushing up to them. His face eased as he looked him over. "That was not what I pictured when you said you were going to crash the wedding."

Thoren laughed, wincing a little at lingering aches. "It wasn't exactly what I pictured either, Vance." He managed a smile at his friend's lighthearted comment.

Vance soon left, joining those gathering to address the aftermath.

Dessuithiel pulled at Thoren's sleeve and led the way to the tower gardens. His face burned hotter the longer they walked in silence. The moment they passed through the rose arch, their scenery shifted, back to the crystal cavern she'd once brought him to. She stopped and he wondered why she'd brought them here.

"Lady Dessuithiel . . ."

She turned around, lifting her hands, wrapping them tenderly around his back and resting the side of her face on his chest. She began to sob, letting out everything she tried so hard to hold in.

Flustered, he held his arms out for several seconds before returning her embrace, allowing himself to comfort her where no one else would know.

He held her in the soft glow of the giant-crystal cavern, lightly stroking one hand over her flowing hair and holding her with the other. Minutes passed until she'd cried her last tear. Her grip upon his tunic lessened and she began to pull back.

"I'm sorry for putting so much on you." She lifted a hand to wipe at the residual tears sliding down her cheeks.

Thoren caught her hand, gave it a tender squeeze, then moved to wipe away her tears. He cupped her face, brushing his thumbs across it while gazing into her reddened, puffy eyes.

Marmidon, she is still beautiful.

He wanted nothing more than to be the one she relied on. The urge to kiss her was growing stronger with each passing minute. He had completely fallen for her in every possible way.

"Dessuithiel, I chose this, be it fate or not. I only wish that I could give you more than this comfort."

She moved her other hand to his, rubbing her thumbs over his knuckles and smiling slightly. "Thoren, you have eased the pain in my heart long before the pain was there. Thoren Belfry, as of this moment, I am yours." Dessuithiel brought her hands to the sides of his face as she had briefly done in the plaza. "In such pain, fate granted me, you."

The eclipse had ended, but their future together had just begun. Drawn into a most tender kiss, Thoren's heart was set ablaze.

Pulling back enough to see her face, Thoren stared into Dessuithiel's bright blue eyes, a reflection of the endless sky and the love that they *could* have in a world of their own, sealed under Ilzu and Maz.

"If it's fate we share . . . then by Marmidon, seal us forever." His heart swelled as he confessed his desire.

He reached out for her face, gently threading his fingers into her fiery red hair and drawing her lips back to his in a passionate kiss.

LOVE AND DUTY ENTWINED

Chapter 25

Thoren Belfry

Eighteenth of Trete

Thoren woke at daybreak. His heart fluttered at the thought of seeing his dearest lady. He jumped up and got ready, nearly inhaling his breakfast.

"You're in a hurry." Janessa walked into Vance's kitchen. "You know that the announcement isn't happening until noon, right?"

“I know.” Thoren smiled.

He finished and cleared his dish. Jogging to the front door, he slipped on his boots, and double checked that his white garb was perfectly set.

“I think I know who you’re going to see.” Janessa leaned on the wall. “I’m still not sure it’s the best course.”

Thoren chuckled and shot back at her. “Don’t think I don’t know about your date with Balek.”

She stood upright, ready to chase him down as her cheeks burned red. Thoren dashed out the door before she had the chance.

Thyrel had postponed the announcement of Marmidon’s mentor in favor of holding a funeral for High Lady Miereene and High Lord Ayzgar. Afterward, they spent a couple days cleaning up the city and repairing the damage caused by the fallen High Lord Nesalariel Valdan.

Thoren had waited anxiously over this stretch of time to see Dessuithiel again. He picked up his pace with his gaze fixed upon the tower. While the announcement of Marmidon’s mentor was set for noon, she’d called him in for something she’d deemed “urgent.”

Dessuithiel Vizule

Light warmed her face as she stared out of her bedroom window, watching the sun rise. Sorrow still hung around her heart, and the funeral of her parents was fresh upon her mind. She twisted a rose in her hand, one from the bouquet that currently sat atop her parent's grave. The soft, yellow petals fluttered at her touch, and with a steady breath, she pulled the petals off.

Aba, Ba, I wish there had been another way. Her breath shook and a single tear rolled down her cheek. *I pray that Marmidon has received you into her arms.*

She held the petals out and slowly opened her hand, letting the breeze take them.

The future she had seen pieces of for so long had come and gone. The marriage she feared had dissolved and from memories she scanned of both Balek and Thoren following the third trial, Aiden was able to determine who Marmidon had chosen. A knock sounded at her door. Dessuithiel pushed back from the window, leaving the stem upon the sill.

"My lady, shall I answer?" her lady's maid asked.

She nodded and slowly approached to greet her caller. The doors opened and Guan stood with his hands held firmly at his sides.

"High Lady Dessuithiel, you've been summoned to the throne room." He smiled kindly.

Dessuithiel glanced down at her gown. She wore the very gown her mother had worn upon her coronation. It hugged her form, and the skirt was longer than any gown she'd worn before, trailing after her, but there was comfort in it. She let a smile brighten her face as she thought of her mother's loving embrace, the last one received before she was taken home to Marmidon. It was as though her mother walked with her, hand in hand, arms wrapped around her.

Guan escorted her to the top floor of the zilkan tower. Every beat of her heart could be felt across her body. The double doors opened and magnified daylight flooded out, lighting the silver and gold worked into her hair.

There was a single thought filling her mind as she approached the throne, walking between all the remaining ethrean royals. She scanned over the faces of those present. Gailiaethere and Dundaelon were nowhere to be seen. She eased, stepping up onto the dais.

Turning around, her skirt spiraled at her feet delicately. She listened to the oath presented to her by none other than Guan.

"High Lady Dessuithiel, this day marks the beginning of your reign over the ethrea of Thyrel. Royal by birth, and heir to High

Lord Ayzgar and High Lady Miereene, it is publicly acknowledged that this is your right in wake of the passing of our beloved high lord and lady." He cleared his throat, pulling out a well-worn scroll and peeling it open. "Before the ethrean royal houses, and the monarchies of Marmidon, you hereby decree that you vow to uphold honor in all your dealings, to seek truth in every quandary, to care for your people, to serve in all your capacities as ruler of Thyrel until Marmidon sees fit to call you home?"

He lowered the scroll, looking up at her as everyone awaited her answer.

Dessuithiel smiled gently, holding her head high as she spoke the oath of her station. "Let light prevail."

The ethrean royals, soldiers present, and Guan repeated her words back to her, letting the echo of their sustaining be heard across the world.

Dessuithiel sat on the throne following a celebratory banquet. She'd spoken with every royal present, and thoroughly worn herself out. Guan stepped up beside her, offering her a drink.

“You have one more guest,” he said as she took a sip of the sweet tea.

“Last one?” Her brow raised as she looked up at him.

He nodded.

“All right.” She sat up, ready to receive her last guest.

The doors opened and Aiden shuffled in. He moved slowly, looking more worn out than she’d ever seen him. She lifted her hand, standing to greet him.

“My lady . . .” He bowed while muffling a deep cough.

“What brings you all the way up here?” she asked.

He rose and tapped at his heart. “I fear my time is about up.” He covered his cough with a handkerchief pulled from an inside pocket.

She quickly noticed the bloodstain upon it. Picking up the skirt of her gown, she stepped down the dais, rushing to his side. Guan met her on the opposite side of him.

Aiden spoke. “Bring in Thoren Belfry. Marmidon’s chosen mentor.”

He arrived at the tower doors and waited until he was granted permission to enter. Guan was there to greet him and Thoren's heart sank like a stone tossed into the Fleurra Sea.

"Don't tell me I'm here to meet with you?" Thoren huffed.

Guan forced a smile. "If I had my way, that's all it would be." He turned to the stairs. "Follow me."

They climbed to the very top of the tower. Thoren took a moment upon reaching the top to rest his legs before following Guan to a set of elaborate doors.

He held out a hand, telling Thoren to stop and wait. Guan raised his fist to the door and knocked.

"Lady Dessuithiel, Thoren Belfry is here as requested."

The doors clicked and swung open, gliding without another sound and revealing the bright zilkan throne room. Thoren's face beamed at the sight of Dessuithiel sitting on the throne.

His heart raced. Her gentle curves were fitted in a white silk dress hugging her form down to her hips where it flowed free over the dais. Loosely braided, her hair rested over one shoulder, down into her lap. Silver and gold leafy jewelry was mixed between her fiery strands.

She waved him in, the sheer sleeves that draped to the floor ruffled from the motion and light caught on the silver metal bracelets upon her upper arms. Metal jewelry crowned her shoulders with leaf and flower bud detailing.

He obeyed eagerly.

As he started walking, Thoren took notice of the red cloaked figure standing beside Dessuithiel's throne.

She lifted her hand once more, asking him to stop a few strides away from her.

What's this about? His eyes drifted to the cloaked figure to which her hand was now raised.

"Thoren Belfry, tested and found worthy by Marmidon herself, I present to you, Aiden Aodh."

Thoren silenced his shock and clamped his mouth shut. *It's Marmidon's Gift Bearer! I was right!*

The man pulled the hood from his head. His green eyes were bright and kind.

Just like that child.

Aiden bowed his head. Adding to the likeness of the child Thoren had seen. Aiden had the same shade of auburn hair and tan sun-kissed skin. His ears held a soft, pointed tip of a half-blooded ethrean.

He wasn't young, despite the rich color of his hair, and looked much like a human nearing the end of their hundred and fifty or so—limited lifespan—years.

Aiden spoke. "As I understand it, Marmidon has shown you the next Gift Bearer."

Before the funeral or cleaning efforts began, Dessuithiel had scanned his memories and revealed him as Marmidon's chosen mentor. He wasn't sure what exactly had marked him as such, but now he understood.

Balek didn't see the child, did he?

His inward question was answered by Dessuithiel in like manner, "*You're correct. Balek, while strong and able, was not chosen for this position.*"

He stammered over his words answering the Gift Bearer, "Y-yes. I believe she did, sir." Thoren wasn't sure what title to give him.

Aiden smiled. "Today, your calling as Marmidon's mentor will be announced. Following this announcement, you will leave and seek out the child shown to you."

Thoren blinked and lowered his gaze, confused. *But, I . . .* His eyes drifted to Dessuithiel.

She nodded, confirming the task being assigned to him.

"My time is *very* limited." Aiden coughed, stumbling forward from the force. "Even now, I feel myself waning."

Dessuithiel rose to help, but Guan beat her to it. He held one of Aiden's arms and presented one in support. Dessuithiel offered up her seat, helping Guan guide Aiden to it.

Once he was sitting, Aiden resumed, "As I was saying. I will pass on from this mortal frame soon. This child, you must find him, train him, and prepare him for the coming Calamity."

Calamity?

"It's hard for me to say exactly how long we have, but you will need every moment to prepare him. The Gift will awaken within him upon my passing."

"Where will I find him? All I saw was a plain little village in a clearing." Thoren scrambled through his memories, seeking any defining details that would tell him where the child was.

"I wish I could tell you." Aiden coughed violently, holding a handkerchief to his mouth. "All I can give you is his name. The name of my son, Malik. He does not carry the surname of Aodh, for his own protection, nor does he know of me as his Ba."

He left his child in hiding? Thoren was starting to get a sense of how dangerous the Gift Bearer's life was. If it was anything like what he'd experienced over the last week, keeping a Gift Bearer alive was going to be quite the challenge—a challenge he was ready and willing to take.

Thoren held his hands firmly at his sides and bowed. "You have my word! I will find Malik, bring him back to Thyrel, and train him."

"That . . . is good . . . to hear." Aiden's words came slow and labored.

"Aiden!" Dessuithiel knelt at his side as he slumped in the throne, kept there by Guan who held to his shoulder.

Thoren rushed over as well, but was unsure of how to help.

"Let me . . . pass." Aiden rested his calloused worn hand upon Dessuithiel's shoulder. "You've done . . . incredibly well."

"Marmidon, take his soul into your care." Dessuithiel held Aiden's hand until the light faded from his eyes.

A wave of warm energy burst from the Gift Bearer's body and firelight flashed through the throne room. They remained still, giving him the silent respect due to one of such importance to their world's balance.

"My Lady, I will lay him to rest," Guan offered.

Dessuithiel lowered Aiden's hand, released it, and backed away, giving Guan the space he needed. Guan gently moved Aiden to the floor and crossed his limp arms over his chest.

"Lay him beside my parents."

"Of course." Her guard tilted his head toward her with respect. "I shall return with a casket and pallbearers."

Thoren waited in the silent throne room with Dessuithiel while Guan stepped out. After a few minutes, Guan returned, along with the needed pallbearers adorned in Thyrel's crest: a single feathered wing. They entered the throne room with a finely crafted casket. Decorated for royalty, they laid the Gift Bearer's body within it.

Guan and the pallbearing guards left the room, leaving Dessuithiel and Thoren alone once more.

Thoren faced her as the doors shut. He took a hesitant step toward her and spoke. "My lady."

She smiled softly and closed the remaining space between them, wrapping her arms around his waist.

"What is it?" she asked and leaned her head into his chest.

He tensed for a moment, and looked about the room to ensure they were alone. Thoren's heart raced as he returned her tender affection in like manner.

He brushed his hand over her silky red hair and asked, "Am I really leaving as soon as my title is announced?"

She sighed and said, "I'm afraid so."

"My position will be full of challenges."

She hummed affirmatively.

Thoren continued voicing his thoughts. "Nobody, other than my close friends and Guan, is aware of our relationship."

She pulled back and looked up at him. "I know."

“Will there ever be a point in the future when we can be open in our union?”

She pulled away, turned sideways, and tilted her head teasingly, “I can’t deny I’ve been tempted to reveal it . . .” Her eyes dropped as she continued, “But at this time, I simply do not know.” She folded her arms tightly to her torso.

The drumming of his heart increased. “Times change, and I can only hope that the customs will, too.” He pulled at her shoulder, turning her to face him directly. “You are mine as much as I am yours.”

“Maybe in time, it will be as you hope and our love will have the light of day shed upon it.” She smiled, but it was tinged with some sadness.

Thoren’s heart ached. How long would it be?

She looked longingly at him. “Our love is not one that can be shared with the world. Not yet.”

“Other suitors will approach you.” Thoren could see it now. Dessuithiel, leader of the western ethrea was young, beautiful, and eligible to the other royal ethrean houses in the world’s eyes. A woman without a man to produce an heir. He hated the idea that she could be given to another. Thoren turned his face from her as his emotions built up within him.

Her hand brushed over his chest—over the thundering beats within him. "I will turn away *every* suitor." Her hand moved to his face, urging him to meet her eyes again.

Thoren relented, powerless at her hand.

"I meant what I said. I am yours, and yours only."

"There is no power in all of Marmidon that will take me from you." She spoke within his mind.

His heart calmed some, and he wrapped his hand over hers upon his cheek, leaning into it.

"All right. I will serve Marmidon in the public eye, and you behind royal doors."

Her face filled with the heart-melting smile he craved. She rose to the tips of her toes while pulling his face down to hers, letting their love live for a moment in time.

A knock at the door called an end to their passion and Thoren pulled back. He straightened his garb and stepped back from Dessuithiel as she did from him.

"Enter," Dessuithiel called.

Guan entered and said, "The time is approaching. We should descend for the announcement."

"Very well." Dessuithiel sighed.

She grabbed hold of Thoren's hand, pulling him along.

"My Lady, that is inappropriate." Guan contested the forward action.

I'll show you what is inappropriate. Thoren mused internally, tightening his free hand into a fist.

"Sorry, Guan." Dessuithiel pulled her hand from Thoren's and walked ahead beside her guard.

Every step down the spiral staircase, Thoren drew closer to leaving in search of the awakening Gift Bearer, Malik. The tower's horns blared as they hit the base floor and Lady Dessuithiel was announced.

Guan held his arm out, stopping Thoren from following.

"You're really getting on my nerves, Guan," he whispered.

Guan shot a glare back at him. "Don't think for one second that I don't know what's going on between you two." He lowered his arm as Thoren was announced. "Well, Marmidon awaits." Guan stepped aside.

Thoren's chest tightened and his pulse quickened as he stepped into view. He walked out into the noonday warmth and the cheers that broke from the gathered crowd. He saw his two best friends, as well as the other contestants from the trials wearing their regular clothing. He noticed Janessa and Balek were rather cozied up to one another—likely holding hands. They wore big smiles and waved at him. Shirra had tragically not survived, but he could imagine her smug face nodding in approval, though begrudgingly.

Dessuithiel was handed a polished wooden box by a nearby guard. She took a step to the side and out in front of Thoren. With a smile in her eyes and a bashful blush upon her cheeks, she opened the box to reveal a custom-designed golden pin, shaped into the symbol of the Fire Heart—the force of light and dark clashing over a beacon between them.

She spoke as she pinned it to the short stiff collar of his garb. "Thoren Belfry. You applied for the position of Marmidon's mentor. Unknowing of the trials that were ahead, your courage was never lacking. Valiantly, you fought through the darkest of beings, persevered through unimaginable pains, and found your way back from within Marmidon's test of your heart and will." She turned from him and faced what felt to Thoren like the whole world gathered in the crowd. "Forged in Marmidon's fire, she has found you worthy. You shall be known as the Gift Bearer's Mentor from this moment until you draw your last breath."

Cheers filled the air as the task now fell upon him. Thoren reached up and brushed his fingers over the smooth metal pin.

The weight of his honored position filled him with pride and duty.

I accept, Marmidon!

The End

Glossary Part 1

Pronunciation Guide

Main Characters

Aiden Aodh
/ˈeɪdən od/ (Ay-den O-de)

Ayzgar Vizule
/ˈaɪzgɑːr vɪˈzuːl/ (Eye-z-gar Viz-oo-L)

Balek Thrain
/beɪˈlɛk θreɪn/ (B-ay-L-eh-ck Th-rain)

Byran
/ˈbaɪrən/ (By-ran)

Dessuithiel Vizule
/des,wɪθ,i,el vɪˈzuːl/ (De-s-w-ith-ee-el Viz-oo-L)

Dundaelon Valdan
/dʌnˈdeɪlɒn ˈvælden/ (Done-day-lawn V-all-dan)

Fern
/fərˈn/ (F-urn)

Finian
/ˈfɪniən/ (Fin-E-an)

Gailiaethere Valdan
/geɪliːˈɛθɛr ˈvælden/ (Gail-lee-ah-th-ear V-all-dan)

Guan
/gwɑːn/ (Gw-on)

James
/dʒeɪmz/ (Jay-m-z)

Janessa Helms
/dʒəˈnɛsə/ (Juh-ness-uh)

Malik
/ˈmælɪk/ (M-al-ick)

Miereene Vizule
/miːˈɛriːn vɪˈzuːl/ (M-ear-ee-n Viz-oo-L)

Nesalariel Valdan
/ˈnɛsɑːləriːl ˈvælden/ (Nessa-la-reel V-all-dan)

Olathe
/oʊˈleɪθ/ (Oh-la-th)

Shirra Namarie
/ ʃieːˈrɑː ˌnɑːməˈriː/ (Sheer-ra Na-mar-re)

Thoren Belfry
/θɔɹ,en belf,ɹi/ (Th-or-in Bell-free)

Vance
/væns/(V-an-ss)

Additional Ethrean Royal Houses

Dailuma
/deɪˈluːmə (Day-loom-ah)

Drosmane
/drɔzˈmeɪn/ (Dr-oz-main)

Gudrovs
/guːˈdroʊvs/ (G-oo-drove-s)

Malduin
/mælˈduːɪn/ (Mal-do-in)

Stabranga
/stɑːˈbrɑːŋgɑː/ (Sta-brawn-ga)

Varonar
/vɛrˈroʊnɑːr/ (V-air-on-ar)

Weaves

Akemins Morfejemis

/Akmɪnz mɔrfˈfidʒɛmɪs/ (A-ck-min-z Morph-fi-dge-eh-miss)

Stone Morph: a weave to manipulate hardened minerals. Select minerals cannot be woven with this weave. A mid-tier level weave.

Aktuly No Patiesibu

/ækˈtuli/ (AK-too-lee) /noʊ/ (NOH) /pætiˈɛsiˈbu/ (Pah-Tee-eh-SEE-boo)

Sight of truth: a weave that reveals truth where there is error. A high level weave.

Aust Savingju Stauv Dauriz Lisma

/aʊst ˈsævɪndʒu staʊv dɔːˈrɪz ˈlɪsmə/ (OWST SAV-in-J-oo ST-ow-V DAH-riz LIS-mah)

Return to true form through light: a high level restorative light weave.

Bajerra

/ba,ʒeɹ,a/ (Bah-j-era)

Barrier: a weave that creates a protective, translucent, barrier. The strength of the barrier depends on how much energy the caster is willing to give when casting it. The size/shape is determined by the weaver's output of energy and skill.

Gaiza Skret Jez

/ˈgaɪzə skrɛt dʒɛz / (GUY-zah SKRET JEHZ)

Wind runner/air walker: a weave commanding air for one's benefit. Air is pressurized under the caster's feet, allowing them to run above ground. A high level weave.

Ledus

/ˈliːdʌs/ (L-ea-d-us)

Ice: cast to change the condition of a liquid to a frozen solid and used in joint weaves for more complex casting.

Listose Yeudins

/lɪˈsstoʊs juːˈdɪnz/ (List-o-ss U-din-z)

Flowing water: a weave to fully manipulate water.

Nevizot Netrimus

/ne,vɪ,zat ne,tɹi,mus/ (Neh-v-eh-zot Neh-tri-mu-s)

Shift dirt (works on small loose minerals).

Piersings Ledus

/ˈpɪər.sɪŋz ˈliːdʌs/ (Peer-sing-z L-ea-d-us)

Piercing ice: a more complex weave that freezes water/liquids into sharp projectiles which can then be directed according to the caster's will.

Redztu

/rɛdˈzu/ (REHZ-too)

See/Look (introspective): a weave used to see internally, often used by medics when assessing injury or illness. It can be used to assess an inner well other than the castor's. A basic level weave.

Saisette

/saɪˈsɛt/ (S-eye-s-eh-T)

Bind: a negative energy weave, often called a raze, that will bind the target/receiver of the raze to the location it is in when the raze connects. This is a higher level weave, and often used by Shades which can tap negative energy weaving.

Salabotte

/sæləˈbɒt/ (sah-lah-BOH-t)

Heal: a restorative weave used to heal wounds of all kinds. Inner well energy is directed to the wounds reversing the damage. Speed of healing varies based on the caster. A basic level weave.

Veis

/ˈvaɪs/ (V-ice)

Wind: a weave that causes a strong force of wind. The strength of the gust varies based on the caster and the amount of one's inner well applied to the weave. The caster can control it to an extent. A basic level weave.

Veisis Gaiza

/ˈvaɪsɪs ˈgaɪzɑ/ (V-ice-iss Guy-zah)

Wind Gust: a weave drawing in a controllable gust of wind. The strength of the gust varies based on the caster and the amount of one's inner well applied to the weave. A mid-tier level weave.

Yeudins

/juːˈdɪnz/ (U-din-z)

Water: a weave to pull the element of water from any nearby nature source or draw it from the air determined by the caster's will.

Glossary Part 2

Terms

Ama/Aba Ba

/ / (Ah-ma Ah-bah B-ah)

The name for mother and father for those of ethrean descent. In Jushosh the ethrea call to their mothers by the name: Ama. In Marmeada they use: Aba. The minor difference has to do with some of the cultural shifts between them. However, the term for father, Ba, has remained consistent.

Calamity

/kəˈlæmɪti/ (kə-LAM-i-tee)

A destructive event causing widespread natural disasters across Marmidon.

Farthven Ladayose

/ˈfɑrθvɛn lædəˈjoʊsɛ/ (FAR-thven LAH-dah-yoh-seh)

The ethrean marital celebration, held every century during the solar eclipse.

Nosh

/nɒʃ/ (N-osh)

The name of an eatery or establishment that provides food.

Sheerma

/ˈʃɪərmə/ (SHEER-mah)

A curse word from the ethrean culture. Equivalent to saying: oh, crud.

Veritian

/vəˈriːʃən/ (V-ur-ii-sh-an)

A sweet and creamy yoke-based drink with finely crushed ice and fizz.

Zilkan

/ˈzɪlkɑn/ (ZIL-kahn)

A luminescent rare mineral with neodymium. It was once mined from the Bearing Mountains and is one of the hardest known substances in Marmidon. With a hexagonal arrangement of atoms, it refracts light giving it an otherworldly glow. The weave to morph this particular mineral has been lost.

Creatures

Beynin

/beɪˈnɪn/ (Bay-n-in)

A small mammal with light gray fur, the body of a deer, but the long floppy ears and tail like a rabbit. They have a mane of hair like a sheep, and large eyes. Beynins are no taller than two feet, and bound through the tall grasslands of Marmidon feeding on grains and flower buds.

Crierspry

/kraɪərsˌpraɪ/ (Cry-er-spr-eye)

A large fowl that stalks and preys upon animals near death. Their shrill call often sounds like something crying in desperation.

Naudder

/ˈnɔdər/ (NAW-der)

Relatives of pigs/boars, with large tusks growing up from their lower jaw. Their body is like that of a boar except for the scaling that mixes with the fur around their upper torso. They are docile unless provoked, at which they can become dangerous to an unarmed individual.

Naux

/ˈnɑks/ (N-Ah-X)

A large, scaled, quadrupedal or bipedal animal. These beasts can grow to be more than twenty feet long from snout to tail. Horns, frills, and scale patterns vary between and within the different elemental types: fire, stone, ice (variants of water nauxen found here), and air. Not all nauxen carry an elemental fire (flame/ice/water), but their traits give them different strengths. From rocky textured scales, to malleable reptilian skin-like scales, nauxen breed and reside atop mountain peaks throughout Marmidon. As the fearsome beasts they are, most steer clear of them, except for those residing in the country, Verra, where they raise, train, and coexist with the nauxen.

Searral

/sɛˈrɑl/ (seh-RAHL)

A canine relative found in the wild and cities. Searral grow to be larger than typical canines and are often trained as companions. Some may call a searral a house pet, but these creatures are clever, agile, and defensive. The searral will use their horned skull to puncture a threatening predator, as well as fight other male searral when vying for a young female.

Vilka

/ˈvɪlkə/ (VEEL-kah)

A large bear-sized canine with wolf-like features and two tails. The skin atop their muzzles is rough and hairless, and their eyes have a green shine in the dark. They hunt solo, and raise their pups alone with their mate. The males hunt and the females protect the den. Vilka don't tend to fight with others of their kind, unless it is over territory or a potential mate. They hunt larger livestock, aiming for the young, and are a plight to livestock farmers across Marmidon. They will attack people.

Glossary Part 3

World

Marmidon
/mɑːrmɪdɔn/ (M-ah-RM-i-dawn)

Countries

Allvelore
/ˌɑlvɛˈlɔr/ (Al-veh-L-or)

Dershja
/ˈdrʃə/ (D-r-sha)

Etrinn
/ˈɛt.rɪn/ (Eh-t-rin)

Jushosh
/dʒuːˈʃɔːʃ/ (J-ew-sh-aw-sh)

Kern
/kɝn/ (K-R-n)

Marmeada
/mɑrˈmeɪdɑ/ (Mar-may-da)

Narimond
/ˈnɛəriˌmɒnd/ (NAIR-ee-mond)

Verra
/ˈvɛrə/ (V-e-rah)

Cities & Towns

Criysous
/kɹ,aɪs,ʌs/ (Cry-s-us)

Elpha Zavar
/ˈɛlfɑ sɑˈvɑr/ (El-fah Sa-var)

Etrinn
/ˈɛt.rɪn/ (Eh-t-rin)

Morvae
/mɔɹ,ve/ (More-v-ay)

Thyrel
/θaɪ,ɹel/ (Th-eye-reh-ll)

Tortiaine
/tuɹ,ʃeɪn/ (Tour-sh-ay-n)

Sea/Landmarks

Astiri Sea
/ʌst,i,ɹi/ (As-tear-ee)

Auksis Mountains
/ˈɔksɪs/ (Ah-k-sis)

Evid Sea
/ev,ɪd/ (Eh-v-id)

Fleurra Sea
/flˈɛrə/ (Fl-er-ra)

Lake Benne
/ˈbɛnɛ/ (B-eh-n-eh)

Yaldeer Mountains
/ˈjɔldɪr/ (Y-all-deer)

Zemin Sea
/ze,mɪn/ (Zeh-min)

Days of the Marmidon Week

Noremme
/nɔˈrɛmɛ/ (noh-REH-meh)
The first day of the Marmidon week.

Tarreth
/ˈtɑrɛθ/ (TAH-reth)
Second day of the Marmidon week.

Vehme
/ˈvɛmɛ/ (VEH-meh)
Third day of the Marmidon week.

Therrem
/ˈθɛrɛm/ (THEH-rem)
Fourth day of the Marmidon week.

Derrethire
/dɛˈrɛθɪər/ (deh-REH-Th-ear)
Fifth day of the Marmidon week.

Sautome
/sɔːˈtoʊmɛ/ (SAH-toh-meh)
Sixth day of the Marmidon week.

Soumone
/suːˈmoʊnɛ/ (SOO-moh-neh)
Seventh day of the Marmidon week.

Months of the Marmidon Year

Frawr
/ˈfrɑːr/ (Fr-ah-r)
The first month of the Marmidon year.

Haure
/ˈhɑʊr/ (H-ah-ur)
Second month of the Marmidon year.

Mashen
/ˈmɑːʃɛn/ (M-ah-sh-en)
Third month of the Marmidon year.

Touah
/ˈtoʊɑː/ (Toe-ah)
Fourth month of the Marmidon year.

Trete
/ˈtrɛt/ (Tr-eh-T)
Fifth month of the Marmidon year.

Feene
/ˈfiːn/ (Fee-n)
Sixth month of the Marmidon year.

Dreshen
/ˈdrɛʃɪn/ (Dr-eh-sh-in)
Seventh month of the Marmidon year.

Autuoe
/ɑˈtuːɑ/ (Ah-too-ah)
Eighth month of the Marmidon year.

Owah
/suːˈmoʊnɛ/ (SOO-moh-neh)
Ninth month of the Marmidon year.

Nevemme
/suːˈmoʊnɛ/ (SOO-moh-neh)
Tenth month of the Marmidon year.

Quette
/suːˈmoʊnɛ/ (SOO-moh-neh)
Eleventh month of the Marmidon year.

Jezez
/suːˈmoʊnɛ/ (SOO-moh-neh)
Twelfth month of the Marmidon year.

Sky

Ilzu & Maz
/ˈɪlzʊ/ (IL-zoo) & /mɑz/ (MAHZ)
Marmidon's double moons. Ilzu is the larger of the moons. Maz orbits around Ilzu.

Seasons

Tieneere
/ʃɪˈnɪər/ (Shee-N-ear)
Snow blankets the northern lands for almost the entire season. Winds pile snow drifts, and make traveling difficult. Rivers and lakes freeze over and the ice doesn't melt until the middle of Speerin.

Speerin
/ˈspɪərɪn/ (SPEER-in)
Everything is in bloom the entire season of Speerin. The Grasslands fill with wild flowers that paint the rolling hills. The end of Speerin is the best hunting season for most of Marmidon, the wild herds migrate north seeking a cooler climate before Tummimar sets in.

Tummimar
/tʊmɛˈmɑr/ (Tuh-Meh-MAR)
Days are long and hot. Farming is most productive, despite the heat, during this season. Lush bushes and trees are fully filled in and put off deep rich colors. The nights are often lively with trade markets and festivals.

Auhen
/ˈɔːhɛn/ (AW-hen)
The longest season in Marmidon. The rain is, more often than not, icy and on the brink of snow. Pleasant temperature through most of the day with cold nights.

Races

Atle
/ˈætl/ (AT-L)
The seafolk of Marmidon. They average nine feet tall, have blue-tinted skin, gilled necks, partially webbed fingers and toes, and pointed ears like the ethrea. Even though they have the ability to walk on land, they prefer their underwater, domed, cities which are a haven from the wars that often plague the surface. They can live relatively long lives, up to around two-hundred years, sometimes a few more.

Ethrea

/ɛˈθriə/ (eh-THREE-ah)

Marmidon's longest living race and most proficient weavers. The only defining physical difference between them and humans are their pointed ears. Ethrea can live for centuries, and some manage to break over a thousand years, avoiding death usually caused by war or misfortune. The longest they can live is unknown.

Human

While humans do not possess any magical advantage, their ingenuity and determination make up for what they lack. Humans age normally until twenty years old, after which the aging process slows. Their average lifespan runs up to one-hundred and fifty with some living up to one-hundred and seventy at most.

Therrinndore

/θɛˈrɪndoʊr/ (theh-RIN-Door)

Short and stocky, Therrinndore rarely break above five feet tall. Their bodies are strong, with each muscle fiber able to pull twice that of most humans. They tend to dwell within the mountains and provided Marmidon with ore supply for many centuries, but with each passing Calamity, their population has decreased, forcing many to live outside of the mountains to preserve their dwindling race.

About the Author

Tiffany has always had a thirst for fantasy adventure, magic, and heroes that rise from the ashes of opposition. She's loved crafting stories since she was little. Putting her imagination to paper started in junior high, around 2005. A lot of her spare time is spent writing and sketching her characters. Now, as a mother to five beautiful children and wife to a loving husband, Tiffany began publishing in the summer of 2021 following her husband's encouragement.

The world of Marmidon has become Tiffany's pride and joy, full of rich tales and characters to explore, and she doesn't plan on stopping any time soon.

Coming Soon/Available Now

Aodh Generations

Heart of Fire Series:

The Gift of Marmidon

Marmidon Ablaze

The Storm of Marmidon

Marmidon's Calamity

The Lone Prince Series:

Beyond the Broken Throne

Beneath the Shattered Crown

Beyond the Sundered Edge

Beneath the Weight of Honor

Tales of Marmidon:

The Mentor's Forge

For more updates and progress follow me on Instagram:
https://www.instagram.com/authortiffanymrhys/

Acknowledgements

This thrilling novella would not have turned out as well as it did, without the listening ear and thoughtful suggestions for revision given by my younger sister—accomplice—Lindsay. With hours of dedication to my endless stories, this one was no exception.

Special thanks to another of my little sisters, Alyssa Jones, for her expert eye and attention to detail. She has the mind of an experienced editor and has put in more of her time in support of my books than I could have ever asked for. My stories become masterpieces under her careful examination of both developmental and line editing.

Additional thanks go to those who read in advance, giving insight that transformed this book from one character's point of view into two, making this story something truly special.

Made in the USA
Las Vegas, NV
20 February 2026

42348941R00293